Books by B. V. Larson:

STAR FORCE SERIES
Swarm
Extinction
Rebellion
Conquest
Battle Station
Empire
Annihilation
Storm Assault
The Dead Sun
Outcast
Exile
Gauntlet
Demon Star

REBEL FLEET SERIES
Rebel Fleet
Orion Fleet
Alpha Fleet
Earth Fleet

Visit BVLarson.com for more information.

Sky World

(Undying Mercenaries Series #18)

by

B. V. Larson

Undying Mercenaries Series:
Steel World
Dust World
Tech World
Machine World
Death World
Home World
Rogue World
Blood World
Dark World
Storm World
Armor World
Clone World
Glass World
Edge World
Green World
Ice World
City World
Sky World

Illustration © Tom Edwards
TomEdwardsDesign.com

Copyright © 2022 by Iron Tower Press.

This book is a work of fiction. Names, characters, places and incidents are either products of the author's imagination or used fictitiously. Any resemblance to actual events, locales or persons, living or dead, is entirely coincidental. All rights reserved. No part of this publication can be reproduced or transmitted in any form or by any means, without permission in writing from the author.

ISBN-13: 979-8359168038
BISAC: Fiction / Science Fiction / Military

"Ruin comes when the trader, lifted up by wealth, becomes ruler."
—Plato, 367 BC

-1-

Etta liked the outdoors. She always had, which was why she'd become a computational biologist. Working for the secretive labs buried under Central, she'd climbed high in their priesthood of scientists. She'd worked on many classified projects including teleportation, gene manipulation and a dozen other criminal activities—criminal at least from the point of view of the Galactics that ruled over us.

So, it should have come as no surprise to me that one morning at dawn she appeared on my porch, tapping at my door.

I came awake with a gun in my hand. I glanced out the window and saw it was Etta, and she was alone. I slipped the gun in my back pocket, opened the door, and put on a big smile.

"Hey, girl," I said, "is breakfast already on the table?"

The birds were peeping hard. The sun was a glimmer on the horizon, buried by trees and the Blue Mountains.

Etta glanced toward the house, then gazed out toward the swamp. She had a worried look on her face.

"There's no breakfast," she said. "Not yet, Dad."

"Well then, what—?"

"I found something… out there." Her eyes darted away from me. She gazed out into the dark swampland behind my family's plot.

Right away, I felt a spike of worry. Etta was good at finding things she was not supposed to find. She wasn't a housecat—she was more of a prowler.

When she was young, she'd found the bones of a kit fox along with a dozen other remains in the bogs of our backcountry. That was precisely the kind of thing I did *not* want her to locate in our family swamp.

"Uh…" I said. "You, uh… you say you found something? Like what?"

Her eyes slid back to me. She looked more worried than ever. "Is something buried out there, Dad?"

"What? You mean like under that old barn?"

"Maybe…"

I faked a laugh. "That's just plain crazy, girl. We knocked the barn down. We were going to sell that property, remember?"

She shook her head. "That deal fell through."

"Well… yeah. Grandma and Grandpa didn't get any money for it—but they were going to sell it."

"What does that prove, Dad? Any idea why did the deal fell through, anyway?"

I shrugged. I spread my hands. The truth was I had done my best to sink the deal. I'd gone down to the county land office and made a bunch of stipulations. I'd even reported some things about the property that weren't true.

That had done the trick. Government permits to sell the property were denied. The deal had been blown.

Later on, this last spring, I'd decided it was high time I made up for my rude, underhanded move. I'd gathered up some credits I'd earned by going on various deadly off-world missions. I'd quietly injected the funds into my parents' bank account. They'd accepted the gift because they needed the money, but they weren't really that happy about it.

I argued that this way, we weren't selling off the family land for cheap. They'd still grumbled, but they went on with it. The developers had looked elsewhere.

The truth was, even after doing a lot of work to cover my tracks out there in that swampy land, I was worried what they might find. Sure, the barn was knocked down and all the bones were at the bottom of a well. But what if there were more bones that I had missed?

What if when they dug a new sewer line, at some point, they had to remove that well and all the stones around it? Well, I'll just tell you what. They'd find what I'd hidden down there.

To prove me right, here was my own daughter standing in front of me, telling me she'd found something. Something incriminating.

I knew in that moment that I had made the right call by burying the whole thing. I put my hands on my hips with my knuckles pressing under my belt loops on both sides. "What did you find out there?" I asked.

"Something weird."

"Uh… something human?"

"I'm not sure."

This surprised me as Etta had an education. She'd taken every anatomy class there was. She knew all kinds of things that I'd never bothered to learn. If she'd found some bones, I was pretty sure she could identify them.

"All right. All right," I said. "So, you found something. There's always been strange goings-on in that swamp, you know? In fact, that barn was once the hideout of some pretty big-time criminals."

Etta looked intrigued, but wary. She knew about my propensity for telling a tall tale. "Criminals? What kind of criminals?" she asked.

"I'm talking about the worst kind. The rebel kind."

"What?"

I lowered my voice and took a half-step closer to her. "Girl, I'm talking about people hiding out. During the unification wars, see?"

Etta looked alarmed. She lowered her voice as well. Even she knew that no person on Earth would dare talk about the Unification Wars openly. "That's crazy. That's a century gone at least."

"Sure is," I said.

"How do you know about stuff like that, Dad?"

I shrugged. "I'm a legion man. I have been for fifty years now. Sometimes... Well, a few secrets leak out."

Etta was staring out in the swamp in earnest. "Are you trying to tell me I found something out there that was from some rebel leaders? Some hunted foot soldiers, guerrillas from a century back?"

"It's possible," I said.

The key to lying and lying big was to plant that initial seed of doubt. You had to convince someone there was a possibility you were right. One of the best ways to do this was an intriguing story. A rumor was perfect for this sort of dodge. It could grip the mind and cause the victim to ask other questions.

Soon, they'd be coming up with the answers themselves. They'd fit the pieces together. They would build a worldview that fit around the seed you had planted in their heads.

Etta was studying my creaky porch. I got out two bottles of ginger ale and offered her one. She took it and cracked it open. We sat on my groaning porch swing and sipped our drinks.

"I always like a bottle of ginger ale in the morning," I said. "The only thing that's better is real beer."

"Dad... I know about the bones. The bones at the old barn—among other things."

"Huh?"

My blood ran cold all of a sudden. Here I'd been thinking I almost had her bamboozled, and it was a shock to realize she was onto my game.

"I don't know what you're talking about," I said.

"You sure as hell do know. There are bones out there, and they tell bad stories about what happened to them."

"Uh... I don't know anything about that. You said you found something weird... You're talking about aliens, right?"

"No, not aliens."

"What was so weird, then?"

"For one thing the bones are weird because they're identical."

"What?"

"You heard me. I found two sets of skeletal remains that are virtually the exact same structure—like they were twins or something."

All of a sudden, I got it. There had been a time not that long ago, before the Clone World campaign, as I recalled, when Claver had sent out some of his muscle-bound look-alikes to my house. They'd come to hassle me here on the farm.

I'd told them I had something special to show them out in the swamp. I'd led them out there and murdered them. Had she found a pair of Claver-Threes? The remains of those boneheaded apes?

I chose to release a belly-laugh. I even put my hand on my gut. "That's crazy talk," I said. "I don't think there were any rebel guerillas out there. Not ones that were twins, anyways."

"No…" she said. "They're probably not rebels. I think the bones are too fresh for that. And in too good of shape. I salvaged them and did a little dating. As best I can tell, they've been out there much less than a century."

I was alarmed all over again. "Did you say you *salvaged* these bones? Are you telling me you dug up an unmarked grave? In the middle of nowhere? That's just plain crazy. That's *dangerous* girl. However those men died, it couldn't have been under happy circumstances."

"No," she said, "I suppose you're right. Do you think the government could have done it? Do you think Hegemony could have taken a couple of men out there and shot them in our swamp?"

"What makes you think that they were shot?" My eyes flicked from side to side as she thought it over. I was beginning to sweat, and the day hadn't even gotten hot yet.

Etta shrugged. "There was one neat round hole in each man's skull. It doesn't take a genius to read that evidence."

I gave my ears a scratch and pretended to think things over carefully. "Okay," I said. "You found some old bones out there in our swamp. What are we going to do about it?"

"We could report it to the police and to Hegemony. Maybe they would know what to do."

"Oh yeah, sure," I said, "they'll have themselves an investigation. Maybe they'll close down the property and call it a historic landmark, or a burial ground, or a crime scene—maybe all three at once."

Etta sighed. "Yeah," she said, "that would be terrible for Grandma and Grandpa."

"It sure would. Just think about it. If they so much as catch one of those little owls that runs around on dirt out here, they'd shut down the whole farm."

"I agree, I don't think we can afford to tell anyone." She shook her head, studying my boots and hers. "This is going to be a lot of work."

"How's that?"

She turned away and walked toward the toolshed. She walked into the shed and came back out again with a couple of power tools, one in each hand.

"Hey, little girl, where are you going?"

"Out to the swamp," she said. "I found something else out there—not just the bones. It looks like I'm going to have to dig everything up myself."

I jumped up off my porch like a water moccasin had bit me.

-2-

It was a bright, early morning. Dawn had just broken over southern Georgia. Normally, I'd still be asleep at this hour, but instead I found myself following my smarty-pants daughter into the swamp.

The clinging mud from the bogs weighed down my feet. This was not just a physical effect, but also an effect of the spirit. My heart was as heavy as my boots, which were covered in slime and muck. I didn't even want to know what Etta had found out here.

She'd told me about the bones, but she'd also insisted there was more to it than that. I'd asked her several times what that extra something special might be, but she'd refused to answer. She wanted to show me in person.

I marched along, listening to the bugs and the birds, which always seemed loudest in the early morning. I was carrying my own thoughts, wondering how bad things would be when she finally confronted me with some dark truth.

"Dad, where are you going?"

I stopped, and I turned. Etta was no longer in front of me. She was off to the side. She'd taken a different path, following a narrow trail through the thistles and reeds.

It was a route I'd rarely to never taken myself. I blinked a few times in confusion. I opened my mouth, and I was about to say, "That's not the way to the barn," but I stopped.

The barn was what I was worried about. The aging ancient structure itself was nothing but a pile of quarried stones, crumbling mortar and rotting timbers—but many bad things had happened in and around that barn. I'd been involved in quite a few of these mishaps.

I'd wrongly assumed that was where Etta was taking me, but apparently, she wasn't going that direction at all.

A real, honest-to-God smile graced my lips for the first time that morning.

"Oh…" I said. "I'm sorry, honey. I must have been daydreaming."

She shook her head, snorted, and turned away. We walked deeper into the more wooded area of the swamp land.

I followed her, trudging behind. I found that my spirits and my step were lifting. I almost never came out this way. Whatever she had found was probably not rotting alien bones, or worse, human bones. It was probably something else entirely.

Soon we'd walked deeper and deeper into the woods, entering an area where the pines were literally centuries old.

I chided myself for having been so worried in the first place. It made perfect sense that Etta wasn't coming out here because of my crimes. All her life she'd had odd interests of her own. In my opinion, this was because she had too much of her grandfather's blood in her veins. The Investigator, as he was known on Dust World, was a strange old coot.

I frowned for just a moment as I wondered about Etta's questionable heritage. She'd had a bad death and sketchy revive a few years back. Afterwards she'd come back… different.

She was still my daughter, mind you, but she was… *different*. She was wilder at heart and possibly even smarter than she had been.

Her grandfather had revived her illegally after her one and only death. We'd lost some of her body-scans, so although her knowledge and memories were intact, her DNA was not quite what she'd been born with. At this point, to the best of my understanding, she was one third my daughter, one third Della's daughter—and one third something else.

The Investigator had told me this extra element came from Natasha, a friend of mine, but I had my doubts concerning that entire story. The man was an odd genius. He was apt to experiment with just about anything. He was at least half-mad, and I suspected my daughter might be too much like him.

"Dad? *Daddy*?"

I looked down again. Etta had stopped, and I'd almost walked right into her.

Looking around, I saw nothing of interest.

"Uh… where are we? I don't even know this place."

Etta pointed a finger to the west.

I looked at that direction, and I peered because underneath all the big old-growth trees, it was still a bit gloomy. The cool moist air was pungent.

I squinted in the direction she indicated, but I didn't see anything special.

"See that pile of dirt, there?" she asked. "That mound?"

Then, I did see it. A black mound of rich soil. It was on top of a roll in the land. I wouldn't call it a hill or even a hillock. It was a *roll*, a spot where the ground was perhaps one to two meters higher than the land that surrounded it. In a swamp, that's a big deal.

Glancing down, I noticed that Etta's hands were grimy. There was black dirt rammed under every fingernail.

"Hey girl," I said, "did you dig up that hill with your bare hands?"

She shrugged. "No," she said. "Not entirely. I have a shovel."

I glanced at her again. Her eyes met mine. She still had that strange, suspicious sly look like she had a secret and a raft of suspicions in her head as well.

"What the hell is this about, girl?" I asked.

"That hill there—this whole place. Do you know anything about it?"

"No," I said. "I've been along this trail, sure, but I've never dug anything up—certainly not on that little hump of dirt over there."

"Okay then, let's have a look." She walked toward the mound and gave me a look I didn't quite understand. I followed her for a dozen steps, maybe two dozen off the trail.

We stopped on top of that unusual roll in the earth. It was the highest point in sight. For some reason, Etta had chosen to dig a hole right here, forming a mound of black earth. It looked as if a giant gopher had been at work, but I knew it was just my crazy daughter. Large trees grew to either side of the mound, and their tangled roots ran all over under the swamp grass.

Etta peered down into the hole she had dug. I joined her and bent over with a grunt. Right then, I caught sight of a long-handled spade she'd clearly swiped from the toolshed. She'd brought it out here and dug random holes without asking. Like any father who finds tools rusting on wet dirt, I opened my mouth to complain.

But these complaints died in my throat because I saw something. Something down there at the bottom of the hole she'd dug.

It was flat. It was round. And it looked like a rusting metal manhole cover.

"What the hell is that?" I demanded, pointing.

"That's what I wanted to show you, Daddy."

"It looks like a manhole cover or something. There're no sewer lines out this far."

"I know…" she said, and we both gazed down at the mysterious find. There was a handle of sorts on top of it, and to me, it looked like a hatch of some kind.

"It might be an old oil tank," I said. "Maybe someone buried it here years ago."

"Yeah? But why?"

She had me stumped. I kicked a fistful of dirt down in the hole. The clods and sand rattled on the metal. It sounded hollow inside.

"Don't do that!" she said. "I worked super hard to get that dirt out of there."

"What made you find this? What made you search out here?"

She shrugged. She studied the hole, not my face. "I have a few instruments left over from when I worked at the labs under Central. Using a… um… metal detector, I detected a large body of metal right under this small clump of trees. It goes along the hump of the earth. From there to there."

She pointed in two directions. My gaze followed her hands, and I saw what she was referring to—the entire length of that odd hump in the land.

It was oblong and reached perhaps twenty meters or so in both directions. We were standing in the middle of the raised area.

I frowned. "Hmm… have you looked inside yet?"

"No," she said. "There's a latch on the top, but I didn't dare."

"What do you think it is?"

She shrugged. "I don't know, Dad. You've got more experience with stuff like this than I do."

I nodded. "Yeah… it kind of looks like a bunker. An old bunker… either that, or an oil storage tank."

Etta didn't say anything. She was waiting, and I now realized she was waiting around for me to open it. There was a lot of tension in her, which gave me the feeling she knew more about this mystery than she wanted to let on just yet. Maybe she had her suspicions, but she didn't want to talk about it. She wanted me to find out for myself.

I heaved a sigh and got down to my knees. I put my hand into a rusty loop of metal that served as a handle.

Etta crouched next to me, and her eyes were gleaming with excitement. "What the hell is a bunker or a storage tank doing out here in the middle of a virgin swamp?" she asked me in a hushed voice. "Who could have buried it out here? And why?"

I shook my head. "I've got no idea."

This, of course, was a flat lie. I *did* have an idea. An idea that was beginning to worry me quite a bit. I pulled my hand back out of the hole without tugging on the handle.

"You know," I said, "we probably should be real careful."

"Come on. Just open it, Dad."

"As a military man, I can tell you that if someone goes to so much trouble to bury something like this out here in a swamp… Well sir, they probably didn't want anybody to find it."

Etta spread her fingers. "So what? It must have been out here for like a century or something. What do we care what anybody thinks about us finding it? This is our land and whoever left it here… well, screw them. It's finders-keepers now."

I laughed. "That's not quite what I mean. There might be a booby-trap. And I don't want to be the booby."

"Oh…" she said. "I never thought of that. This might be some kind of illegal drug manufacturing place. Something like that…"

"Yeah, sure. Something like that." In truth, my thoughts were going to a much darker place. My father had mentioned that this land, and even the old barn itself, had once been a hideout for unsavory characters during the Unification Wars. If that was true, if this really was an old rebel base, hidden out in the woods… The Lord only knew what was in there and what the rebels might have put in place to protect it.

"Hey," I said, "I've got an idea. How about we just forget about the whole thing? We'll mark this spot as off limits to everybody in the family. We'll just bury this right back up."

I took the shovel that she had lifted from the tool shed and began scooping up dirt and gravel, tossing it back into the hole. The hatch at the bottom rang like a rusty old bell.

Etta grabbed at the shovel with surprising strength. Of course, she couldn't stop me, but I could tell she wasn't happy.

"Are you crazy?" she said. "I worked all night and into the morning digging this up. I've got to know what's inside, Dad. I'm going to find out—eventually."

We eyed each other. I knew she meant business. The girl had crazy eyes, and she could be an unstoppable force of nature when her curiosity was piqued.

She wasn't like normal people—the sort who wanted to know things like who their favorite holo-star was dating or even what was happening on the stock market. Nooo, she was only interested in the extraordinary—like what someone had secretly buried in our swamp a century ago.

"Aw, shit…" I said, putting the shovel down.

I knew there wasn't much I was going to be able to do to get out of this one. Now that she'd found this place, she was going to be obsessed with it.

"All right. We'll come back out here tonight with some better equipment. And we'll figure out what's inside this hole."

"Tonight?" she said. "Why the hell are we going to do it tonight? Why not right now?"

"Because we need some better gear. This thing could be dangerous. There can be anything. Snap-traps. Mines... anything.

Etta took a step or two back in alarm. "You really think so?"

"I do."

To my good fortune, she trusted my judgment in this case. She knew that I had been to the stars many more times than she had. That I'd seen practically everything evil there was to see, and if there was a military threat around, she could trust my judgment about its origins and nature.

Accordingly, she followed me back out of the swamp. We returned home and washed up. We were just in time for my mother to lay out a fine breakfast. We ate flapjacks and sausage, with thick ham steaks and a dozen eggs. Between the four of us, we polished off everything. When I pushed back my chair at last, my mother marveled.

"My stars, James," she said. "You two both have quite an appetite. It's first thing in the morning... how long have you guys been up?"

"I just rolled out of bed," I lied immediately and easily.

Etta said nothing. She studied her hands. They still had plenty of black dirt under the fingernails.

My mother eyed her nails as well. She knew that we weren't telling her the whole story.

"All right," she said, "whatever. Frank, have you got some work for these two early risers? They seem full of energy and boredom to me."

"Early risers, huh?" my dad leaned forward and smiled. "There's always a lot of work to be done on a spread of land like ours."

Etta and I both groaned.

The morning passed by in physical labor. I've always been a man who enjoyed living in the country. I preferred the peace, quiet, and solitude. It was infinitely better than living in some crowded, filthy city.

But at the same time, it was undeniable that the more acreage you owned the more work and care and sweat you are going to have to put into it. After all, my family was not landed gentry; the kind of people who owned an army of robots to groom the lawn. We owned exactly one rattling old tram between the four of us, and we only turned on the air conditioners when we couldn't stand the heat any longer.

Eventually, it got to be around noontime, and we ate lunch. It was too warm to keep going all afternoon, so we relaxed as the heat of day began to set in. It was only mid-May, which meant that it wasn't boiling hot yet. But in southern Georgia, you could feel the summer heat that was coming soon.

Once we'd escaped my father's relentless list of chores, Etta and I went our separate ways.

"Tonight, Dad," she whispered as she passed me by.

"Huh?"

"Tonight, remember? You promised!"

"Oh… oh yeah, okay."

-3-

After dinner, when it began to get dark, Etta came scratching at my door like a stray cat. By this time, I'd cracked a beer or three and was watching a good game projected on my dingy ceiling.

When I didn't answer right away, Etta opened the door and slipped into the dark interior of my shack.

"Daddy? Are you forgetting something?"

"Huh? What you want now, honey?"

"Come on, let's go!" she said this with urgency, snapping her fingers at me, but I was honestly baffled for a few seconds.

"Uh… go where?"

"Out into the swamp. We've got to go have a look at the… the *thing*…"

"Oh… oh right."

"I've been thinking about it all day, haven't you?"

The truth was I'd been thinking about lots of other stuff, including a couple of ball games. There were also some flirty women I'd contacted on the grid during the commercials…

"Of course, I have! Let's get out some gear."

I pulled out every portable computerized gizmo I had, and I added them to Etta's equipment. Some of the stuff was official military hardware, built for sniffing out dangers, like mines and hidden pits underground. It was the kind of gear that an old soldier tended to accumulate after having gone to the stars a few dozen times in the past.

Loading up two packs, we took a circuitous route that went behind my shack and around the main tool shed just in case my parents were looking out their back windows and watching for us. We snuck away into the woods, and soon we were into the gloom underneath the trees again.

"Hurry, Dad hurry," Etta said, "it's getting dark."

"I thought you liked the dark."

"I do, but I want to see everything."

Grumbling, I trotted after her matching her pace.

We soon found the mysterious spot and unloaded our packs. I began scanning with every device we had. Between the two of us, we detected nothing all that unusual. Yes, there was something large and metallic underneath those two trees just as Etta had already determined. The only entrance I could find was the round hatch on top of it in a spot that appeared to be the exact center of the whole structure. Fortunately, we found no hints of explosive chemicals or anything else dangerous.

"Okay," I said, "here we go. You stand way back over there."

"Why?" she asked. "Why do you get the first look?"

"Because, honey, if it blows me up, you might live if you stand back a ways. Then, you can go home and tell people about it. I'll get a revive down at Central or maybe at the chapter house long before you will."

If Etta died now, things could go badly. She wasn't a legionnaire, and she wasn't even part of Central's cadre of nerds anymore. She was an independent regular citizen, and for people like that, dying really meant something.

Although we'd made an effort to copy her new DNA sequence, we didn't have a constant, continuously updating cellular structure. She might lose memories. She might even lose details that had happened to her body over time.

"All right," she said, and she stood well clear.

Grunting, I reached down and fumbled with the old metal slide bolt. I heaved up on the rusty steel handle, and the hatch swung open with a screeching sound. You could just tell these hinges had not moved for many years.

A musty smell rose up out of the hole, but there were no explosions.

"Well, I'll be damned…" I said gazing down into the hole. "It looks pretty deep."

"Let me see! Let me see!" Etta had trotted up the moment I hadn't been blown away upon opening the thing. She couldn't contain herself. She was right there at my side, peering over my shoulder, aiming lights down into the interior.

There was an all-metal ladder that led down to the bottom of a dark chamber. Not much else was visible.

"Well?" I said, looking at her.

She thought things over, gritting her teeth. "You go first."

I smiled. "That's a smart girl."

She stepped back two or three paces as I put my big boots into the hole and began to descend the ladder.

Each rung on that rusty old ladder squeaked and scraped as my boots touched it. The center of each rung was silver with wear. Likewise, the sides of the ladder were blackened by the touch of an unknown number of oily hands in the past.

If you've ever descended down into a sewer system, you know the claustrophobic feeling that overcame me as I entered that underground tomb. I looked around using a small handheld flashlight. There was a lot of equipment and crates everywhere. Gear was hung from the curving walls and was strewn all over the floor. The shape of the chamber was definitely cylindrical. The interior was like the top half of a tube lying on its side. I was reminded of a huge railway tanker car, or maybe a submarine.

The space was maybe six meters wide from side to side with an arching ceiling. The floor below me was more of a deck, being made of a thick wire mesh. When I stepped down on that floor it rattled and creaked and groaned even more than the ladder had.

Looking around, I put my hands on my hips and whistled long and low.

"What's wrong Daddy?"

I glanced up at Etta's face silhouetted by a circle of stars. The outside world was up there behind and beyond her. I grinned and laughed to show that I was in no danger.

"Just a bunch of junk, honey," I said. "I think we ought to just leave this all where it is and head on back home. It's going to be bedtime soon, and—"

"Forget it. I didn't come all the way out here and dig this place up with my bare hands for nothing."

I sighed. I knew there was no way Etta would ever forget about this place without thoroughly exploring it. She probably wouldn't forget about it after that, either.

"All right," I said, "come on down. There doesn't seem to be anything dangerous in here."

Etta climbed down the ladder like a monkey. She moved faster than I had because she knew it was safe.

The two of us stood on the rattling metal deck looking around for a minute or two.

"What is this place?" Etta wondered aloud. "Who could have buried all this stuff down here? Is it just a storage area for junk?"

"Yeah, that's probably exactly what it is," I said. I began to study the artifacts that hung from the ceiling and lined the shelves on either side of us. It was mostly military gear.

"What about this?" Etta asked, holding up a green Canvas belt. "Is this some kind of old-fashioned gun?" She pulled an angular hunk of black metal from the belt and waved it around.

"Careful honey, I think that thing might be loaded."

"Huh… a gunpowder gun?" she said. "You don't see too many of these anymore."

"No, you don't, but if you fire that off, the slug will probably bounce off these walls a few times and nail one of us in the ass."

She put the gun back into its holster and hung the gun belt back on the rack it came from. "I guess we could get some money for this antique stuff."

"Not likely. It's mostly illegal. Only government issued weapons are allowed these days."

We kept looking around, and she soon found a helmet with some kind of optic gear attached to it. "This looks primitive, but I think it might be a night vision helmet."

I took it from her and examined it. "The battery's dead," I said after I fooled with it for a while and examined the power cord.

Etta quickly took out a diagnostic kit and severed the wire. She shoved the wire into a tiny, automated splicing device and poked a universal wire into the other end. The splicer analyzed the purpose of each of the separate copper filaments and connected them up to the universal outlet. Less than a minute later, the universal outlet lit up.

Immediately, a greenish glow came from the lens piece of the tube attached to the helmet.

"Let me see that," I said, taking the helmet. I put it on my head and flipped the single optical tube down over my right eye. I looked around the place. "This isn't too bad," I said, "everything's green and black and there's a couple little fuzzy sparks inside here... but you can see pretty well."

"Is it alien tech?" Etta asked.

"No, I think we developed it. A modern unit would have full color though, and it would be brighter."

"That makes it illegal, right? Earth doesn't hold any patent for night vision gear."

"Right," I said. "More jailbait. It's worse than useless. Let's get out of here."

Etta ignored me. She found another night vision helmet and hooked it up too. We both turned off our flashlights and crept around in the gloom, looking for stuff in the dark that we'd missed. It was kind of fun.

The gear was decent because it wasn't just infrared. It was actually light-magnifying tech. We could see rather well even in the darkest corners

Etta found a ring in the wire deck and a square outline of steel around it. "This must be the way down."

"The way down into what?" I asked.

"Let's find out."

I complained, and I groaned, but again there wasn't much hope of my fatherly objections slowing my daughter down. We soon had the trapdoor open, pulling up on the ring, and found another ladder leading down into an even deeper, dingy pit of darkness.

Etta wanted to go first this time. She had quickly lost all her fear of this place.

It seemed like the steel rungs of the ladder were fresher and less well worn, but the scents rising up from the chamber below certainly weren't.

The rust which had accumulated on the first ladder had been due to the relentless moisture seeping in from the swamp outside. The second ladder was more protected and even more sturdy.

Gazing down at her through that square hole in the wire, I watched as she moved around.

"More junk," she said, "bigger stuff, though. There are guns down here, Dad."

"Guns? Don't touch them."

"I'm not a kid," she said.

"Yeah, well," I said, "You look like one, and you'll always be a kid to me."

She scoffed and walked out of my range of view. Annoyed and somewhat concerned I climbed down the ladder and stood on a metal floor that curved upward in either direction. I realized now that it was essentially the bottom half of the tube-shaped chamber. The upper half above had a curved roof, while here the bottom curved upward to match.

The wire grate had formed a floor—a deck between the upper and the lower halves of this bunker, or whatever it was.

We soon found sealed doors at either end of the long chamber. These were serious doors, built to hold back pressure or invaders. They reminded me of the kind they had on spaceships. Each door had a big metal wheel and heavy pressure clamps with all sorts of heavy metal projections.

When I reached Etta, I was alarmed to find she was already trying to spin the wheel on the southern door. She was tugging and grunting at it determinedly. "This thing won't budge."

"That's because it's locked, honey. See this keypad right here?"

She looked at the lock. "That's a lock?"

"That's right. You've got to have the combination, or you're not getting through."

"Combinations..." she said. "That's an old, weird idea."

I laughed. "It still works."

Etta frowned at the lock. She put her hands on it.

"Uh…" I said.

"Hmm. I'm used to biometrics…" she said, and she began fooling with the device. After pressing the buttons several times, she determined there was a five-digit combination. Typing various number combos, she found that it not only didn't open, but after five tries there was a clanking sound and a hiss. The door shot an additional set of bolts in every direction.

Then, the key panel turned red.

"Hey honey," I said, "let's just not touch that right now." I physically reached out and pulled her hand away from it. "It might be trapped."

"Trapped. Why?"

"Well, just imagine. Imagine you don't want anybody coming down here and messing around and trying to break into your little special hidey-hole. If somebody doesn't know the combination, maybe it locks that door. Maybe it locks it forever. Maybe it even turns it into a frigging bomb. We just don't know."

"This is bullshit," she said in frustration.

"It is," I agreed, "but we're not going to push any of those buttons anymore, right?"

Etta made some very unhappy noises. "I want to know what's in there."

"I know, girl, but some things are just not knowable. Hey!"

She'd already scampered off and was at the other end of the tube. Before I knew it, I was hearing beeping sounds again. She was pressing the buttons on that one, too. I walked up behind her with my big boots clump-clumping.

I grabbed her by both hands. She wriggled angrily. "Let go of me."

"I'm trying to help. Stop and think for a minute. You already perma-locked one door. We've got to get more information before we mess them both up."

My appeal to basic logic finally won through. Her fit of wild-side Etta faded away. "You're right. If both doors clamp down, we might never get in."

"That's right."

"Hmm… but how the heck else are we ever going to get to the bottom of this place? Do you think we could bring backhoes and a cutting torch out here?"

I rolled my eyes. "That might be hard to get past my folks—or the authorities."

"Maybe somebody knows the right combination. Maybe we can research it on the grid."

"All right. All right," she said, relaxing with an effort.

I was glad to see she was still able to settle down. I'd seen this sort of emotional flash from her before. She'd been ready to attack me. She'd been ready to insanely attack this door. Anything that frustrated her and got in her way was in physical danger—and that worried me.

If you got in Etta's way… well… it was a dangerous place to be. People had gotten between Etta and her goals before, and they'd ended up dead.

When she really, really wanted something, she meant business.

We spent another hour in the chamber. We searched everything, going through every crate we found on the floor, the shelves and lockers—everything. But we found nothing that would give us the combination to either one of these damnable doors.

Etta was crestfallen. "Junk, she said, "everything we found is junk. There's nothing down here. Whoever made this place, they didn't want unauthorized personnel to move past these doors."

"Yeah, looks that way," I said. "I think we'd best just give this a rest, and a little bit of thinking."

She finally agreed. We retreated from the bunker, sealed it up and carefully scooped some dirt on top of the hatch.

Etta was breathing hard when we stood outside. It was midnight now, and I could tell by the wild darting movements of her eyes she was thinking of different ways of defeating this problem. She'd never been a girl to give up easily.

She turned to me at last. "Dad? Someone has to know what the combination is. They have to know what this bunker is for."

"Uh…" I said.

"I can't get into Central anymore, Dad. Why don't you do it?"

"Do what?"

"Go back to your legion headquarters and ask around, that's what."

I was surprised by this idea. I'd been planning on a few beers, bed, and instantly forgetting the whole thing. "That's crazy," I told her. "I think this whole thing is best left forgotten."

"There's no way I'm going to forget about this. I'll tell you what I'm going to do. I'm going to go back to Dust World. I'm going to talk to my grandfather. He's probably seen some stuff like this before. When the colonists left Earth, this kind of thing was modern."

"Oh Jeez… the Investigator? You're going to go out there to pester him?"

"I sure am. Those people might have built something of this kind. I filmed everything and recorded all my readings. I'll take the problem to him and see what he says."

I scratched the back of my neck and yawned. "I suppose if you have to…"

"You can help here at this end, too," she continued. "I want you to head up to Central and ask around."

My eyes sprung back open, fully awake and alarmed. "Now hold on, Etta. I make it a firm rule not to go anywhere near that place when I'm off duty. You know that. They're liable to come up with damn near anything for poor old McGill to do if I show my nose at headquarters."

She rolled her eyes. "I know you're lazy, Dad. I know you don't want to do anything until you're called back on deployment."

"Good! As long as that's understood, we—"

"Hold on. I still would really like a little help, here. This is a mystery. It's kind of fun, isn't it?"

Naturally, I didn't think there was anything fun about any of this. If I went to Central and managed to freak out some Hegemony official about an old war bunker on my family land… Well, they might come down here and do damn well anything. No matter what they did, it would probably be upsetting to me, my parents and even Etta herself.

She was smart enough to do calculus, but she couldn't see my point. She kept wheedling and crying until I gave in. That's one of the things about being a daddy to a single girl. It was just really hard to say no to her.

So, I promised to go to Central and ask around. She wanted details, of course, because there were certain trust issues between us. I'm sorry to say it, but she did not fully believe in her father's sacred word.

"Who are you going to talk to?" she asked.

"Well, I'm not really sure right now."

"Come on, you've got to know somebody who would know about the Unification Wars."

I threw my hands wide. "I don't!" I lied.

"Dad, it could be anybody old. Who are the oldest people you know?"

Faces flashed up behind my eyes. Armel, he was a tribune for a mercenary legion of Saurians these days. In the past, he had run Germanica—one of Earth's finest and oldest legions.

Then there was Claver himself. A man so old they had barely figured out revival machines when the legions had started fighting and dying for Earth.

Lastly, I thought of the man who was the most likely to know about this, namely Primus Graves. He had once been Lt. Graves from a navy that had been disbanded long ago.

As Lt. Ryan Graves, he'd told me he'd actually fought in the Unification Wars before the formation of the first Legion. Who else to better know something about this mystery?

Then Etta snapped her fingers. "I know. How about Galina's father, Alexander Turov?"

"Alexander?"

"Yes, of course. He's ancient and a government big wig. His daughter was just here for Thanksgiving last year. She's been your girlfriend forever, Dad. You must know that old man personally?"

I laughed. "Alexander, yes, he's older than dirt. He does probably know a thing or two about the old days, but he's kind of a scary old fart. You know what I mean?"

"Come on, Dad. Just take one of your weird, random trips. Call Galina and get an invite to go back to her family's homeland."

One of the keys to parenting is to know when you've been beaten, and to retreat and fight another day. This was not the kind of mission I wanted. There was no pay and no upside to any of it, but I clapped my big hands together. My smile spread to an improbable size.

"All right, honey. You've convinced me, but you're going to owe me a big Christmas present next year!"

She studied my face for a moment. Her eyes were narrowed and suspicious. I'd probably changed my tune too quickly.

But after a few dodgy seconds, she smiled back and hugged me. "Okay, Dad, if you find something out, I'll get you that beer cooler you asked for last year."

We shook hands on it. A deal had been struck, and Etta left for Dust World the very next day. She was going to investigate things with her weird grandfather. With any luck at all, that would get her out of my hair for a few months, maybe longer.

At the same time, I was going to pretend to question every weird old fart I knew here on Earth.

Naturally, I planned to forget about the whole thing and hope that Etta would discover some new obsession. By the time I saw her again, she'd probably have dropped the whole thing.

To my way of thinking, the problem had been neatly and permanently solved.

-4-

Nearly a month went by after Etta left Earth without me giving a single thought to the rusting bunker, the Unification Wars, or the old farts who knew dark secrets that no one needed to remember. None of that stuff impinged upon my mind at all.

Of course, my parents were in a different state. My mother and father—well, mostly my mother—fretted about where her granddaughter had gone and how long it would be before she came back. Even though it was mid-May, she worried about Christmas and if we should be laying out gifts for Etta under the tree or not—all that kind of thing.

I grunted, and said, "Uh huh," whenever she asked me about such things. For the most part, I focused on eating, working, sleeping and chasing women down in Waycross.

The month of May went by, which slid into June, and soon it was July. In early July I got a strange text on my tapper. "McGill?" it read. "Have you found anything unusual down there in Georgia?"

I stared at that. Then I blinked a few times. My mind was a blank. As far as I could remember, I hadn't found a damned thing of interest that I could recall.

The message was from Primus Graves. With a frown I began typing back to him, starting off with a firm denial. After all, I hadn't gone into the Chapter House and stolen any booze—not since the last Christmas party. Nor had I pestered the girls who were working at the recruitment desk. None of that, nothing like that. There had been no shenanigans at all.

Just as I finished tapping this message in response to Graves, I paused. My finger hovered over the send button. I frowned to myself.

Come to think of it, I *had* found something recently... There was all that business with Etta and the swamp and the bunker. Graves had asked about me *finding* something, not *doing* something. That bunker, buried on my parents darkest, tree-covered swampy ground, was definitely a find.

But no, that couldn't be it. There was no way Graves could have heard about that. Not unless he had drones watching me... or something else?

I was instantly suspicious, but even the idea of being spied on didn't add up very well. If he had seen me out there searching around in the swamp, wouldn't he have contacted me a month or so back? It'd been many weeks since that fateful day.

Checking the date on my tapper, I saw it was the 4th of July. That meant nothing to me, of course. The only summer event on my calendar was August 6th, Unification Day. That was the date upon which everyone in southern Georgia got drunk and blew stuff up.

I was looking forward to the celebration, but it was a month away. So, I was left scratching my head in confusion. What should I say to Graves?

My first instinct, of course, was to lie. Or better yet, to ghost him.

I considered erasing the text and claiming it had never got to me. Just one more lost message eaten by bad service. To help back up my claims, I could cover my tapper up with aluminum foil—all my usual dodges.

But I knew that wasn't going to get me anywhere with Graves. He was a calm, steady, implacable man. He was worse than Etta in his own way. As stubborn as a mule and as distrustful as a housecat.

I finally decided I had to answer somehow, so I typed out the following message: "Primus Graves, I've got no earthly idea what you're talking about."

That was pretty close to the God's honest truth.

After sending it, I didn't have to wait long for a response. "Come up to Central City," it said. "Meet me at 6pm at Unification Square. Bring whatever you found, or at least videos of it. Don't be late."

Dropping my arm back down into my lap, I released a big sigh. The last thing I wanted to do was show my nose up around Central in the middle of the summer. I'd been a free man since Thanksgiving last year, and I was really enjoying my time off.

Unfortunately, I couldn't think of any easy way to get out of such a simple and direct order. I told Graves I would be there, and I'd be on time.

My shoulders slumped as I walked from the house back to my tiny shack. I opened the creaky door and looked around.

My eyes landed on a pile of junk in one corner. Digging in the pile, I pulled out the helmet with the night vision monocular tube still attached. Experimentally, I flicked it on and off. It worked. It had held the charge.

I shrugged. I supposed I could show him this thing. Maybe that would get him to leave me alone for the rest of the summer.

The next morning, I was on the sky train. I used my tapper and checked to see if my status had changed from furloughed to active duty, but so far it hadn't. This was both good and bad. The good side of it was this didn't seem to be the beginning of an official mission. Graves had not added me to the roster of some Suicide Squad I didn't know about.

The bad side, of course, was that I was up here at Central without getting paid properly.

Welcome to the Legions, McGill, I thought to myself on the long trip northward.

I spent an hour or two sleeping and then another hour or two wondering what the hell Graves wanted. I thought over a dozen possibilities, and I rejected them all. Being summoned for some random and unpleasant duty wasn't unusual for a man like me. When you were part of Legion Varus, you had to expect assignments that could lead you to the stars or an early grave. You never knew which or even if you were going to get compensated for any of it.

Reaching Unification Square, I walked around the place briefly. I didn't see Graves in the crowd. What I did spot was the nearest bar, and I made a beeline for it.

When I reached the doors, I pushed on the big glass panels, but to my surprise, the doors pushed back against my hand.

This was just the sort of thing that lit up a country boy like me. People in the big city didn't have any manners, and I wasn't used to that. I'd spent at least seven months away from crowds like this. So, I wasn't used to how city people liked to push and shove and get in each other's way. They rarely said "thank you" or "I'm sorry" about any of it, either.

With an effort of will, I fought back against my urge to shove even harder and force the man on the other side to stumble away. I just decided to go with it. I stepped back and let him walk out into me.

That's when the door was flung wide, and Graves stood there staring flatly at me.

"Come on, McGill," he said. "Stop fooling around and get in here."

"Oh... hello, Primus. Fancy meeting you at this place."

Graves snorted at me as he led me through the bar to the restaurant section in back. "I knew you'd be coming here first."

I grimaced in disappointment. Instead of escaping my fate for one more hour, I was going to have to talk to Graves. He was quite possibly the most boring, straight-laced man on the face of God's green Earth.

With an empty belly and a sober mind, I was led to a booth in the back of the place. I followed him, clumping along, while my duffel swung against my leg. The joint was mildly crowded, and my over-sized duffel banged up against a number of patrons.

They glanced up in irritation, but they said nothing. After all, I was wearing my beret, and the wolf's head patch of Varus was clearly on display. No one wanted to mess with a pair of officers from my legion. We didn't have the best reputation among the general population. We were usually treated somewhere between a felon in an orange jumpsuit and a patron at a biker bar. Either way, people tended to get out of my way, and didn't dare to do anything more than snarl wordlessly when offended.

Graves slid into a tight booth. I slid into the slot opposite him. It was one of those places that had high old-fashioned wooden walls on three sides. This would go a long way to providing us with some privacy, but apparently for Graves this wasn't enough.

He took out a tiny device, set it on the table between us and switched it on. It was a jammer, something that emitted interference in the form of radio waves, infrared flashes and hypersonic buzzing sounds. It was designed to foil any attempts to eavesdrop or record our conversation.

I glanced down at the anti-spy device and threw up my hands in alarm. "Primus Graves? Do my eyes deceive me? I'm sure you must be aware, sir, that devices of this nature are highly illegal."

"Shut up, McGill. Just tell me what you found down there."

"What?"

He leaned forward and lowered his voice. "This is serious stuff. Tell me the whole story, and don't lie."

"Sir, I'm not quite sure what you're talking about."

Graves flicked one index finger up. "That's lie number one. I'm keeping track. You don't have as many lies left to tell as I have fingers."

Our eyes met and locked. I knew he meant business. Was he going to shoot me on the spot? Or have me arrested for insubordination? I wasn't sure what he would do if I kept on dodging, but I was pretty certain I wasn't going to like whatever he had in mind.

"Sir," I said, "I'm not quite sure what you've gotten yourself mixed up in, but I'm not going to be able to protect you in this instance."

Graves narrowed his eyes back in my direction. "What the hell are you talking about?"

I took out the helmet with the night vision monocular attached. Disconnecting the device, I set the night vision tube on the table between us.

"Do you know what this is, sir?" I asked him.

Graves reached out, snatched away the device and shoved it in his pocket. "You shouldn't bring stuff like that out in the open."

"What is it, sir?"

"You know very well what it is." He glared at me. "It's a piece of outdated military hardware."

I nodded. "That's what I figured. When Legion Varus was first commissioned, did they use gear of that nature?"

"You know we didn't. We had more advanced tech by then. Full color, video. Higher light-gathering numbers. The works."

"Yeah, well," I said, "I thought maybe this was sort of a prototype for that kind of gear."

"You did, huh? No, you didn't. You're lying again."

He put a second finger up. This one was his middle finger. You would have thought a man should use his thumb for the second finger. But no, not Graves. He had jumped right to the middle finger.

"Sir," I said, "what exactly is going on here? Why do you care about me finding an outdated piece of military hardware?"

He heaved a sigh. "McGill, I'm going to tell you something. And I don't want you to tell anyone else what I said. You got that?"

"Sir, when you tell any McGill a secret, it goes straight to the vault."

He shook his head slightly. I could tell he didn't believe me. I should have been offended—but I wasn't.

"McGill, there are certain places on this Earth that were long kept secret. Places that were designed to harbor individuals who were on the run, so to speak."

"Okay, that's really interesting, sir. I feel like I'm getting a history lesson, here—but what's this got to do with me?"

"Do I have to spell it out for you?"

"That would be for the best."

"You found one of those places. On your property. So, tell me when the hell you were in there and what you found."

I squinted at him. "But how could you possibly know that, sir?"

"Because that secret location on your family land sent me a status update yesterday. Several times every year, the system is programmed to do that."

"Huh... what did the update say?"

"It said there had been a security breach—a security breach inside the bunker."

I sat thinking that over. Then I thought about how Etta and I had pretty much broken into the place, after which we'd gone down and fooled with those strange, locked doors until one of them went bright red after we failed to get the correct key code repeatedly.

"Hmm," I said, "I don't see how a man such as myself has anything to gain by a confession. In fact, I want to very clearly state right now that I am not confessing to have found jack squat on my land."

"That's a good start," Graves said. "That's the right attitude. You need to forget about that bunker. Never go out there again. Above all, stop fucking around with the locked doors at the bottom."

"Who told you about that?"

"It was in the update message, McGill. No one is allowed past those doors. Understand me?"

I lean forward, eyes intense. "What's in there, sir?"

"You don't want to know, McGill. You're never going to know. Trust me, you don't want to know *why* you don't want to know."

I nodded and sat back. Graves had confirmed my worst fears. Etta had found something that was politically dangerous, and I'd stumbled into it with her.

Right about then, the food showed up. We ate quietly.

Graves stopped talking about bunkers, strange dates, and mysterious locked doors. He talked instead about our Legion and the fact that he expected us to go on deployment again in the near future.

This time he told me we were getting a truly cushy assignment.

"Really, Primus? A color-guard job? I just can't believe it."

"That's right, one of those old-fashioned posts where you deploy to a relatively friendly, peaceful world and protect the rich people who live there. We're going to be glorified policemen."

"Wow, I said, "I'd never thought I'd see the day. What planet are we talking about?"

"Storm World. You remember that place?"

"I sure do. You mean the place with all the colorful salamanders?"

"The Scuppers, that's right."

We ate while we talked, and I began to smile as the conversation went along. I was more than willing to forget about the bunker, and the red lit door and how weird Graves was being about it. If we could get a color guard assignment to a peaceful planet… Damn.

"Who are we protecting out there, sir?"

"Their queen, of course," he said. "She wants us out there for some kind of ceremony. I guess she plans to die and then pass on the throne to someone else."

"She *plans* to die?"

"That's what I understand. Scuppers are weird. They get to a certain age, and they just die. And they know when that's coming. Then they'll declare a new queen."

"Hmm," I said as I took another big bite of my steak sandwich.

We proceeded to talk about Storm World and other innocuous things for the rest of the meal. Naturally, I knew I was breaking my promise to Etta right now. I'd told her I would seek out information about the nature of that bunker. And here I was, facing a man who obviously knew quite a bit about it, but I'd dropped the whole thing.

That was because I was neither as dumb nor curious as my daughter. She just didn't know enough yet to keep her nose out of things that were dangerous. I still held out hope she would grow out of that stage, forget all about this and still live to tell about it.

Dust World would probably do the trick, I figured. That place was a hive of mysteries all by itself. I hoped Dust World would redirect her curious nature towards some new goal.

With any luck at all, she was going to forget about what we'd found—and she'd leave it the hell alone.

-5-

Some people might call me an incurious person, and for the most part, they'd be correct. After all, I'm often willing to let things slide, to take the easy path and ignore trouble—but not always.

After I left the place and Graves behind, I couldn't help but wonder about the nature of his connection to that secret bunker in my swamp. How had he found out that I'd located it and broken in? Why did he want me to leave it alone so badly?

Naturally, I hadn't told him about my daughter being involved. There was no point in giving him extra details like that which wouldn't help anybody—and me least of all.

To satisfy my curiosity, I turned to a source of information that normally could be used by anyone in my time to investigate any topic under the sun. That was my tapper.

The organic device connected me to the grid, and I was able to do some searches. I did quite a few of them. I did searches on lost bunkers, the Unification Wars, and the significance of the Fourth of July.

To my surprise, I didn't find much data of interest on any of these queries. There were a few articles that talked about long debunked conspiracy theories. A few references were made to infamous traitors who'd been located and then executed or imprisoned for unknown lengths of time, and not much else.

Deciding I was wasting my time, I erased the whole topic and all my queries with a sweep of my fingers across my arm. I did my best to forget about the whole thing.

For anyone who knows me, my next move was probably predictable. I attempted to contact several women that I knew in town. To my chagrin, I struck out three times in a row.

Grumbling and considering my next move, I was surprised when my tapper went off. It answered itself, and an attractive young woman's face appeared on my forearm.

This was none other than Galina Turov.

"Hey, Imperator," I said, "How'd you know I was in town? I was just about to call you."

We hadn't seen each other lately, but she was a long-term girlfriend of mine and my superior officer. These two facts all by themselves spelled danger for old McGill. The fact that I'd just made repeated attempts to contact a series of women who were not her gnawed at the back of my mind.

Had there been some vile new update to my tapper's software? Something that allowed her to not only track my location, not only call me and force me to answer, but which also might alert her whenever I attempted to find another woman in town? I wouldn't put it past the sneaky intel boys of Hegemony, who ran everyone's tapper, to have created such a fresh new evil.

None of these thoughts or worries showed on my face, however. I grinned like an idiot. I even lifted my other hand and waved vigorously.

Galina looked at me with a sour expression. She had suspicion engraved on her face. "James," she said, "I've just gotten a very strange message about you from the Department of Internal Security."

"Uh… what internal security department might that be, Imperator?"

She squinted at me. "I don't know," she said, "but I've been asked to provide a subversity rating on you."

"Uh… sub-what?"

"Subversion is tracked by a numeric value, James. It's a number which high-level officers are required to keep in regard to lower-level officers. It ranks your loyalty to Earth."

"Well, Hell's bells. You know, as well as the next person that I'm as loyal and true and honest as the day is long."

She sighed. "I knew you were going to say something like that. Come to my office, I'll meet you there."

"Okay," I said, but she'd already signed off.

I began cursing up a blue streak. It was already 8pm, and I was supposed to meet her at her office in Central. What a pain. All my hopes of evening activities faded away.

After having struck out with most of the girls I knew in town, I'd kind of figured that maybe I could find a new girl. There were plenty of bars around town, and it was right about eight o'clock. That's when things started happening. But noooo, that's not how this evening was going to go.

Trudging toward the looming structure known as Central, I halfway figured all this talk about subversity ratings was bullshit. Galina always kept tabs on me. She knew when I was in town, and when I was making calls. Maybe she just felt like she wanted to order me around.

I tried to look on the bright side of things. If she was nosing around, at least that meant she was still interested. At this point, I'd made a long sky trip up from Georgia for absolutely nothing. Maybe I could salvage something from the evening.

I arrived at Central and went through a bunch of security checks. To my surprise, my weapons were removed and put in lockers in the lobby. Normally, when traveling around on the government property like Central, an officer was allowed to keep basic gear like a pistol or a combat knife on his person. Full-fledged infantry rifles are frowned upon, as were explosives, but personal protection was considered a right for any loyal officer.

Shrugging, I figured those regulations had changed. I gave up my weapons and walked on over to the elevators. There, as I rode up through hundreds of flights, I had to frown around at the other passengers on my elevator car. There were a couple of officers in the group. Unlike me, they were still armed. There was a pistol on every hip in the place—except for mine.

What did that mean? I had no idea, but I didn't much care.

I arrived at Galina's floor and walked down a long corridor. At the end of it, I tapped at the outer entrance.

Galina herself opened the door. Gary and the rest of her staffers had long since logged off for the night. Galina crooked her finger over her shoulder, and I followed her.

That was a real treat, as she possessed hindquarters built to mesmerize a man like me. By the time we got into her office, and we'd sat down at a small conference table I was feeling pretty good about this new twist of fate. Perhaps the whole trip could be salvaged after all.

"James," she said, "whatever you're involved in, you need to stop it right now."

"Uh… I don't really know what you're talking about, sir, but you can rest assured that I *will* stop it. As soon as I figure out whatever it is."

She shook her head and looked down at the carpet. "That's not good enough. This time Internal Security is involved. Those are serious people. You could end up being flogged, imprisoned, or dead with no one even being told why."

"Fair enough," I said. "Been there and done that."

"All right. I give up on trying to warn you. Is there anything you'd like to tell me, James?"

Her eyes seemed serious, but I couldn't think of anything, so I looked as dumb as I felt.

"Uh… no. Things do seem kind of… touchy around here these days. What's up?"

"You mean the increased security? I'm sure you've heard about the various new defense projects and our part in them."

"What exactly are we talking about, sir?"

She pointed upward with one finger aimed at the ceiling. I followed her gesture and stared at the roof.

"No, no," she said, "I'm talking about up in space. Come here and look."

She walked across the room and pointed up through the slanted window of her office. Central was a pyramid-shaped building. It had always been a marvel of construction magic. The building was taller than anything that had been built in the previous century. Due to its insane size, it was not straight up and down. Instead, the four sides slanted at a significant angle like the facets of a cut gemstone. If you leaned out a bit and put your forehead up against the glass, you could look down and see the city streets far below.

Even more impressive was the view upward. It was a vision of the heavens themselves. There were a few clouds up there, but the sky was mostly clear. There were a lot of stars and a few visible spaceships hulking in orbit far overhead. The ships didn't *look* that big from the surface of Earth, but they were actually a kilometer long or more in some cases.

Catching the light of the sun, which had already gone down, the ships were high above the curvature of the Earth. The sun outlined them with a slivery-white glow.

Frowning, I gaped at the heavens. I did notice one structure that was different from the others.

"That's no ship," I said, pointing. "What's that big X-shaped thing?"

"That's part of the Big Sky project."

"The what?"

Galina rolled her eyes. "You can't possibly tell me that you've been hiding in Georgia all year and haven't watched the news? Not even a single time?"

"I won't tell you that, sir, because I don't like to disappoint."

"Right… well, as any news feed would have explained to you, we're building a series of large satellites. Like that one. The project is called Big Sky."

"Space stations, huh? What? Have we got a bunch of missiles up there on a platform or something?"

"No," she said. "The project is purely defensive in nature. It's designed to generate a shield."

"A shield?"

"A force field that will cover the entire earth when we're done with it."

"What? That's plumb crazy."

"Some would agree with you," she said.

Stepping closer to the glass, I put my forehead right up against the cold slanted surface. My breath puffed and steamed the window a bit. But I just kept staring up at that big white X of metal.

"I've seen something like that before," I said.

"Where?"

"Out at Rigel—and at City World, too."

"Yes," she agreed. "That's exactly where you've seen it. Rigel has long had a planetary screen. It's been a key strategic weakness of ours."

"How many of those stations have we built?"

"Not many," she admitted. "Only four so far. They stretch out over the Atlantic. Eventually, they're going to fill the sky. There will be 78 of them when we're finished."

"Wow. That's really impressive. And they're all going to link-up and form a big screen, huh?"

"They'll cover the whole earth and protect everybody. That's our intention."

Galina watched me gape and grin. I didn't care. She was always suspicious, always thinking that I had an ulterior motive of some kind.

That's because she always did and couldn't even imagine someone who didn't. The plain truth was I was like a kid at a carnival. Just looking at the sights and watching the world go by. I really was impressed by the ambitious nature of this engineering project. I actually thought it was a darn good idea.

If our enemies knew they couldn't just punch a fleet through here and drop bombs on us willy-nilly, maybe they would be less likely to do it.

-6-

Galina kept on watching me. I could tell she was thinking serious thoughts, but I didn't much care. After all, she was always overthinking everything. Always studying my every move, always trying to figure me out.

The truth was, there wasn't much going on underneath the surface in my case. I was a man of elemental tastes, desires and thoughts.

When I was on furlough, the things that almost always occupied my mind consisted of beer, women, the play-by-play of a recent ballgame… That was about it… Oh and food, food was always big on the list.

"Hey, I said, turning to her. "How about you and me go out and have a bite to eat?"

Galina's eyes fell. She sighed. "It's too late for that, James. I'm sorry."

I frowned at her and opened my mouth to make a reply, but there was a thumping at the door. My eyes moved in that direction and then went back to Galina.

And then I knew. She wasn't meeting my gaze. She was looking down, staring at her carpets. Her nice, thick carpets that were always beyond regulation, in both depth and comfort.

"Really?" I said. "Did you turn me in? What for?"

"It wasn't me, James. I was trying to clear your name. But you confessed to nothing. You've done nothing but confirm all our worst fears."

My mouth hung open, and it wasn't even an act. I didn't know what to say.

Something thumped at the door, and someone had managed to override the lock. Three hogs strode in. They were all armed with their short-barreled carbine lasers unslung. The muzzles weren't leveled in my direction, at least. Not yet.

The whole thing seemed like a big series of mistakes to me. First off, any security officer worth his salt should have known that you needed more than three hogs to deal with one ornery man from Legion Varus.

My mind immediately flashed through half a dozen approaches to the situation. I could throw up my hands and surrender, which was what they were suggesting. Or, I could grab Galina and snatch her weapon, which was temptingly available on her hip. But I knew that approach wasn't likely to meet with success.

So instead, I decided to go with trickery. An old standby for me in such situations.

"About time you boys got here," I said sternly. I pointed a thick finger at Galina. "Here she is. Be careful, now. She's armed."

I made no moves that could be considered aggressive.

"Stand aside, Centurion," said the leader of the three hogs. He was what they loosely called an officer hog. An adjunct in the security forces stationed here at Central. He approached with his laser aimed directly at me.

I ignored him and stayed focused on Galina. "Whatever she's done," I said, "I want you guys to go easy on her. She used to be my girlfriend, and I want you to know—"

Galina jerked her head up and looked at me in shock. We normally didn't talk openly about our inappropriate relationship. Her surprise quickly melted away into anger. She faced me and she lifted a finger of her own. "You are so full of shit, James. Is that what you're really going to do now? Throw embarrassments at me?"

The hogs were a bit taken aback. Galina's hand had moved up to her sidearm, after all. It was an automatic gesture of hers when she faced a man like me, a man of imposing size and reputation. Being a smart woman, she was very quick to rely upon superior weaponry when dealing with brutes such as myself.

"Whoa, whoa, whoa!" the adjunct hog said. "Let's just stay calm. No personal matters need to be involved here, folks. We're here to arrest Centurion James McGill."

"What?" I said. "This here woman is my superior officer. Whatever you think I've done, I'll tell you right now, this is the crazy lady who ordered me to do it."

"Shut up, James. You're not helping yourself."

I ignored her and addressed the hogs. "She's been involved in an awful lot of shady goings-on here at Central. Remember that business when the squids came and bombed us. They blew this building to Hell and back—and she invited them in. Did you guys know that?"

The three confused hogs were pretty close to us now. They were shouting at me to get on my knees, and ordering Galina to drop her weapon. No one was listening to them.

When they were three or four steps away, they glanced from one to the other. Right away, I could tell from the nature of those sidelong glances they'd heard rumors about Galina. They were no longer completely sure about what was going on.

"Now here I am," I continued, "revealing a brand new plot on the part of my commander, but who gets blamed for whatever shenanigans she's been caught up in? Me, of course. That's just typical, isn't it? The brass never pays, no sir. It's always some poor veteran who just wants to make a buck and go home to dinner."

Galina has many positive qualities and many bad ones. But one of her greatest failings was a short temper. Her hand was like a white claw on that pistol of hers, and she chose this inopportune moment to shove it into my face.

"You will shut up, right now, McGill. You are to be taken into custody, dead or alive. I think I prefer you to be dead."

The hogs stepped closer. They still had all their guns aimed at me, which was only to be expected, but all the excitement had served to put them off-guard.

The adjunct hog in the back nodded to the others. They let their carbines slide down to dangle from the strap and reached for the gravity-cuffs. The adjunct himself stayed back a pace or two, that was mighty wise of him.

Now, you have to understand that up to this very point I had shown no signs of aggression. I was just making a few accusations, waving my finger, that sort of thing. So, to the casual observer, I didn't seem like I was much of a threat.

Galina, on the other hand, was angry with my revelations and accusations. I don't think she was thinking too clearly. She was standing close with her weapon aimed into my face.

My first move was quite predictable. I extended my hands to be cuffed by the first hog who approached. He obligingly snapped a cuff onto the wrist that I offered. A thinking man might have gotten me down on the ground first, probably with the application of a few shock rods and a knee in the spine just to make sure.

When the cuff snapped onto my wrist, I made my first surprise move. I flicked the cuff around, striking Galina's pistol which she held in one thin hand. The gun went off, and for one hot second, I thought I'd been hit.

Instead, the poor bastard who'd cuffed me look shocked. He staggered backward two steps then fell to his knees.

I took this moment to snatch Galina's weapon from her while it was off target. She fired a couple more times but hit nothing.

The second hog was up close and personal with me by this time. He lunged in, grabbing at me. But I think he was a little scared of Galina's pistol because his heart didn't seem to be in it.

He seemed to believe that by grabbing my free hand in both of his, he was in some kind of control. But he had underestimated my strength. Grabbing up a fistful of his tunic, I lifted him half off the deck. I twisted to place him between me and the adjunct, who was lining me up with the muzzle of his carbine.

With my involuntary hog in place as a human shield, I had to give credit where credit was due. The hog adjunct was on the ball. He'd watched all this play out over a few seconds, and he decided it was time to act decisively.

He squeezed the trigger on his laser carbine and released, I don't know, maybe thirty bolts from the business end of it. He sprayed the place on full-auto, hosing me down. He killed the hog I was using as a shield and hammered a dozen bolts through my body as well. Sizzling, burning flesh sent acrid smoke into my nose. Smoke from vaporized meat and bone and uniforms filled my nostrils.

The bolts penetrated to ruin my chest and mortally injured me. Galina's pistol dropped from my numb fingers. Galina herself backed away. She was breathing hard with her fingers spread over her chest.

Behind me, the thick glass window dribbled. Red hot molten glass splattered into my hair and burned my skin. One droplet fell onto my left cheek and cooked that spot, but I was beyond caring.

I slumped on my back, staring up at the two of them as they came to stand over me.

"You were a lot of trouble," the hog said.

I grinned, even though it hurt to do so. "That's right, I wheezed, "you've got to be prepared if you come to arrest a wrongly accused Varus man."

My words came out in wheezes and gasps, but they seemed to understand me. Galina put her face into mine.

"James," she said. "Are you a traitor? Tell me now. You've got nothing to hide anymore."

"Nope," I said.

"Then who is it? Who told you to search for those things, that date—that place?"

"Uh…"

Suddenly, in my dimming brain, I figured out what all this was about. It wasn't because Galina was pissed off over me looking for other women. It wasn't about my meeting with Graves. It wasn't about what I'd found, either. Or even the red gleaming keypad that had locked me out of the lower reaches of that bunker

No. It was about the searches I'd made on my tapper. Somehow, those queries I'd made had triggered my imminent arrest.

I thought about ratting on Graves. I thought about just bringing up his name. That might be enough to get me out of all this, and whatever lay ahead.

But I didn't do it. I just smiled as best I was able.

I shook my head. "I've got no earthly idea what you're talking about, Imperator. "But I must say, you sure are pretty when you get mad."

With those final words I died at their feet.

-7-

I have to say upfront, that I have died many times under many different circumstances. I've also been brought back to life when I had no right to think I ever would see the light of day again.

This time out, however, I figured I was in the clear. Sure, I'd been shot dead by a hog guard who was just doing his duty, and I'd certainly been resisting arrest. I'd taken down two hogs who now knew how I felt about matters.

But I would account it as a good death, and I purely expect to be revived.

Being a veteran of these kinds of misunderstandings, I expected to be given a stern lecture, and possibly spending a night or four in the brig. After that, I thought I might be released with yet another black mark on my record.

Worst case, I figured, they might decide to demote me or flog me or whatever. No big deal.

But when I came awake, circumstances were clearly a bit different. Instead of a pretty nurse, or a sneering orderly, I was greeted with no faces at all.

My first moment of awareness was the odd sensation that I'd been turned onto my stomach. Normally, when a man awakens from a revive, he finds himself flat on his back being worked on by various medical people.

Not so this time. The only hard surface I felt was in front of me.

I was indeed naked, and I was wet with slime. None of that was unusual—but the lighting was all wrong. There were harsh lights that were almost too much for my freshly regrown eyes to tolerate, and the weird part was they were shining down on my bare ass.

The hard surface was definitely pressing against my hands, forearms, my chest—even my chin was up against it. In my confusion, I thought at first that I was lying on a gurney facedown instead of on my back.

My awareness slowly improved. My groggy brain did a little flip in my head, and I realized that I was *standing* and leaning against something. That hard surface against my belly and my cheek—it had to be a wall. Then I realized my toes were all folded-up on the floor, beneath me.

Flopping and weak, I squirmed a bit, bumping my knees into this wall. My feet were slippery and felt rubbery. My muscles didn't obey me yet. My feet scratched a bit at the floor, trying to get a purchase trying to stand myself up straight.

That's when I heard the first slash of the whip.

Crack!

That sound came with a little something extra, a buzzing jolt. When that whip struck home, it laid open my back and delivered an electric shock at the same moment.

I stiffened up and lurched like a gigged frog. The chains on my wrists jangled and scraped, and my eyes flew wide open.

I'm going to tell you that whoever was flogging me had definitely gotten my attention.

"Centurion James McGill," said a voice.

I mumbled something incoherent and obscene. The voice took no notice of this.

"Centurion, you've been sentenced to thirty lashes prior to your interrogation. If I'm not satisfied with your answers, you'll get some more. Eventually, if you become unresponsive, you'll be executed. Each time we're forced to execute you, the number of lashes administered will be increased the next time around. Do you understand?"

My crusty lips grunted some suggestions concerning the speaker and his mother, but he didn't seem to mind.

"Again, there will be lashes delivered *before* the interrogation begins. Once you've fully experienced this punishment, you'll be allowed to speak. It is this officer's recommendation that you make a full and complete statement immediately after your punishment."

I burbled, spit and coughed violently. My obvious state of fresh revival, confusion and damn-near helplessness had no effect on the sadist with the whip.

The buzzing lash crashed home again. And again. I felt that extra little tingle and splash of electricity with each blow. The whip must have had some kind of built-in shock stick just to add spice.

The lashes were counted off in a dull monotone. I was glad to learn the one that had awakened me in the first place was part of the count, not just a bonus for funsies.

By the time the count reached twenty-two or so, my mind was operating pretty clearly. I could feel blood running down my back. A lot of my skin was numb, as well as the muscles and tissue under them. Unfortunately, the numbness wasn't enough to get me to enjoy the experience.

Instead of squalling and squirming against that wall, I realized it was time to do something. Accordingly, I went limp. I let my head loll and let my feet splay into an uncomfortable, almost ankle-breaking stance.

Retaining that pose, I slumped motionless as more lashes slammed into my back. As a testimony to my toughness of mind and spirit, I did not flinch when these landed. Oh, my fingers might have curled a little, but that could have been due to some kind of a shock response.

"He's out, sir. I must stop the flogging."

There was a bit of shuffling around behind me, and I heard a familiar voice. It was female, and it belonged to my assumedly ex-girlfriend, Galina Turov.

"He's just playing possum," she said. "Don't fall for it. He can feel every stroke, trust me."

"Sir, I cannot keep beating him if he's unconscious. The strokes won't count legally against his record. That's against regulations. Secondly, and thirdly, if we keep beating him when he wakes back up, it might either kill him or cause him to be incapacitated to such an extent that—"

"All right, all right, shut up," Galina said angrily.

The situation seemed odd to me. Sure, I'd picked up on the fact that Galina had me pegged as a traitor. She'd turned me in and had me arrested. All that made some kind of twisted sense.

But I figured she should have cooled off a bit by now. After all, I'd done her a good turn. When the hogs had come in to arrest me, I hadn't killed her. I could have done that easily. Adding her small form to the pile of bodies on that carpet would have been child's play.

So why was she so angry with me? She seemed to want to see me beaten before I'd even gotten off the revival table properly.

My mind cast back to recent times. What had I done to piss off my girlfriend this badly? It had to be something serious. Something truly heinous in nature.

"This is so frustrating," Galina said. "He's manipulating you even now."

The hog officer snorted. I could have told him that was a bad idea. When Galina's tail was out and lashing—while she was in the midst of beating one of her longtime companions half to death—you probably didn't want to suggest that she was wrong about anything.

I heard stern footsteps on the move. Sharp heels made popping sounds as they struck the hard puff-crete floor.

I heard the door to the chamber creak open, and then I heard the hog speak. "What next, sir? Are we done for the day?"

Galina didn't answer him. Instead, she leaned out into the hall. I heard her shout down the corridor.

Throughout all of this I didn't flinch or groan. I didn't do so much as turn my head to listen. I was still playing possum.

"Guard! Guard!" Galina shouted.

The hogs came running because she was an imperator. "What is it, sir?"

"I want this torturer removed. I need another man who isn't so weak-minded."

"Sir, that's not what we call ourselves here. We're corrections officers."

"Yes, yes, whatever. Get another one."

The officer hog who'd been working on my back for quite some time sniffed in disgust. He walked out, dropping the whip on the puff-crete floor.

I listened carefully, and I definitively took note of the fact the door had never clicked closed.

I heard the tapping of small, sharp-heeled footsteps again. Galina was moving around, probably pacing behind me.

I took great pains to not move a muscle.

"You can stop faking now, James," she said. "There's no one here but us. I don't plan to beat you as much as I'd like to."

Deciding this was as good a time as any to stage a miraculous recovery, I snorted, jerked my head up and stood on my bare feet. I flexed my shoulders, rolling them a bit. I felt the blood run all the way down my butt and along the back of my legs.

"I'm a bit stiff this morning," I said.

"Shut up."

I glanced over my shoulder. "Oh, are you still here Imperator? Maybe you could help me out. There seems to be some kind of misunderstanding between myself and these dedicated hogs around here."

"There is no misunderstanding, James," she said, coming closer. She dared to step almost within reach. Of course, since my arms were chained to the wall, I wasn't in the best position to do anything to her.

"Uh…" I said, "did I accidentally run over your cat, or something? You seem to be in a bad mood."

"I *am* in a bad mood. Not only have I received evidence of treachery on your part, but you have proven to be personally disloyal as well."

That set my head to spinning. Naturally, I could think of a dozen different crimes she might be upset about—and that was only considering the events of the last year or so.

We hadn't been together as a couple since the holidays last year, and that was just too long for a man of my caliber to wait around. Since then, there had been a number of things—mostly women—that Galina might have found offensive.

Still, I was pretty sure she didn't know about any of that stuff. But maybe she was watching me closely. She probably had drones following various girls around Waycross, all that sort of thing.

To the best of my knowledge, she hadn't been doing that. She'd spent most of the winter at her parents' house in Eastern Europe. In the spring, she'd returned to Central and as far as I knew her life had been business as usual.

During that time, she'd sent me a few notes, and I'd sent her a few as well. But there hadn't been much animosity.

Our relationship was a strange one. When we got together, we were passionate, but it never seemed to last.

All this talk of treachery I dismissed out of hand. She was the bigger traitor between the two of us, not me. She was, in fact, more likely to have foul dealings with enemy powers than I'd ever been.

"Huh…" I said, "there seems to be a misunderstanding, here. The last thing I remember was having a nice night with you after Thanksgiving. After you and your sister ate dinner at my parents' house…"

"Don't bring that up," she snapped with such vehemence that I knew I must be close to the mark.

"Was the cooking that bad, or…?"

"If you know what's good for you McGill, you'll shut up."

Right about then, another hog torturer walked in the room. He experimentally cracked his whip a couple of times in the air.

"What's the count?" he asked.

"That other fool was keeping track," Galina told him.

I began to wonder if I was going to catch a few extra licks out of this. That was always the way with bureaucratic hogs. When they screwed up, you paid the price for it.

"Let me see… ah, here it is in the notes. The previous operator got to twenty-four, but the perpetrator officially lost consciousness according to the record."

"Whatever. Give him the last six, and we'll get to the questions. This is taking all day."

Following Galina's instructions, the new man began to work his whip.

Snap, snap, snap, crack, crackle, snap.

Six more hard strokes landed on my back. All the coagulated blood and crusty scabs that had just begun to swell up and seal my wounds were laid open again.

When this was done, the hog expressed some level of concern. "I think I hit an artery over the kidney, Imperator. Let me put a little new skin over the spot."

"You'll do no such thing," Galina said.

Damn, this girl was being unpleasant today.

"James McGill," Galina said. "Here's your first question: What do you know about rebel bunkers from the Unification Wars?"

"Rebel what?" I asked.

The heavy feet of the hog sounded on the puff-crete floor behind me. I could almost feel him cocking back that whip, and I wasn't relishing another blow.

A weaker man might have cried for his mommy. A less experienced man might have fessed-up to damn near anything—but not me.

I understood from countless similar situations that when Hegemony served up justice, confessing to anything never brought relief. If it did, it was quite short-lived and simply went on to some worse horror. The rule of living under any harsh government was to never admit to anything. What's more, you had to admit nothing in a very convincing way. That was your only defense.

I suspected the rules had been the same back in medieval times. It was just part of the human condition as far as I could tell.

"If I let him hit you thirty more times, James. You'll probably die. Do you really want to be beaten to death?"

I shrugged my bleeding shoulders. "Wouldn't be the first time."

She hissed and spat angrily. "There's no point to this. We might as well be flogging a block of puff-crete."

"We could try something else," the hog torturer said. There was a hopeful tone in his voice that I didn't like—even a hint of excitement. Maybe he thought he had himself a live one.

"Like what?" Galina asked.

"We have lots of other options. Some of them are a little, shall we say, off-regs? Like glass, needles, hooks—lots of things. Sometimes, a man can work wonders with just the hot barrel of a laser or a pair of tin snips."

Galina appeared to be thinking this over, which I found somewhat alarming.

My mind cast back to our last evening together. To the best of my limited memory, we'd had a fine time in my shack that night. She'd come back after Thanksgiving, tapping at my door.

I recalled having worried that I was about to jump in the sack with her sister, if it had been Sophia knocking at my door, but fortunately it had been Galina herself. We'd had a grand old time, too.

As my two tormentors discussed their plentiful options, a twinge struck my dog's mind. I had flirted with Sophia, or at least she had flirted with me that night…

Then, sometime after that, when I was revived at the Turov mansion in Eastern Europe, I had the opportunity to meet Sophia again. She had made some serious eyes at me. Call me egotistical, but when a girl gives you that look, well, sir, any man worth his salt knows that he's in if he wants to be.

Her father had made it very clear that I was no longer welcome in the house. I had rushed out of the place, and I hadn't seen her since. Nor had I seen Galina after that.

Maybe, just maybe, Galina had found out about how close I'd come to nailing her little sister. Could that be what this was all about?

By the time I'd done all this hard thinking, the sadistic hog and my angry ex-girlfriend had gotten around to talking about burning me with flaming brands and such-like.

"Hey, Imperator," I said, with my jawbone working against the wall. "I just thought of something."

"What is it now, McGill? Are you ready to confess?"

"I was just thinking about your family. Have you had a chance to talk to your sister Sophia lately?"

Galina did not answer, but I felt a frosty sensation enter the room. Suddenly, I heard her small heels snapping on the puff-crete behind me.

She came close. Real close. She whispered up toward me. "You'll shut up about that, McGill, if you know what's good for you."

Now, this seemed like an empty threat on steroids to me. After all, I was already buck-naked, hugging a wall and being beaten to death. Just exactly how much worse were things going to get?

"Imperator?" the hog said, clearing his throat. "I can't recommend that you get that close to the prisoner. He's got a reputation for violence, sir."

"Oh, I know. He's a brute. What do you think landed him in here?" Galina lingered behind me for a minute or so, thinking hard. At last, she gave a little grunt of frustration. "Leave," she said.

"What?"

"You heard me, get out! Leave me with the prisoner immediately."

"Imperator, I can't take—"

"Shut up, and get out of here, or I'll strip you down to a recruit and put you on this wall. You'll be cleaning toilets by noon tomorrow."

The hog, not being the dumbest sort, didn't say another word. I heard his heavy steps on the way to the door, and then I heard the door crash closed. Galina and I were alone.

Rest assured, I did consider killing her at that moment. I had carefully measured the amount of slack I had in the chain on my right side, where her little face was as she spoke up at me. She was almost in my armpit.

I figured I could probably knock her down with a body-slam. Maybe I'd even be able to use my heel to put her out.

But what would be the point of that? I'd still be chained to a wall. There were sure to be extra criminal charges. More nonsense. Worse, I couldn't imagine her mood would improve any.

Instead, I cranked my head around as far as it would go to look at her. "Galina? What do you really want to know?"

We stared at each other. Believe it or not, despite all the blood and the bad feelings, I think she was still angrier than I was. Go figure.

"James, I want to know if you slept with my sister Sophia."

Properly answering a question like that could be tricky for a man like me. The problem was I had a well-deserved reputation for both fabricating untruths and unbridled horn-doggery. Therefore, no matter what I answered, Galina was going to suspect I was lying.

I knew I had to come up with a way of convincing her I'd been falsely accused.

"Why, Imperator!" I said. "Whoever gave you the idea that such a heinous event could have happened?"

"My father, for one," she said. "You visited the mansion, and you spoke with my sister. He told me that you had eyes on her, and she had eyes on you. He indicated the interaction was very personal in nature. What were you even doing at my family's house?"

I shrugged, and my chains jingled. "That's supposed to be a secret, but…well, I did catch a courtesy revive from your dad. That was about six months ago. I wasn't there to see Sophia or anything."

Galina blinked a few times, and she frowned. "My father didn't say you had been revived…"

"Well… he and I worked out a little mutual aid package for each other. Let's just say I work for him sometimes."

"I know you've done that in the past… All right. All right. So, you didn't fly out there to meet her. But why does she have that glow in her eyes every time she talks about you?"

"She does, huh?" I grinned, and Galina poked a finger into my bloody back making me wince.

"I don't know… Maybe she just likes my mom's good home-cooking. This sure is a mean moment for you, Galina. The last time you were out at my place, you seemed happy enough."

Her eyes dropped. They studied the bloody puff-crete floor. They moved back and forth.

"All right," she said at last. "Maybe I jumped to conclusions. I'm sorry."

This was a huge admission on her part. Thirty lashes, lots of electricity with sweat and blood all over my bare-naked back. It was a small price to pay on my part for getting an apology out of her.

"I accept your apology. No hard feelings. Now, can you get me detached from this wall? Like… now?"

She shook her head. She didn't meet my eyes. "No, I can't. I'm sorry. The treachery charges—they're all real. You're in big trouble, James. None of that has anything to do with my sister."

"Uh…"

She turned away. Her steps were making sharp reports again, snapping against the puff-crete floor. When she got to the exit she buzzed to be let out. As she left, she turned back.

"I truly am sorry, James."

Before I could answer, the door slammed shut.

-8-

After Galina left, I kind of figured they would take me off that wall, maybe give me some clothes and put me in a cell. Something like that—but that wasn't how things went.

An hour and a half of hanging on the wall went by before someone came in and squirted a bit of nu-skin on my back. That was something at least, but no one offered me so much as a drink of water.

I lounged in the manacles, humming to myself a bit. With a great effort that started my wrists bleeding, I managed to reach my tapper with my chin and my tongue.

That was a sweet relief as I was able to get a ball game to play. I watched that and was having a good laugh at some of the announcer's off-color jokes when the door creaked open again.

"Hey," I said, "there's a really good game on."

"That's too bad, McGill, because I think you're going to miss the rest of it."

It was that same hog. The replacement man who Galina had put in charge of the final strokes on my wrecked back.

There were more footsteps following him, and I realized someone else had come in as well. Craning my sore neck, I thought I caught a glimpse of Primus Graves.

"Hey, is that you, Graves? Fancy meeting you down here. What brings you down to my neck of the woods?"

Graves put his hands on his hips and stared at me. "Centurion McGill... what are we going to do with you this time?"

"Uh... let me go on my personal word of honor?"

Graves laughed. "Let me have a look at that sheet of charges, officer."

The chief hog in charge of torture and abuse rattled a piece of plastic. He gave the computer scroll to Graves, who grunted while he went over the list.

"Resisting arrest, endangering a superior officer, two counts of misdemeanor murder—but those can easily be upgraded by Hegemony to felonies."

"Why's that?"

"Because you killed those hogs *while* resisting arrest. That compounds the charges."

"Aww... it was just a big misunderstanding, sir," I said.

"Right. Those aren't the bad charges, anyway. Oh, here we go, this is the big stuff: Sedition, illicit grid searches, and the distribution of forbidden disinformation. That's why you're really in here."

"I don't rightly understand it, sir. All I did was watch some kind of horror show on my tapper. It gave me a few ideas. So, I thought I'd look it up to see if the crazy things in the show were even possible."

"Shut up, McGill. They've done a full analysis of everything you've witnessed in the last couple of years. Nothing in that body of vids would absolve you. That brings us to this impasse. Where did you get this forbidden idea about bunkers and ancient wars, huh?"

He walked closer as he said this, and I glanced over my shoulder. Our eyes met. He gave me a flat stare.

I knew right then that I could drop a deuce on Graves' head. I could tell him and the portly gentleman that stood well back, caressing his whip like it was his date, that I'd gotten the idea from Graves himself. I could tell them about the bunker on my back-forty as well.

But I didn't want to say any of that. I knew all too well that Hegemony never forgave a sinful man. Confessing your sins would only serve to make them certain they were on a true and righteous path. A path that could only lead to my destruction.

Only lying, confusion and sheer pig-ignorance could save a man in a spot like this. Besides, there was no point in getting Graves chained up to the wall beside me. That wasn't going to help anybody.

Without a moment's hesitation, I shrugged and shook my head. "I'm completely flummoxed, sir," I said. This action caused my back to start bleeding again in a couple of places where the skin had cracked.

Graves pointed at the bleeding streaks. "This man is not in any condition to be interrogated further," he said. "Freshen him up."

Graves walked away, and his final words did not ring happily in my skull.

Freshen him up?

I hoped against hope that he didn't mean what I thought he meant.

Then the hog walked closer, and I saw he was grinning. He was still fondling that whip of his, and I saw him twist the bottom knob on the handle. That served to jack up the power.

It seemed clear to me that he intended to shock me to death. He lifted the whip up between us.

"You know what, McGill?" he said, "when this thing is turned up white-hot, it can give you an amazing jolt. Let's see how you like that, joker."

That was as far as he got. Contrary to popular belief, I'm not always a docile prisoner. Since my feet were not chained, just my hands, I was able to bring up a long leg up with a very hard knee attached.

I struck the bottom of that whip at a pretty precise angle. The business end of the device rammed right into the hog's left eye socket. That was an error on my part, I have to admit, because I had been aiming for his mouth.

But, oh well. A man had to take what he could get under these circumstances.

So, I watched him sizzle. He did a little dance and expired. He ended up curled into a ball on the puff-crete at my bloody feet.

Graves walked up a few minutes later. He looked annoyed and almost bored. "All right, McGill, you've had your fun," he said. "That's a third murder charge. You just don't know when to quit, do you?

"I guess I don't, Primus, sir."

He nodded, and then he shot me in the face.

* * *

Next time I opened my eyes, I was pleased to feel a hard cold steel gurney pressing against my sticky back. At least I wasn't up against a puff-crete wall this time around.

But where was I? I was supposed to be on a revival table.

"What have we got?" one of the bios asked the other. Both sounded bored and both were male, which caused me to lose interest almost instantly.

"He's an eight—maybe an eight and a half. I don't know… What difference does it make?"

"None at all," said the first guy.

They hauled me up off the table and left me staggering. Then they threw one of those ugly blue prison jumpsuits over me.

After they kicked me out of the revival chamber, I ran into the welcoming arms of a pair of hogs. They were loaded down with chains for both my wrists and my ankles.

Sooo, it was going to be one of those kinds of days…

At least my back was feeling good again. My hide was all one piece. I rolled my shoulders, enjoying the sensation.

In my opinion, prisoners always seemed to overestimate the inconvenience of being incarcerated. Just try being whipped to death a few times. You'll be enjoying your time on a safe bunk behind bars in no time. Three bland-tasting squares a day don't taste that bad to a man with some perspective.

Shuffling along behind my captors took me to the end of a long corridor. I asked several questions and made a few jokes, but they ignored everything.

My chains weren't long enough for me to be dangerous, just annoying. I might have been able to knock one of them on the floor, sure. But what would that have gotten me? A well-deserved beating with shock rods, so I didn't bother.

Eventually, we reached the end of the corridor and entered a room marked "court seven".

I frowned up at that. Why would they have auto-courts down here underneath Central? That was just plain weird.

It could be a good sign, however. With any kind of justice in the world, I'd be given a chance to make bail. With a quick hearing and a court date for the next step, I could see myself getting out of here tonight.

With my head held high, I was seated in the defendant's box. In this case, it was quite literally a *box*—a clear cage constructed with crysteel glass. There were some thoughtful holes punched through it, so you could breathe.

The box was supposedly to keep me from harming myself or others, but I wasn't even in the mood. The precautions seemed like overkill to me. Sure, I could be a dangerous man, but only when circumstances warranted violent action.

As I watched, three men shuffled into the courtroom. None of them were smiling. I didn't really recognize them right off, until one of them tossed me an angry glare.

"Hey," I said, "are you the three hogs I killed earlier today... or... was that yesterday?"

"It was yesterday!" One of the hogs spat out.

He sounded irritable, and I guess I couldn't blame him. Sure, it was sour grapes to worry about a death. But Hegemony types tended to take this sort of thing seriously.

"No hard feelings," I said to them, but none of them answered me.

Just then, the robot sitting up at a high desk at the front of the room came to life. Now, if I were the one designing such a device, I would have at least put a light bulb on top of its head or maybe even a rubber mask or something. Anything to make it look more human, more natural.

But no, this was a government robot, and they were always budget conscious. Their judges got a single camera and a single arm with a gavel permanently welded onto the end of it. The robot's black robe didn't really fit on its coat hanger-thin shoulders, either.

"Centurion James McGill, approach the bench."

"Uh…" I said, "I can't really do that, your honor, sir. I'm like… locked in this box, see?"

A hog bailiff unlocked my box. I was allowed to shuffle forward. My chains jangled and rattled like a handful of Hegemony pennies going down a sewer grate.

As I passed my accusers, I turned toward the three hogs I'd murdered the day before. They scowled at me. Jeez, these guys were touchy.

"Are each of you eyewitnesses to the crimes committed upon your person?" the robot judge asked.

They all nodded "Yes, Your Honor," they murmured in unison. They were holding their hats in their hands and studying the floor most of the time.

"Hold your horses," I said. "Judge, this was all one big misunderstanding. You see, I'm a special friend of Imperator Galina Turov's. I have a history—"

"The defendant will be silent," the judge said suddenly.

Being James McGill, I quite naturally failed to shut up. But the next time I opened my big mouth, a collar which I hadn't really noticed before cinched up around my throat. Apparently, the hogs had snuck that onto me when they'd put on the manacles.

Wherever it had come from, the damned thing was a powerful nuisance. It choked the words right out of my mouth. Strangling a bit, all I could do was make grunting noises. This turned into a gurgling sound within seconds.

I moved my hand up to my throat to loosen it—but my hands were chained, and I couldn't reach.

"Normally," the judge said, "sentencing in this matter would be light. No more than a month in the stockade per offense."

The three hogs shuffled around a bit. They looked kind of upset. I figured they must have felt their lives were worth more than a month of inconvenience. For my part, I disagreed with them, of course—but everyone had their own opinions.

"However," the judge went on, "there is a much more serious offense involved in this instance. That of seditious grid-searching."

The hogs perked up. Maybe, they hoped, I wasn't going to get off scot-free.

"This suspect stands accused of plotting against Hegemony itself."

The hogs began to smile and nudge each other. Meanwhile, I was looking long in the face.

"Our society isn't often abused by offenders of this nature in the modern era, but the old laws are quite clear, and they still apply. The punishments for his High Crime are carefully described, and the fact that the defendant committed all these acts nearly simultaneously, compounds the situation. In short, the three misdemeanor murders charges have been upgraded to felonies."

I tried to complain about all this skullduggery, don't think that I didn't, but the only sounds escaping my throat were rough gargling swallows. Every time I attempted to speak, the collar squeezed tighter, like a shock collar on a dog. I could only stand mute. The longer I stayed quiet, the sooner the collar would begin to ease, and I could breathe again.

Making a determined effort, I shut my fool mouth and kept it that way. I didn't want to pass out on the floor during the sentencing. I was kind of curious as to how much time I was going to get for the three murders.

"Therefore," the robot judge said, "Centurion James McGill of Legion Varus is hereby sentenced to one year for each count of murder."

Oh, I couldn't even tell you how happy those three hogs looked. They were all smiles now.

I made a squawking sound, but again, my words were choked away.

"For the more serious crime of searching for disinformation online," the judge continued, "you are sentenced to seven more years. All four of these sentences are to be served sequentially in the high security data vaults here at Central."

The judge then banged his gavel, and that was pretty much it. Everybody in the room seemed happy as a clam—except for me.

With his one skinny steel arm, the judge swung his gavel again. He hammered it down on his desk, and the loud report was like the sound of doom to me.

"Court is dismissed."

As I was hustled out of the place, I felt numb. Ten years? *Damnation...*

That was a shocker. Sure, with good behavior and the right parole officers I could probably hope to get out at five but still...

My body was going to be mid-thirties by that time. I'd probably have sprung a sore back or something before I got out of this place. I hoped they'd keep my body scans around until I got out.

Already, I was considering returning to Legion Varus for the opportunity of engineering just *one* quick death. Then I could be myself again.

This thought gave me another pang of worry. Would Legion Varus take me back after being kept on ice for ten years? I wasn't sure.

I was certain to lose my officer's commission, of course. But would I be allowed to serve at all? I wasn't sure about the bylaws and that stuff... although I'd been told to read it all, I never had.

The three hogs that I'd killed walked behind me and my two guards. They were hooting and catcalling—telling me nasty things.

"How's that feel, hero?"

"You're going to like it here, I'm certain of that!"

They said things like that and much more. I tried to shout a few choice comments back at them but again, that stupid collar kept strangling me.

So, I just went with it and shut up. I tried to look forward to the bright side of the whole thing. Sure, I was going to be sitting around bored to death in a prison cell for some years to come. But I'd endured worse things.

With any luck I wouldn't get too many beatings. And who knew? Maybe somebody important would take pity on poor old McGill and decide that I was better used as an agent on foreign soil—or just to shine somebody's shoes.

Maybe Galina herself, or her horndog sister, or her father would take pity on me and get me the hell out of here. Any one of those three probably had the clout to do it.

There was always Graves, too. He knew the truth. He knew that I had saved him from this fate, a downfall that was truly meant for him.

Graves owed me one. Hell, there were *a lot* of people that owed me one.

While I told myself all this happy-talk, I finally realized I wasn't being led to a prison cell.

"Uh…" I managed to say, "is this what I think it is?"

"That's right, genius," one of my guards said. "It's an execution booth."

This news set me to frowning all over again. "I thought I was getting a bunk and free food." I managed to get out.

All five of the hogs laughed at me. "This is your last and final resting place, McGill."

One of the hogs patted me on the shoulder. He was grinning at me. Grinning big. I thought I recognized him then. He had to be the hog that I'd tricked into shoving his electric whip into his own eye socket. That must have been a bad way to go out. I couldn't really blame him for being happy about my misfortune.

"Can we do it now?" asked another hog.

"No, no, not yet," whip-boy answered. "Wait a second. One more witness must be here."

"Damn it. I'm supposed to knock off at four."

They grumbled and shuffled and stood around. I tried to wheeze and hiss a few words. I was hoping to make small talk with them, but they weren't really in the mood to hear anything from me.

After about five minutes, I heard a heavy footstep in the hallway. To my surprise, Primus Graves walked into the place.

He looked me up and down and then glanced toward the hogs.

"This prisoner is James McGill," the head-hog said. "You can identify him, correct?"

"Yes," Graves admitted, nodding.

The hog rattled a computer scroll. "Honorable Judge Number Seven has sentenced this man to ten years hard time, to be served right here at Central."

Graves nodded again. He was grim-faced. He rarely smiled normally, but today, it seemed like he was almost ready to give me an honest frown.

"Centurion James McGill," the hog said in a formal tone. "You have been sentenced to ten years of nonexistence. Do you understand?"

"Non-what?" I said. "What's that mean? I thought I was going to go to a prison cell…"

That set the hogs to laughing. They could hardly contain their mirth.

"Shut up," Graves told them, and they all straightened up, hiding secret smiles. Graves turned back to me. "We don't keep prisoners here for that long, McGill. It's too expensive. Too much food, too much clean-up. You're here to be executed. When your sentence is up, you'll be revived again."

"Oh…" I said, and I couldn't keep the disappointment out of my voice. "I get it."

"Look at it this way," Graves said, "as far as you're concerned, you're going to go to sleep and wake up when it's all over. Not much of a punishment if you ask me. See you in ten."

He turned away and walked out.

I lifted my rattling chains, and my hands balled into fists. The hogs were swarming now, and their smiles weren't so secret anymore. I gave them a little wrestling contest, I even managed to give one man a knee to the groin and another a bleeding ear—but then one of them tweaked that collar that was still around my neck.

It began squeezing in earnest. Soon, I was on my knees. Then I slumped down onto the puff-crete floor.

I think they purposely set the collar to take a long time to do its work. Instead of clamping my throat shut and choking me out hard and fast, it just strangled me for several long minutes.

In the end I was laying on my back, turning blue and wheezing. I felt the blood in my neck fighting to make it to my fool brain.

All five hogs stood around, grinning and laughing. They handed coins to one another. They were betting on how many minutes I could last.

"He's a strong one. Look at them neck muscles!"

"He'll make six minutes easy. You mark my words."

Eventually, everything went black, and I died.

I never did find out who won the contest.

-9-

The next time I was revived, I don't mind telling you I was a little bit concerned. After all, the last two rounds of life and death hadn't gone too well for old James McGill.

But despite these bad precedents, as I came into awareness once again, I was happy to notice that I wasn't chained to a wall. I wasn't being beaten, either.

I listened while my head drooped, playing dead on a table. I noted there wasn't talk on the part of the bio people who revived me about execution trials or anything else horrible.

Beeping machines, the usual chemical stinks and the bright lights were all there, as they should be. The bio people working on me uttered nothing but sterile medical talk. It was all almost homey to a man like me. But then, one of them said something concerning.

"Is this a mistake?" One bio woman asked her partner. "This date… it's all wrong."

My relaxed body shifted into a more alert state. I was still lying limp on the table, mind you, all naked, sticky and drippy. I was barely breathing in fact, and I made a show of rolling my eyes way back up into my head when they shined lights into my face.

Despite my act, I was listening closely.

"Yeah…" a male voice said. They both seemed befuddled. "Yeah… you're right. He's not due out of purgatory for years yet."

I could hear their fingers swiping plastic computer scrolls. They were looking up my records. Already, my thoughts had turned to murder. I know that's a sorry state of affairs, but you shouldn't give anyone a lecture on morality until after you've been beaten to death multiple times. Let's just say that I wasn't in the mood for any more abuse at the cold hands of hogs from Central.

"I don't get it," the male said.

"I found it," the female said. "See? It's right here. His sentence has been commuted. It's stamped right here."

"Sentence commuted? What the hell does that mean?"

"It means that somebody decided to erase his crimes to let him out early."

"Huh… well, okay. Just as long as it's not our fault."

They went back to work taking my vitals, and I relaxed a fraction. My fists uncurled, becoming fingers again. No one was going to have to die. Not today… or at least not yet.

A few minutes later, I staged an amazing recovery. I was given a uniform and sent staggering out of the place. Unsurprisingly, a pair of hog guards were waiting right outside the revival chamber.

One of these portly boys handed me a packet with all my Legion Varus emblems and insignia in it. I snapped these into place, feeling proudful. Apparently, I was still an officer in the legions. That right there sounded like a win to me.

"Am I still under arrest, hogs?" I asked.

Their faces darkened a bit, but they didn't reach for their electric truncheons. They just scowled at me.

The veteran on the right answered me first. "We're here to escort you upstairs, sir. You're technically still a prisoner until you've been fully processed."

"Okay, then let's get to it."

I followed my hogs like a good little boy. I didn't ask these two why I'd been released. I didn't say a frigging thing about who had set all this up, either. I kept my damned mouth shut.

When you're given a gift from Heaven, even a fool knows you don't start complaining about having to go to church. You just stand the Hell up and start singing in the pews.

On the long elevator ride up into the highest floors of Central, I started to whistle a tune. It was an old song about ancient battles and forgotten times. The two hogs didn't seem to know or like the music. They just looked annoyed. As a testament to my reputation for sudden and decisive violence, neither one of them did more than fidget. No one dared to object.

Finally, the bell rang, and the doors opened. I walked out and they followed.

"Where we headed, exactly?" I asked.

"The big office at the end of the hall."

I strode there with purpose. I knew where this corridor had to lead before my outstretched hand hit the big double doors. It was Praetor Drusus' office.

"Damnation..." I said. "I haven't been up here for years. I swear every time I come in here the old boy has more statues. Look at the gold leaf frames on his paintings... And the carpet... isn't it a centimeter thicker than it was last year?"

The hogs didn't say anything.

Drusus' staff greeted me in an utterly unfriendly fashion. Primus Bob led the pack looking older and a little bit more bald than he had the last time I'd met up with him.

"Hey, Bob," I said, "do you remember how I like my coffee?"

"I don't get coffee for prisoners, McGill."

I lifted my hands, which were now free of manacles. I'm not a prisoner today. I'm an ex-con, see?"

"Whatever. The praetor is waiting for you behind those doors." He poked a crooked finger toward the inner office.

I walked in that direction and stepped inside without knocking.

"There you are, McGill," Drusus said. "You're late as usual."

I glanced at my tapper. "I'm not sure about that, sir," I said. "According to my best guestimation, I'm about nine years and one month early!"

Drusus grimaced rather than smiled in response. "Yes, yes, come right this way."

He walked over to his large holographic battle computer, which doubled as his desk or as a conference table, depending on the situation. Today it depicted our immediate area of the solar system.

Earth bulged up at the dead center, graphically displayed as something about the size of a basketball. The Moon was a grapefruit way off in one corner. Running in circles all over the place on the screen were various smaller contacts. These were spaceships, freighters, and miners coming in from the asteroids, that sort of thing.

Earth's primary space station was firmly in place above Central, as it should be, but there were some things on the display I didn't recognize right off.

The most notable of these was a collection of X-shaped green contacts. They were floating around over the Southern European zone.

"What are all those things, sir?" I asked pointing at the hologram.

Drusus frowned. "Haven't you been briefed?"

"Sorry, sir. The pet hogs that dragged me up here weren't in a talkative mood."

"All right. Well, I'll give you the short version. Those X's are what we call 'Big Sky'. We're planning on doing our startup tests of the screening system in the next 24 hours, in fact."

"Wow, really? You guys have been hauling ass building this thing in less than a year."

"Yes, well, it's high time we had a defensive system protecting Earth. Up until now, we've relied purely on our fleet. But all an enemy would have to do is sneak one good missile past us. One warhead per city, and you've got total destruction down here on the ground."

"Of course, sir, of course. I've always been admiring of Rigel's defensive systems. They've had a screen over their world for decades."

"Exactly," he said pointing a finger at me. "That's exactly right. That's the argument that got this thing built in the end. There was a lot of pushback from Fleet, mind you... everyone always fights over budgets."

I nodded. I understood completely.

For my own part, I was happy we'd finally started building a planet-wide screen in space. Rigel was way ahead of us.

"Within 1000 lightyears," Drusus said, "there's nothing to stop any attackers other than our own ships. That's a crazy way to operate a growing defense network."

Drusus talked more about how hard it was to build the satellites. He went over boring details like getting them funded, but I stopped listening. I just grunted and nodded now and then to keep him happy.

Internally, I was in a positive mood since someone had changed their mind about my prison time. When I'd first heard my sentence was to spend ten long years stored in the data banks here at Central, I'd been feeling kind of depressed. Essentially, I was to be left in a state of nonexistence until someone bothered to print me out again.

All those Christmases, all those Thanksgivings… My parents and my daughter, they were all going to be sad living through that decade without me. This cheapskate approach of keeping a man dead for so long, to my way of thinking it was more of a punishment for his family than it was for the guy himself.

And there were other relationships I'd missed out on as well. How many girls in my contacts list would even remember my name ten years later?

I was glad that my lost decade hadn't fully passed by.

Thinking that over, I felt a tiny unfamiliar sensation. It was unease. A dark thought had come to sit on my dim-bulb of a brain. There was something I hadn't asked about yet, and I needed to know the truth.

"Sir? Praetor Drusus, sir? I've got one quick question for you."

Drusus stopped talking about power requirements and how many tons of metal they'd mined from the asteroids to build his space stations. He frowned at me and checked his tapper. "All right, but hurry up, McGill. We've only got a couple of minutes left."

"Uh… okay. Well sir, they said my sentence was *commuted*. Does that mean like… permanently commuted?"

Drusus chuckled. "You're asking if you're going back into cold storage after this meeting, is that it?"

"Yes, sir. I can't help but feel a little curious about it."

"Don't worry, McGill," he said, "due to some legal technicality, once a man has been released from storage, it's no longer permissible to execute him and resentenced him unless he's committed additional crimes."

"Oh... that's a sheer relief."

Drusus gave me a dark look. "You did make it up here without murdering your guards, right?"

"Oh, yes, sir. I sure did. I did everything but shine their little hog-shoes."

Drusus nodded. "I'm sure you did... Okay, I see they're about to arrive."

Turning back to the high-resolution screen on the tabletop between us, he directed my attention to a bluish contact that was moving toward Earth. "You see that ship? The one that's coming down from outside the plane of the ecliptic?"

"I guess so."

"That is a ship from Rigel."

I made a squawk of alarm. "Rigel? Where are our cruisers? We have to stop that thing!"

"No, no," he said. "We've signed a negotiated truce with them. It's been in place for some time now, ever since the City World campaign."

"Oh..." I said thinking to myself that would have been about a year and a half ago. What with my lack of interest in politics and being dead for nearly a year, I'd missed out on lots of details. "All right, I guess that's good news. So... why are they coming here?"

"They're sending us diplomats, not a warship. Rigel is the reason you're breathing right now, in fact. They reportedly asked for you to be at this meeting."

"Really? What the hell for?"

He shook his head. "Beats me. Your lucky day, I guess. It was my impression that the bears from Rigel hated you above all else. Let's hope it's not their fondest wish to trade you away as a prisoner in exchange for an alliance or something."

I looked alarmed all over again. "Uh... well... Earth wouldn't go for that kind of deal, right?"

Drusus didn't answer. He was busy with his tapper and his screens.

Before I could ask anything else, his tapper buzzed.

"Major guests are arriving McGill. Stand here, look alert, and don't wreck anything."

He walked away, opened his office doors, and let in several other officials. Among them was one Alexander Turov. He was a man I hadn't seen for quite some time. I waved at him, and I even walked toward him hoping for a possible handshake.

He didn't look at me, so my hands slowly dropped back down to my side. Perhaps he was infected by the same anger that Galina was.

It was all about Sophia, Galina's younger sister. She'd shown an unhealthy interest in old McGill. Apparently, it had been acceptable to this old goat that I'd had numerous indiscretions with his oldest daughter. However, upon learning that I'd also captured the interest of his younger daughter, he had apparently been pushed a step too far.

Oh well, go figure. Some people were sensitive that way.

There were plenty of other officials in the crowd that I knew, but I didn't pester them too much. For the most part they were all high-level brass. The one man who nodded to me sourly was Praetor Wurtenberger.

I was sorry to see there wasn't a single tribune in the bunch. Not even Tribune Winslade, who ran my beloved Legion Varus, had been invited. That was too damned bad. At least if he'd been present, I would have had someone to talk to.

Casting my eyes about the place, I soon caught sight of the refreshment table. I made myself at home, filling up a plate with melon balls, cheeses, all that kind of stuff. Frustrated with the small plate, I took about a quarter of the salami, and the plate it sat upon. Discarding the rest of the salami on to the table itself, I finished my raid with a mounding pile of at least thirty fresh prawns onto the pirated serving platter. Dumping what was uneaten from the first inadequately sized plate onto my new McGill-sized plate, I headed over to the waiting area.

I grabbed a fine seat where Drusus had parked a circle of cushy chairs with a floating coffee table between them. There, while the brass was playing meet-and-greet, I feasted on everything I'd managed to purloin.

As I chewed, I looked around for a bar. So far, my greatest regret was the total lack of alcohol at the meeting. This seemed like a grim oversight.

The brass pretty much ignored me. They talked about themselves in small circles until Drusus called the meeting to order. At that point, I licked my fingers and left the plate covered with shrimp tails on the floating coffee table. Smearing tartar sauce across the expensive luxury furniture. I wiped my hands on my pants and walked over to the main conference table.

When I joined the circle, the high-level officers present tossed me hostile glances. They seemed as mystified as I was regarding the reasons for my presence. But no one addressed me about it. I felt like the proverbial turd in the toilet bowl.

"Officers," Drusus said. "The representatives from Rigel are just about to arrive in orbit. We're here to discuss our strategy during the diplomatic functions to come."

My face went blank, but inside I was feeling uplifted. I'd attended any number of diplomatic functions, and they were always boring as hell. They were universally attended by old boring bigwigs like fat-boy Praetor Wurtenberger, who sat bulging in his chair on my left. But on the positive side there were always attractive waitresses wandering around. Sometimes even a few bored trophy wives to talk to with excellent food and drink along the way. Since I was a man who was never important in any kind of diplomatic sense at these functions, I pretty much played the part of a vacuum cleaner, sucking up every morsel of good food and drink I could.

On the side, I chatted up every good-looking woman in the room. It passed the time, anyways.

The crowd of officers watched as the blue triangle representing the ship from Rigel arrived at our spaceport and docked.

"What do you think they want from us, Drusus?" Praetor Wurtenberger asked.

"They haven't made that clear, but they did say their mission is urgent and involves the outstanding treaties they have with Earth." Drusus replied.

"That could mean they're announcing war!" Wurtenberger huffed.

"I doubt it," Drusus said. "If that was their intention, I believe they would just show up here with a fleet and attack."

Wurtenberger frowned and poked at the ship icon from Rigel. Nothing useful popped up in the way of information, other than to say it was an alien vessel.

"Then they're here to spy on us," another voice announced.

Everybody turned, and I realized it was Alexander Turov who had spoken. In a sense, he was the highest-ranked person present. He was a Servant of the People, a member of the Ruling Council of Hegemony. What's more, he'd been holding that office for nearly a century.

His particular specialty involved budgetary contracts for Earth's military. That meant he was worth any dozen imperators and equestrians. He was beyond rank, and while he was no collector of salutes from low level soldiers like me, he held a power of even greater significance. He controlled the purse strings for everybody else present.

"It can be said that every diplomat serves the secondary capacity as a spy," Drusus said. "But the urgency of this request from Rigel indicates that something else is on their minds."

"They should bring up their grievances in a less provocative manner," Turov said.

"We don't maintain permanent embassies in each other's territory. We've asked for that, but sadly, they've always refused."

Alexander Turov leaned over the planning table. Everyone else had stopped talking. "Let us discuss another matter, Drusus."

Then, the old buzzard extended a long arm in my direction. At the end of that skinny arm was an even thinner, crooked finger. The finger was bent with age and seemed accusatory in nature. "What is this man doing here? Why has he been prematurely released from nonexistence?"

I almost opened my mouth to say something, but I controlled the urge with difficulty.

Drusus glanced at me then turned back to Servant Turov. "Servant," he said, "the Rigellians specifically requested that McGill be present at our first meeting with their delegation. If you wish to override this request and deny it, I will of course immediately remove McGill."

To make his point more clearly, Drusus pulled his jacket away from the holster on his belt. He put his hand on the butt of a laser pistol.

My eyes widened a fraction and my mouth dropped open a centimeter or so. But still I managed to hold my tongue.

Old Alexander seemed to consider these words for a moment. He finally turned to me, and his eyes met mine for the first time since his arrival.

Not being a man who could read emotions on any face easily, it still seemed to me like he wasn't happy to see me. Not at all.

"McGill," he said. "What trickery and nonsense is this? Has some agent of yours gotten the Rigellians to make this absurd request?"

"Uh…" I said. "Well, sir, I wouldn't rightly know. I've been sleeping on ice for about eleven months now, and I don't really have any agents or other benefactors anyways."

Alexander nodded once. "That is my assessment as well. All right. I'm curious as to what these horrific little bears want from us. So, I will allow McGill's offensive existence to continue for now."

Thinking back over Alexander's words as the meeting wore on, I was pretty damned certain that he was offended by me. Maybe he'd been responsible for this entire business of me being executed, accused of sedition, and all the rest of that hullabaloo.

Maybe, he'd been just waiting in the wings for the smallest infraction. Something like doing a simple web search, in order to throw the book at me and get me burned off the face of the Earth.

Damnation, this old boy sure was defensive of his younger daughter.

The meeting dragged on, with everyone discussing various details of their current treaty with Rigel. Our two fledgling frontier powers had agreed to divide up the empty province of star systems between us. Several key pieces of real estate had gone to Rigel, including Dark World with its starship factory. We had secured properties of more dubious value, such as Blood World which at least provided us a great number of excellent ground troops. Storm World was also included, a soggy planet that gave us nothing but headaches as far as I could tell. Glass World was likewise neutral territory these days, as no one lived there permanently.

Most of the rest of the star systems either had uninhabited planets, no planets, or some feisty independent group of aliens that didn't recognize either Earth or Rigel as their masters. Most of these worlds were too low value to be worthy of a campaign to conquer them.

That was the way things went out here on the Frontier, outside the edges of the Empire. The outer half of the galaxy was barbaric and disorganized. It was catch as catch can, with countless petty tyrants, kingdoms and tiny empires.

Rigel was technically at war with the Empire after having refused their demands some years ago. But that didn't matter much, since the Empire had no military presence out here in Province 921.

The truth was we simply weren't valuable enough to our masters, the Mogwa of the Core Worlds. They couldn't bother to spend resources on a fleet to defend us. Instead, they'd decided to deputize us to handle local security issues on the cheap. Giving Earth something like a feudal fiefdom allowed us to run whatever planets we occupied. That is, as long as we maintained a strong enough military force to defend Province 921. All things considered they didn't much care what we did out here in our ghetto of scattered stars.

The bigwigs at the meeting planned out various dull, ceremonial steps. They decided who would be speaking for Earth at each stage of the ceremony and generally bored the hell out of me.

As soon as I was able, I crept back to the snack table with my pilfered plate and stacked it high once again.

Drusus caught up with me while I was stuffing my face with the best that his table had to offer.

"McGill?"

"Yessir?"

"Just what is this business with you and Servant Turov? I thought that you guys were… well… if not friends, then at least acquaintances."

"That's right, sir," I said. "Old Alexander and I go waaay back. Did you know I was at his daughter's wedding a few years ago?"

Drusus frowned. "Didn't his daughter and her fiancé die in a hail of bullets during that ceremony?"

"Uh… well, not exactly. The ceremony hadn't even started at that point, see."

Drusus shook his head. "Well, I'm sure that he has his reasons for being annoyed with you. Please try not to irritate him any further."

"Don't worry about a thing, sir. No one has ever accounted themselves as properly schmoozed and back-rubbed until they've met up with ol' McGill."

Drusus rolled his eyes and left me to continue my assault on the snack bar.

-10-

Just then someone small stepped up on my six. I turned around, and to my surprise, I laid eyes on Galina Turov.

"Hey there, Imperator," I said with my mouthful. "You're late."

"I'm not late McGill," she said. "I just got in from Big Sky Station Four."

"Huh? Big what?"

She pointed up and out the windows. "You do recall the project that Earth has been working on for the last year and a half, right?"

"Oh yeah, right, of course. Big Sky Station Four... That's what they call it? That's cool. What's it like up there?"

"It's boring," she said. "Very boring. The machinery isn't even running yet." She grabbed a proper tiny snack plate and stabbed a cocktail frank with a long pointy toothpick. She chewed on this item for a moment.

"How did you manage to get out of Purgatory anyway?" she asked me.

"Well, sir, as you may recall, I've never been a man who is easily kept incarcerated."

She nodded. "True enough. Anyway, since you're here, what do you think these bears want? It can't be a coincidence that they're coming here today, the very day we're doing our first tests on the Big Sky system."

"Uh…" I said. "I don't rightly know what they're up to. I've kind of been out of the picture for a while. You know what I mean?"

"Right, right, useless as always. Just stay out of my way." She walked off, and I watched her hindquarters as she headed toward a knot of officers who were standing around talking. They seemed happy to see her coming, as she'd lost none of her natural charms.

Eventually, the meeting broke up, and I walked out of Drusus' office like I owned the world. I half-expected to see a couple of hogs waiting in the corridor, either to arrest me and take me back to a cell, or simply to escort me out of the building.

No one was around, so I was apparently a free man. Grinning big, I headed for the elevators and began riding down to the streets. I had big plans. *Big, big* plans. I was going to hit every stripper-bar in town.

Just as I reached the lobby, my tapper began buzzing. I glanced down in irritation. Hadn't I just talked to just about everyone here at Central who cared to pester me? Who could have possibly gotten through.

But then, I saw the identification on my tapper. It was my daughter Etta. I smiled and opened the channel. "Hi honey. Long-time no-see!"

Etta looked sunburned. She had a few new lines around her eyes, too. How old was she now? Thirty? Thirty-five? I had no earthly idea, but I kept right on smiling. I didn't give any hint that anything was wrong.

I could tell she was still on Dust World because I could see the hot sky behind her. The star was glaring with bright yellow light. Unless she was in one of the roughest deserts on Earth, she had to be off-world.

"I can't believe you're back, Dad. It's been so long."

"That's right honey. It's been a long, long time. Not for me though. Seems just like yesterday when we spoke last."

"Listen, Dad. This phone call is costing me a lot because it's going through the deep-link system. So just listen for a second. I've learned a few things."

My mind was blank for a moment, but then I thought I had it. "Oh, you mean about that place out in the swamp?"

She waved her hands wildly urging me to shut up. "Don't say anything, Dad. Just know that I've learned a few things. I need to talk to you. When can you come out here to see the Investigator?"

"Out to Dust World? I don't know... It'll be a while. I've kind of got a couple of important meetings to attend, see."

"Listen," she said, "this is extremely important. It affects the whole family. I can't talk to you about it on Earth. I can't talk to you about it on deep-link, either. You have to get to the gateway posts and come here as soon as you can."

I side-glanced back at the elevators. Indicators with flashing numbers crawled above each door. If I did a U-turn in the lobby and headed to Gray Deck now, I could get to one of the gateway rooms and probably get myself transported to Dust World for free.

However, that would put me in danger of missing the big meet-and-greet that Praetor Drusus and the rest of them had set up with Rigel.

Still, I almost did it, until I remembered that the alien bears had specifically demanded that I be revived for this meeting. They weren't going to just forget about that.

Drusus wouldn't be happy either if he had to gloss-over my absence at this diplomatic function.

"I'll tell you what, girl," I said. "Your grandpa has waited for months. I think he can wait a day or two more. I'll come out there as soon as I can."

"All right," she said, looking a little upset. "Just don't forget."

Then, she ended the phone call. A large number flashed up on my tapper, and I realized it represented the astounding number of credits that had just been charged to my account. Hell, I hadn't even realized the girl was calling collect.

I did manage to eat a sandwich, seven beers, and hand out some big tips to some blushing ladies. None of it lasted long enough from my point of view.

My tapper was soon hopping right out of my skin. All kinds of high-ranked monkeys back at Central demanded my immediate return.

Dragging my feet just a little mind you, I returned to the hulking building. The night was cool, and the stars were out, but I couldn't enjoy any of it. I went back upstairs and wandered into yet another social event, as bored as a three-year-old in church.

Things perked up when the bears arrived. The nasty natives of Rigel weren't interested in parades, ceremonies, or anything of the kind. They wanted to get down to business immediately.

Turov called for a feast, and I was ready to vote for him on the spot—except I don't think people got to vote for their Public Servants anymore these days.

A grand meeting was called and plenty of food summoned. I groaned about the meeting and salivated in anticipation of the food.

Nine bears had come down from their diplomatic ship to talk to us. None of them looked like Squanto to me, but that didn't mean much. Should Squanto still be alive, he would be quite old by now. None of the bears seemed ancient enough to fit the description.

You have to understand, the people of Rigel were different in culture and lived their lives differently than humans did. Their typical lifespans were only about forty years, instead of our typical ninety. So essentially, they lived half as long as we did. On top of that, they felt that any bear that fell in battle deserved his death, and it was considered dishonorable to bring them back to life.

Therefore, they totally avoided revival machines and considered all the races that used them to be demonstrably inferior. They often made comments suggesting humans like me were of poor genetic stock.

The bears themselves did not look *exactly* like a wild bear from Earth. Their hair was thinner than a bears, being almost see-through in places. This was not a pretty sight. If you've ever seen a man's hair cut super-short, down to where you can see the scalp as if each hair were a blade of grass… Well, that's the sort of effect you got from looking closely at the bears.

They did have fangs and claws, and their stature was perhaps a meter tall when they stood on their hind legs. But they definitely were a lot uglier than bears from the zoo.

To make up for being heinously ugly, they were a sneering, unforgiving and downright mean species of apex predators, making them vicious fighters. They also liked to torture and kill their captives. They uniformly mistreated any race they managed to subjugate. If you've ever fought a soldier from Rigel, either one-on-one or on the battlefield, you know they're tough.

It was no surprise to me that the bears who came down to meet with us from the diplomatic ship didn't wear robes of civilian office or anything like that. Instead, they were all wearing their impervious black armor. Every molded centimeter was laced with star-stuff.

That meant that if this group decided right now to kill everybody in our group, they would likely succeed, since we were wearing our fancy-pants dress uniforms. That fact right there was enough to put me on my guard.

Even though I was pretty sure Squanto wasn't in the group, the fact the other side was in combat gear made me feel like we weren't on safe ground. I also thought that Alexander was being naive to even consider bringing these bears up to see our new top-secret facility. We were supposed to switch-on within days, and it just seemed like a bad idea to this bumpkin.

I looked forward to seeing a protective field form over Earth, but I knew I wasn't in any kind of good graces with Old Alexander—or Galina either for that matter. I figured my best move would be to keep my mouth shut.

"Who is in charge, here?" one of the bears demanded, eyeballing our group.

At first, several people glanced toward Drusus. He was usually our spokesman and was nominally in charge of Earth's defenses.

A few others glanced toward Praetor Wurtenberger, as he was technically senior to Drusus, but when neither of these two spoke up, everyone turned toward old Alexander Turov.

Servant Turov stood tall despite his exceeding age. He stared at the bear without speaking for several long moments.

No one else moved. When the bear finally noticed Turov, the two squared-off.

"I am Squantus," the bear said. "Alpha-cub of Squanto. I am the governor of this province."

A murmur went through the assembled officers. They glanced at each other, and I smirked. They hadn't yet personally encountered this arrogant race of space-bears.

"I am known as Servant Turov," Alexander said. "I must note at this point that we do not recognize any authority over this province other than our own."

The self-proclaimed Governor Squantus nodded. "You must understand that it is customary for our species to take roles that are possibly premature from your point of view. Since the conquering of what is currently known as Province 921 of the Empire is an inevitability, I have been given a title of rulership over this region of space."

"It does indeed seem premature. What steps do you plan to take to create this… inevitability?"

Squantus showed his rough black palms to the humans. "Until Rigel has succeeded in her goals of conquering this region it's my task to play the part of a military commander. When the coming campaign is finished, I will eventually become the governor or overlord of this province."

"And what if you should fail?" Turov asked. "Or die in the attempt?"

"Such a thing is… almost inconceivable. But, if such a near-impossibility were to occur by some freak chance, then my heir would take over this grand task."

There were more confused looks among the humans. No one dared speak because Alexander was still standing there and everybody else was subordinate to him. There was a little bit of quiet grumbling but no outright shouts in anger.

Turov took a moment to think this over before responding. "That is a very arrogant and presumptuous position to take during what I had imagined would be a peaceful diplomatic talk."

Squantus made an easy gesture, opening his clawed hands wide and sweeping them around to the sides. "Do not be alarmed," he said. "The eventuality of this provinces' fall may be decades away. At this time, as you stated correctly, we are at peace. Think about my title and my statements as merely clarifications of my mission goals."

"I understand," Turov said, inclining his head slightly.

These guys certainly weren't like earthmen. In comparison, we kind of did things on the fly. Sure, we had some long-term plans. I was certain that think-tanks right here inside Central had gamed things out for decades.

That said, we sure as hell didn't go around declaring ourselves to be governors for properties that we didn't even own yet. That right there was just a pure example of the fantastic level of arrogance that I always met up with among the people of Rigel.

No wonder nobody liked the little bastards.

"Now that we've finished the introductions," Servant Turov said, getting directly to the point. "Why are you here? Why have you summoned us into this audience? Is it only to tell us of your declared intentions to conquer the space between our two empires?"

"No," Squantus said. "I am here to implore you to maintain our useful peace treaty."

"All right... what do you require to continue enjoying the fruits of peace with Earth?"

"We require that you don't continue construction or testing of your planet-wide defensive screens."

This was too much. Several of the officers present stood up, but Alexander waved them back down with a pair of bony hands.

"Why would we comply with such demands?" he asked.

"To keep the peace, of course," Squantus replied. "Your submission on this point is a critical requirement of our peace treaty."

Turov shook his head. He seemed bemused. "Listen, Squantus," he said, "please try to see this matter from our point of view. Rigel already has a defensive network quite similar in nature to the one we're building here. Yours, in fact, may still be superior—even after we're finished with our construction efforts."

"No!" Squantus responded emphatically. "There is no 'may be' in this matter. Our defensive systems are infinitely superior, and they will always remain superior to anything Earthmen can construct."

"Be that as it may, it seems quite unfair and in fact, preposterous that you should come here and demand that we do not build a purely defensive structure. Especially one of a type that you yourselves have already deployed."

Squantus blinked a few times. It seemed like he was confused by these statements.

"Don't misunderstand," he said, "we are not demanding anything from Earth. We are imploring… requesting… what are other words I can use? We are beseeching Earth to not take this step."

"Otherwise, Rigel will attack?" Turov asked. "Is that what you're saying?"

"No. I'm not saying this. I'm saying that it's a precursor for the maintenance of our current peace treaty. That Earth—"

"Yes, yes, I got that," Turov said. His calm seemed to be cracking at last. "You're making a demand. You plan to break the treaty if we do not comply, and you waited until we're well into the construction of the system before you even came here to tell us about your concerns."

"I think you now grasp the situation firmly. It was difficult, but I have communicated successfully."

Turov showed his aging yellow teeth. "All of this seems difficult to swallow on the face of it, but I will entertain the entire concept for now. What, High Lord Squantus, do you propose to offer Earth in return for our compliance in this matter?"

Again, the bears seemed a bit confused. Other members of Squantus' party shuffled about, and they leaned towards each other. They clicked at each other in their bizarre native tongue.

At last, Squantus turned back around, and he made a broad circular motion with both paws. Perhaps that was meant to calm us or something, I wasn't quite sure

"We offer you continued peace," he said, as if this was the simplest matter in the world to understand. "The people of

Earth will continue to draw breath. No bombs shall fall upon your forests or your oceans."

"Yeah, that's great—but we already have these benefits from our existing peace treaty. You're asking us to alter it in your favor. What do you offer in return?"

"I have nothing else to offer," the bear said. "If the continuance of one's lifespan is an insufficient motivator, then perhaps we are at an impasse."

Turov took a deep breath for the first time during this meeting. I thought he glanced my direction perhaps just for a moment. Now he was beginning to grasp how difficult these bears had been to deal with. He knew that I'd often come to blows with them in the past... Maybe now he knew why.

He moved his eyes back to Squantus. He put a hand that was curled with age to his chin. After a moment's thought he spoke again. "How about this? You shall allow us to occupy Dark World and give up the factory that orbits above that planet. In return, we will abandon our attempts to build a planetary defense shield."

The bears were positively stunned. They huddled, and there was a lot of loud, angry clicking. I could tell by the way their ears were clamped down flatly to their skulls that there wasn't much positive thinking going on inside that angry group of little bears.

"Your request is absurd," Squantus said. "You are requesting ownership of the Vulbites, who make our infantry armor. That armor is vastly superior to your own, I might add. You also request to take our primary starship production facility? And for this, your sole offer is to not build a defensive structure? This hardly seems equitable."

Turov shrugged, and he spread his hands making that circular motion the bear had done. He was a quick learner for such an elderly guy. "All right," he said. "Negotiations have commenced. What is your counter proposal?"

The bears huddled again for a moment, but when they came up for air, they looked universally upset. "We have none at this moment. We will have to reconvene."

"When?"

"Possibly tomorrow, after we have consulted with our home government."

Turov nodded. "That is acceptable. Tomorrow, by the way, we plan to have the first test of the Big Sky project. We would enjoy having you as our guests to witness this historic occasion."

Squantus took three waddling steps forward and pointed an angry claw at Turov. "You have not listened to anything I've said. Rigel demands that you don't switch on this defensive system."

Alexander smiled coldly. "Don't worry, it's only a test. It will be on very briefly, simply to make sure the whole thing works. Feel free to take pictures or make sensory recordings to return home to your government. We want you to report the status of our grand accomplishments."

Squantus paced among his partners, speaking in his native tongue.

"For now," Alexander said, "let's stop talking about serious matters. Let us break for social activities."

The bears accepted his invitation with poor grace. They sat at a table especially built for them which was low to the ground. Small chairs circled the table, which looked about the size of something a kindergartener would sit at.

The aliens were provided with a separate buffet of food. It was laden with foods that should, to the best of our knowledge, please the bears.

The Rigellians attacked the food. They sniffed, climbed over, poked at and tasted practically everything.

-11-

The bears were serious double-dippers, I could tell that much right away. All of them seemed to delight in sticking a claw into a given dish, licking it for flavor. If they enjoyed the taste, they'd return that same dirty paw to the same public dish. If they didn't like it, they spat it out on the deck. I reminded myself to avoid inviting these characters to any future Thanksgiving dinner at my place.

As for myself, I'd rushed the buffet with the bears. There was quite a spread to be had. Roast duck was front and center, and I took a double helping before I went to the next item on the list. I moved on to the mashed potatoes and then the greens. But before I'd finished filling my first plate or even putting a speck of food upon my second plate, I felt a tiny poke and a tug on my pant leg.

I looked down. There stood a diminutive figure that came up just past my knees. He was almost to the level of my genitals. I knew him. I squinted down at that nasty face. He was the one called Squantus.

"You," Squantus said, blowing foul breath up at me. "You are of unusual size, even for a human."

"Yep, that's right," I said. "Two meters tall and no cheating."

He stared at me. "My computational aide," he said, touching the rattling snake-like necklace of artificial bones that every Rigellian wore, "has identified you as a member of this species who has been recorded in our database."

"Is that right? That's quite a coincidence, because you look kind of familiar to me, too. There was once this bear that tried to steal my picnic out in the Smoky Mountains. You wouldn't be related to him, would you?"

"The suggestion that such an animal might be my relative is not only offensive, but also genetically impossible."

"Oh, well. Too bad. Looks aren't everything, you know." I tried to make a quick exit from the conversation after that. I stepped away from the buffet even though I'd only managed to pick up half my food with my hands.

This bear, however, wasn't so easily dissuaded. He poked at me with his claw again, hooking it right through my pants leg. There was a ripping sound as I moved away. He'd torn a nick out of my dress uniform.

Under different circumstances, I might have stomped on him for that. But I was on my best behavior today.

Instead of attacking the little bastard, I turned around and forced a smile. "What's the problem, little friend?"

"I'm not your friend, human. I'm not even your acquaintance. But I do know who and what you are."

"Oh, yeah. Who's that?"

"You are the McGill," he said. "An almost mythical creature who once plagued my father through countless campaigns and years of his lifetime."

"The McGill? Sorry, never heard of the guy."

"Yes, yes!" he persisted, jabbing that single curved talon at me repeatedly as he spoke. "Your behavior confirms my suspicions. You lie with fanatical persistence—telling mistruths even when there's almost no point to it. That is also part of your personality profile."

"Is that so?"

"Yes. I now believe you're not a descendant of the ape I seek, but rather the original scoundrel himself."

I sighed and shoved a leg of duck into my jaws and began chewing on it. "Okay, Squantus. I guess you're right. I knew your daddy. What do you want to make out of it? Do you want to duel or something?"

The bear seemed to think this over. "No," he said at last. "Not at this time. I would instead entreat with you."

"You want to *what* with me?"

"I wish to talk with you privately."

"Uh…" I said knowing that any kind of dialog between a bear and old McGill was damn near certain to turn into a disaster. "I'm not a diplomat, you understand? I'm just a soldier. I've got very little pull here among all these higher-level officers and politicians. I'm pretty much a nobody in this crowd."

"And yet you're here," he said. "That simple fact is either evidence of your true importance, or a subtle insult designed by your superiors to offend me."

I blinked a few times. I'd become confused about a detail of recent events myself.

"Hold on a minute," I said, waving a duck legbone at him. "Didn't you specifically request that I be here at this meeting?"

"No," he said, "why would I make such a demand?"

"Huh," I said thinking that over. "That does change things a bit. Why don't we go and have a little talk?"

We retired to a table that was too big for him and too small for me. We sat across from each other. He had snagged the whole platter of beef, while I had a plate of just about everything else on the menu except for the beef.

We both ate for a while, studying one another with suspicious glances.

"My father knew you," Squantus said. "Would you like to know the wisdom he imparted in his dying gasps?"

"Well… not particularly. But if you really feel like telling me, go ahead."

"He said that you were a ferocious competitor. He said you were a trickster. He said you were a vile being, unworthy of eating the excrement of all the bears you have slain."

I nodded. "Sounds pretty dead-on so far."

"He also said, however, that you had a sense of honor. That upon your final meeting, you chose not to assassinate him when you could have done so. He was impressed because you were clearly under orders to dishonorably slay him."

"Yup, that's right. I remember the feel of that bomb in my belly… I let your poppa know what was coming, and he got away scot-free."

"This brings us to the purpose of this diplomatic mission. We are here to stop Earth's ignorant leadership from activating their new planetary defensive screen. Do you believe there's any way we can implore your government to abandon this folly?"

"Whoa! That's a tall order right there. I don't think it can be done. Certainly not by me, as I don't have that much pull around here."

The bear glumly sucked gravy out of his fur and claws. "A fair answer and plainly stated. You are as my father indicated. An ignoramus who lies when he shouldn't, but who also tells the truth when he must."

"Don't look so down in the snout, Squantus. What are you guys worried about? It's only a test. We haven't even covered most of the planet yet. We're just going to see if it works, that's all."

He jabbed that little claw at me again. "You do not need to worry about our motivations. You need to worry about what will happen if the system is tested. Events will proceed that are uncontrollable and unpleasant."

I shook my head. To me, he sounded like your typical alien. These bears usually offered up the same old threats and bullshit. Here they were demanding we bend the knee, while offering us jack-squat-nothing in return.

"You know," I said, talking around my next bite, "you guys might be able to offer something that would get them to not switch this project on, but it would have to be something good. Maybe you could hand over a few outposts in the Eridani region."

The bear shook his head vigorously. "There will be no planets surrendered to the humans."

"Well then, I don't know. There's not much else I can think of that would persuade my people to do anything differently."

Squantus looked dejected. "My mission here was doomed to failure. I am wasting my time."

"Well, at least you can eat some good food. Here, let's toast to your father. Old Squanto was a good wrestler, I bet you knew that."

He brightened a little, and we talked about more pleasant things after that. We ate a lot of food and drank a few drinks. To my mind, the bears were a little hard to take, and they were kind of weird around the fringes, but if you got a few drinks into just about anybody, you could usually get along with them.

Around about midnight, the bear left with the rest of his delegation. That's when someone else came close and stood at my table. She put her fine hands on the back of the chair Squantus had vacated.

"Hi, James."

"Oh… hi."

To my surprise, it was none other than Sophia Turov, Galina's little sister. She was cute like her older sibling. She wasn't quite as much of a perfectly-figured girl, mind you, but she did have more of a wholesome look to her—kind of a vibrant and less plasticky feel. She was definitely far less negative in her outlook.

Right away, I was on my guard. When she sat down across from me, I stood up like there was a jack-in-the-box stuck up my butt.

"Where are you going?" she said in disappointment. "I've just sat down."

"Well… " I said, faking a big yawn and a stretch. "Duty calls. I've got early morning PT at six, followed by—"

"Oh, stop it," she said. "Look around. My father and my sister have both left already."

I did look around warily, and I didn't spot any of the rest of the Turov clan among the twenty-odd attendees who were still in the banquet hall. Reluctantly, I sat back down.

"Why are you looking at me like I'm a snake about to strike?" she asked. "That's not how you acted the last few times we met."

"No," I admitted.

I didn't want to tell her that I'd been repeatedly killed and then left dead for eleven months due to having flirted with her once or twice. It didn't seem fair that she should be burdened with such knowledge.

She leaned close and lowered her voice. "Has my father warned you off?" she asked.

I snorted. "Hell no. Such a thing could never sway my judgement, even if he had."

She nodded, not buying my boasts for a second. "That's what I thought. It's just the kind of thing he would do. That's so infuriating. He's always trying to manage my life for me."

"Uh…" I said. "It's not just that. As you may have heard, I've enjoyed a few friendly evenings with your sister as well."

"Ah," she said. "Galina. So that's it. You do realize it's been a year and a half since you've been with her?"

"There-abouts, I guess that's right…"

"Yes. She's quite angry with you, and she doesn't want to be around you anymore. How long does it take before a man can talk to another girl after his girlfriend has ditched him? It's been a frigging year and a half, James."

"Yeah…" I said, "but, well…"

Naturally, I was thinking about being executed by slow strangulation. About gavels swinging in the single metal arms of automated judges, all that sort of thing.

I didn't want to come off like a coward or anything, mind you. But after being flogged to death a couple of times for what I considered to be innocent moments between Sophia and I… Well, I was a bit gun-shy, I have to admit.

"Come on," she said. "Your reputation is that of a scoundrel."

"Oh yeah?"

"Yes. Everyone has warned me about you. They say you're a cad. A man who crawls over every woman he sees. Am I ugly or something? Or… are you just scared?"

I turned and looked at her. Our eyes met for just one quiet moment, and I knew I was in trouble.

This girl *seemed* innocent, sure. I'd always assumed she was a lot less conniving than her sister Galina, but now, I was beginning to wonder if that assumption might be untrue. Had I found yet another small, cute bundle of evil?

Just considering her pedigree, I had to admit to myself that the odds were pretty high.

"Uh…" I said. "Okay. I guess a friendly conversation never hurt anyone. Tell me something about yourself."

That was it. I'd brought up her favorite topic, and she started talking a mile a minute.

Soon, the night wore on. We had a few drinks, and then, around about midnight, we crept away. We found an empty officer's quarters in amongst the vast barracks at Central, and we spent a robust night together.

-12-

The next day rolled around all too quickly. I managed to sneak a private breakfast with Sophia, but then, after a squeeze of the hand and a peck on the cheek, she vanished. She raced away to rejoin her family members.

After she did so, I quickly scrambled away to a different part of Central altogether. Once I felt I was at a safe distance, I removed a special lead-lined sheath that I bought just to wrap around my tapper at moments like this.

The sheath was designed to look kind of like one of those braces that weaklings wore on their wrists because they typed too often, or some such nonsense. But in actuality, it was a cunningly designed tapper-blocker.

This simple device didn't require any duct tape, aluminum foil, or other noisy, messy stuff that was difficult to remove. In the past, my dodges had been kind of obvious to the eye. The sheath slid neatly under your sleeve and dampened all signals and tracking until you removed it.

It was the perfect solution for a guy like me who liked to go incognito now and then. There were risks to wearing this kind of thing, of course. First of all, the people in an official capacity at Central would be able to see that my link was dead. It looked like I had left the planet or something—or maybe that I was dead entirely. That could cause loud misunderstandings when I suddenly popped back up on the radar.

Also, when you had the sheath on your arm, your mind wasn't being tracked by the data core. So, if I ever managed to get myself killed while I was wearing it, I'd lose all the memories that would have otherwise been recorded.

Trotting around the track down on Green Deck, I checked to see how far I was from Sophia. It looked good, what with about two hundred floors between the two of us. While jogging through a fake forested area, I ripped off the blocker and dropped it in a trash can.

Immediately, I was back on the grid. I just kept calmly jogging through the trees after that. I ignored everyone and everything, just giving an occasional wave to anybody who recognized me. There were a lot of joggers out at this time in the morning.

About three minutes after I ditched the evidence, a call came through on my tapper. This wasn't really much of a surprise. I didn't answer it, but it answered itself.

When I lifted my arm up to my face, I saw an attractive, unsmiling woman looking up at me. It was none other than Galina Turov herself.

"James?" she said. "Where the fuck have you been?"

"Uh…" I said. "Right here, sir. Running around this track down on Green Deck."

"No. No, you haven't. I've been looking for you since I woke up this morning. Where did you go last night?"

I gave her my dumbest look. "Nowhere, sir. Just take a look around."

I lifted my arm, and I panned my camera all around the greenery as if she would be interested—which she wasn't.

"McGill," she said, "I better not find out that any of our Rigellian guests were murdered during the night. If I do discover such a thing, I'm going to blame you personally and insist that you're put back into incarceration."

That gave me a little chill. I hadn't really enjoyed my trial, my execution, or my long separation from my friends and family. I shook my head and laughed. "Do your worst, sir. I can't help it if there's a little technical snafu now and then. After all, I was just revived yesterday. Come to think of it, maybe that's the trouble. Maybe my tapper thinks I'm supposed to be dead, still. Maybe the grid has marked me as nonexistent because my sentence wasn't served out to the end."

It was bullshit, but it was good bullshit. Galina frowned hard, not knowing what to think.

"All right, whatever. Come up to the roof. We're all gathering to fly to Big Sky Station Four. The lifter is landing in ten minutes. You are to be aboard with the rest of us."

After this announcement, the screen went dead.

I heaved a sigh. There wouldn't even be time for a shower after my jog. Of course, as I'd only been jogging for a couple of minutes, it didn't really matter.

I took the time to spruce up my uniform a little and then headed straight for the elevators. I barely made it up to the roof and joined the delegation of VIPs who were about to climb up the ramp of a parked lifter.

I'd never actually seen a lifter land on the roof of Central before. Shuttles, pinnaces, air cars—sure, all that kind of stuff. But not an actual lifter.

There were already burn marks all over the roof's landing area, which was really designed for domestic air traffic rather than large heavy radiation-producing thrusters. I supposed that the various janitors and clean-up men would have their work cut out for them tonight, what with repainting all the lines and such.

Walking calmly to the rear of the delegation, I followed them up the ramps. It was easy to join the throng and blend in.

Once we were aboard, I found Galina and tapped her on the shoulder.

"Hey," I said, "where are the bears? Aren't they supposed to be in on this?"

"Yes, they are. But they went back up into space last night to their ship. They said they would meet us on Big Sky Four, where we're going to hold the ceremony."

We found seats on the command deck. About ninety seconds after we'd strapped in, the lifter roared up into the sky. It broke through the top of the atmosphere and pushed higher and higher up into orbit.

It took about half an hour to reach Big Sky Station Four, I made idle chitchat with Galina the whole time.

Her father, Alexander Turov, spent most of his time talking to the top brass members. They were huddled at a table surrounded by big comfy chairs near the observation windows—which weren't really windows at all.

The walls of the lifter were actually screens of such high resolution they *looked* like windows. Outside, we could see the station as we approached it. The shape of it was unusual. It was built in kind of an X-pattern. Each of the four arms of the X narrowed almost to a point.

In the center of the structure was a disk, sitting like a hubcap in the middle of the whole thing. I knew the idea was that each of these stations would generate a protective field in quadrants. The fields were to be projected outward from two of those four arms to three other stations. That way, a square shield was formed between them. Once all the stations were in place and activated, the Earth would be entirely surrounded by a globe of force—kind of like a greenhouse built with interlocking plates of glass.

Today's test would only involve one pane of this invisible shield. Stations one, two, three and four were all in position and angled precisely. The satellites were approximately 1000 kilometers apart. Eventually, with a webwork of more stations in place, the shield would be complete.

I had to admit, it was quite an impressive feat of engineering.

During the flight, I did glance around the command deck occasionally. I'd spotted Sophia several times, but my eyes did not pause when they landed on her.

Sure, I wanted to linger there and admire her form. That's only natural after a man has spent a night with a girl. Anyone would want to check on her the next morning. But I didn't dare.

Galina was sitting next to me, and like most women, she had excellent senses for this kind of thing. So, my eyes glided right over Sophia without seeming to even pause as I scanned the members of the delegation.

"Wow," I said. "Look at all the brass we've got aboard. There must be, let me see, four praetors, a solid seven equestrians, a dozen imperators... Jeez. I've got to be the lowest ranked guy on the ship. I bet the pilot outranks me. Hell, I bet the cabin-boy outranks me!"

Galina listened to all this nonsense without answering. She was staring at me. She wasn't saying anything while I made this little speech and performed this little act.

Putting on an ignorant smile, I turned and looked down at her.

Her eyes were narrowed. Damn it. How could she have sensed my checking out of Sophia?

"James," she said. "Where exactly did you spend the night?"

"Well, it's kind of embarrassing," I said, inventing an instantaneous cover story. "I think I had a bit too much drink last night. You know, that happens now and then to everybody."

She snorted. "That happens to you at least once a week."

"Yeah, well, like I said it's a little bit embarrassing, but I stretched out in the lobby. Did you know there are lots of decent couches down there?"

"You didn't visit the barracks, then?"

"The barracks? Hell no! Those places are for grunts and recruits, not officers."

She nodded. I knew that she would agree with that opinion because it was precisely the one that she had held for many years.

"I'm asking," she said, "because I checked on my sister's location last night. I discovered to my horror that she was in the barracks."

"Really?"

"Yes. The common area—apparently, with the common soldiery."

"What?" I said as I guffawed and slapped my knee. "So, she hooked up with some rando down there? Is that what you're telling me? I didn't know you had that kind of sister."

"Shut up. I don't have that kind of sister. It's not like her at all. I don't understand it. You will never mention this again, McGill. Not to me or to anyone else."

"Uh… okay, okay, whatever. Maybe it's not that bad. Maybe she's just grown up a bit. Maybe she'll even find herself a new husband. Maybe she'll—"

"Shut up, damn you!"

I finally did shut up. I had Galina barking up the wrong tree. I'd convinced her that some other legionnaire had perhaps managed to woo her sister, which was upsetting for her but a sheer relief to me.

Looking at the big screens again, I saw that we were gliding in for a landing. We slowed and docked under the center of the X-shaped space station. Within a minute or two, we were shuffling after all the other passengers, going through a docking tube.

There was a little disorienting flip-around when we climbed through the hatches, as the "up" direction reversed itself. The artificial gravity on the space station was flowing in the opposite direction. That made your gut feel a little funny when you went through the transition, but it was nothing that a spacer such as myself found upsetting.

A couple of the political types looked sick, and one of them puked after they went through the second hatchway. I was the only man in sight who laughed, and the guy shot me an angry look as he wiped at his expensive suit.

Galina elbowed me in the gut, which sobered me up real quick.

As a group, we walked along the metal decks. Our boots clacked and rang as we went.

"They should put some carpets up here or something," I said.

"They'll never do that," Galina told me. "This is a military station, not a sightseeing tourist trap."

A tall, attractive figure with a long neck, long arms and long legs stepped out from one of the side passages ahead of us. She wore a lab coat of the kind our tech smiths wore. They were high-level scientists from Central, originally born on Rogue World.

She looked like Floramel for a second, but then I blinked and realized it wasn't her. It couldn't be her, as she was out on Dust World living with the Investigator.

That thought brought me a pang. I recalled that Etta had contacted me, asking me to come out to Dust World. I'd kind of forgotten, what with all the screwing and dying and stuff. I made a mental note to look up my daughter when I escaped this dog-and-pony show.

"Hello everyone, I'm Elin, originally from Arcturus IV, otherwise known as Rogue World."

"Hi, Elin," I blurted out eagerly.

Several people looked at me, including Galina.

"Ah, hello," Elin said, she gave me a small, confused wave. "Citizens, welcome to Sky Station Four. I am one of the directors of this project, and I will be your tour guide today."

Galina was checking me out all over again. I was smiling at Elin, and I lifted my hand to get her attention again, but she didn't notice me what with all the pot-bellied old farts asking technical questions.

"How could you possibly know that woman, McGill?" Galina asked with venom.

"I don't," I said. "She just seemed a friendly sort, you know."

"Yes. I do know. Keep your distance McGill. She's trying to do an important job. We don't need you playing the part of the saboteur."

"Okay, okay. No offense meant."

We walked after Elin as she talked and showed us stuff. Galina seemed even more sour about this trip now than she had been before.

The tall skinny scientist-girl indicated a dozen technical details about the station, waving her arms and pointing out various viewports. She talked about how many terawatts of power the station generated, how much it would take to project each panel of the force field when it was finished, and how the station itself was protected by another shield of force in case it was bombarded from space at some point.

By the time she got deep in the weeds, like about how many meters thick the projected shield was, and how many gigatons of force it could repel—I was yawning. There was all kinds of boring nonsense going on.

Fortunately, the little walk-around tour only took maybe twenty minutes. Finally, when we came full-circle to where we'd started, we took a different path. We moved up a steep metal staircase to where the control center was.

A whole flock of lab coats and blue jumpsuits were in this chamber. It looked to me like the lab coat people were all about touching screens, while the guys in the jumpsuits did all the work.

I guess that's the way all big facilities like this operated.

Elin talked some more, but pretty soon the assembled crew of bigwigs began to get edgy. Praetor Wurtenberger became particularly annoyed. He lifted up his tapper and flicked it with his fat fingers as if suspecting there was an error.

"Can this be right? We're sixteen minutes over the allotted time already? When are we going to begin this test?"

"Technical achievements like this, sir," Elin said, "are not always precisely on time."

Public Servant Alexander Turov stepped to the front of the group. Up until now, he'd been silent. The moment he moved, everyone else shut the hell up. It was easy to see who the big hound was at this fox hunt.

"Please accept our apologies," he told the group. "We are waiting for the delegation from Rigel to arrive. That's the real nature of this delay."

"Ah," Wurtenberger said, "so the bears are late as well as rude? Can we at least project the location of their ship from here?"

"Certainly," Elin said, and she moved to do as he requested. She activated a large holotable which displayed Earth, the four stations, and all the various space traffic in the area.

A blue triangle representing Rigel's visiting ship was halfway between the space station orbiting Earth and Big Sky Four.

"I don't understand this," Wurtenberger said. "It'll be another half hour until they're here at this pace."

"I'm getting messages from Squantus himself," Servant Turov said. "He says that they're having some kind of steering jet failure, and they may not be able to dock at all. At least not for an hour—possibly longer."

These words elicited a lot of grumbling. Fists were placed on hips, and the mood in the chamber had generally soured.

These people were top-level officers, politicians and the like. They weren't accustomed to being kept waiting by anyone.

Everybody appeared to have a meeting, or lunch engagement, or something else important to go to immediately after this ceremony.

"All right, all right," Alexander said, "let's get on with the ceremony. Proceed with the ribbon cutting, please."

A long blue ribbon of the famous blue and white of Hegemony ran across the main control console. On the console itself, a large green button was prominently displayed.

It looked like a real button, and it was something like five centimeters across, but it couldn't be physically there. It had to be a hologram.

Still, pushing it would most likely fire up the system and cause the big shield to light up outside in space.

Alexander Turov himself did the honors of cutting the ribbon, and Elin approached the panel. "Who would like the honor of pressing the button?"

"Wait," Drusus said. "Are we going to wait for the Rigellians or not? The whole point of this ceremony is to have them participate."

Alexander glanced at him. "They don't want to participate. They don't want us to do this at all. They consider it a military escalation. I suspect the real reason they're late to this event is that none of them wishes to be seen or recorded as having attended."

Drusus frowned. "Why would that be, Servant?"

"Think, Drusus. Think like a politician, not like a military leader. Rigel is a despotic regime. This delegation, headed by Squantus, was sent out here to implore Earth not to build this network of defensive space stations. It's one thing to fail in your diplomatic mission. It is quite another and quite a bit worse, to be recorded celebrating the failure."

Drusus nodded. "I get it. They're worried they're going to go back and have their reputations ruined—or possibly, they'll be met with prison time and reduced career opportunities."

"Who knows?" Alexander said, shrugging his skinny shoulders. "In any case, we'll pretend we believe there are nonsensical technical mishaps. I'll tell them they can view the glory of Earth's first forcefield from the comfort of their own ship." He turned to Elin. "Let's get on with the ceremony."

"Do you wish to do the honors?" she asked again.

"Yes, of course," he said, "are the cameras ready?"

Drones rushed forward. They were little guys I'd barely noticed before. They lingered at the edge of the entourage floating around and buzzing.

They captured the action from a dozen different angles, as each of them had multiple cameras.

Alexander, viewed from every possible angle, smiled as he walked up in a very stately manner to the ethereal green button. He applied his finger, pressing it down.

The response was immediate and quite impressive. The whole room glimmered and shook a bit. There was a surge of power in the station which came alive under our feet.

We looked out through the viewports, and we saw a lightning-like glare that grew in intensity until we were shielding our eyes with our fingers. Automatically, the viewports were dampened by a rolling shade effect that came down. It looked as if we were gazing through sunglasses.

Two of the arms of the X-shaped station lit up. They ran with power, causing the lights to dim and flashes of lightning randomly grounded to the arms to blossom in a dramatic display.

There were gasps from the crowd, then applause as within a flickering instant, the shield came to life.

A thousand kilometers away, the other stations powered-up as well. The shield formed, becoming a single square of glowing light.

"It's like glass made of lightning," I said, clapping my big mitts together.

There were more gasps, oohs and ahhs. We all turned toward the holotable in the middle of the control center. From the strategic bird's eye point of view, we saw all four of the stations were now lit up. They were all green, a light, bright green. A single square of the forcefield was alive between them all.

Everyone began to tap their hands together in a polite show of applause. I, on the other hand, hooted a few times and waved my fist over my head.

"Now that's hog engineering at its best," I said. "Give it up people, give it up!"

I slammed my hands together enthusiastically. The tech people, smiled at this and nodded to me with gratitude. With my encouragement, many of the more boisterous officers in the group whistled, cheered and clapped more enthusiastically.

It was, after all, quite a technical achievement.

"It works!" I shouted. "The friggin' thing works!"

"Yes," Alexander said, looking at it thoughtfully. "It does work. No wonder the bears don't like it. Let's test it."

He turned toward Elin and nodded.

She smiled, and she waved to her army of monkeys in lab coats like a conductor directing a symphony to begin a lively tune. They all turned to their workstations and began to speak into microphones, finger their tablet screens and signal one another.

I dared to hope something new was about to happen. By this time, I was pleasantly surprised and certainly no longer bored. This was actually getting good.

On the central display, we watched as an object approached. It was a sliver of metal. The new contact gleamed red on the tactical displays. Warning tones began going off.

"Looks like a missile," I said to old Alexander, and he nodded to me.

"Yes, exactly," he said, "a missile has been waiting out in space for this moment. It has a live warhead. It is incoming now and will strike the shield in approximately 45 seconds."

"That's cool!" I said. "Is it antimatter or just fusion?"

Elin turned around to face me. "Neither," she said. "It's only a test. It'll be a simple kinetic blow. Just a little something to see how the shield holds up."

"Aw, dang. I was hoping for some big fireworks. Can't this shield keep out something bigger?"

"Well, it's designed to do so of course, but we don't want our very first test to overload the system. Remember, we only have one pane of this vast geodesic pattern in place. There will eventually be hundreds of them when it's finished. Right now, the shield is relatively weak as it's not being supported by dozens of others around it."

"Not even a little fission warhead?" I asked, seriously disappointed.

Galina slapped my elbow, so I shut up. We watched as a big countdown was splashed up on the screens. The numbers began ticking down.

When we got to the end, I got the whole group chanting with me.

"5… 4… 3… 2… 1…"

Then came the glorious moment of impact.

Everything went white—at least, that's all I can remember.

-13-

Another bad death had been added to my life-long tally.

When I was revived at Central after the disaster on Big Sky Four, the place was in an uproar. There was a full-on scramble, with Earth's military headquarters in the middle of it.

Accordingly, I was brought back to life in a very abrupt and businesslike fashion.

"What's the score?"

"He's a nine."

"Great. Get him into a uniform and out the door. Recharge the tanks too—we've already got another customer in the buffers."

These people were serious. Even though my eyes were still closed, I could hear the seriousness in the voices of the bio people.

Normally, if I'd managed to get myself killed in an aircar accident or a drunken brawl, or something of that kind, they wouldn't have been in such a hurry. On a regular lazy afternoon, I might well have been the only revival that these bored-ass bios had to deal with.

That was not the case today. They were humping and bumping, and they wanted to get me out of there as fast as possible.

I was provided with zero answers to the questions I managed to croak out of my rubbery lips. They gave zero shits about my confusion. I was told to check my unit's briefings and head to my assigned post.

Stumbling, staggering and still sticky from the birthing fluids, I walked out into the echoing halls on one of Central's Blue Decks. I was disappointed to note I'd been revived near the legion barracks, and not upstairs with the cool kids. I was pretty sure Drusus, for example, had been given the VIP treatment up top, where they often served mints and coffee.

As I made my way out of the place, I saw other zombie-like fresh revives wandering around. Everyone had that vacant look in their eyes, the look of the recently revived dead.

I tried to shake it off. The trouble was the whole thing had been so sudden, so unexpected. One moment we'd been watching a cool demonstration of Earth's cutting-edge technology—and the next instant it had all turned to shit.

My tapper did have a pile of messages, of course, but they were pages long and printed small. I couldn't bother with that official nonsense right now. Heck, I couldn't even see straight.

My first question was what in the nine flavors of hell had gone wrong? My second was just as predictable: what the hell was happening now?

I sent these queries to my military superiors such as Graves and Tribune Winslade. but to my further frustration, Neither of them answered me.

I decided next to ask people beneath me. People who were obligated to respond. The first name on my list was Natasha. She was a notorious tech hacker, and she was always as curious as a bird on a wire.

Selecting her name, I gave her a call. She answered immediately.

"What are your orders, Centurion?" she said, out of breath.

I could see she was half in uniform. She was struggling to pull her service jacket on even as I watched.

"What rumors have you heard today, Natasha?" I asked.

She blinked at me in confusion. "Sir, you're the one contacting me. All I know is I've gotten my mobilization orders. I've got to report to Central as quickly as possible."

"Full scramble alert, huh?"

"Yes. They've sent out an emergency call."

"Do you know which legions are involved?"

"Well, Varus obviously," she said. "As far as I understand it, Victrix, Germanica and Solstice are involved too. At least six legions have been summoned to Central."

I smiled. Here she was, claiming she didn't know anything, and yet she had already told me more than any thirty pages of worthless reports in my inbox would have done.

"Why the massive infantry call?" I asked her.

"I don't know, sir. Maybe they expect an invasion. Everything's gone crazy."

"Did you die in this attack?"

"No, sir."

"Okay, then. Brief me. Everybody's in such a panic here, I can't even get on the news feeds for current info. All non-classified traffic to the outside world is being blocked."

"Well," she said, "they don't normally do that. But you're allowed to talk to me because I'm part of your unit, right?"

"That's right."

"Okay, well... I've actually seen the news feeds. Apparently, something big struck our new shield even as we put it up for the very first time. All four of the Big Sky stations were destroyed."

I whistled long and low. "That's quite an opening strike. That's a lot of expensive hardware. A damned shame."

Natasha looked around like someone might be listening. She selected the private channel encryption option, and I saw the little blue icon gleam on my tapper as it activated.

"Listen, James. That's not the big thing. The debris did the real damage. Those four stations—they were flying chunks of metal. Big flying chunks."

"Uh... right. So what?"

"They've fallen. They've dropped out of orbit and impacted on Earth."

"Holy shit... where?"

"One of them hit the eastern Mediterranean. It caused a tidal wave. James, I don't even know the level of devastation yet, but they're saying that Cyprus, southern Turkey, a lot of the Greek islands... They've all been swept away."

"Swept away...?" I said, "like... what do you mean?"

"I mean, the cities, the people—they're all gone. We're talking about tens of millions of dead."

My jaw fell open, and I stopped shambling along. I leaned against the corridor walls. Looking around, I noted that the lights had been dimmed to emergency levels. No wonder there were colored arrows on the decks. We were at war.

This was serious. As far as I could remember, Earth had never been hit so hard, at least not with a sucker-punch like this one.

"What about the other three chunks of metal?" I asked.

Natasha shook her head. "Minor damage. They mostly burned up in the atmosphere and struck relatively uninhabited areas in the Mideast. That one that hit the water, though, that was the bad one."

"When can you get here? I need you at my side. We're at war, now. This is a real war."

"I know," she said. "I'm coming. Give me two hours."

The call ended, and I scrolled around on my tapper. All those messages were still waiting for me. Most of them were from members of my unit. Harris wanted to know if he was in charge of getting everybody's butt to Central as fast as possible, and I immediately approved his request to take on that duty. He was the best of us at kicking tail.

Leeson had asked if I was awake and back in the game yet. He'd sent that same message over and over again.

That almost made me smile. Most likely, he was worried that he was going to have to be in charge of 3rd Unit. I knew he didn't like playing centurion.

I sent him back a confirmation of my return to existence, and his response was brief and immediate: "That's a big relief, sir. I'll be there as fast as I can."

Lastly, there was a note from Adjunct Dickson. This was a new man on my roster. I'd only known him briefly on City World, and I hadn't much liked what I'd seen.

He was a transfer from Victrix. I had foolishly traded Adjunct Barton, who was probably my best officer, for the dregs of Victrix. Oh well. Hopefully, we would develop a good working relationship over time.

At least Dickson's note was promising. "I'm already here at Central, sir. I'll meet with you at your convenience."

I liked that. Of my entire unit, as far as I could tell, he was the only man who was already in our assigned barracks. It was nice to see someone who was truly on the ball when the chips were down.

I tapped in his name, and a mapping tool located him. That gave me at least an immediate destination.

Moving again my next step was much more steady. My legs were working fully now. My balance was better, too.

I took long even strides to the elevators. Unfortunately, they were so busy that after waiting a minute and a half I decided just to hit the stairwell. It was only nine stories down to the barracks. Nine stories of smacking the panic bars and taking the steps two or three at a time.

Reaching the barracks level, I stepped into a busy, chaotic scene. Troops were everywhere. A number of them were half-dressed. Some jogged along the corridors in teams and squads.

There were a dozen other units present, and all of them were Varus people. Officers and grunts mixed, rushing this way and that. They were assembling into formations, checking their gear. We hadn't received a scramble order to mobilize like this since the wars against the Cephalopods, back when our home world itself was directly threatened.

I thought about that as I searched the empty barracks chambers for Dickson. How bad were things? How coordinated was this attack? Could there be more shocks on the way?

It seemed quite suspicious that the Rigellian ship had been reluctant to come join us as we launched our first test of the new defensive system. Had they known what was going to happen? It seemed that they must have.

In my mind, I replayed all the dire warnings I'd gotten from Squantus. Was Rigel poised to attack Earth even now? Was their fleet on the way?

Maybe that was the real reason they didn't want us to build a defensive system, because they'd planned an invasion here on Earth. That was a startling thought.

We'd been living under an uneasy peace with Rigel since the Clone World campaign. It was more or less a Cold War that had lasted for a decade or two. Oh, sure, we often fought each other on the ground of some planet or another. Each of us served a different brand of Galactic, and our masters hated one another.

The Rigellians normally fought on the side of the Skay. Earth forces normally fought on the side of the Mogwa. As a result, we were often on opposite sides of any given conflict.

Neither of us had struck directly at the other's homeworld for a long, long time.

Today, all of that had changed. It was a chilling thought.

I finally found Dickson. He was smoking a stim alone in a dimly lit barracks chamber. He had chosen a seat at a table. I chose the seat opposite him, and I sat down, breathing heavily. I'd just jogged my way through this giant building, jostling with a thousand others to get to this spot.

"You look calm, cool and collected," I told him.

"Yes, sir. Thank you, sir." He stood up and gave me a salute. I offered him a hand to shake instead. Startled, he took my hand, and he shook it.

"Welcome aboard, Dickson," I said. "The last time we met out on City World, we didn't really have much time to get to know each other. I think that's all about to change."

"Undoubtedly, sir," he said. "This war seems to be more serious."

"It's as real as it gets."

We sat down then, and we began to make our plans. We mapped out where our various troops were. Essentially, they were scattered across the globe, but at least half of them were within ten hours travel of Central.

"Send a note to distant stragglers," I told Dickson. "Tell them I'm authorizing legion funds to pay for faster transportation."

"Emergency funding?" Dickson said. "You have the authorization for that… just on the basis of your signature?"

"Well, no, of course not. But I'll get it past the quartermaster, or from Graves. I'll even go to Winslade himself if I have to. Just promise the troops that if they take a jump gate, or a sky train, or even an Interplanetary Transport, they'll be reimbursed in their next month's paycheck."

Dickson made an appreciative noise and nodded. "I can see why you're here, Centurion. You have a reputation as a man who gets things done."

"That I do, Adjunct. All right, I expect us to be up to half strength in ten hours. Full strength within twenty-four."

"Right sir, I think that's doable."

"Okay then, let's talk about your position in this unit. This is a mixed arms combat formation. We have a platoon of heavies, backed up by a platoon of lights."

Dickson put up a hand to stop me. "I'm well versed with the battle formations of our unit, sir."

"Right. Of course. I'm putting you in charge of the lights, replacing Adjunct Barton directly. Is that acceptable."

Dickson smiled. "Would it matter if it wasn't?"

"Not as much as a gnat's balls."

He nodded. "In that case, sir, I'd be honored to serve in Barton's place."

"Did you actually know Adjunct Barton, when you served in Victrix with her?"

He shrugged. "I knew of her. I wouldn't call us friends, only mild acquaintances. We were in the same cohort, but not the same unit. You know how it is. With three adjuncts per unit, that's thirty per cohort. It's not like you get to know everybody on a first name basis."

"Right, right," I said. "Good enough. Now, let's plan for the worst."

Dickson stared at me. "What do you mean, sir?"

"I mean that you have joined a legion that is commonly deployed as a rapid response force in situations like this. Among all the members of Legion Varus, 3rd cohort, 3rd Unit is infamously over-utilized for things like teleport commando missions and the like."

Dickson looked somewhat alarmed. Apparently, he didn't know everything about the outfit he joined up with. He'd been more or less kicked out of Victrix at the end of the last campaign, and after we'd returned to Earth, we'd immediately demobilized. He'd had little chance to exercise with the rest of us.

I took my measure of Dickson. I recalled that back on City World, he'd been very harsh with the troops. But working with him here, one-on-one, he seemed competent and confident. I hoped he would be a good supporting officer—but the jury was still out on that.

After about an hour of working with Dickson, about a squad's worth of my troops had shown up. None of them were officers, but there were a few noncoms. The unit was beginning to assemble, but we were nowhere near our full strength yet.

I was talking to the new arrivals, briefing them, when my tapper began to buzz. Then, it chose to answer itself. That was always a bad sign, as it meant that a superior officer had contacted me and had done so in the rudest possible fashion—by forcing the call through without my consent.

I brought my arm up to my face, curious as to who it might be. To my surprise, it wasn't Graves. It wasn't Winslade, either. Those two were the next up in my chain of command.

It was Praetor Drusus. A man with four big stars on his shoulders.

My jaw sagged a bit. "Praetor?" I said. "To what do I owe this honor?"

"McGill, I want to meet with you. I'm gathering together everyone who was present at the tragedy earlier today. I want to see if anyone can remember any clues that we might be able to follow… Also, there are several important announcements to be made."

"Yessir! I'll be right there."

I closed the channel and gave Dickson orders to continue gathering and organizing the unit. Then I raced for the door.

-14-

I couldn't believe my bad luck. Here I was, sucked into yet another high-level meeting. This was exactly why I'd never sought a promotion to the primus or tribune level. Such people were always tormented by endless, boring-ass meetings.

When I was ushered into Drusus' office by Primus Bob, I found that I was one of the last members to arrive. The meeting was already in full swing. They were going over a briefing showing visually what had happened to the Big Sky project.

Several of the people there hadn't known the details, and they were gasping in astonishment. The numbers—the real numbers that they'd hidden from all the news feeds—were finally rolling in.

The death counts were only estimates, of course, and bound to rise, but according to the best data analysts at Central, Earth had lost something greater than ninety million people. Much of Turkey, Egypt, Greece, Southern Italy and many other places surrounding the eastern Mediterranean were gone. They'd all been consumed by a wave that reached as high as one hundred meters.

Crete and Cypress had been virtually wiped clean. Places that had mountains close to the coast had fared better than those that were flat, but everyone had suffered greatly in the region.

Watching images and graphics of the devastation, I became unglued after fifteen minutes of gloomy news.

"We need to strike back, sirs!" I shouted, swinging a big fist down and bashing the table with it.

I had to glance down and make sure I hadn't cracked the surface. Fortunately, it was tough and built to military specs.

"Rest assured, McGill," Drusus said, "Earth will extract her pound of flesh for this outrage."

Praetor Wurtenberger, a portly man with a euro accent, stepped into the conversation. I was surprised he was still fat. Usually, they edited that out after a revive. Maybe Wurtenberger had been stored with his gut carefully recorded. The idea made me smile.

"We've been hit hard by a foreign attack, but that is not the entire story. Someone here on Earth had to put a real warhead aboard that test missile. We now know it was an antimatter warhead of approximately a gigaton yield. If the entire shield had been up and active, I doubt it could have penetrated. But as it was, it brought down the entire thing. The point is, we must find out who here on Earth helped Rigel with this cowardly attack!"

There were murmurs of agreement from the crowd. Before anyone could come to a further consensus, however, another even more important figure arrived.

It was Public Servant Alexander Turov, showing much less of his great age than usual. To my surprise, and probably everyone else's who was present, this version of our most famous Servant was quite a bit younger than he had been the last time we'd seen him.

He was not a kid, mind you. He apparently wasn't as vain as his daughter and didn't come back looking like a teenager. But if I had to guess, I would say he appeared to be in his mid-forties. His hair was gray only at the temples instead of all over, and he had a lot more of it.

His eyes, which had always been wicked things in the past, were even more quick-moving and crafty.

He scanned the group, and he seemed to take particular note of my presence. He lingered on me for a full, uncomfortable second before moving on.

"Public Servant Turov," Drusus said, "you've just returned from an emergency meeting of the Ruling Council in Geneva.

Can you tell us what the mood is there? Do you have a mandate for our military?"

Alexander strode up to the table. The high-level brass officers scooted away from him. He hadn't even bothered to ask anyone to step aside. They'd all scattered like chickens from the skirts of a farmer's wife—a farmer's wife with a butcher knife in her hand.

"I have indeed returned from Geneva," Alexander said. "The mood there is grim. This is an act of war. In response, the Ruling Council has formally declared war upon Rigel."

Praetor Wurtenberger stood up suddenly, making his gut bounce. "Could that step possibly be premature? We have yet to form an investigatory committee. We have yet to determine the exact nature of this strike. What if it was a domestic terrorist situation, and—?"

Alexander cut him off with a hacking motion of his left hand. "Let's not fool ourselves, gentlemen. This was an act of war. Earth has never been so greatly threatened. Not since the Cephalopods wandered our green hills, just north of here, have we faced a greater enemy."

Drusus nodded. "Possibly, this situation is worse, because it was a surprise attack made by a supposed friend who came in the guise of someone offering peace."

"Exactly," Alexander said, nodding. "Remember that we still had an active peace treaty with Rigel when they struck this blow. What can be worse than an enemy that strikes you while under treaty?"

The group mumbled to themselves, but from my reading of the room, most were in agreement with Drusus and Alexander.

Praetor Wurtenberger slowly sat down again, frowning.

"So," Alexander continued, "the question becomes what are we going to do about this outrage? The Ruling Council has taken decisive action. In addition to announcing war, we have decided that a purge is in order."

Everyone suddenly quieted. A purge? That was a cold word.

Everyone pretty much froze. Some of them, in my estimation, stopped breathing entirely.

Purge was a word that no military officer wanted to hear from his governing official.

Praetor Wurtenberger dared to speak first. "What might this purge entail?"

Alexander produced a black box about the size of an old-fashioned bible. "It will start with a loyalty test. Everyone here is now required to place their hand upon this device and swear an oath to Earth, to Hegemony and to humanity at large."

"What about the Empire?" Wurtenberger asked.

"Yes, of course... to the Empire as well."

Solemnly, Alexander passed the box to each officer present. One at a time, all of us placed a hand upon the mysterious box and made the pledge.

When it was my turn, I stood tall, not sitting down. I raised my right hand and placed it over my heart while I put my left upon the box. Most of the others had remained seated and simply slapped their hand down on the box, mumbling the words that were required.

The box did nothing much other than flash a light once for each officer who had made their pledge. The whole thing seemed pretty pointless to me. What was a box going to tell you about loyalty? About the true nature of a man's soul? I didn't know, but I didn't believe it could be definitive.

After the box had made the rounds and been returned to Alexander's hands again, he lifted it and examined it.

Reaching out toward the battle display, he swept away all the tactical charts, including the visions of chaos and destruction from the Mediterranean, with an imperious hand. Then, he tossed a glowing handful of words onto the table in our midst.

After a moment, I realized that the words were actually the names and ranks of everyone present.

"Hey look, there I am! Centurion James McGill: Cleared!" I laughed.

The others began intently looking for their names on the list. Some sighed with relief, while others looked bored.

But Praetor Wurtenberger squawked loudly. He stood up again, moving so fast his belly slapped the shoulders of the two men on either side of him.

"What's the meaning of this?" he demanded. "My name is on this list, and it says *disqualified*."

Servant Turov did not answer immediately. He made a large show of going over each of the names. "There's only one here that has not cleared the test," he said. "We shall readminister it, in case there was an error."

He handed the box to Wurtenberger again. Angrily, the officer took the box and held it in his hands. He began to make a speech. "Know this: I have served Earth for well over eighty years in official capacity. I have never—"

"Praetor," Alexander said, "you are simply required to place your hand upon the box and swear the oath again."

Gritting his teeth, Wurtenberger did as he was commanded. He made the loyalty oath, then he looked anxiously at the box for any kind of response.

It did nothing but flash its light once, indicating that it had recognized him and recorded some result.

"How do you get this thing to tell you what it's thinking?" he demanded.

"I will show you," Alexander said, taking the box calmly. He ran his fingers over the top of it and made a tossing motion onto the table again.

Between all of us was a single name, that of Praetor Wurtenberger. The box's judgment was displayed with bright, clear print: *Disqualified.*

"This is preposterous. Why am I being singled out? What have I done? What's going on here, Drusus?"

Drusus was the only other military man whose rank matched Wurtenberger's. He was frowning fiercely at the box and the glowing words on the table in our midst.

My mouth was hanging open, but I was just barely smart enough not to say anything. I looked at Drusus for guidance. He was one of my favorite officers in the world. A good man by any measure.

Drusus took in a great breath and let it out slowly. "None of us wants to believe that a member of our military is a traitor. But then again, it seems likely that someone on Earth was involved in all this."

"Exactly," Tribune Winslade said, speaking up for the first time. "It must be someone at a high level. How else could this test of the Big Sky Project have gone so disastrously wrong?"

Servant Turov cleared his throat. "This is an awkward situation," he said. "Rest assured, Praetor Wurtenberger, that this is not a final verdict. You have not yet been found guilty of anything."

"Well, at least the Ruling Council hasn't completely lost—"

Alexander raised a thin hand, silencing the officer. "There is, however, a dark cloud of suspicion over your name. We can take no chances at this time. You will therefore be executed and placed in purgatory until such time that we can hold an appropriate investigation and a trial. Rest assured, the final truth of this matter will be determined… eventually. Understand that this is not an admission or declaration of guilt, but rather—"

At that point, Wurtenberger cut him off. He was red faced. His fat lips were purple with anger. "This is a trick!" he shouted. "Why don't you put your hand on that thing, Turov? Why are only the military men being scapegoated? Something is going on here. All of you should see it!"

Turov's face grew stern. "Praetor Wurtenberger, are you declaring yourself in a state of mutiny?"

"Ah… No, of course not. I merely want this farcical—"

"Are you then making a threat to the defense of Earth?"

"No, no, I didn't say anything like that. I said that this entire procedure is outside of regulatory norms."

Turov eyed him coldly. "I am the civil authority in charge of military matters. I will not make military decisions. But I will make political ones about who is in charge of what. I've decided on the basis of this loyalty test that you're under a cloud of suspicion. We cannot tolerate any risk or lack of unity at this time. Therefore, my verdict and my decision stand."

He turned towards Praetor Drusus and made a small hand gesture indicating that Drusus should get on with the show. Drusus nodded glumly.

"Place Praetor Wurtenberger under arrest," he said.

On cue, a crowd of hogs stepped forward. They were all armed with much more than the decorative pistols that the assembled officers wore.

To his credit, Wurtenberger's hand slid to his pistol anyway. But almost as quickly, his fingers numbly slipped away again. He was no trick gunman. There was no way he was shooting his way out of here. Attempting to do so would only serve to embarrass him further, and worse, possibly confirm his guilt.

Snarling and grumbling with many dark looks cast over his shoulder, he was escorted away to the brig. I knew he'd be executed in a cell just as I had been. I wondered if they would use a powered garrote the way they had in my case.

The whole thing seemed so unfair that I dared to lift my hand in the air and waggle it there.

Servant Turov pointedly ignored me, but Drusus waved for me to speak. "What is it McGill? Do you have something material to offer?"

"I sure as hell do, Praetor, sir. This purging business seems poorly timed. It's the wrong moment for this kind of action. We should all work together. We should all be unified. Does anybody here really believe that Wurtenberger is a traitor to Earth? I've known him for years. He never—"

That was as far as I got because Alexander Turov decided to speak again. When a public servant speaks in the presence of military officers, they all shut up immediately.

"What's done is done, Centurion," he said. "I understand your emotionalism, so it is forgiven in this instance. You have a natural desire to believe the best of people. But for now, we just can't take such chances. Don't worry, Praetor Wurtenberger will eventually get his day in court."

Everyone looked cowed, and I clamped my jaws tightly.

"Now," Alexander continued, "I have an even more important announcement to make. This is one that affects all of you—and in fact, all of Earth."

Even I was curious about what he might say next. Anything that was important to Servant Turov was certainly important to the entire world.

"Hegemony has made another momentous decision," he said. "The vote was unanimous, as always."

"What vote?" I blurted out.

Several officers frowned at me instantly, and I shut the hell up.

"Due to the extreme nature of this war," Alexander continued, "and to the fact that we're facing an opponent who possesses a technological advantage over us—such as having their own functional defensive shield—the Ruling Council has decided to appoint an individual to the highest possible rank."

Everyone was stunned. "A consul?" Drusus dared to ask. "Are you talking about elevating an officer to the rank of consul?"

"Yes," Alexander said.

There were gasps all around the room. Hegemony military worked on some of the same principles as the ancient Roman Republic. In times of great peril, Rome would appoint a consul and give him near dictatorial powers. This was a temporary rank above all others. To the best of my knowledge, no one had ever been declared consul in recent memory. The last time had been during the Unification Wars more than a century ago.

Once we'd gotten over our initial shock, everyone's immediate question was who was going to be given this high rank? This was an honor that virtually no one here had ever seen bestowed before.

After only a moment's thought, all eyes turned toward Drusus. He had, upon occasion, organized our planet-wide defenses. In addition to that, he was the only four-star officer present, now that Wurtenberger had been dragged away to the dungeons.

Drusus himself looked a bit shocked. I don't think he suspected this turn of events, but he stood there ramrod straight. With a stern face he waited for Alexander's next fateful words.

"Praetor Drusus," the Servant said. "I, by the authority invested in me by the Hegemony, do hereby award you with the office of consul. I have brought with me this insignia not worn for over a century's time."

He took out a box. It was a small box this time, nowhere near as big as his truth detector had been. He slid it across the table.

It stopped a few centimeters from Drusus, who stared at it.

"I'm stunned, he said. "I… I had no idea the Ruling Council believes events are so dire—or that I would be a suitable candidate for this high office."

Alexander smiled. It was a thin, wicked smile. "Such a lack of ambition. No wonder you are a favorite of our beloved government. It's not just your impeccable record and your legendary capability as an officer. No, I think it's also your streak of humility that has caused us to have such strong confidence in your leadership. Open the box Drusus."

With hands that were almost shaking, Drusus opened the box, and he found the five stars inside.

He had been a four-star praetor, and now he was a five-star consul—the first man to hold such an elevated rank on Earth in many, many decades.

-15-

There was quite a bit of speeching and a little bit of cheering after Drusus got his promotion. Pretty soon, I stopped listening to the hullabaloo and began to eyeball the food again. It wasn't really a dinner spread—just a bunch of snacks—but it's all there was, so that's where my mind focused.

I tried to come up with a way to edge out of line and wander over to the side bar to snag a few choice items, but I was forced to wait until the meeting shifted gears first.

"All right," Drusus said finally. "Enough glad-handing. We're in a serious state of war. I have some orders that involve all of you."

He began handing down directives to everyone. Every officer present got an order of some kind, mostly to gather together a fleet, unit or a legion. Some however were directed to check on garrisons, troop-readiness, or logistical supply chains of munitions and general gear. All kinds of boring crap like that.

In the middle of this flurry of directives, Alexander slipped out of the place. He knew when the getting was good.

Feeling jealous of his escape and seriously bored, I kept looking at the food. At the first opportunity, I stepped over to the table and began popping stuff into my mouth.

I hadn't figured that Drusus was going to call upon me at all—but I was wrong.

As the last few members of the military elite left, Drusus walked on over to the snack table. He approached me directly.

"And now we come to Centurion James McGill," he said.

"Oh… hi, Praetor… uh… I mean Consul. What can I do for you, sir?"

"Why do you think you were invited here, McGill?"

"Uh… I dunno, sir, but I am probably your biggest cheerleader. I wouldn't have missed this for the world."

He nodded. "That's very gratifying, but I brought you here for a much more express purpose."

"How's that, Consul, sir?"

"First of all, you should know that I personally requested that your sentence be commuted."

My mouth sagged a bit. "Really? You did that for me, sir? That sure was nice. I had no idea it was you."

Drusus cocked his head slightly and squinted his eyes a little. "But you knew *someone* had to make the request, right?"

"Well… yessir. I was told that that ambassador fella Squantus from Rigel asked for my release."

Drusus nodded. "That was our initial cover story. The truth was when I found out that the son of Squanto was flying out, I wanted you to be here. I thought there might be a chance for closure on an old wound between our two empires. Apparently, I was wrong about that."

"I don't know about all that, sir," I said, "but I do know Squantus told me personally that his old poppa Squanto eventually wished he had accepted my offers of peace. He said the little frigger had second thoughts about me in the end—but now he's dead and gone."

"Hmm…" Drusus wondered to himself. Finally, he came to a decision. "Today, McGill, I'm calling upon you for a very special purpose."

"Oh no, here it comes!"

"We can't let this insult stand. We need to strike back hard and fast against Rigel."

"Sounds good so far," I said with enthusiasm.

"A reprisal is necessary. We cannot appear weak in this moment. A swift response from Earth is needed to remind Rigel they cannot simply attack us with impunity."

"Uh… what did you have mind?"

"A teleport commando mission," he said.

Right away, my heart sank into my boots even though I'd figured it was probably something like that. I wasn't really much good for anything else, but I'd kind of held out hope I wouldn't be packaged up and shipped off to Rigel immediately.

Drusus turned to his holotable. He brought up a tactical diagram of Rigel, which was a large star with a fairly large planet circling it. This was the home world of the bears.

"We can't get past their barrier," he said, "but our technology in the area of teleportation exceeds theirs in both range and accuracy. This leaves us with unique options they do not enjoy."

"Yeah," I said, "if it wasn't for that shield of theirs, we could just pop a bomb down on their capital right now. That would let them know what's what."

"Yes, we could. That's why we've been working on our own planetary shielding. It's only a matter of time before they will do the same to us. The target of this early strike should therefore be obvious." He just looked at me after that until the pause became awkward.

"Uh... could you help me out a little?"

Drusus reached out a finger like the hand of God and wagged it at the bluish glass-like globe around Rigel. "We'd like to bring down part of their shield."

"Oh," I said. "So, it's like that, is it? I've got to go out to their space stations and blow one up? I'm supposed to wreck the equivalent of Big Sky Four?"

"Yes. You and a handpicked squad of commandos will deliver our response to this attack upon Earth's sovereignty."

"Well, sir," I said, "I can certainly do it. I gotta warn you though, wanton destruction tends to get out of hand fast — especially when you put old McGill in charge of it. Once you let this genie out of the bottle, there's no putting him back in."

"Yes, I'm aware—and I would remind you of what happened in the Mediterranean. Perhaps Rigel didn't really intend to kill tens of millions of civilians, but they did. They struck first, but we shall strike back harder, and we shall do it almost immediately. I want you to pull troops together from your own unit. If you want some other specialists from a different part of the legion, or even from hog... ah... Hegemony forces... that will be acceptable as well."

"Wow. Blank check, huh?"

"Turn your requests in to Imperator Turov and Tribune Winslade. They've already been informed of this proposed action."

"Whoa," I said, "wait a minute. I'm in charge of this op, but who's planning this thing?"

"You are," he said, jabbing at me with a finger.

"Why me, sir? I'm just a centurion."

He smiled. "Do you remember my first aircar? The one that you wrecked?"

"A strong word for a little bit of accidental—"

"You cut up the seats. There were exterior scrapes on every painted surface, and the tires were worn down to a nub. Oh, and—"

"No need to go any further, Consul. I remember that sad event quite well. Purely an accident, of course."

"Right," he said. "Accidents like that follow you around everywhere, McGill. You're an absolute wrecking machine, and a wrecking machine is just what I need right now. Can you do it?"

"Absolutely, sir."

"Go down to the barracks. Gather your group. Hit Gray Deck in an hour. I'd like to see a launch within... three to four hours from now."

I sucked in a deep breath. All my fantasies of catching up with the family and chasing skirts were evaporating in my mind.

"Dismissed, McGill. Move out."

I saluted and jogged out of the room. Out in the hallway, I whistled loudly as I looked around. I was a little bit deflated.

Sure, this was just the kind of mission I was born and bred to perform. But it was hard to look forward to it. After all, I'd just got my ass out of death prison. I hadn't even gone down to Georgia to see my folks yet. I hadn't communicated with Etta either, to find out how she was getting on out there on Dust World.

All of that would have to wait. Except for some decent food, all I'd gotten today was a swift kick in the ass from various stuffed shirts. As a bonus, I was now going off on a suicide mission to a star system over a thousand lightyears distant. It was enough to make a man contemplate retirement.

Consulting my tapper, I jogged down corridors, rode elevators, and eventually gathered my staff. I soon found that I was still missing both Harris and Leeson, my other two supporting officers. The only adjunct I had was Dickson, and he was truly untested.

I had some hopes, as he was from Victrix and all, but I'd already seen a nasty streak in him. I guess he would do as well as anyone else to help me command this mission.

I gathered Carlos, Natasha and Sargon, along with a dozen grunts to my banner. Everybody who I both trusted and who had actually shown up on time to my mobilization call.

I let them know Dickson was my second in command with Sargon serving as my veteran specialist. He would be operating as both a weaponeer and my noncom lead, which made him the third man in command.

Natasha's face was ashen. I could tell she was shocked at her bad luck. She'd been drawn into a fresh war that had just started a few hours ago. That was the nature of serving in Legion Varus.

Carlos had his arms crossed, and his lips twisted in disgust. He acted as though this entire thing had been arranged just to inconvenience him.

"Seriously, McGill?" he said. "You're telling me you couldn't manage to talk your way out of this one? You can talk yourself into any girl's bed, or out of a well-deserved flogging. Hell, you got yourself out of a ten-year sentence with less than a tenth of it served. You should be able to slip and slide out of this cluster…"

I shook my head. "It's not going to happen this time."

Most of the men made unhappy noises as we gathered our kits, tested straps, bags, equipment, ammo, and so forth. Before we could go down and report to Gray Deck, however, another high officer arrived.

He was a whisper-thin man with a quick step. He came into the room, tossed a salute at the group who stood and immediately came to attention.

Then, he walked up to me and jabbed a sharp finger at my face.

"You there, McGill," Winslade said. "Come talk to me. In private."

We parked ourselves inside a small conference room, away from prying eyes and ears.

"McGill," Winslade said, "just what happened up there in Drusus' office?"

I shrugged. "Well sir, I started off by eating a lot of bean dip. But by the end of it, I was given orders to fly out into deep space and die horribly."

"That's not what I meant. What do you think about all these strange and sudden changes at the top?"

"Uh... like what?"

"I mean they've declared Praetor Wurtenberger a traitor and executed him—and yes, they actually did the deed just minutes ago. Immediately afterward, Drusus was elevated to a rank unheard of in living memory. The whole thing is disturbing and arguably insane."

I thought that quite possibly some of the old farts like Graves, or Alexander Turov could recall the last time there was a living consul on Earth, but I did not bother to argue with Winslade about it.

"Mighty strange, sir. Mighty strange."

Winslade gave me an odd look. "I think you need to be very careful, McGill."

"How's that, sir?"

"You were recently brought out of purgatory just in time to witness this highly unlikely sequence of events. They can put you back on ice just as easily as they brought you out. Do you understand what I'm saying, Centurion?"

"Not entirely, sir," I admitted. "But I appreciate the sentiment. I will be careful."

"Good. I find this entire string of circumstances to strain even the limits of credulity. I'm going to inquire about some of these oddities while you're vacationing out at Rigel."

"Like… what string are you talking about, sir?"

"Try to turn on that simian brain of yours, McGill. Someone had to have installed a live anti-matter warhead in that missile that struck the Big Sky Project prematurely."

"Seems like a simple enough mistake," I said shrugging. "Just like loading a live round into your gun instead of a blank. Could have happened to anybody."

Winslade shook his head. "No, it couldn't have. Maybe *you* could have managed such a colossal cock-up, but no normal engineering technician, would have done that sort of thing. No, such people are *competent* McGill. They would not have accidentally loaded a gigaton warhead into a missile and then fired it at a half strength shield without knowing what they were doing."

I thought about that, and I nodded. "It does seem kind of unlikely…"

"Exactly. That leaves us with deliberate sabotage—but sabotage by whom?"

"By Rigel, of course, sir."

Winslade rolled his eyes and crossed his skinny arms. "How did Rigel manage to load a warhead into that missile? Did perhaps a squad of bears dress up as human technicians and fool everyone with their amazing disguises?"

I didn't have a good answer for that. "I'm no tech, sir," I said, "but I would think they must have bribed somebody to do it."

"Bribery… Winslade said, thinking it over. "Just how big of a bribe would you accept to perm ninety million of Earth's citizens?"

I whistled. "It would have to be a big number."

"Yes. A very big number. I've looked into this, as best I'm able. I want to know the exact circumstance under which that warhead came to be upon that missile. I want to know which Hegemony officer ordered it. Who was in charge, who was the quartermaster? Do you know what I found?"

I shrugged helplessly.

"Nothing, he said. "I found absolutely nothing. Either all of the official documents related to that missile test have been deleted, or they were never written up in the first place."

"Huh…" I said, "that is a plain mystery, sir."

"Right. So now you know what I'll be working on while you're out there cavorting around in deep space."

"I'm pretty sure we've got the right man assigned to each of these tasks."

Winslade laughed. It came out as an evil chuckle.

"I'm actually not sure which of us has the more dangerous task ahead of them," he said.

I wasn't sure quite what he meant. It certainly seemed like I was going on a suicide mission. It was definitely more dangerous than his snooping… wasn't it?

After this strange little talk, he let me go, and I marched my crew down directly to Gray Deck. Sixteen of us were suited-up with long-range teleportation gear and given bombs to carry.

These bombs were more than just small, decorative chemical explosives. They were small atomic weapons. Each one was capable of releasing about half a kiloton of destruction with a simple twist of the timing knob on top.

I briefed my team after having been given the weapons, and they all looked sick.

"Each of us will carry one of these," I said. "Essentially, it's a time bomb. You grab the round part here with one hand, and you give the knob on top a hard twist. Don't do it now, you dumbass, Carlos!"

He grinned. "Just fooling, sir."

I glared at him sourly for a minute, then continued the briefing. "Make sure it's twisted pretty good. Because whatever minute it goes to—that's how long you've got. You can't add time to the bomb. You can *subtract* time from the bomb after that initial twist is given, if you want to, but you can't add it back on. That's to prevent any enemy who finds it from adding time until he can throw it out into space or something. Once it's been set—"

Here, I paused to reach out and slap Carlos a good one. He'd put his hand on the knob again, causing all our hearts to race. Blood flew from his lips.

"What the hell, McGill? Don't be such a tool."

"Don't fool with the frigging bomb, asshole."

"I wasn't going to twist it. I was just checking it out."

"There's quite a bit of torque required to twist that knob," I continued. "Once you do it, though, you're committed. It's going to go off on you—so don't play with that knob unless you mean business."

Sargon stepped up then, bouncing a bomb in his hands. "Don't worry, it can't go off from a kinetic impact. Only the timer can do it. Can I suggest one more thing, Centurion?"

"Be my guest."

Sargon faced the crowd. "That first twist has got to be a hard one. I would suggest you dial it *way* out there. Twist it to, like, thirty minutes. That's the max. Then you can nudge it down a little shorter should you decide that's what you want later on."

The team all nodded. They all seemed fascinated with their bombs. Most of them had never carried anything more powerful than a plasma grenade.

"Essentially," Sargon continued, "it's a giant grenade. Once you twist the knob, it's going to go off. It's just a matter of time."

"Pretty cool," Carlos said. He took his bomb and tossed it up in the air and caught it a few times. It was about the size and weight of a baseball.

"That's it for now," I told my soldiers. "We've got four minutes until jump time. Everybody, sync-up your tappers, and do a final check on your gear. Make sure you've got your oxygen tanks full, and just in case we arrive in vacuum, we're going to ride with faceplates down."

I started going through the list after that. We'd been equipped with enough air to last us about four hours. That should be more than enough.

At least, I seriously hoped that it would be.

-16-

The world around us began to turn blue and flashing lights glared into our eyes. We all began hyperventilating a bit. This reaction was automatic and almost unstoppable, even though it was pointless.

One at a time, we winked out and jumped across the cosmos. Carlos flashed away first, then Sargon then six others—then it was my turn.

When you did a long jump through hyperspace—or whatever the right technical term was for crossing lightyears impossibly fast—some trick of the cosmos rewarded you with the sensation that you couldn't breathe. This was a true feeling, of course, as no one could breathe in hyperspace—but you also didn't need to.

The real problem was the traveler being *aware* of their strange, ghostly state. You knew that your heart wasn't beating, and that blood wasn't flowing in your veins. There was a vague sensation of pressure from clothing that was in contact with your skin—but that was it.

Not being a techie, I wasn't sure how real any of these impressions were, but the one thing I knew for sure was I always felt a growing burn in my lungs. It became panic-inducing. You felt like you were drowning, even though you didn't really require oxygen, and you couldn't die that way. You couldn't even pass out—although you might want to.

I'd often wondered how bad it would be if I ever teleported all the way to the Core Worlds—not by dying and being revived out there, mind you, but rather by utilizing a high-powered teleportation technique. If I ever had the balls to do such a fantastically long jump, would I arrive as a raving madman? I mean, after having spent *days* feeling as if my lungs were starving for oxygen, as if my heart should be pounding madly in my chest—that would be pretty intense.

The trip out to Rigel took around twenty minutes. It was torment, even though I had no lungs, no heart, and nothing in my nonexistent veins to be pumped around in the first place.

As I sailed between the stars, I counted the seconds. When I got up to about 1200, which was approximately the right number of lightyears between Rigel and old Sol, I finally arrived.

Doubled over and gasping, I almost ended up on my face on the deck. Within thirty seconds, all of us had arrived.

"All right, we made it," I told them as they were wheezing and sicking-up in their suits. "Veteran Moller, get these troops into line."

"Straighten up!" she shouted. "Hold your rifles and your pricks in the upright and locked position!"

I had them sound-off to get their minds operating again. One by one, they reported in. We were in luck. Everyone on the team had made it to Rigel.

There was always some risk that one of us could have had a bad battery, which might run out of juice somewhere in the middle of that long, long jump. Such an unfortunate soldier would find himself flying for an eternity through nothingness, or he might simply cease to be.

Another possible result would be getting kicked out of hyperspace and back into normal, old, boring space. Such an individual would find themselves in a vast ocean of nothingness, drifting between the stars. They'd slowly starve, run out of air and water, and eventually die. Today, none of these grim things had happened. My entire team was here, armed and ready to go.

Our first objective was to determine where the hell we were. The Gray Deck techs back at Central had not seen it fit to describe the destination they had in mind for me and my team earlier—that part was classified.

I realized now how diabolical the situation was. They'd sent us to a place we had no knowledge of and left us here to do or die.

"This is bullshit!" Carlos exclaimed. Then he repeated that single phrase over and over again.

"What's your problem, Ortiz? Are your panties riding up your butt-crack?"

"They sure are. Just take a look over there. That's solid rock. Don't tell me it's not, McGill. Don't try to bullshit me on this one."

I followed his thick, pointing finger toward a nearby dark wall.

We were in a large chamber of some kind. Most of it was metal. Much of it was either plastic or glass.

But Carlos was right. There was a section of polished stone nearby.

"Looks like granite," I said.

"I don't care if it's solid freaking gold, McGill. That's not supposed to be here. That means we're on an asteroid, or a moon or something. We're not on a space station at all."

He began walking around, staring at our surroundings and complaining more and more loudly. "We're in the wrong damned place! We're screwed. Totally screwed. No grease, no nothing—!"

I thumped him one on the skull. That stopped his complaints. "You removed your helmet without orders, Specialist."

The blow wasn't a hard one. He didn't drop to his knees or vomit. He just glared at me.

"Just try to think for a second, Ortiz," I told him. "They said we're going to some sky stations, kind of like the ones back on Earth. But that doesn't mean that the Rigellians build them all out of metal. I happen to know they like to bring asteroids close and park them in orbit around their big planet."

"What for?" Carlos asked, rubbing at his bruised brain. He put his helmet back on sullenly.

"It takes a lot of power to run one of these shields. Massive generators require space. The bears use stations cut out of asteroids to provide the space they need."

Still glaring, he narrowed his eyes in suspicion. "How the hell do you know all this stuff?"

"That's classified. Shut up and fall in."

As I didn't recognize the area we were in, I chose a likely direction at random. This led us to a metal wall. It wasn't a natural one made of stone this time. I marched in that direction confidently. Sometimes, choosing a direction and moving out was the best thing a leader could do.

Fooled into believing I knew where I was going, my crew fell in and marched behind me. Warily, they looked this way and that. They examined the distant ceiling which was made of dark rock and also the deck under our boots which was made of some type of alloy.

I could tell the squad was kind of freaked out. We were inside a large chamber that was clearly pressurized. It didn't make much sense to me as an Earth man. In space, you normally only put air and heat into regions that required it for people to live.

All this environmental energy being released seemed insane—but as I'd noticed before, the Rigellians didn't seem to quite think the way we did about efficiency.

After we'd marched for a minute or two, we reached another wall. This one was tall and definitely made of polished stone.

We walked along the wall until we found a hatch in the deck. With a little bit of work, my tech specialists got the hatch open, and we climbed down inside.

"Well," I said looking around the small chamber, "this place looks as good as anywhere for us to set our first bomb."

The storage chamber was full of junk and maintenance equipment. There were racks of oxygen tanks, cutting torches, power carts—stuff like that. The ceiling was low because it was built for bears.

I took out my baseball-sized bomb and put my hand upon the knob to twist it.

"Hold on a second," Carlos said. "How do we know this is the optimal place that will do the optimal damage?"

"We don't frigging know that, Carlos," I said.

"But what about the rest of the mission?"

"We don't have any other objectives. We're not supposed to *do* anything. We don't even need to shoot anybody. All we have to do is set off some bombs."

"Yeah… but how will they know we're dead? I mean… how do we get okayed for revival back home?"

I shrugged. "I'm sure that Central is spying on this place somehow. When this pineapple goes off, they'll see we have completed our mission, and then we'll get revived lickety-split."

Carlos looked nervous. I toyed with my bomb, and I made ready to twist it.

"Just a second, though," Carlos said. "Don't you think we should have a better look around, first?"

"That will only increase the odds that someone will stop us. Is that what you secretly want? You're sounding like a hog right now. A hog who eats chicken."

"Yeah, yeah, yeah," he said, "but this is a fantastic opportunity. I've never been to Rigel, McGill. At least let me smell the flowers around here."

I snorted.

"Chicken!" Sargon said. "You see that, McGill? This pug is *chicken*. He doesn't want to die."

A few of the grunts in the back of the group chuckled at that.

"I think Sargon is right," I said. "You'd think that after all these years serving with Legion Varus, you'd have gotten over this kind of squeamishness. It's kind of embarrassing to be honest, Carlos."

Right about then, we heard a strange, loud noise. It was coming from outside the supply room we'd all hidden ourselves in.

"What the hell is that?" Sargon asked.

"I think they found us," whispered Kivi. She had deployed buzzers in the big chamber above, letting them crawl all over the place, gathering data.

That was enough for me. I grabbed my bomb and twisted the knob all the way around, giving us half an hour before it went off.

"All right, enough flower-smelling," I said. "Let's get out of here."

"Why the hell are we doing that?" Carlos asked. "We got one ticking. Let's just set it off, and be done with it."

"We don't know how big this place is. We don't know if this bomb will fizzle and just kill everyone in the room. We've got to be thorough, our orders are to drop them all over the place and make sure the station is a full kill. Come on."

I climbed up, opened the hatch, and threw it clear with a clang. Looking around with my rifle in my hands, I didn't see any bears. I exited the storage compartment and half-dragged my crew up behind me.

"More than one is just a waste," Carlos complained. "It just increases the odds we'll be found."

I ignored him. "All right, you—what's your name?"

"Vines, sir. Regular, First Class—"

"Yeah, whatever. Go over there to that cubby in the rock and plant one. Make sure to twist the timer hard, all the way around."

Vines trotted away. I didn't wait for him to come back. I began marching rapidly toward a dark tunnel mouth that led into the polished rock wall.

Sargon was right on my tail. "I think I get your strategy, sir. They can dismantle one bomb, but they can't get all sixteen if we hide them all over their complex."

"That's right."

An alarm sounded.

"Oh, crap," Kivi said.

I began to run, and my squad all hustled after me. More alarms went off as we raced by, beeping and whooping at us in an accusatory fashion. There were even some flashing lights as well. Every time we found a storage closet, an unattended vehicle, or even a large ventilator shaft, I had one of my men twist the knob on their bomb and place it accordingly.

Carlos still seemed unhappy, but I barely cared. "You really are a firebug, aren't you, Centurion? One of those crazies who gets sexual gratification from blowing things up."

"Yeah, that's it, Carlos. You should know this by now."

We kept going and dropping bombs, but eventually we came to a door that didn't open, and we decided to pass it by.

We trotted about another dozen steps when it popped opened suddenly behind us. Guns poked out into the corridor in our wake, and they immediately began to fire.

We returned fire, and a battle began. Bolts were spraying down both sides of the corridor. The tunnel wasn't well-lit, and muzzle flashes were like lightning in the dark. Each bolt lit the place up with orange fire.

In the end, three Saurian soldiers lay facedown on the deck along with one Varus specialist sprawled near them.

I walked over to this pile of bodies and inspected the group.

"Correct me if I'm wrong, sir," Sargon said, "but there are no bears in sight here."

"You're unusually observant today, Veteran," Carlos said.

"Armel…" I said. "It has to be Armel."

"What are you talking about, sir?" Sargon asked.

"Kivi," I said, "they've got to have a communications system active around here. Try to hack in and find out who is aboard this station."

She did as I asked, and while she worked, more sirens wailed. Groups of Saurian soldiers found us, but we ambushed them and mowed them down. After maybe five minutes had gone by, Kivi had managed to finish the hack. She was now perusing through contacts, looking for anything that we could understand.

"I've got a channel. It's not Rigellian… I think it's something Imperial…"

Sargon's belcher flared white, releasing a massive surge of radiation downrange. Two Saurians were flash-fried in their scaly hides.

Kivi was pecking at my shoulder, so I leaned close to her. "What have you got?"

"Sir, I think I recognize this pattern. This is from Imperial equipment, but it's a little different."

"What do you mean?"

"I think it's Saurian gear."

I nodded. "That makes perfect sense. Armel is here somewhere. Locate him. I don't know if he's on this rock, exactly. But these Saurians are his mercenary troops, so we'd best have a look."

She looked startled. "You mean like back on Edge World? Do you think he's still working for the Skay?"

"Probably."

Sargon came and squatted down with us. He tapped at his tapper, which was running a helpful timer app. "We've only got about twenty-one minutes left, McGill," he said.

"Got it."

I turned back to Kivi. "No way to give us any more time on those bombs?"

"Hell no, not now that we've dropped like ten of them all over the place."

"Right. Okay, so we all know we're dead in twenty minutes. Let's do whatever we can."

"Yeah," Carlos said in a bitter tone, "let's live big. I've got a huge personality, and I want to let all these aliens know about it."

We took a new route through the passages we hadn't tried before, and I used Kivi's information to lead me. We found a region where there was a concentration of Imperial message transmissions.

That clearly wasn't coming from any natives of Rigel.

We found yet another locked door. As we were under time-pressure, I just waved for Sargon with his belcher. He burned the door down without any preambles. When it fell inward, clanging into a large chamber on the other side, a storm of fire came back in our direction.

We threw in a few plasma grenades and spray from our morph-rifles, but neither side was landing any hits on the other as we were both standing well back from the entrance.

"Hey," I yelled. "Let's talk, lizard-breath."

It was quiet for a few moments. Finally, a rasping reply came back. "What do you want, human?"

"I want to talk to your leader," I said. "I want to talk to Maurice Armel."

"Our tribune is not here."

"Well, call him. Tell him James McGill wants to talk."

"What would the purpose of this conversation be?"

"I'm not going to tell you, but if you don't contact Armel, he'll know about it. Then later on, you're going to get your tail pulled off."

"You could never do such a thing," he said angrily. "My tail is far too strong. Far too well attached. Far too—"

"Yeah, yeah," I said. "Just relay my message to your master."

"My tail is incomparable, human!"

I was sorry I'd ever brought up tails. Saurians had a real thing about their tails. In human parlance, it was said that men liked to have dick-measuring contests. Well, amongst Saurians, they *literally* had tail-measuring contests.

"Just contact your master," I shouted, "or you'll be wishing you were still in your mama's egg sack."

There was some hissing after that, and no doubt foul words were spoken in his native tongue. But the Saurian did finally make an attempt to transmit a message. I had Kivi trace this while we all stayed way back from the doorway.

After a minute or so, a response finally came out of the chamber. "The master is coming. You have earned his wrath."

"Sounds good!" I called back. "We'll wait right here but tell him to make it quick."

We waited for maybe two more precious minutes, during which Carlos went on about how useless this all was and how we were about to be blown up for nothing. Then, a blue flashing light appeared in the chamber.

A moment or two later there were sharp reports as boots struck the deck. In the smoking doorway, which Sargon had burned down with his belcher, a figure appeared.

The human had his hands on his hips. His guns were still safely located in their holsters, so we didn't shoot him down. He looked around at the group of us humans with a sneer on his face.

"Legion Varus pigs?" he said. "Of course… I should have known. What do you rodents want here?"

"Hi, Armel. Remember me?" I stood up and, and I can't swear he didn't flinch in surprise.

"James McGill…" he said. "You are the bane of my existence. How long has it been, madman?"

"Too long. Way too long."

I walked forward and offered him a hand to shake. He ignored this gesture for a few seconds, but he finally reached out and shook my hand.

"I imagine you are engaged in some farcical suicide-mission?" he asked.

"Just like you are!"

Armel smiled a bit. Both of us knew that we were going to die in some fashion or another in short order. But one thing about Armel that I appreciated was how little fear he had of death. He didn't *like* the process, mind you. He would struggle against it as hard as the next fellow. But he was more worried about who won a given moment in time—a contest between two competing men—than he was interested in keeping his skin intact at all times. In a way, I could admire that about him.

"Why have you summoned me, McGill? Why don't you just do whatever goofy display of futility Earth has ordered you to perform and be on your way."

"I wanted to talk to you for a minute or two, sir."

"Talk? That is not your usual ape-manner What do you wish to converse about?"

"Well sir, this whole thing seems kind of strange. What do you know about this new war starting up between Earth and Rigel?"

Armel shrugged. "I know almost nothing. I know that the bears sent a ship to implore your government to return to sanity. These diplomats were rudely rebuffed. Then, Earth has made a great show of blowing up its own fledgling and probably inoperable planetary shield in order to create an excuse for attacking Rigel."

"Huh? Are you for reals? Are you saying this is a false-flag operation?"

Armel shrugged. "Take my words for whatever value you find in them. Rigel did not destroy your planetary shield."

I flipped up my visor and one finger came up to my face, which was suddenly itchy. It got like that when I felt a thought coming on.

"Huh…" I said. "All right. I suppose the truth will come out in time. There's an investigation going on you know."

Armel laughed in my face. "McGill, your ineptitude is almost charming. There is always an investigation going on. All of them find what the investigators want to be found. How can you have lived so long and not figured that out yet?"

"Yeah, well, listen. There's something else I wanted to ask you about."

"Pray continue. You have not yet sufficiently wasted my time."

"Do you know anything about some bunkers? Some old, old bunkers back on Earth. They're full of military gear from before the Unification Wars, as far as I can tell."

Armel blinked once, then twice. I could tell right off he hadn't been expecting *that* question. He cocked his head and looked at me curiously.

"Have you found something dangerous, McGill? Looking at your simpleton's face... yes. Yes, I do believe you have."

"Sir," Sargon said, "we've only got about nine minutes left."

Kivi and Carlos were listening to me, and I could tell they were going to burst with questions.

But I didn't care about any of that. We were all going to be blown apart, and we wouldn't be able to remember any of this. Therefore, it didn't matter what was revealed to anyone present.

Except for Armel, that was. His mind was being recorded right now, because this was his turf, his territory. Sure, we were all going to die, but he was on his own grid, he would remember this conversation. None of the rest of us would.

Armel regarded me closely with real curiosity. "You have intrigued me, McGill. I have not been intrigued for a long time. I've been bored to tears out here, sitting in this dismal star system with these nasty little bears and disgusting, retarded lizards. What good is vast wealth if you must spend your time with such deplorable creatures?"

"Eight minutes!" Sargon called through my headset.

"Glad I could be of service..." I told Armel, "but I don't think we have much time left for gabbing."

Armel nodded. "Will you come with me, McGill? To my ship?"

"Uh… what?"

"It's an invitation. Must I engrave it for you?"

Carlos was listening in, and he turned his head to the others. "They're exchanging rings, and they're about to bone! I'm sure of it!" he said loudly.

Armel's eyes narrowed. "I would enjoy shooting that man. A close and personal stabbing would be even more satisfactory."

"You'll have to take a number on that. Honestly, I would let you do it, but we don't have much time. You said something about a ship though?"

Armel smiled. "This will be a matter of honor between us. I will talk to you, and afterward I will send you back to Earth in a nice, neat box. Just the way you like it."

He held out his hand as if to shake again, but I noticed that his other hand was reaching a finger to touch a button on his harness.

Some of my troops saw this as well. They lifted their rifles, wheeling around. "He's trying to perm McGill!" Carlos shouted.

I grabbed Armel's hand, and he pushed the button. Blue lights flashed as we began to flicker away. All the grunts in the passageway were shocked, but not for long.

After seeing that both their commanders were going to skedaddle, chaos broke out.

The truce was over. Saurians and Earth men all began firing on each other at once.

Then, Armel and I faded from view.

-17-

A minute ago, Armel had been under our guns, but now the reverse was true. A pack of at least twenty oversized lizards stood all around us. Every gun in the place was targeting yours truly.

"Let us enjoy a beverage," Armel said.

He beckoned, and I followed him to a table surrounded by vintage chests and cabinets. I eyed his cache of goods and furniture admiringly. "You brought this stuff all the way from Earth, didn't you?"

"I certainly did. I believe it helps a man's spirit to be surrounded by objects from his home."

I looked around curiously. As far as living beings, I saw nothing but lizards, although, I had seen Armel use human staff members in the past as well.

"No… women?" I asked.

Armel pursed his lips under a wormy mustache. "I had one, but I believe she left my service to enter yours."

"Oh yeah… Leza. Well, don't worry about that. She didn't stick around for long. I think she's still part of Legion Varus, but I haven't seen her on this deployment. For all I know she mustered out permanently."

Armel nodded, and he poured me a glass of brandy. He drank his own with quiet sips while I gulped mine. "McGill," he said, "let us be civilized. I assume that your raiding party came here for the purpose of sabotage, yes?"

"Uh…" I said thinking that over. I wasn't sure if I should confess or not.

Finally, I shrugged and figured what the hell? "Yes, of course we did. You'll never have time to find all the bombs. They've been set in too many places. And they're all going to go off within the next few minutes."

"As expected, Armel said. "I told the Rigellians that you would do this. I'm actually pleased that you came here to confirm my status as an oracle. They cannot go on without the likes of Maurice Armel."

I frowned. He didn't seem concerned at all. We were about to punch a hole in Rigel's network of stations that surrounded their world. What's more, it would be a larger hole than they had punched into our shield.

Each of their stations was larger and transmitted a projected shield over a comparatively larger region. Therefore, destroying one of theirs was at least equivalent to destroying four of ours, just because of the way each system had been designed.

"So, you predicted this move, and the bears didn't care?"

"Hmm? Oh, they have a care, certainly. But you see, by now we've isolated where your little strike was going to land."

"You what?"

"We're able to disconnect any given station from the grid. With a little bit of thrust the station you've attacked is now heading out into deep space."

My jaw sagged. "You like… pulled it out of the whole network of stations?"

"Exactly. Come, look out of this observation window." He walked with me, and we stood before a very large, very tall pane of glass. I knew that it probably was a screen, not actual transparent material, but it looked real. I wasn't even *sure* if it was real or not—and it didn't matter. "There," Armel said, pointing.

I could see quite clearly, one of the modified asteroid stations was moving out of formation. I wished right then that I could contact my men and tell them to set one of the bombs to one minute. We'd been fools to set so many and waste so much time.

Armel swilled more of his brandy. "What is it you wanted to talk about McGill? Realize that we don't have forever if I'm to kill you and send you home. Once the Rigellians see your vicious act of sabotage, they will demand that I capture you and hand you over into their custody."

I nodded, understanding his logic. "I was asking about bunkers. Back on Earth during the Unification Wars, certain secret bunkers were placed in remote locations. Do you know anything about that?"

Armel squinted at me. "This is a strange topic for you to pursue, McGill. Who has been talking to you?"

I shrugged. "No one. Imagine that I've found such a place, and I'm naturally curious about it."

Armel laughed. "In regard to this matter, McGill, you very much want to avoid curiosity. Hegemony, at its very heart, is still terrified of the rebels they once fought. In order to secure their final victory against them, they were extremely harsh. If anyone shows the slightest inclination toward bringing those old ghosts back to life, they will almost certainly go to great lengths to destroy that individual."

I thought that over, and I figured he had to be right. After all, on the basis of only a couple of grid searches, I had been beaten to death, convicted of a slew of crimes, executed a couple more times and then sentenced to what was essentially permadeath. If Drusus hadn't pulled some strings to get me out of purgatory, I would still be there.

"But what's the deal with these bunkers?" I asked. "So what if there are some hidden old places on Earth still? They can't be dangerous to anyone, certainly not to Hegemony bigwigs."

"Partly, it's out of sheer paranoia—but not entirely. You see, some of the bunkers contain the seeds for the rebellion to reawaken and reassert itself. Now, keep in mind that I'm only speaking of legends. I have not been in these bunkers. But it was well known that when the rebels were losing, they hid repositories from the past in various secret locations. They planned to use them to return to power someday."

"Huh…" I said, "I think I'm beginning to understand… might there be doors, deep in these places? Doors with sophisticated locks?"

Armel peered at me. "Possibly."

"So, there's like a secret cache of weapons down there? Or maybe critical intel that would help bring Hegemony down? Something like that?"

"Something like that…" Armel agreed. "As a young man, I served during the earliest history of the legions, but I cannot claim to have fought in the Unification Wars—very few men can."

"Like, who?"

Armel looked thoughtful. "Hmm… I'm thinking of Claver, Alexander Turov, Primus Graves… there are others, but they're few and far between."

"Right," I said, thinking about the fact that I actually knew three men who had fought in the Unification Wars. Maybe that association had made some paranoid piece of spyware flag me as a threat.

It was strange to know that these men still existed at all. They were like fossils from a different time who still lived and breathed in this one.

"Well," I said, "if that's all you can tell me, I guess you can send me home now."

He nodded, but he lifted a finger to point at me. "I will ask one favor in return for what I've told you."

I laughed. "You didn't really give me much."

"True," he said, "but I would still ask that you not tell anyone on Earth we had this conversation."

"Okay. In fact, I'll erase it right now."

I worked my tapper and deleted some videos that I'd made of Armel and his headquarters. "Anything else?"

"Yes. I would ask you to speak to Leza on my behalf. I would like to make amends if she is interested—entirely on her terms. As I said, I'm both lonely and bored out here.

"Okay, okay, sure. I'll give it a shot. It's never been said that old McGill is too smart to pester women who aren't interested."

"Now, one last point… I want to show you something. I want to show you something which you should take back to show Hegemony. Turn on your recording cameras again and come this way."

We walked over to a large section of wall. It had to be twenty meters high and forty meters wide. He tapped at it with a single finger. The wall was a dormant screen which immediately flashed to life. There, I saw Rigel itself, a glorious planet full of greens and blues with white clouds hanging above.

"As you can, see the shimmering shield operates without a flaw."

Rigel's defenses were quite impressive, really. But then, Armel pointed out another crescent shape that was smaller and hung up high in the left corner of the screen. It was above the arcing curvature of Rigel itself.

I was not immediately impressed. "So, what?" I said, "I know that Rigel has some moons. I've even been on one of them."

"Of course, you have. But McGill… that is not a moon."

I squinted at the curved object in the top corner. I squinted hard, and then I walked a few steps closer, peering up at that upper left corner of the giant screen. Finally, I saw what he was talking about. There was a black, rectangular opening in the face of that strange moon…

That's when I realized he was right, and it wasn't a moon at all.

I turned around, eyes wide, to face Armel. I waggled a finger up at the screen. "That's a Skay! A big, giant Skay parked in orbit over Rigel!"

Armel smiled, and he nodded grimly. "Yes. The patron saint of Rigel is here, patrolling."

The last time the Mogwa had sent Battle Fleet 921 to visit Earth had been decades ago. Back then, they'd been considering destroying us all.

I thought about that. There were only two occasions when Galactic fleets had visited Earth. The first time was the Annexation Event when the Empire had announced itself and declared Earth to be one of her possessions. The second time had been after the Rogue World campaign, when the Mogwa had decided that all of earthlings had to be exterminated because of the illegal activities of the Rogue-Worlders. That had taken a little bit of work and wangling to get out of afterwards.

Naturally, after Battle Fleet 921 had been destroyed the Mogwa forces had never returned in strength again.

"So… you're telling me that the Skay care more about Rigel than the Mogwa care about Earth?"

"That is definitely true."

"Huh… That's not good."

"Exactly. Think about it, McGill. Earth is about to embark upon a foolish war. Firstly, Rigel's defensive shield is intact and fully operational. In addition to that, they have powerful patron allies while Earth has none."

"Hmm," I said, thinking that over. Armel had a strong point. Rigel had both allies and better defenses. The bears seemed to be in a better position all around.

"Ah, it is the moment of truth," Armel said. He directed my attention to another screen that followed a camera placed in deep space.

I watched as a white light flashed there. The Saurians in the room all hissed and shifted around menacingly.

Armel was triumphant. "I see that your bombs have ignited. I'd half-expected them to fail and fizzle like most earthly creations."

"Nope. We still know how to blow shit up."

We watched as the one stray station disintegrated into chunks of flying debris. Just as Armel had said, it had wandered away from the network, leaving the rest of them untouched. Streamers of flame and a growing cloud of dust and destruction marked the spot where the station had been.

I was still videoing the event with all my body cameras when Armel took his pistol from his belt. Without so much as a kiss goodbye, he lifted the weapon, put it to my head, and blew my brains out.

-18-

After my revival, I was relieved to be home again. I made my way directly to the barracks, where I was pleased to find most of the Legion had assembled. That included most of my unit.

Dickson had proved particularly effective in this area of organization. I complimented him on his success. He'd gotten most of his light troops to report in early.

"Usually, the recruits are worst at showing up—but not this time," I told him. "Harris couldn't have done it better."

"Say nothing of it, Centurion," Dickson said with a smug hint of pride. "The key to leading any group of soldiers is to learn what motivates them best—and then to apply it vigorously."

I nodded, but I didn't ask for any details. "Have you heard anything about the general officers' briefing? I believe we're going to get a legion-wide assignment soon."

"About that, sir," Harris said. He'd walked up behind us wearing a sour expression. Apparently, he'd been listening in. "One of the things I've heard—mind you, this is just a rumor, sir—but I heard that Tribune Winslade has been arrested for sedition."

There was that word again. "Winslade? A traitor? Well, it wouldn't be the first time he's been accused of such things… But in this case, I don't buy it."

Harris shrugged. "It's just what I heard."

"I'm going to go for a little walk, gentlemen," I told them.

As I left, I heard Harris mutter something. It sounded like: "See? What'd I tell you?"

I stopped and turned to frown at Dickson and Harris. "What *did* you tell him?"

"Nothing, sir," Harris said.

"It sounded like something, Adjunct Harris."

"I was just telling our fine, new Adjunct Dickson that you have a very well pronounced sense of justice."

I frowned for a moment, but I couldn't find an insult buried in those words anywhere. Nodding, I walked out again.

When I reached Legion Varus headquarters and walked under the banner that bore the wolf's head emblem, I found one of Winslade's staff members there. She was looking real nervous. On top of that, I spotted one additional member of the crew. It was Gary, an adjunct who normally worked under Galina Turov.

"Gary? What are you doing here?"

"I wish I knew, McGill," he said. "I wish I knew…"

Turning toward the closed inner door, I approached and thumped on it.

"Come in," said a distinctively female voice.

I threw the door wide. There, sitting in Winslade's chair, was Galina Turov herself. "Huh…" I said. "Fancy finding you slumming around down here with us Legion Varus losers."

She didn't look happy to see me. After all, she'd had me beaten to death repeatedly. She might be thinking I was in a vengeful mood.

"What do you want, McGill?" she asked.

"Nothing Earth-shattering. I came here to talk to the tribune, sir. Whoa, hold on! You didn't get demoted to tribune again, did you, sir?"

"Certainly not," she snapped. "I was directed to stand in for Winslade during his leave of absence."

"Heh…" I said, mildly amused. "You mean, until his trial verdict is decided with finality, right?"

Her lips twitched upward slightly. "With finality… I find I like the sound of that word, but I don't want to be stuck here forever because of Winslade's fuck-up."

"Uh… what did he do, exactly?"

"He didn't *do* anything. He was caught making unacceptable statements. If I were you, I wouldn't ask any more about it. You're an ex-con yourself, you know."

I thought that over and considered my options. "Galina?" I asked. "Are you happy sitting here flying Winslade's desk? Are you just itching to take Varus out to the stars again?"

"Hell no. It's a demeaning task for an imperator. I haven't even been assigned three or four legions as I should have been. Just a single outfit with the lowest of reputations."

I leaned a big set of knuckles on her desk. "What if I could fix that for you?" I asked, and I finally had her attention. She looked up and met my gaze.

"I would like that, James."

I nodded. "Okay, sir. Consider it done."

Spinning around, I marched out of the place. I didn't listen to any queries from the staffers. Instead, I marched down the corridor, got into the elevator, and punched up a very high floor number. A very high floor number indeed.

After a couple of minutes, I reached the nosebleed levels. Primus Bob got in my way as I closed in on the office of Consul Drusus.

"McGill?" he said. "Are you serious?"

Bob interposed himself between me and Drusus' inner door.

"I'm here to make a private report, Primus. Please step aside."

"Are you aware, Centurion," Bob said in an unusually snotty tone, "that Drusus is now the consul of all Earth?"

"That's what I heard sir. In fact, I recall being there during the swearing-in ceremony."

"Ah, yes. Well, as you can quite possibly imagine, he has many more high priority things to worry about. Things that are much more important than whatever piddling nonsense you want to peddle today."

"You got me there!" I said. "He probably doesn't have time for any eyewitness reporting from the orbit of Rigel. I'll put my report on the backburner, I'm sure you know best. I'll be on my way." I staged a turn-around, but I didn't make it three steps across that lush carpet before old Bob was in front of me again.

"I forgot. You were sent on a mission, weren't you? It was an abject failure, but I suppose Drusus might want to hear your excuses."

"Uh… a failure?"

Bob's eyebrows shot up on his bald, overly-large forehead. "Don't you know? You must have set the timers for too long. A cowardly move. The enemy had enough time to shunt their station out of place, and thus the strike only created a small hole in their defenses, not a gaping wound."

"That might be your opinion, Primus. Where should I wait?"

"Huh? Wait for what?"

"Wait for Drusus. For his next unscheduled moment."

Bob frowned at me. "Do you really have something to report? How could you remember anything? We blew you up out there on purpose. I don't think you know anything, McGill. I think you're just trying to get in here because you like to brown nose around power. You're a throne-sniffer, McGill nothing more, nothing less."

"A what?"

I felt like letting him know what I thought of him with my fists, but after a moment of rage I decided that such an approach would get me nowhere fast. I looked down on my tapper instead. I pressed the stopwatch mode, and numbers began flashing by quickly on the screen.

"Now, what are you doing?" Bob asked in irritation.

"Starting a timer, sir."

"What for?"

"Well sir, when Drusus asks me why I'm so late to debrief him, I want to be able to show him exactly how long you stood in my way."

Primus Bob glared at me for several long seconds. At last, he cleared his throat. "All right. I'll send him an announcement message. I can, however, virtually assure you that nothing will come of it."

I smiled, nodded and sat my big butt down in the waiting area. I barely had time to flick my tapper to a ballgame when Primus Bob was up and out of his seat. He came toward me with a quick flurry of steps.

"Come this way, Centurion."

I made a show of checking the stopwatch app on my tapper, then I ambled slowly to the doors. Primus Bob waved furiously for me to hurry up, but I pretended not to get it.

Once I'd stepped inside, I spotted Drusus. He wasn't alone. He had a dozen staffers standing around giving him various reports. With a quick flick of his finger, the consul indicated that I should sit on those comfy chairs in his inner waiting area.

I immediately walked over to the line of statues he had clustered nearby and inspected them. I couldn't help noticing that today, at the end of that line of marble mutes, a Rigellian bear now stood. It looked like a depiction of Squanto himself.

That bust hadn't been there previously, I was certain of it. I suspected old Drusus had kept it hidden. When the emissaries from Rigel had run off that had all changed. Perhaps now that we were at war, he no longer cared who saw the thing.

A dozen minutes went by, and then another dozen after that. I put my feet up on one of those floating coffee tables, leaned back in my chair and fell asleep.

I awakened sometime later when someone cleared his throat nearby. Snorting and sitting up, I saw Drusus was standing over me. His hands were on his hips.

"McGill, I really don't have a lot of time for you today. So, make it quick."

"I understand, Consul, sir. A man in your position probably doesn't have much time for anything—not even taking a piss."

Drusus made a spinning motion with one finger, suggesting that I should get on with it.

"Well, sir, it's like this. When I went out there to Rigel, I met with someone that you and I both know well."

Drusus frowned.

"Perhaps it would be better if I showed you sir," I said reaching to my tapper.

Drusus nodded and led the way to his holotable. I flicked the video recording of my meeting with Armel to the main screen. The clip played just the final part of our conversation, where he showed me around his headquarters and pointed out the Skay.

Drusus squinted. "Stop playing the file."

I tapped the video to freeze it. Using his fingers, he spread that one area, zooming in. It was easy to see that the image was indeed of a Skay, not an errant moon.

"I'll be damned..." he said. "A Skay, sitting right there in orbit, over Rigel."

"He's a big bastard, too, sir. The biggest I've ever laid eyes on."

"This changes all of our strategic planning."

"Uh... were we thinking about striking with the fleet, sir?" I asked.

Drusus glanced at me. "It was under consideration—but not now. Thanks for this timely intel, McGill."

"No charge, sir."

"There's just one thing I need cleared up: how is it that you can recall this? How did you get this recording from Rigel to Earth? Everyone else in your unit was killed without recording anything."

I explained how Armel had bargained to have me send a message to Leza on his behalf, and then murdered me after updating my information and effectively sending me home.

Drusus shook his head bemusedly. "It's always about a woman in the end with you, isn't it?"

I scratched my cheek a bit. "It is my biggest hobby."

"All right, what else have you got for me?"

"Well, sir, besides my report from Rigel, I've got one other thing."

"What's that? Speak up, you're almost out of time."

"Uh... okay. Here it goes, I think you should order that Tribune Winslade be released."

Slowly, Drusus turned his head and eyed me. His expression had shifted. He seemed concerned and a bit suspicious. "You do realize, McGill, that any individual caught in league with someone convicted of sedition is, by definition, guilty of the same crime?"

"Does innocence spread in the same manner?"

He smiled, amused by the idea. "No. It never works that way."

"I thought not. Anyways, you found the case against me to be pointless and frivolous, and so you got me released.

Whatever Winslade did was no worse than anything I did—and probably not worse than whatever Praetor Wurtenberger has been accused of."

Drusus studied me and thought about that list of names. "Hmm... you're actually equating these three circumstances—same crime, same source of accusation."

"Right, and the same lack of evidence to support any of these cases."

Drusus turned toward a gaggle of officers that were at another tactical table going over my new data. They were quite concerned about the apparent fact that a Skay was parked at Rigel. They were all making hand gestures and loud statements. I didn't get the impression that any of them were listening to me and Drusus, as they were too concerned about this new information to be eavesdropping.

But Drusus was a cautious man. "Gentleman," he said, and they all froze and stopped speaking instantly. He was, after all, the most powerful man that Earth had seen walking these halls for a century or so. "Gentlemen, may I have the room? I would ask that you all excuse us immediately. Carry on in conference room B, please."

They all jumped like jackrabbits. They grabbed their tablets, and their plastic computer scrolls and marched out right-quick. Nobody asked a damned thing about why they were being kicked out. They did throw me a few disgusted looks, however.

"All right, McGill. Tell me what's on your mind and be as quick and clear about it as you can."

"Yes sir. It's like this... A certain public servant, who shall remain unnamed, has made some startling moves over the last week or two. For one thing, he had me arrested and beaten to death multiple times over nothing."

Drusus frowned and shook his head. "Actually, it was Galina Turov who signed that order."

I smiled frostily. I had naturally suspected this, but I still didn't think that she was the original source of the idea. "Possibly, sir," I said, "but her motivations, I believe, came from another source."

"Go on."

"Immediately before your appointment to your high and well-deserved office, sir, a man who I am not in love with by any means was treated in just such an unfair manner. Praetor Wurtenberger was arrested and executed. Apparently, he remains in purgatory awaiting a trial, which I doubt he's ever going to get."

Drusus was frowning now. He looked down studying the image of the Skay again. "Go on, but be careful, McGill. You're treading on dangerous territory here."

"Don't I know it, sir. Thirdly, Winslade—who happens to be Wurtenberger's butt-boy was similarly accused, arrested and executed just today."

"All right, all right," Drusus said. "You're saying, if I dare to paraphrase, that someone has decided to promote me and then get rid of everyone else they see as a threat to my position."

"I think it might even be worse than that, sir. I think that someone has worked mighty hard to start this war."

That did it for Drusus. He stopped playing with the image of the Skay and stared up at me very seriously. "Now you're making your own accusations of sedition, McGill?"

"I'm only telling you what I feel in my heart. I call them how I see them."

"All right. What proof have you got?"

"Not much," I admitted, "except for the high improbability of three men in your immediate sphere of influence all being declared traitors and removed from your presence in short order."

"But… what kind of motive could make someone do all this?"

"I don't know. I just know when something is fishy. You're being propelled up to the highest levels of government so fast—it just seems like a mighty long string of coincidences to this country boy. Uh… no disrespect intended, sir."

Drusus was chewing his lower lip. At last, he nodded. "All right. Unlike countless leaders before me, I can take bad news without shooting the messenger. I can also take what amounts to an insult without becoming enraged. I can even listen to one of the most scandalous and dishonest men I've ever known without doubting he can sometimes speak the truth."

I wasn't sure, but I felt like I'd been insulted. I didn't let that show in my face, however. I just smiled and nodded.

"Glad to help, sir. Now… can I have my Tribune Winslade back?"

Drusus frowned. "Have him back?"

"Yes sir. You're the consul of Earth. With one wave of your hand, you can commute his sentence and announce him innocent."

Drusus looked down at the Skay again. "I'll take your suggestions under advisement, McGill. Now return to your unit and prepare. Legion Varus is deploying to province 928. At dawn tomorrow, you are to be aboard that ship and flying with the rest of your legion."

"Happy to serve, sir. I was getting bored down on my farm, anyways." I saluted, turned around and walked out.

-19-

My unit was chased out of bed bright and early the next morning. We ran through the showers and ate a paltry breakfast. The red arrows on the deck directed us to a subway station, where we were whisked away to the spaceport.

We weren't treated to first-class transportation out at the blast pans, either. Instead, we were packed into a lifter like a thousand sardines with no place better to go.

The roar and rumble of the ship filled the hold as we took off. I found myself with Harris on one side and Adjunct Dickson on the other. Harris was bitching as usual, ticking off a long list of complaints on his fingers.

"We weren't given proper warning. We don't know who we're going to attack. Our gear is incomplete. We haven't been issued live ammo, nothing."

"Are you done, Adjunct?"

Harris shook his head. "Not by a longshot. The worst is a quarter of our unit hasn't even checked in yet. How are we supposed to have a training session without our full unit aboard the transport? Whatever happened to using gateway posts to join a mission in progress?"

"Maybe it costs too much power, or something."

He threw up his hands in disgust. "That's just not how you do things."

That was his favorite line today, and Harris had used it three or four times in a row now. Dickson squinted throughout Harris' tirade. I could tell by the little telltale twist of his lip that he wasn't completely happy with Harris or his complaints.

"If we're heading all the way to Rigel," he continued, "this is all plain crazy. We won't be ready when we arrive."

Dickson finally spoke up. "I thought you said we didn't know where we were going." Harris glowered at Dickson as if daring him to speak further. Dickson plowed ahead without a care. "I overheard you complaining earlier that you had no idea where the legion was headed—but now you're worried about whether we'll arrive at Rigel too soon?"

"Yeah," Harris said. "I *did* say that because I'm not certain where we're headed. There's been no confirmation. But of course, we're probably going to Rigel or one of their occupied star systems in the frontier zone."

Dickson brightened. He looked prim and pleased with himself. I realized that he figured he'd scored a point against Harris by proving that he'd contradicted himself.

I hoped that Harris didn't much care. If he did care, it could only serve to engender a deeper sense of hatred for Dickson. Thinking that over, I noted that my newest adjunct had a near magical way of upsetting other officers and crewmen that met him and dealt with him. "What about the training issue?" I asked, looking at Dickson.

He shrugged. "That's the easiest thing in the world to solve."

"Oh yeah, right," Harris said. "What's your bright idea?"

Dickson looked at me, turning away from Harris' baleful stare. "Centurion? Perhaps you'll allow me the honor of setting up our training session. That way, I'll be able to prove my point and solve a problem for the unit at the same time."

I thought it over and smiled. "You're on, Dickson. It's your baby. Training is all yours this time out."

Dickson looked pleased while Harris looked even more irritated than before. He glowered and mumbled things under his breath that no one could understand. The lifter flight wasn't a long one, fortunately. All we had to do was reach orbit and dock with our transport ship.

As we filed off the crowded decks, we felt relieved to get out of the cramped lifter and into the wide open, roomy space of *Dominus*.

I made an immediate effort to lose both my adjuncts and headed for the officers' cantina. Along the way, however, my tapper buzzed. I was irritated to see a superior officer was contacting me. Knowing there was no escape for the wicked today, I answered with a fake smile. Galina Turov herself was on the line.

"Hey, Imperator," I said. "What a difference a week makes, huh? Why, the last time I saw you, I was looking over my shoulder with my wrists manacled to a wall!"

She winced a bit as if it was painful that I should mention such a thing. "I guess. Is that memory still sharp for you, McGill?" she asked.

"It sure is. I can feel the sting of every lash. For me, that was just a few days back, you know."

"Right... well... a lot has happened since then. I'm... well I am calling to apologize."

This really floored me. I blinked not once or twice but three times before my brain could register her answer. "You're calling to *what*, sir? Did I hear you right?"

"Yes," she said. "I'm calling to apologize. Don't rub it in. I think now... I think I was wrong about you. You've done me a favor, and all I've done to you is abuse you without cause."

"Huh..." I said, not at all certain why she was happy about anything I'd done. As far as I was concerned, I'd recently attempted to impregnate her sister and done my best to get her replaced by Tribune Winslade.

"Come on up to the Gold Deck," she said. "I want to talk to you about serious matters."

I pretended to be happy with this news, then disconnected and grumbled all the way to the elevators. I lamented that I hadn't managed to down a single beer all damned day, and here I was, already being summoned to Gold Deck by a woman who was at the very least psychotically jealous. It didn't help matters that I'd recently given her further reason to feel that way.

I was also somewhat baffled as to why she was aboard *Dominus* at all. I'd been kind of hoping that when Drusus had said he would think about rescuing Winslade, Galina would be left safely back on Earth.

But no. Here she was, aboard ship ahead of me and setting camp up on Gold Deck. I figured she was busy lording it over everyone on *Dominus*. It couldn't be just me who was unhappy about this turn of events.

After going through a few security checks, I managed to reach Galina's office. I was immediately redirected to her apartments—her private apartments. *Oh boy*, I thought to myself, where was this going?

When I knocked timidly on her door, I didn't know whether I was going to be shanghaied and thrown into the brig again, possibly for another round of torture and death, or to be welcomed with open arms.

Galina's attitude would largely depend on whether or not she knew about how I'd gotten on with her sister. When she let me in, I knew the answer immediately. She was in uniform, but she was not in her formal service uniform. She was in her fatigues.

Now with most people, when they put on something they considered fatigues, that meant that they were in looser-fitting gear with a comfortable, relaxed fit. Not so with Galina. Her fatigues were probably the smallest uniform I'd ever seen on an adult human, and they hugged her like a chimp hugged onto its momma. They were so tight they pulled in over every curve and seam. The outlines of her shapely form were thus displayed at their best.

"Uh…" I said, dumbfounded by the view. "You're looking good, Imperator."

"Don't be inappropriate, James. Take a seat."

Being a man who was at home in her quarters, I ambled over toward the tiny bar she kept near her couch. She made a small gesture then, like a magician flicking the air with gloved fingers. Through some evil new trick of her smart-home software, the cabinet locked itself.

"Hey," I said, "I haven't had a drink since I left Earth."

"And it's going to stay that way for a little bit longer. James, not everything between us is repaired."

"Oh… okay." I was immediately thinking of Sophia again. Was it possible that Galina knew? Or that maybe she suspected, but wasn't sure yet?

She was a very tricky, cat-like individual. She was a predator and an assassin of the worst kind. It was perfectly possible for her to lull me and put me at my ease before springing a deadly trap. I sincerely hoped that was not the case today.

She looked at me with her head cocked and her eyes squinty. It was as if she was trying to figure out a puzzle. "James did you beg Drusus to release Winslade?"

I shrugged. "Well now, sir, I wouldn't exactly say that I *begged*."

"No, I guess James McGill doesn't beg for anything."

"That's right."

"Well then, let's say that you negotiated, or threatened, or maybe even convinced Drusus. Is that correct?"

"Yeah… I guess so. Did you know that Winslade was serving a seven-year sentence?"

"Seven years, huh?"

"Yup, for sedition." That reminded me of the extra sentencing I had received because of the deaths involved. I had resisted arrest, which had added some extra years to my imprisonment, but I recalled that seven specifically were for sedition.

"Winslade was tried by a robotic court and found guilty," I explained. "They executed him with the intention of keeping him dead for the better part of the next decade. That's when I realized that things had gone too far."

"I didn't know you cared for him so deeply."

I snorted. "I don't. Winslade is a dick. He's an arrogant asshole of the worst order—but he didn't really deserve seven years on ice."

"Is that why you did it? For justice?"

I looked at her, trying to figure her out. She sure was worried about Winslade tonight. What the hell was her angle? What was the right answer? My automatic response when I don't understand a situation is to attempt to be evasive—so I went with that first.

"Well, not just that…" I said, giving my big shoulders a shrug.

"Come on," she said, stepping closer to me. She was still looking at me with that cocked head. It was the way a cat looks at something they're trying to figure out. It wasn't a predatory stance, mind you. It was more a look of curiosity and bewilderment.

"I think I know why you did it," she said finally, reaching up and running one fine finger along my collar.

"And what would that be, sir?"

"I think you did it to help me."

My jaw hit my collar and stayed there. My brain is usually slower than a mailman with a nail in his foot, but this time was different. Some part of me knew this was important, and that gaping and croaking like a fool wasn't going to cut it today. If Galina wanted to believe that I was doing her a special favor, then I was damn-well going to do everything I could to encourage that fantasy.

"Ha," I said. "I can't keep joking around. Of course, I did it to help you out!"

This was a sheer lie, and what's more it was a *dangerous* lie because I barely knew what I was lying about. I didn't see how she'd been helped at all by getting Winslade out of purgatory.

She tapped a small finger on my chest. "Right," she said, "right, I knew it." Then, she walked over to the bar she'd just locked me out of and waved her hand to open it again. She poured us two large fruity drinks and returned to my side, handing me one.

I gulped it happily. Inside, I was hoping that she would give me some clue as to why she felt I'd helped her—or even in what way she figured she'd been helped. This would go a long way to carrying on the conversation.

Being blank in the mind and thirsty, I buried myself in my drink. I gave it little noisy sips and slurps. I rattled the cubes around, making sure the beverage occupied the entirety of my attention while she talked.

"I was puzzling about this last night," she said. "At first, I thought it was some kind of insult that you would rather have Winslade than me as your commander."

This of course, was the truth, but I was still slurping and playing with ice cubes on my tongue. I began sucking on them noisily.

"But no," she said, "that didn't make any sense. You hate Winslade, and he hates you. Why the hell would you do such a snake a favor? You're not a man who goes out of your way for such a thing. In fact, I would expect you to come up here—no matter who was in command, me or him—and tap on my door like a little stray dog trying to get any kind of favors or scraps you could. That's just the kind of man you are, McGill."

"Can I have another?"

"Another what?"

"Drink, sir?" I rattled the last ice cube which was lonely in the bottom my glass.

She had barely consumed a tenth of hers, but she waved imperiously toward the bar, so I moved on past her and helped myself, looking for something a little stiffer.

"But then," Galina continued, "I had to think about it. Maybe you were feeling bad. Maybe you felt somewhat guilty for having tempted my poor, younger sister Sophia. Maybe you thought that you owed the Turov family something, and so you acted to relieve me of my temporary reduction in rank."

My mind was finally catching up. Galina hated losing rank and prestige, even temporarily. Stepping down from Central to play the part of a tribune on the battlefield was a fate worse than death to her. She'd done it before lots of times, and she'd never liked it.

"You really nailed it this time, sir," I said, casting my voice over my shoulder.

I was sad to see she had run out of whiskey, and I was going to have to substitute in rum or brandy instead. The flavor wouldn't be all that pleasant, but I figured it would get the job done.

"You knew how much I hate to go on these missions," she continued, "riding herd on a single legion. With Winslade gone, their only choice was to promote Graves or some other primus. No one in Hegemony liked either option. They want as little to do with Legion Varus as possible, so they put me back into the cage with the rest of you animals. It's an insult, really."

"Totally unfair."

"Every time anything goes wrong with the top leadership of this pathetic Legion, I'm tossed in because of my prior experience. I feel like a principal who's constantly having to substitute for teachers who have the sniffles."

I thought about the idea of Winslade having been tortured and killed—possibly repeatedly—for having the sniffles. I began to laugh.

"What's so funny?"

"Nothing, sir."

It was the alcohol. Even though it came from the stale bottles Galina kept in her office, the stuff was beginning to have an effect. I needed to play this better.

Turning around and facing her again, I smiled, but I didn't laugh. I had her full attention now. "Truth was, I was just kind of missing you. It seemed like we got off on a bad foot last time we met."

"A bad foot? I had you beaten to death… repeatedly."

I shrugged. "I can get over it if you can."

She lowered her head. "I apologize again. I can't believe I'm saying this, but—I simply overreacted. I was feeling jealous and mean and spiteful. I shouldn't have done that—not even if you did sleep with my sister."

One tiny part of my brain considered coming clean right then. But I avoided that like the plague. "Well then," I said reaching out a big arm and slipping it around her shoulders. "Maybe we can make amends."

She shrugged me off. "Not so fast. I don't feel that way about you right now."

I knew this was a bald-faced lie, but I took it in stride. "All right. Is there anything else you wanted to talk about?"

"Yes," she said, "I've been told that you have a very special suggestion for a new training exercise in which the entire legion Varus will participate."

"Who told you that?"

"I believe his name is Dickson. He contacted me on the way up here from the lifter."

"Oh… right." I recalled having told Dickson he could run an exercise—but I hadn't said anything about him contacting the brass about it.

"Technically, I'm still in charge of Legion Varus because Tribune Winslade hasn't yet been fully processed and revived down on Blue Deck. I'm going to do you and your unit a favor. I'm going to let you have your moment to shine, McGill. Whatever exercise your adjunct cooked up is going to be practiced in three days' time in front of the entire legion."

I was alarmed, but I pretended not to be. "That sounds *great*, sir! Thanks for the opportunity to impress the whole outfit."

"Very well, Centurion. I'm sure whatever you've planned, it will be excellent. You are now dismissed."

I stood, and we eyed each other for a few seconds. It's important to understand that Galina and I had a very unusual relationship. It wasn't entirely normal, appropriate or even enviable. As we'd both had a few drinks, I took this opportunity to sneak a kiss. I bent down and pressed my lips against her cheek.

She allowed this, but then danced away when I went for more.

"Out," she said, "Out, McGill!"

We parted ways smiling at each other.

-20-

Adjunct Dickson was overjoyed when he learned his suggestion had been taken so seriously by the imperator. "I've been given the green light for the entire legion?" he asked. Pride slowly puffed him up, like a cobra that was ready to strike. "That's excellent…"

Rather than being embarrassed or overwhelmed by stage fright, or any of another dozen natural emotions that a junior officer might have felt in such a situation, Dickson swelled up with importance. He strutted in front of the entire unit, talking about how great his idea was without giving us any details.

Leeson and Harris were not enthusiastic about the whole thing.

"Mark my words, McGill," Harris said. "This is going to turn into something nasty. There's something unnatural about that boy. I'm pretty sure I know why they kicked him out of Victrix and sent him down here."

"Why's that?"

"He was excommunicated for evil—ditched and left behind like garbage on a country road. It's because that boy isn't right in the head."

I shrugged off Harris' worries. I figured whatever Dickson had in mind, it couldn't be any worse than some of the things I'd done. Better yet, I couldn't be blamed this time for how things turned out. After all, Dickson had sent his message directly to Turov, and she had accepted it. My name was not even attached to this, whether it turned into a disaster or not.

Leeson had an entirely different, but no less negative, take on things. "You've been upstaged, McGill," he said. "That Victrix boy has stars in his eyes—your stars. He plans to replace you as the centurion."

"Why do you think that?"

Leeson snorted. "Because it's frigging obvious. This is his first deployment, and he's a junior officer. What does he do? He goes out trying to earn brownie points with the brass. That's a bad sign. We've been here before. Winslade was like that, remember? Turov too."

"Yeah…" I admitted.

"That's right. Climbers are like that. Besides, he's from Victrix, so he thinks he shits chocolate ice cream."

Losing interest in their jealous griping, I nodded sagely. I let their concerns ooze out of the opposite side of my head. The truth was, I was completely unconcerned. Let Dickson schmooze his way out of my unit. That was fine with me.

My mind was dwelling on happier thoughts, most of which revolved around Galina's improved attitude. She seemed positively happy with me right now. She might even warm up to me on this mission at some point. Best of all, she seemed to have no inkling that I'd gotten to the finish line with her sister.

Being beaten to death and left for dead for nearly a year did wonders to clarify a man's priorities. To me, things were rosy right now, and I didn't want to disturb anything when the universe was tilting in my favor. If Dickson wanted rank, he could have it for all I cared.

As the next few weeks rolled by, Dickson drilled his light troops on Green Deck every day. He worked them harder than anyone else in the unit. I wouldn't say that I admired him or that I liked him, but I did respect his work ethic and his well-disciplined troops.

The only frown he put on my face was when it came to punishments. He seemed to only have one penalty for any transgression. Any recruit that dared step out of line by, even a tiny bit, was delivered a swift death. Legion Varus had taught me the ropes in a similar fashion when I was a recruit, but damn… it did seem like Dickson enjoyed delivering the harshest of punishments.

We knew next to nothing about his plans for our ship-wide exercises. We only knew one key element—it was going to involve nothing but fresh recruits. All light troops in light armor. He didn't want any regulars in the games. There were to be nothing but first-timers, which amounted to about nine hundred individuals ship-wide.

On the tenth fateful day of the legion's journey across the frontier stars, Imperator Galina Turov appeared on every wall on the ship. She was essentially visible everywhere by everyone all at once.

"I have an announcement to make," she said. "Tribune Winslade has officially been revived back at Central with all charges against him formally dropped."

My troops were responding somewhat surly in my opinion. There was only scattered clapping to be heard in my unit's module. Deciding to put on a show, I slammed my hands together, put my fingers my mouth and whistled loudly. This got my troops to at least applaud tepidly. No one was in love with Winslade, mind you, but I figured he at least deserved some clapping after the suffering he had gone through.

Galina nodded as if she could hear all of us. Perhaps she could. "I will therefore be stepping away as commander of this legion. I will still remain aboard the ship and offer my guidance, but Tribune Winslade will return to his position and command Varus directly."

The troops murmured to one another, and the veterans did some mild cuffing and attitude-fixing.

"In other news," Galina continued, "today is the day that we've long awaited—the day of the recruit training on green deck for the entire legion. Here to officiate the event is the mastermind behind it: Adjunct Dickson."

Galina indicated someone off to the side with a wave of her hand. She stepped off camera, and Dickson quickly replaced her. Harris and Leeson looked around with alarm. It seemed to us that Dickson had been here just a few minutes ago.

"That weasel," Harris said.

"I told you so," Leeson said.

I looked sour, but I said nothing. Could they be right? Was Dickson making a move so quickly? He was a bold one.

Another new thought hit my mind right then. I'd been a fool not to think of it earlier. Was Dickson giving Galina shoulder rubs at night? Already? I was starting to wonder.

Dickson strode onto the screen like a rooster taking credit for the sunrise. You could just tell he was as proud as could be. He gazed out at everyone sweeping his eyes over the assembled thousands through the screens. He allowed his moment of glory to linger before speaking.

"Today you will be treated to something different," he said. "For too long, Legion Varus has been growing stale with her training events. Oh certainly, you've been digging into the basics—blood and guts and the rigors of death... but you normally, to my way of thinking, fail in the most important department of all."

Here, he tapped at his overly large forehead. "The mind. The psychological aspect—that's where my design will be different. Here are the rules: every recruit in this Legion will be provided with nothing but their spacesuit and their bare hands. They will be released onto Green Deck. Hidden in various spots all over the jungle are many items. Some are more useful than others."

There were some concerned looks among the recruits in 3rd Unit. They were showing their teeth and looking a bit panicky. They knew Dickson, and they knew a painful death awaited for many of them today.

"One item," Dickson continued, "is different from all the others. It's a key, a way to escape Green Deck. Whoever finds it need only touch the locked doors to exit the arena victorious."

Some of the recruits dared looked hopeful. They were figuring, I knew, that this amounted to a scavenger hunt. How fun...

"The trick however," Dickson said, grinning hugely now, "is the key will not work until there is only one person alive on the entire playing field."

The whispers and glancing around returned. Most of the light troops seemed horrified.

Galina stepped back onto the stage, and she clapped her hands together. "You heard him. Recruits are to leave all weapons, food and other supplies behind. You are to report to Green Deck immediately. Anyone who is part of this exercise and does not enter Green Deck within the next fifteen minutes will be executed on sight."

-21-

Boiling like ants out of every unit module, hundreds of recruits dashed down to Green Deck. Almost all of them made it—but not quite all.

There were twenty doors allowing entrance onto Green Deck on this extremely large ship of ours. The exercise area itself was quite large, with a lagoon, a hill, a secret grotto, a waterfall, lots of plants, and even a few picturesque islands. It was a lovely place most of the time. The freshly planted quick-grow flora had grown in fully by the tenth day of our flight, and it was now ready for us to tear it up.

Precisely fifteen minutes after Dickson had announced the start of the contest, the doors came crashing down. One of the recruits was so desperate to make it inside that she attempted to dive, roll and crawl under the doorway at the last possible second.

Dickson noticed this. He'd deployed a swarm of drone cameras into the jungle. He swooped a buzzer down for a close-up. Everyone grunted and winced. The recruit was crawling legless and squalling in the dirt.

"Ah," Dickson said, "our first disqualification. "There will be others, but none more dedicated than this young lady. Let's all give her some applause."

We did tap our hands together, and she waved briefly at the buzzer that floated over her. Then, the light faded out of her eyes, and she died.

Thirty-odd more recruits arrived late. Maybe they'd been taking an emergency shit or having second thoughts—it didn't matter. When they trotted up to their assigned doors and found them sealed shut, they were met by stern-faced veterans.

The slowpokes put up their hands. With wide eyes and some wet cheeks, they were arrested and awaited their fate in front of the locked doors. All of this action was displayed with cunning camerawork on our module's walls.

"Things are going to go harshly for those who were slow on the ball," Dickson said. He made a gesture with his hand and immediately our point of view was taken to the entry regions outside Green Deck. There, held at the point of morph-rifles, were those who hadn't made it inside.

Dickson ordered them all shot down in ignominious shame. After this mass execution, the cameras switched inside Green Deck. A few recruits were already struggling with each other. They tripped and kicked at one another in hand-to-hand combat. Most ran off into the jungle to avoid the rest.

"Let's have good sportsmanlike conduct," Dickson said. "Until the tone is heard, the next stage of the game has not yet begun. 5… 4… 3… 2… 1…"

A gong-like noise rang out across *Dominus*.

"It's on now!" Harris shouted. He was grinning, and he did seem to be honestly enjoying the show. I had to wonder about this. Was Dickson a genius or a sadistic maniac? The jury was still out.

Things became bloody immediately. People fought with their fists, and they bashed each other down with rocks. Two smaller recruits chased one big guy into the lagoon and drowned him. It was a general melee.

Dickson's main contribution was playing the part of the cheerleader. He rapidly switched between different scenes of action with his buzzers, and he always narrated the action with fast, funny comments.

Soon everyone on the ship seemed to be enjoying themselves with the notable exception of the recruits on Green Deck. After something like fifty percent of the recruits were dead or hopelessly maimed, things quieted.

The survivors had separated and were prowling every corner of the park-like space. Being approximately two square kilometers of overgrown jungle, there was quite a few available hiding spaces.

Dickson had arranged some way whereby he was alerted whenever a special item was found. When this happened, a buzzer immediately swooped to the spot. He would then discuss the find.

The first of these was rather unremarkable. A young woman, panting and desperate, had found a satchel which held within it a bio's drug-administering device. She frowned at it, eyeballing the instructions, turning it this way and that in her hands.

Dickson seemed gleeful. "Ah," he said. "An injector. Those of you from Blue Deck know the truth about these wonderful devices. They have many different uses. They can become deadly, or life-giving, in the hands of an expert user."

"She's going to figure it out," Harris said.

"No, she's not," Leeson scoffed. "I can tell a dumb-bunny when I see one."

Dickson continued as we watched the young recruit struggle with her find. "Press the correct combination of buttons and this beauty will inject a deadly poison. Press a different set, and you've got a stimulant, or a critically needed antibiotic. Will this recruit use her gift wisely? Or will she fail? That is yet to be seen."

He went on like that for the next twenty or thirty minutes. We saw a number of murders. A half-dozen recruits discovered easter-egg treasures.

Even I had to admit that if nothing else, this particular Green Deck exercise was extremely entertaining.

"This is great," Harris said. "You see that little one? That little dude? The one that tripped and found a knife under the rock? I'll put my money on him. I've got ten thousand credits down, right now. Who's got me?"

"I'll see your ten K," Sargon said, "and I'll double it. That weasel doesn't know a knife from his asshole."

Harris accepted the bet eagerly.

"I want the chick with the bio device," Kivi said. "Those things have killed me more times than the enemy."

Bets began to fly. Very soon, every troop in our unit had a favorite. For the most part they chose individuals who had either found a special treasure to murder the others or who were from our own unit.

Regardless, everyone seemed to be having a good time. Everyone, that was, except for Leeson. He'd sidled up to me and tapped me on the shoulder. "You see this?" he said. "This is how it begins."

"How what begins?"

"I'm talking about Dickson. This is how a truly criminal, rank-climbing whore of an officer is born. First-off, you've got to understand why the imperator is favoring him. Why should anyone care about a character like this? He's just some transferred-in loser from Victrix."

"Okay, I'll bite," I said. "Why should anyone care about him?"

"Because he's cool that's why. He's new. He's someone different. You see, if you or I were to throw a turd out of the window, it would just be a turd. In fact, it'd be worse than a turd, because it'd be a turd which we had ejected from our presence with extreme prejudice."

"Uh… does all this talk of turds have a point to it, Adjunct?"

"It sure does. Imagine somebody's outside that window, somebody who thinks we're cool because we're in Legion Varus. If that somebody were to catch our rejected turd, they might shine it all up. Maybe they'd even spray paint it and put it on the mantle."

"Adjunct Dickson, is the turd here, right?" I asked, becoming a little confused.

"Yeah, that's right. Victrix kicked him out, but because he's from Victrix, he's cool."

I thought about Leeson's tirade, and I knew that he did have a point. Galina Turov was clearly favoring Dickson far beyond the man's station.

That said, I had to admit Dickson was performing well—but that might make things worse. Galina liked having a new, male figure around. She liked to promote them far beyond their logical station in life. Was this going to be another case like that? A case like Winslade or Gary had been many years ago?

Turning my attention back to the contest, I saw that there was a new dynamic in play. A fair number of the recruits had finally realized there were no rules against teaming up. Soon it wasn't just individual recruits that slunk around the deck looking for someone to murder but gangs of troops instead. They worked as teams to kill anyone they found. Some of the most interesting battles were between two rival gangs facing each other.

One such contest involved a man who was leading such a team. He'd managed to find a crossbow. He used this weapon with deadly effect, killing four enemy gang members in a single clash. But the crossbowman was in turn brought down when two rival gangs came together and overwhelmed his own group, two to one. The battle was vicious and savage, but in the end the man with a crossbow was cut down. In short, everyone aboard *Dominus* was riveted.

In the upper right corner of the screen was a large red number. The number kept ticking higher. This was a count tracking the number of deaths that occurred so far. When the number reached 930, there would be only one recruit left alive on Green Deck.

So far, the count stood at 478. In two hours' time, approximately half the recruits in Legion Varus had perished. In fact, a few members of my own unit had already returned from the revival chambers. They came back to the module slinking and looking disheveled. Their eyes were haunted and bewildered.

We clapped their shoulders, handed them extra rations of alcohol and sugary drinks, and then pointed to the big screen. We urged them to watch as the struggle continued. Soon, the drama of the event even caught fire in the imagination of these murdered recruits. It was like magic. Dickson really *was* raising the level of the morale of every troop in the legion. I had to admit, I was impressed.

Several more hours passed during which we were fed lunch and then dinner. In each case, every member of the unit wanted to get back to watching the show. It was being displayed live on the wall of the cafeteria, of course, but that wasn't the same. We wanted to get back to our unit's module to cheer and bet on our favorites.

After dinner, the event had begun to drag somewhat. It was getting old. People's attention began to waver, even though there were still heinous murders occurring on the big screen every five minutes or so. People began smoking stims, taking showers, polishing their gear…

Perhaps, I thought, Dickson had made his event too large and too long. But then he managed to surprise everyone again. He came onto the screen and made a critical announcement. "We are now down to the last fifty participants," he said. "At this point, the game's rules are changing. I'm broadcasting my voice into Green Deck, as well as all over the ship. Listen up, participants. There are very few of you left. The contest is almost at an end. Any of you might still win."

"Yeah, right," Carlos shouted. "Half of them are half dead. They'll bleed out in an hour if nothing else—trust me, I'm a bio."

"I don't trust you an inch," Harris told him.

"Remember," Dickson continued, "one of the items secreted somewhere on Green Deck will allow you to leave and escape with your life. But everyone else must be dead first. Now, as I see that most of you are in hiding, perhaps waiting until the others go to sleep to kill each other, we're going to up the ante."

I could see the group perking up. They wanted to know what new hell awaited the long-suffering recruits.

"Every living recruit on Green Deck can now be located via your tappers. Get busy!"

Dickson clapped his hands together. He almost laughed. You could tell he was really enjoying this.

A bright, glowing red dot appeared representing every recruit on the ship. One dot marked each individual. This worked even in the modules. A few of the recruits in my module pointed to each other and laughed, declaring their comrades to be their next victim.

On Green Deck, the effect was electric as most of the recruits had resorted to hiding somewhere. Many of them were hoarding a weapon, waiting in a dark tunnel or under a leafy bush, something like that. A few had set up high in a tree.

Now they were easily located by their enemies. Half of them were too close to another participant to ignore one another, and they engaged each other almost immediately.

Of the few gangs left, most disintegrated either through loss of numbers or through distrust and treachery.

In one case a leader had led his troops into a skirmish that got most of them slaughtered and then backstabbed the last one or two who had survived the fight. Then, he worked to recruit a new gang. He got away with this several times until other recruits figured it out. They ended up tearing him apart in a rage. Traitors were never well-liked, it seemed.

The last hour of the contest was quite intense. Some of the battles went on for a considerable length of time. It ended up with one burly recruit of unusual size and athletic capacity pitted against a male-female team who seemed to be boyfriend and girlfriend. I wasn't quite sure if they had befriended each other on Green Deck, or if they had come in as a team from the start.

Regardless, they fought together against the brute who opposed them. After a bloody beat-down, all three of them were badly injured. The mated pair managed to kill the brute at last, grinding his ruined face into the dirt. Panting and swaying, they didn't take time to enjoy their victory. Instead, there was a final moment of treachery.

The girl was the one who had first found the biomedical device. Apparently, by this time she had figured out its function and become something of an expert in its use. She popped a needle out from the injector's business end and stuck it into her boyfriend's neck. The bulb pulsed three times. He fell face first, breathing his last. She kissed the back of his sweaty, bloody, dirty head and then trudged toward the exit.

Everyone in my module broke into cheers. There were high fives, torn up bets, and money exchanged between tappers as winners and losers were sorted out.

The last girl had with her no less than seven items. She seemed exhausted, but everyone on the ship was cheering for her.

"She's not going to make it," Harris said. "Look how she's bleeding. Thirty thousand credits says she doesn't make it out."

"You're full of shit, Harris," Leeson said. "She's gonna make it. That girl's as tough as nails. I bet McGill's going to try to date her next year."

I ignored them all and watched the scene with interest. The girl finally made it to one of the doors. She began methodically touching the different devices she'd found to the door. The Biomedical injector did the trick. The door slid open, and she stumbled out to a waiting crowd who congratulated her and began working to save her fading life.

-22-

To everyone's utter shock, Dickson returned to 3rd Unit's module with Imperator Galina Turov at his side. He was walking and talking with her like they were old friends.

"Imperator on deck!" Veteran Moller shouted.

Everybody came to attention immediately. She tossed off a salute, barely acknowledging the group. The pair stopped in front of me, and they were both smiling. Galina pointed to Dickson. "You've got a real gem here, McGill. I knew Victrix people were different—but damn, it's another thing to see such a comparison. I predict this man will go far. Don't let him out of your unit for anything."

Dickson thanked her profusely and watched with appreciation as she marched back out. After she left, Leeson whistled. "Looks like you got yourself a stiff piece of competition there, Centurion."

I tossed him a glare and turned back to Dickson. I smiled and held out my hand. He took it, and we shook vigorously. "That was really well done. I have to admit, I had my doubts, but you pulled it off and then some. Morale has been lifted all over the ship."

Harris came up next, and he shook Dickson's hand as well. "I bet not one of those recruits will forget the experience. Not until their final death."

"Thank you, gentlemen. Thank you," Dickson said. He even had the gall to take a little bow.

I dismissed everyone after that, sending them to bed. The whole module soon went into relaxed, evening mode. We were nowhere near a target world yet, so our schedule was loose. In fact, we hadn't even been told yet what that target world might be. We could tell by the length of time we'd been flying that it had to be pretty deep into the frontier territory. That was all we knew.

The next day started off with a bang, however—quite literally. The door to my private cabin was unlocked and kicked open in one smooth motion. A couple of our men rushed in.

My reactions were swift, almost automatic. The best way to understand the situation is to realize that I am of course a combat soldier and that I've been assaulted in life-or-death situations literally hundreds of times. Such lifelong experience can leave a man mentally scarred, but in my case, it had left me very well prepared.

A morph-rifle rode on hooks over my bunk. This, of course, was not regulation. We were allowed to have pistols in our cabins and combat knives, but normally not full-on combat rifles.

Part of the reason for this was the overpowered nature of morph-rifles. They were quite capable of dispensing grenades, wall-piercing bolts, or in this case, explosive shells. All of these could be dangerous to *Dominus* and certainly to the other soldiers in my module.

The walls were thin inside the modules, and there were a lot of strange sounds a man could hear at night, if you took care to listen. Along with that thinness was a vulnerability. Anything brighter than a pencil-thin laser beam or a needler would cut right through the metal.

But I've never been a man to concern myself overly much with safety regulations. If one of my men around me died due to a mistake on my part, well, that was all part of the business. He would just have to lounge in the revival queues until he could come back home to his bunk. Maybe, he might even learn something from the experience.

In any case, when the doors popped open, and two men rushed in, I lifted my morph-rifle off the hooks above me and twisted around in bed. My cabin lights were set to sleep mode, and I only had one eye open as the other one seemed glued shut by sleep—but it didn't matter.

I leveled the gun and let loose. The rifle chattered away. I'd left it in close-assault mode. Accelerated streaks of burning plasma flew at a rate of around six a second. They fired back, of course, but they were already dead on their feet.

Pissing, shivering and bleeding on each other, they formed a heap on the deck of my tiny cabin. I took a deep breath and felt around in the shadows. The lights came up at my touch, and I looked myself over. Sure enough. I'd taken a hit in my right forearm and another in my right calf.

One of them had been able to use his pistol effectively enough to nail me twice. I was impressed. Glancing over my shoulder, I counted at least nine burn marks in the wall behind me. I whistled and shook my head, rubbing the sleep out of my eyes.

Harris appeared in the doorway, breathing hard. He had one of those heavy shotguns in his hand, the kind we used to kill Rigellian bears in armor. He poked the barrel at the two men on the floor.

"Who are these guys, sir?"

"Just some practical jokers, I suspect."

Leeson stepped into sight next. He eyed the two critically, taking snaps of them with his tapper. He ran an ID test on them.

"It says here, these two men are Fleet."

"What?" I said. "Toss that over here."

He did so with a flick of his finger on his tapper. I applied some NuSkin and pulled my clothes on, letting the smart cloth straps slide over my body and knit together.

So far, I hadn't bothered to call for help or any other such nonsense. On a ship such as this one—an Earth warship—gunfire in the modules wasn't all that uncommon, but it did automatically alert ship's security. Maybe some people were on their way by now. I looked at the information Leeson had tossed to me. It was true.

"Hmm," I said. "You know what's funny about old Merton upstairs? He just got a blinking light on his console, letting him know some of his men are down and there's been a ruckus in the modules. That'll speed up the response."

Sure enough, before I could get fully dressed, another unexpected guest arrived. The man was none other than Captain Merton himself. He was in nominal command of *Dominus*.

"Hello, Captain," I said with a grunt of pain, "it's a fine morning, isn't it?"

He stared at the mess on my cabin deck. "McGill, why are two of my agents dead inside your cabin?"

"*Your* agents?" I said, feigning shock and ignorance. "Are you sure about that, sir? The way I understood it, these boys were just a couple of hogs who were down on their luck. I think they came in here looking for a card game, but—"

Merton wasn't interested in my line of bullshit and banter. He lifted a big finger, and he waved it at me. "McGill, we've had our run-ins in the past. Let's not start off on the wrong foot this time. You're under arrest."

"Under arrest, huh? What for this time? Did I forget to spit polish your boots for you?"

"I'm not behind this arrest order, McGill. It comes straight down from Central."

"Well, it certainly wouldn't be proper unless you went through correct channels of command, such as talking to Primus Graves or Tribune Winslade."

He shook his head. "Today isn't your day, McGill. Tribune Winslade still hasn't been released from Central. Primus Graves was arrested mere hours ago—just before you were."

"What now? That's crazy."

I could only think of one good reason why both Graves and I were being arrested by surprise this morning. I thought we'd put all this business about bunkers and secrets behind us—but that clearly wasn't the case.

Had they found the bunker in my back swamp? Had they discovered a bunch of hidden stuff from the Unification Wars down there? If they had, it could lead to very bad things in my future. My parents' farm wasn't far, and it could lead them right to it. Even my daughter Etta wasn't safe. Who knew how far Hegemony might go to cut out what they considered to be an ancient cancer? Outwardly, I tried to appear calm and even bored.

"Look, sir," I said, "when you send a couple of men to my door in the middle of the night, you'd best tell them to knock first."

Merton sighed. "All right, point taken. But you are still under arrest. Report to me up on Gold Deck immediately."

I promised I would do so, and he left.

I walked out of the place, stepping over the dead men who were still bleeding on the deck. Everyone in the module was awake by this time and asking questions. Everyone, that is, except for the two recruits who had been stationed directly across from the door to my cabin.

When I fired my morph-rifle, the plasma charges burned right through the thin walls, and unfortunately, I'd taken them both out.

"That's a damn shame," I said to Carlos. "Have somebody clean that up."

As he was my unit's bio, he was sort of the janitor when it came to cleaning up dead bodies and things like that. He made a face and cracked a few jokes, but he didn't argue. Even he knew it was his job. "Read the room, man. Read the room," he said. "Somebody's got it in for you big time, McGill."

"Ya think?" I said, glaring at Carlos.

I walked out of the place and headed toward Gold Deck. To my surprise, I found someone was following in my wake. It was Adjunct Dickson. He looked fresh and well-rested. Unlike my own kit, which was disheveled—my unwashed hair slipping out from under my cap in spots. Dickson's appearance was immaculate. I wondered how a man could look like that at 4:30 in the morning? There wasn't even supposed to be a drill until eight.

"What do you want, Dickson?" I asked.

"Sir, I was wondering if you wanted me to accompany you up to Gold Deck."

I frowned at him. "Thanks, I know the way, Adjunct."

"Yes sir, of course. But I thought I might warn you regarding a couple of points."

I stopped and turned to face him. I was frowning more deeply now. I was beginning to notice Dickson quite a lot lately. Since his arrival, a lot of strange things had been going on. Now, I knew that in this complex world surprising events often turned out to be coincidences. The trouble was, I didn't believe in coincidences.

I stared at him. "All right. Time for you to fess-up. Who are you working for, boy?"

Dickson blinked a few times, seemingly taken aback. "For you sir. I'm part of Legion Varus now."

"Why the hell are you getting into everybody's business? Every time I turn around, you're up to something I don't like."

Dickson seemed honestly surprised. But then, any good lawyer or undercover man had to be a master at that, or he wasn't worth his salt.

"Let me assure you, Centurion, I'm doing everything to help you and Graves out of this situation."

I squinted at him. "What do you know about these arrests?"

"I know that there's been… ah…. a political problem back on Earth. Certain officers are being singled out as troublemakers."

"Hmm," I said, as that part had seemed obvious enough. "How do *you* know all this?"

He shrugged. "I have my connections. I still know people back at Victrix—and I know people inside Hegemony as well. All I can say right now is there's a lot of buzzing around you—Graves, Winslade and others. People are talking about you being disloyal. I think it's crazy, of course."

"Of course, you do. Is that it?"

"That's all I have, sir. But you need to watch your back."

I dismissed him and watched as he turned back and walked to the modules. I stared after him as he left.

There were lots of dark thoughts in my heart at that moment. I contemplated a quick murder.

Glancing around, I spotted an airlock that led all the way down to the main hold, which wasn't pressurized. Eventually, that path led outside *Dominus* itself.

If you did it right, you could perm a man that way. The trick would be to bust his tapper in a place that was

189

untraceable. That way, he would simply disappear from the grid.

Then you had to take the corpse to somewhere like an airlock that led directly outside. This worked especially well while the ship was on warp, as it was now. If you could turn off all the warning software and fire a body straight out into space—straight out into the warp field the body would be disintegrated. All evidence lost.

Later, when it was discovered that he was missing, it would seem as if the victim had never existed at all. With no body and no evidence as to exactly what had happened to the man, he couldn't be legally revived.

Contemplating murder most foul, I watched Dickson until he turned a corner and disappeared.

My thoughts regarding him were dark indeed. But that's the way my mind worked. When I began to suspect someone had done me wrong, their life wasn't worth spit.

Captain Merton met up with me in his meeting chamber immediately adjacent to the ship's bridge. That's where he spent most of his time when he wasn't on the command deck.

He had a full squad of Marines at his back, so-called Marines anyway.

These boys had never impressed me much. Oh, they were well-trained and tough enough fighters, and they at least had the balls to go into space. But none of them had ever experienced the meat-grinding hell of a planetary invasion. Therefore, I considered them to be only ship's security, rather than true soldiers.

Merton gave me a long speech. First, he began talking about how ill-advised it was to perform treacherous actions—as if I needed to hear that. Then he expressed regrets concerning Winslade, Graves and myself.

He said he had been ordered to arrest me and interrogate me. In the case of Graves, he had been ordered to arrest and return him to Earth for interrogation there.

"So… that's what you did?" I asked. "You sent Graves through the gate posts back to Earth?"

Merton glanced down at his desk for a moment then back up again. He met my eyes. "No, not exactly. He resisted arrest and died. I returned his engrams and body scans with permission to revive him on Earth."

"Well, what's happened to him back there?"

He shrugged. "That's none of my affair at this point. It's Hegemony's problem. You, on the other hand, are my problem."

"Uh… so… this is your interrogation, huh?"

"Yes. Tell me what you know of these matters. Why is Hegemony so convinced you're operating against the greater good?"

"I don't know anything."

Merton crossed his heavy arms. "But you were contacted by Graves the day prior to your arrest at Central—that's what it says here in this report."

He fingered a computer scroll on his desk, and I felt itchy. Merton did know something—but how much?

"Is that so? I said. "Does that slip of plastic say what we were talking about, or why it was wrong?"

"No, it doesn't."

"Well, sir, I'll tell you what the story is then." I described meeting Graves at Unification Square. Then I went into full bullshit-mode. "Well, sir, see, it's like this. Graves never has had much of a love life. I know. I know. Most officers don't get in other people's business like that. But after about fifty years serving under this man, I felt like I could give my primus a helping hand."

Merton sat down. He brought up his right fist, and he leaned his right cheek into it. "Go on, if you must."

"I'm only answering the question, sir. We sat at that restaurant, and… well, this is kind of embarrassing, but I gave him pointers on how to pick-up women. That's the God's honest truth."

"Really, McGill?"

"Yes sir. Really. I'm feeling kind of bad to tell you about this stuff. After all, I told Graves I wouldn't tell anyone about this. I'd planned to take his secret shame with my soul to heaven before I revealed the truth, but I just don't see how it could hurt him now. Possibly, it could help him."

Merton's left hand was on his desk now. The fingers were drumming rhythmically. "Seriously, McGill, you're telling me Primus Graves asked for your help with meeting women?"

"Well, no sir. Not exactly like that. I just happened to be up in Central City planning on doing some… visiting. I happen to know several women in the area, see. Graves is my superior officer, so he was automatically alerted to my presence. He contacted me and asked me what I was doing."

Merton sighed. "And then what?"

"I told him I was looking around for a little tail on a Saturday night. Then—to my total surprise—he expressed… well, he just hinted actually… that he was having some troubles in that area himself. I'm a neighborly sort, so I offered to meet him at the Unification Square and the rest is history."

Merton's face was sour. "No, McGill the rest is *not* history. History has yet to be written in this case. Hegemony does not go around randomly arresting, executing and purging people without more to go on than that. This entire cock-and-bull story you just gave me is unacceptable. I refuse to report it to Central."

I spread my hands helplessly. "I'm sorry, sir. I really am. You might want me to lie. Maybe you want to make this more complicated. Maybe there's some hog out there who's just made a mistake and wishes that this would all go away because he's embarrassed. But no matter what, I'm going to tell the truth this time. I'm determined!"

Merton's fist seemed to sink more deeply into his cheek as he regarded me. He gave a sigh. "All right," he said, "get out of here. If you want to tell me anything that I need to know at a later date, you may do so. It will probably be too late for you by then, however."

"So…" I said, "I'm no longer under arrest."

"No, you've been questioned. You've been interrogated, and you've been found useless as a witness for the prosecution or the defense."

I brightened, as this was exactly where I like to be. When it came down to witnessing the best kind of witness to be was the totally useless kind.

"Thank you, sir," I said. "Thank you kindly." Then I hightailed it out of there and headed back down to the modules.

I never made it however, I didn't even make it off Gold Deck. A small, angry, skinny man caught up with me before I could reach the elevators and head back down to the lower, safer regions of the ship.

The thin man's hair was wet. His face was twisted up. He looked like he smelled shit. "McGill?" Winslade said. "What are you doing on Gold Deck?"

I explained in brief that I had been arrested for purposes of interrogation. This made Winslade turn thoughtful.

"Graves…" he said. "Are you telling me they actually arrested Graves now?"

"That's right, sir."

Winslade bared his small teeth. "They've purged him just like they did me."

"And me before that," I added. "But I couldn't help noticing that you and me are free again, sir."

"Yes," he said, thinking hard. He rubbed his chin as if he needed to shave but there wasn't a whisker on it. "McGill, there's something very strange going on. You know that they kept accusing me of all kinds of bizarre things. I had no idea what they were talking about. And that really bothers me."

"Why's that sir? It's best to be ignorant when it comes down to things like this."

"Yes, yes, I know. That's your perennial position on these matters. Sheer blissful, pig-ignorance. But I'm not like that. I *do* tend to know things. I pride myself on it. If I don't know what's happening, I'm left vulnerable."

I shook my head, sadly. "Don't go poking down this rabbit-hole, Tribune. I don't know what's at the bottom, but I do know it's something bad. Curiosity has killed countless cats and legionnaires. You can take that to the bank."

Winslade waved his hand at me in disgust. "Stop mixing metaphors. This is serious. Right now, your cohort has no primus. Do you want me to appoint some random fool to the post?"

"Uh…" I said, considering. "That is a real problem. If we're about to go into battle, possibly kickstarting a very serious interstellar war with Rigel, we need Primus Graves now more than ever."

"That's right."

"What can I do to help, sir?"

"Probably nothing," he admitted. "But it would help to know who is behind this string of arrests. There are three of us under suspicion at this point."

I aimed a finger at him. "Don't forget about Praetor Wurtenberger."

"Ah yes. Him as well. He's still gone, isn't he?"

"Yes, sir. I do believe he is."

Winslade narrowed his eyes. I could tell the wheels were moving in that head of his. I could almost hear the clicking sounds.

"There's got to be something we can do," he fumed. He marched around the deck in little circles. There were a few droplets of revival fluids—greasy, clear, glycerin shining on the deck at his feet. More of them showered the shoulders of his uniform, but he didn't even notice. "I don't want to go into open warfare with my best tactical officer having been purged. Who can fix this for us, McGill?"

"I can only think of one person, sir. Imperator Galina Turov. There's nobody else aboard this ship that would give a shit."

Winslade made a hissing sound. He seemed upset. At last, he fluttered his fingers in the air in defeat. "All right," he said. "Let's go see her. She's about to exit the ship, anyway."

We marched toward her office. The fact that she was leaving was unwelcome news to me. Sure, Galina was sometimes my own personal horror show. She'd presided over my torment, abuse and murder just a few days ago. Worse, she'd shown very little interest in me personally during the journey. However, set-backs like that had never stopped a man like me from trying. I knew how to push her buttons. Eventually—I felt I was almost certain—I could achieve success if this mission went on long enough, and if she stayed aboard *Dominus*.

"She's going back to Earth, huh? Why's that? Has she been reassigned?"

"No, no, I don't think so. She's going back there for a meeting of some kind. Maybe they'll arrest her and purge her as well."

That was an alarming thought, and it was all too possible. It did seem like everyone around me, everyone up the chain of command, was being waylaid.

Giving myself a shake, I matched and then exceeded Winslade's rapid step. He was soon trotting behind me just to keep up. We reached the big gold doors to Galina's office.

They were the only gold doors on the deck. What's more, I knew that they had been carefully layered with a thin layer of true gold. It was no more than a few molecules thick, mind you, but it was impressive. It was a beautiful, unusual symbol that helped cement her status as the supreme commander above everyone aboard this vessel.

After hammering away until there were dents and even a few tears in that gold leaf, the door finally opened. Gary peered out angrily. He lifted a finger to accuse me of having damaged the door, but then he stopped, letting his breath catch in his throat. He'd caught sight of Winslade and noted that the small man seemed to be in a very bad mood.

"Oh…" he said. "Right this way, sirs."

I marched past him and pointed at the torn gold leaf. "You should get that fixed, Gary. Turov doesn't like to see a mess like that."

Gary sneered and ushered us into Galina's inner sanctum.

-23-

"Well, look what we have here," Galina said. She flung her arms wide in our faces. "McGill and Winslade together in the same room with me. I'm almost shuddering with fear. Aren't you two the biggest traitors in Earth's history?"

Winslade appeared sour. "I am here because of something McGill just said to me while he was on his way into your office, Imperator, it may be of great interest to you."

"I very much doubt that."

Winslade gave her a nasty smile. "Have you ever considered that you might—just possibly—be next on this list of officers to be purged?"

Galina froze. I believe she'd begun taking a step while walking around behind her desk, and she lifted one foot—but she didn't put it down right away. She stood there like a flamingo for a full second.

Then she dropped that foot, and she turned to face us. "What are you talking about? What have you done, you weasel?"

Winslade touched his hand to his chest and with a contrived look on his face, pretended to be as innocent as possible. "What *could* I have done? I've been purged, abused, questioned, maltreated, given unfair sentencing and then finally released. Justice has prevailed, but only due to the gracious intervention of our freshly honored Consul Drusus."

Galina's eyes were sliding from side to side. I could tell her brain was working faster than mine ever could.

"Uh... Imperator?" I said. "I think what Tribune Winslade's trying to say is that with me at the bottom of that chain, Grave's is next up, then Winslade, then you—and then Wurtenberger above that. This is a long chain of people who have all been caught up in an internal security boondoggle."

"That's it exactly," Winslade said, aiming a finger at me. He was clearly taking a great deal of pleasure in Galina's new expression, which was one of shock and fear.

"You're suggesting this will lead to me?" she asked. "That's insanity. I'm above reproach."

Winslade laughed. It was a nasty sound. He crossed his arms in front of his skinny ribs and leaned back on his heels.

"Oh, certainly," he said with a wicked smile. "Praetors, tribunes... they're cast about willy-nilly. All suspected and abused—but not *you*. Everyone in Hegemony loves Galina Turov."

She pointed a finger at him. "Is that how you got out? Did you lie to them? Did you implicate me in some nefarious scheme of yours? Is that why they freed you?"

"No, no, no," he said. "They made no offers of clemency. These people are overzealous and half-mad. They're obsessed with some nonsense about bunkers and hiding fugitives—I didn't even understand what they were talking about. Eventually, my complete ignorance seemed to cast them into a rage, so they murdered me. I thought my existence had come to an inglorious finish—and it had—until Drusus decided to commute my sentence."

Galina's eyes slitted and they moved to me next. "You, then," she said. "You were angry because I didn't help you when you got caught up in this whole thing, isn't that right?"

"Well, sir, I have to admit I wasn't sensing a whole lot of love while I was chained to that wall, being whipped to death."

She made a dismissive gesture, shaking her hand in the air. "I had a good reason to be upset."

"What? All that business about your sister? I thought we had that sorted out."

"Yes, fine," she said, shrugging. "So, I made a mistake. It was an honest error. Anyone could have done it."

"Yeah, well, you're not the one who got beaten—at least not yet."

"Enough talk about that," she said, and she began pacing again. "I don't like even thinking about it."

She had her arms both wrapped around herself. She was grabbing her own shoulders, clearly comforting herself. She was haunted by the idea of suffering a fate such as had befallen me and Winslade.

Winslade, on the other hand, was all smiles. He could barely contain his glee.

I was concerned. I didn't like the idea of Galina being trussed-up and whipped. I knew it could happen, since it *had* happened to everyone else in the room, and because Graves was probably going through the process right now.

"Look, Galina," I said. "We didn't just come here to talk about that. I want to try to enlist your aid to help Graves."

"Whatever for?"

"He's in purgatory—right now."

"Yes, yes," she said, "of course he is. He's probably the one that deserves it. He's the only one of us who was actually in the Unification Wars, or didn't you two know that?"

We both nodded. We'd both heard the rumors over the years.

"Right, well if they arrest me, it is absolutely typical of the incompetence of Hegemony. Here I am, filling in for them, doing everyone's work, even participating materially in extracting information from some of these perpetrators."

I scoffed, as I knew that she was talking about me.

"And yet," she went on, "despite all that, do I get any gratitude? Why no, I get treated like a criminal myself. It's incredible."

"Imperator," I said, "we need Graves. We're going into some very serious combat situations. Earth needs her best tactician. He's one of the reasons why Varus always wins."

"Yes," she agreed. "There's some truth to that… I've been summoned back to Central. I guess I could put in a good word for Graves with Drusus."

Winslade and I shrugged, knowing that was about as good an offer as we could hope to get.

Galina watched us. Her mind was full of suspicion. Her eyes gleamed with yellow paranoia. "But you two aren't done scheming yet, are you? You know more about this. You wouldn't just come in here trying to get me to talk up Graves to the brass. You must know *something*."

My face went slack, and I pointed a big finger. "Well, Winslade here looks like a ferret in a henhouse. But that doesn't really mean he's guilty. He always looks like that."

Winslade wrinkled his nose. "Thanks, McGill."

"I've got a new idea," Galina said. "I'm not going back to Central. I'm going to send word that I'm too busy to do it. I'll send a lackey instead."

Winslade's expression changed from smug to alarmed. "Don't look at me. I'm not going near that ziggurat of evil. I just got out of the place."

She nodded. "Right. I've got just the man. I'll send Captain Merton in my place."

Winslade snorted. "He's hardly a diplomat. He's barely functional as a ship's captain."

"He'll make do. He's a zealot in his own way and highly regarded for his eagle scout reputation."

"What's your excuse going to be for the substitution?" Winslade asked. "A bad hair day?"

"That's very disrespectful, Tribune. Perhaps you haven't been flogged enough recently."

Winslade gave a little shrug, but he did shut up.

"I will arrange the transfer," she said, "the excuse, all of it. What I need from you two is a little bit of digging. Try to figure out what's really going on."

"Will do, sir," I said. "Is that all?"

"No… there's something else… we're arriving at our first destination tomorrow."

"Really?" I said. "When was somebody going to tell us? There hasn't even been a briefing."

"That's right," she said, "and there won't be one, either. At least not in a large-scale, public format. Hegemony is extremely paranoid about spies right now. They don't want the slightest chance that someone aboard *Dominus* is working for the bears. No one can transmit our destination if no one knows what it is."

"But you do?" Winslade asked.

"That's right. Me, Captain Merton—a few others on the navigational crew. We will arrive there in the morning and our assault will begin immediately."

"Hot damn," I said. I slammed my hands together and rubbing them vigorously. "I've been getting mighty bored sitting around on this spaceship for the last few weeks."

Galina smirked. "Don't worry, McGill. You'll have a chance to spill plenty of alien body fluids before this is over."

-24-

Galina really must have known something. Bright and early the next morning we were rousted from our beds, before the sun would have risen back on old Earth.

My whole unit was sent scrambling for Red Deck. On the way, we were allowed to shower, dress and eat. That was something at least, but it was rush, rush, rush, go, go, go after that.

We still didn't know where we were, or what we were doing. That was the new way of things over recent years. The brass liked to keep us in the dark to maintain mission-security.

There had been some nasty spying lately, and a proliferation of deep-link systems. Some of these interstellar communications sets were built small and portable—for spies. I'd known one of these characters, a lizard named Raash. He had a unit that could be carried off in a knapsack in a pinch.

Mission commanders had become paranoid about the possibility of spies aboard spaceships. The recent sabotage attack on the Big Sky project, along with the odd behavior of the Rigellians, had heightened their fears. As a result, the destination of any vessel was often kept secret. The brass had gone overboard with mission security.

As Graves was still on ice, Winslade had appointed Primus Collins to replace him. She was a nice enough young lady. I'd gotten to know her back during the City World campaign. She was normally a staffer rather than a combat soldier, but I had worked with her before.

After a few kinks, we'd come to understand one another. I had a feeling that eventually, with enough experience, she would become a good mid-rank officer. I would've rather had Graves mind you, but no one asked my opinion.

Galina had been busy during the night. Instead of leaving *Dominus* and going back to Central as she'd been ordered to do, she'd done a masterful shuffle. Somehow, poor old Captain Merton had found himself shipped home on a rail in her place.

Her argument had been a simple one. Once we were in the landing and assault phase, she was in command of the mission. Since he was no longer flying a ship around, he wasn't needed. Therefore, he had been charged with reporting back to Central in her stead.

Oh sure, Merton had complained and quoted regulations, but things like that had never impressed Galina Turov when her own shapely butt was on the line. So, she'd mailed him off with a bow stapled onto his bald head.

She had a ghostly smile on her lips while she described her dodge, and I'd smiled back. It had been a slick piece of maneuvering.

Geared up and loaded down, I trotted for the lifters on Red Deck. My unit tramped steadily along behind me, following a trail of blinking red arrows. I was pleased to see we weren't going to be shat out of the ship in drop pods this time.

Harris, who never stopped complaining, seemed to have rubbed off onto Leeson, who was right behind me.

"If this isn't the weirdest damn thing I've ever seen," Leeson said. "How are we supposed to assault a planet when we don't even know where we're headed?"

"They're supposed to give us the briefing on the way down to the planet aboard the lifter," I told him. "They'll tell me first, then I'll relay it down to the unit."

"Shit only rolls downhill," Leeson grumbled. "I don't know whether I should set my suit to air conditioning, or heating. Is there a breathable atmosphere? Do we need extra oxygen tanks? Are we going to be underwater? I have no frigging idea."

Leeson was right, of course. When a spacefaring soldier decided what gear to take on a mission, a lot depended on the nature of the destination. Climate alone could be a big issue.

For example, if the target environment was very hot, you'd need extra battery power for cooling and possibly extra water supplies to combat dehydration. On the other hand, if we were invading a vacuum or a freezing-cold world, you had an entirely different set of parameters to worry about.

As a result, many of the soldiers had gone overboard. They were weighed down with extra gear. A few of Harris' heavies hoarded until they were waddling like ducks.

Sargon was the exception. He never stopped working out, and he could carry a ton of equipment without struggling. He was the strongest man in the unit—with the possible exception of myself.

When we crammed ourselves aboard our lifter, we looked like we were carrying stuffed couches home with us. Big bundles filled our arms as we strapped ourselves into the jump seats. Occasional slap-fights broke out, and a few punches were thrown when some of the men tried to offload their gear onto their neighbors' laps and feet.

"All right, all right. That's enough of that," Harris shouted.

Veteran Moller walked around, breaking up fights. Sargon would have done the same, but he had so much gear he couldn't even move around without bashing people. It was better that he stayed in his seat.

I took a look down toward the lights. They were presided over by Adjunct Dickson. As the youngest and least experienced members of our unit, light troops tended to screw around more.

There was a little bit of bravado and high-spirits—but not much. I soon saw why.

Dickson was marching along the line between them, sternly looking each recruit in the face. None of them dared to do so much as smile.

This made me frown in disapproval. He was taking all the fun out of this adventure.

Harris sat next to me, and he tapped me on the shoulder. "Take a look. You've got to look at this. I wish I'd thought of that back in the day."

Not sure what he was talking about, I turned and watched Dickson. He was still pacing among his lights, still kicking at any boot that had strayed into his path and slapping at the tops of helmets when he found a soldier who had a hair out of place.

"He's a goddamn tyrant," Harris said in an admiring tone. "Watch—watch what he does."

Dickson walked up to one female recruit who was stretching out a leg and rubbing at it—maybe she had a charley horse or something like that.

I was expecting to see him kick her a good one—but that wasn't his move at all. Instead, he reached down and seemed to tap at her shoulder.

She winced and yiped in pain.

"What the hell was that?" I asked.

"He's a wizard," Harris marveled. "I've only seen such a move a few times before, but maybe I haven't been watching closely enough. Live and learn…"

I frowned. "What are you talking about, Adjunct?"

"I'm saying that Dickson has come up with a brand new way of keeping a bunch of rowdy recruits in line. What he does, see, is he carries a little needle. A needle that's probably got some juice hooked up to it. Or maybe it's twinged with a little bit of skin irritant. I don't know."

My frown deepened. "Are you telling me he's poking holes in their suits? That's crazy."

"No, no, no," he said. "He's way smarter than that. He's using those special little holes, you know, the ones the bio-bastards use."

"Oh… I hate those things."

The bio people had long ago lobbied successfully to install ports in our suits. They'd claimed they needed them to get through our armor and treat wounded soldiers. In my experience, they'd used them for more nefarious purposes.

I considered Dickson with squinty eyes and gritted teeth. "The bio-people usually use those weak spots to kill me."

"Exactly," Harris said. "Dickson is no less evil. Any snot-nosed recruit who pisses him off gets jabbed. Now watch the results: they jump like whipped jackrabbits."

I watched as Dickson moved among his crew. Now and then, he dipped low to administer a painful jab.

"That's kind of weird," I said

"Yeah, it's weird—but it's also sheer genius!" Harris continued to admire Dickson, chuckling and shaking his head.

I kept on frowning. I wasn't too sure about Dickson. He was definitely a mixed bag. I could tell that his odd habits had gotten him kicked out of Victrix for good reason.

It was just my luck that I'd agreed to trade away Barton, the best officer I'd ever worked with, for this freak. I had to admit, however, that Dickson probably belonged to Legion Varus more than he did Victrix. If he was a little bit mental, a little bit twisted, well… this Legion would suit him well.

Primus Collins' voice broke in over the cohort-wide chat channel. As she was our commanding officer, all our conversations were cut short.

"3rd Cohort," she said, "this lifter is going to cut loose from the transport and drop in ten. Take your seats, people."

Everyone began to scramble desperately for a seat. They threw gear onto the deck and snarled at each other. In Legion Varus, when somebody told you something was happening in ten, it didn't mean ten minutes. It meant ten seconds.

"10… 9… 8… 7… 6…"

Everyone fought for a jump seat. We were supposed to already be in them, mind you, but we'd been sitting around for quite a while on Red Deck. Varus people were easily bored and tended to wander.

As these vital seconds ticked by, not everyone in my unit managed to get strapped in. Most notable among the failures was Adjunct Dickson.

He'd been caught flat-footed. He turned and scrambled for his seat, but along the way, somehow, his boot got hooked up with someone else's. He went down, sprawling on the deck.

Naturally enough, he bounced up again, red-faced and furious. There were a few giggles, but it was hard to tell who was making them. Everyone was staring dead ahead. The light troops were all statues.

"5... 4... 3... 2... 1..."

Dickson was still climbing into a seat when the whole lifter lurched under us. He went down again, landing on his face.

As he traveled down the long aisle between them, not a single recruit moved to help. They didn't even grab onto the straps of his backpack.

"You see that?" I told Harris. "That's what he gets for being such an asshole with his men. He'll be lucky if he doesn't get fragged in the first hour after we land."

Harris grimaced. "Maybe you're right. Maybe he's not doing it right. It's one thing to instill fear and respect in your troops, but it's another just to poke at them for the sheer fun of it. You think he'll learn his lesson?"

I shook my head. "I doubt it. If he was going to learn anything, they wouldn't have kicked his ass out of Victrix."

The lifter heeled over, slid sideways, then slewed around to a fresh angle. The thrust kicked in, and we were finally accelerating in the direction of our mysterious target.

Military lifters normally moved like sedated whales gliding through a dark ocean. But not when we were invading a hostile planet. The pilots were all business now.

They used all the thrust, power and maneuverability of their craft. They wanted to get to their assigned destination, kick out the troops, and get the hell out of danger as fast as possible.

They weren't too worried about the troops at any point of this operation. If a soldier went splat and died, well, that was just too damned bad.

Once we were on a straight course, Dickson managed to struggle into a seat and get himself strapped in. That was when he turned his head my way to see if I'd noticed his little fiasco.

I gave him a small shake of the head, then turned away, ignoring him. He knew that was my show of disapproval.

A private channel connection invite showed up inside my helmet display. I activated it and joined the officers chat-channel for the cohort.

Primus Collins was in full swing. She gave us a summary briefing. It was all she had time for before we reached our destination.

"Soldiers," she said, "we have returned to a world that we abandoned long ago, a place where Legion Varus was once beaten and driven back with Iron Eagles fighting at her side."

Whoa, I thought. Was she talking about…?

"This time will be different," she continued. "We'll take the high ground over 191 Eridani and…"

My eyes squinted inside my helmet. I tried to remember which world she was talking about. Oh yeah, I thought to myself, *Dark World.*

The home planet of the Vulbites orbited 191 Eridani. I hadn't been out here in a long time. We'd first met up with the forces of Rigel at Dark World. In fact, I'd met Squanto for the first time right here.

It was called Dark World because its star was a smoldering ember, rather than a bright point of fire in the sky. It was a brown dwarf—a star so small and feeble that it was barely lit by fusion in its guts. Such stars glimmered like a dying campfire rather than glared intensely.

The planet that circled this tiny star was not terribly cold, but it was not brightly lit by its dim sun. When you were on the planet surface, it was like looking at the sun through thick clouds. It was a gloomy place, full of purple vegetation and nasty-looking Vulbites.

The local inhabitants were centipede-like creatures that lived in vast hives. We'd tangled with them many times, and they served Rigel as a subservient species.

Although the planet itself wasn't of much value, it had one very important feature: a vast orbital factory. The factory ringed the entire planet. It was, to the best of our knowledge, the largest starship construction facility we'd ever encountered.

Primus Collins relayed video from the lifter's external sensors. I'd stopped listening to her, but I watched the video feed.

I saw Dark World. It was purply-blue with a few splotches of green. The planet had a hazy atmosphere. Above that, the silver ring of the factory circled the equator like a belt.

The belt was unbroken. I could see that easily. My efforts to sabotage the factory decades ago had apparently been repaired.

"Central Command," Primus Collins continued, "has made a strategic decision. We're going to strike at the orbital facilities here at Dark World. I'm not sure if they're doing this simply to make a point of anger and contention about the fact that Rigel destroyed our Big Sky project, or if they think it's simply the best move we can make."

A general groan went up from the troops who were in on the broadcast. None of Collins' speech giving mattered from the point of view of a grunt.

We were invading a satellite in orbit. That meant we could expect to be fighting in vacuum, facing cold more than heat.

Primus Collins kept on talking. She wasn't much for reading the mood of the chatroom. "Our best advantage is that of surprise and swift action. Accordingly, a large percentage of Earth cruisers and two of her dreadnought class ships are here to support us. Right now, they've engaged the Rigellian fleet in a surprise attack. That's all for now. I'll see you when we get our boots on an alien deck. Collins out."

One thing I liked about this primus was her short briefings. Unlike Turov, she knew how to tell you what you needed to know without making an autobiography out of it.

I relayed the essentials to my men, and there were a number of fresh groans, especially from my three supporting officers. Well, actually, only two of them groaned. Harris and Leeson weren't happy. Dickson, for all his other faults, wasn't much of a complainer.

"This is bullshit," Harris said. "Total bullshit. Since when are they going to fly us into the middle of a fleet battle while we're supposed to attack a satellite? That's not how you do it. That's not how I learned it in school."

"You never went to school for any of this stuff," Leeson told him.

"I sure as hell did," Harris fired back. "I went to the school of hard knocks. I worked my way up from nothing in this legion. I—"

"Shut up," I said, and they fell silent. "Here's the deal. We've got to be ready for anything. Everybody button-up your suits. Pressurize them. Expect this lifter to explode without warning. Then, you're all to shed any extra gear. We're not going to need it."

The whole unit began to follow this order. Cannisters and extra packs clattered on the metal deck plates.

"We're going to land on the interior surface of that ring," I continued. "We'll deploy as fast as we can. Once we're clear of the lifter, our one and only mission is to get inside of that factory as fast as we can, before the enemy can respond. Does everybody understand the mission?"

There were a couple of dismal-sounding "yes-sirs."

"Good, good," I said, as if they'd all stood up and sung hallelujah. "We've got eight minutes according to the lifter pilots until we touchdown. Wake up and stay awake. The instant metal hits metal, we're rushing down that ramp."

Troops began making adjustments to their random hodgepodge kits. Some of them shed extra batteries, and a lot of them shed water and other heat-related gear. A few of them discarded their portable air conditioning. I wasn't sure that was a good idea, but I wasn't going to argue with them about it.

Most of these men had been fighting at hellish off-world locations like this one for decades. They knew their business, and if they didn't, they could take an extra trip through revival machines to sharpen their minds.

Eight minutes could be a very long time when you couldn't see what was happening outside. I relayed video of the fleet battle, as that always made for a good distraction to pass the time—hopefully with less stress.

We watched as Earth's ships flooded into existence between us and the silvery ring of the orbital factory. Obviously surprised and somewhat out of position, a squadron of six enemy cruisers swarmed to meet our larger fleet.

We outnumbered them at least three to one, but Rigellian forces always fought with valor. The two waves of ships met and slammed into one another. We couldn't see the beams and missiles from this distance, only winking lights. These were brief releases of radiation and plasmas flaring brightly. Gases were vented into space where they ignited into blossoms of orange and blue fire.

The two sides traded blows for perhaps ninety seconds. When the brief combat was over, two Rigellian cruisers managed to turn and run. Both of them were on fire and venting badly, but they escaped into hyperspace.

The Earth squadrons had won the battle. A lot of cheering began aboard the lifter as news of the victory spread. I was glad I had shared the video with my troops. It was a morale booster.

I'd calculated that Hegemony wouldn't have been dumb enough to send us out here without enough cruisers to destroy the enemy. My gamble had paid off. Even Harris was clapping me on the back and laughing.

Dickson cracked a wintry smile. He'd been on the sour side since he'd performed a facer on the deck in front of his own abused troops.

The recruits high-fived each other and chattered excitedly. No one interrupted them. All the officers and noncoms knew that this might be the happiest moment of their day.

-25-

When the lifter thumped down and the ramp dropped, we were all on our feet. We jogged and jostled for the exit.

This was always a dangerous moment for any legionnaire. We didn't know when an enemy missile might come and obliterate our whole cohort, killing all of us.

The worst part was being near the center of the lifter, trapped inside while the rest charged out through one of the ramps.

"Go, go, go!" I shouted. "Break right, break right! Everybody, we're moving to flank right!"

Once we'd managed to get out of the lifter, which had become a possible death-trap now that it was down on the station, we found ourselves on an uneven deck of metal and polymers.

The satellite factory was crowded with wart-like lifters. The massive skids had smashed down a dozen air vents, fuel ports and other protuberances. Anything that stuck out into space in a seemingly random pattern was fair game when a lifter came in to land.

The satellite was artificial, and it was machined and constructed in what seemed like a familiar pattern. Still, there were alien oddities to it. Being designed and built by non-human minds, it had a surface that reminded me of a complex circuit board.

There were rows of pipes, wires, bulbous tanks and large, mushroom-shaped valves that released vapor. All kinds of stuff, but I had no interest in trying to identify any of it. To me it was all just cover until we could get down into the satellite itself.

Hopping along, we used magnetic boots and gravity-manipulation to cling to the gravity-free hull. Little puffs of air from our shoulders managed to keep us from flying off into space as we trotted around the surface.

The weirdest thing came whenever a soldier turned his head up—at least from our perspective, it was up—and saw the strange disk of Dark World itself. Noob recruits gaped. They could see the mass of bluish-purple vegetation on the surface. It seemed like the entire planet was cast in the shadow of night.

The sun, such as it was, could be seen in the opposite direction of the planet. 191 Eridani was a weird star. Glancing that way, I found it to be the most alien star I'd ever eyeballed. There were orange patches moving over an otherwise dark surface. I knew I was seeing hot spots breaking through the cooler crust, and they were shifting hour by hour. To me, it looked like a cluster of volcanoes that were about to erupt. There were rivers of gleaming light flowing between the dark spots.

We expected to be assaulted by robots upon landing, but none of them boiled up to meet us. Following the instructions from Primus Collins, I rushed to my waypoint on the tactical map and hunkered down with my troops.

There was a hot gush of plasma fire against our backs. The lifters were taking off again, leaving us to our fates on the satellite. Glancing back at the dwindling sparks and exhaust trails, you couldn't help but feel abandoned.

I saw no less than twenty to thirty soldiers fall off the ramps. They dove for the safety of the satellite rather than being left adrift in space. Apparently, they'd been too slow from the pilot's point of view.

Most of the stragglers were killed in various ways. Some had their faceplates shattered by impact with the ramp or the struts. A few others were incinerated by the jets because they couldn't get out of the way fast enough.

About ten of them managed to survive by avoiding the gushing exhaust. They used every trick they could to guide themselves into a controlled crash on the surface of the satellite.

"That was frigging rude," Leeson said.

"You're right about that," I agreed. "It's always the same with these Fleet pukes. They value their own ass over and above any thousand legionnaire deaths."

I knew, of course, the lifter pilots were probably under orders not to lose a single ship. None of our lives mattered as much as the value of a lifter. In fact, I was sure that any member of the brass or the Fleet would have traded my entire cohort for that lifter straight-up.

These days it was far easier to print out a thousand soldiers than it was to build something sophisticated like a new spaceship. Especially with a reliable source of revival machines. If I had to compare the value between the two, I would say that a lifter was like a fancy color printer while the humans inside were like sheets of paper. We were infinitely more replaceable.

Our next orders were not long in coming.

"Each unit is to find a way to break in," Primus Collins said in our headsets. "If you've got a portal in your immediate vicinity hack it or burn it open. Get inside no matter what. If you can't, then use your belchers to melt metal until you've bored a hole through the satellite's skin."

I consulted my techs and my weaponeers. They soon found that we had no obvious hatches or doorways to enter the satellite safely. Consequently, I ordered Sargon and his team to use charges and beams from their belchers.

"Dig us a hole! We've got to get down inside the satellite as fast as possible."

Dickson was the only adjunct who seemed bewildered by these requirements. "Why the big rush, Centurion? I would think it would be more sensible to make a few intelligent breaches into the satellite rather than dozens of them all over the hull. Wouldn't that be less damaging to the factory itself?"

"You're right about all that, Dickson," I said, "but that's because you haven't been out here to Dark World before. The Vulbites live down there, see." I pointed toward the surface of the violet planet below. "They've got weapons. The last time, they hit us with laser barrages from the surface. They're lining up their cannons right now to burn us, like ticks on a dog."

Dickson was alarmed. He immediately moved his recruits to better positions, trying to put any chunk of metal between them and the lavender disk of Dark World below us.

I watched Sargon's steady progress. He'd been burning through a spot in the satellite's hull that the techs claimed was thinner than most.

Sparks, plasma and gushes of blazing color were all coming out of the hole he was digging. Long before Sargon managed to break through the skin of the satellite, however, there was a problem.

"Centurion!" Harris shouted, getting my attention.

"What now, Harris?" I asked, tossing a look over my shoulder.

Harris was pointing. He was pointing to another region of the orbital factory's surface.

Due to the gentle curvature of the satellite, we were able to see other units. One of them was crouched in and among what resembled a long set of solar panels. I had no idea if they were solar panels or not, but they were fat, angled planes that were definitely aimed toward the glimmering star.

"You see the solar panels over there, sir? Look above them—look directly above them."

I did as he suggested, squinting and using my helmet's digital zoom feature for a better view. I saw what looked like twisted bodies, burnt bodies that were unusually dark in color. These corpses were floating away from the factory's surface. There were dozens of them.

A moment later, the tactical chatlines began to buzz.

"We're taking fire from the planet," Collins said. "Nobody panic, just keep burrowing into the satellite's skin. There are a lot of troops out here. They can't get us all. If anybody breaches, let us know. We'll move all nearby units to that position for entry."

"I'll be damned," Harris said, "this is a bigger cluster-fuck than last time. Do you realize none of us located any easy, hackable points of entry?"

"Uh... no, I didn't realize that."

"Well, it's frigging true. It's almost like the bears and the Vulbites learned something last time around."

"Ya think? Of course, they learned something. Just take cover and keep your eyes open."

Harris crawled close to me and put his back up against the same chunk of metal I was sheltering behind. I was hoping my lucky stars were with me today.

"They're using those anti-personnel lasers from the surface," he complained. "Just like last time. They're punching right through their clouds and burning troops willy-nilly. We're like ants under a magnifying glass out here, McGill."

"Yeah... I remember a lot of us got burned out here the last time we visited this garden spot."

"Don't remind me."

We hugged the walls and waited. Our breath came out loud in our suits, and it seemed like our heartbeats roared in our ears. That was the trouble with spacewalking, the sounds were all wrong. You were isolated in your suit, and it was kind of freaky after a while.

We looked around at the skies. There wasn't much shelter from a radiation blast directed at us from below. We were just too exposed. We had to trust luck.

Over the next three minutes other units were struck. Each time, the ground batteries found a good target and fired beams at us. You could see holes appear in the cloud layer below, burned through by the released energy.

The cannons were a hundred kilometers or more away, but they were still effective. The surface of the satellite was slashed and burned. Each time, a platoon's worth of legionnaires died.

Those who weren't struck dead screamed and wriggled in space. They fought with melted hoses and burning spacesuits—but most were luckier than that, dying instantly.

"Hey! Look at *Dominus*!"

I followed Leeson's short arm, which was pointing out into deep space. There, parked overhead, was the hulk of our transport ship. The ground lasers weren't powerful enough to damage her, so they hadn't tried.

Eyeing the big warship, I soon saw what Leeson was excited about.

"The broadsides are traveling," I said. "Everyone, hunker down!"

We were already hugging the deck as hard as we could, but Sargon shut down his operation at my order. We all braced for impact.

Sixteen fusion cannons spoke at once. A barrage of smart-shells flew from the barrels and streaked downward toward the planet.

Leeson whooped like he'd won the lottery. "Those fucking bugs are gonna eat it now!"

"Shield your eyes," I warned. "Dampen the light coming in from your helmets."

We waited for about a minute, then a long series of flashes struck the planet below. Circular impact points puffed like puddles with rocks thrown into them. A moment later, numerous fireballs appeared at the center of each strike.

"That'll teach them!" Harris shouted.

"Back to work, Sargon. The rest of you, stay low. We might not have gotten all their lasers."

A few minutes later, Sargon began shouting. "I've got a breach, sir!"

"In, in," I roared, "everybody in!"

A few other breaches had been called out around the cohort, but they'd been judged as too far away. As a courtesy, I alerted the 2nd and the 4th unit commanders to let them know they could use our breach.

Sargon dove in first, and his weaponeers went in behind him. Me and a dozen other heavies flew down next. Dickson and his light troopers came in last.

I did take note that Dickson himself hadn't charged into the opening to dive for safety with the other officers. He could have done that by pulling rank—but he hadn't.

Adjuncts Leeson and Harris, of course, hadn't hesitated one second. But Dickson stood outside in the open, exposed to enemy fire. He made sure every one of his hapless recruits went down that rabbit hole before he did.

"Huh," I said, watching him on a buzzer-feed.

Dickson was something of a riddle to me. One minute he seemed to be a devil, testing and torturing his recruits. The next, he was caring about them, or entertaining everybody aboard *Dominus* with his entrancing performance on Green Deck.

He wasn't an easy man to describe in a single sentence. He had his good traits and his bad ones.

I shrugged my shoulders. He was a weirdo. Maybe he belonged in Legion Varus after all.

-26-

Once we were down inside the orbital factory, we felt an overwhelming sense of relief. Sure, it was an alien environment, but it beat being exposed to a big laser cannon by a country mile. Outside, we'd never known which moment would be our last before we were burned to vapor.

My troops held their rifles to their shoulders and patrolled in every direction. After investigating the chamber we'd broken into, I made sure everyone in my unit had made it safely into the factory. Overall, losses had been minimal.

We put up a fabric barrier to block the hole in the roof and let the chamber repressurize.

"Open your face plates and shut off your oxygen," I ordered. "We've got to save every breath we can."

All around me, face plates were flipped up. People took hesitant sniffs of the air. It was full of unpleasant acrid smells from hot burnt metal and smoking insulation. Still, it was air, and it contained enough oxygen to breathe

"It's not immediately poisonous," Carlos concluded.

"Would have been better if you'd run that test before we opened our suits," I commented.

Carlos shrugged. "I was busy. Anyway, we'll be fine. Some people with allergies are going to cough a lot, but no one is going to die… probably."

"Great… Techs!" I shouted. "Where the hell are we? My map isn't updating. How do we get to the rest of our cohort?"

After looking over her maps, Kivi came up with an answer. "Sir, check this out," she said, coming to me and showing me a computer scroll she had in her hands. She spread it out on a flat surface, and it adhered itself there. We huddled over it, trying to figure out where we were.

"The interior of the orbital factory is convoluted and complex by nature," she said. "Most lines aren't straight down here. As far as I can tell, we're in a power generation sector."

"Power generation, huh? What's this chamber for?"

"The one we're in now?" Kivi looked around. We were surrounded by piled gear and machinery with mysterious purposes. Some of it looked like it had big cables sprouting out, but that was about all I could glean from the look of the place.

Kivi put up her hands in a gesture of surrender. "I don't know. The purpose of many of these chambers is unknown to us. Maybe it's a maintenance storage area for generator repair? That's my guess."

I nodded. "A good guess. That would explain all these solar panels and heavy cables. Don't cut into these cables, boys," I told my dumber grunts. "There's liable to be a lot of juice in there. It'll blow your balls off and then some."

Heavy soldiers that had been pecking at the equipment like bored chickens moved away from the cables. After all, some were as thick as a man's leg.

Troops that had encountered alien equipment before were always wary of it, and with good reason. Aliens usually weren't safety nuts. They didn't always insulate high voltages. They depended on their workers and soldiers to *know* what was dangerous and to avoid it without any clear markings or warning signs.

"Okay, Kivi," I said, "get me out of this owl-trap. I need a path to the rest of the cohort."

Kivi pointed to her map again. "Primus Collins is dragging everyone in this direction. Let's just say it's north."

"No," I said, "let's call it east, because it seems to head into the rising sun. This orbital factory forms a belt that runs east-west around the planet's equator."

She rolled her eyes at me. "All right, whatever. We'll call it east. We needed to head east until we link-up with all the other units. They're moving toward these really large chambers down here."

I eyeballed her map critically. The vast majority of it was blank, which wasn't encouraging. "So, what do you think these large chambers are for?"

Kivi shrugged. "As far as intel knows, they're drydocks."

"Drydocks? You mean like shipyards, For the construction of vessels?"

"Exactly."

I thought that made good sense. "That's why we were sent here, I guess. This entire structure is designed and built specifically to build warships."

It was always easier to build large space vessels in space than it was to build them on a planetary body. That's because you didn't have to expend the vast amount of energy it took to thrust the bulk of the spaceship through a planetary atmosphere. Once one of these vast ships was constructed in space, all you had to do was exert enough power to allow it to break free from the local gravitational field. I said as much to Kivi, and she agreed.

"There's another reason why they build them in space," she said. "Most ships have hulls that are too thin in spots. They're not built for the stress of moving through an atmosphere, or the heat of reentry. They're designed to be built in space, launched in space, and spend their entire existence in space. There's a lot of advantages to that kind of design."

Primus Collins ordered my unit to move to a new rally point. As Kivi had said, it was in the middle of a large chamber due east of the power generation sector.

"All right, we've got new orders. Let's move out."

Instead of ordering Dickson and his recruits to trail behind us, this time I sent them ahead to take the lead. They fanned out to play scouts. Dickson wasn't the first to open a new hatch and plunge through, but he didn't linger in the rear, either. He moved in the middle of the pack, directing recruits to cover one another as they advanced.

The heavies moved out next, with weaponeers last. It was the reverse order we'd used when jumping into the breach Sargon had managed to create.

"I'm having a hard time figuring out Dickson," Harris told me as he trudged along at my side. "One minute he seems like the biggest tool I've ever met in my life. But the next, I see him making smart tactical decisions and even standing shoulder to shoulder with his men."

I nodded in agreement. "I'm not sure what I think of him yet either," I admitted

"Did someone say tool?" Carlos said from behind us.

Harris glanced back in disgust. "Don't worry Specialist," he said. "We're not calling for you—at least not yet."

Carlos wasn't fooled, nor was he deterred. He stepped a little closer. "Anyone using the word 'tool' in this unit has to be talking about one special individual—and yes, I am talking about Adjunct Dickson."

"Careful, Carlos," I told him. "I haven't had you shot for insubordination yet on this mission, but there's always the first time."

Carlos didn't seem to hear my warning. He certainly didn't heed it. "That guy is a *serious* tool. Scratch that—he's a megatool. I don't think I've ever talked to recruits who hate their commander more than that guy."

I believed Carlos, but at the same time, I wasn't entirely certain that Dickson's methods were entirely wrong. "I don't know," I said. "When he talks, his troops move their asses. The instant he gives an order, no one dares to hesitate. In the end, that might save some lives."

Carlos was disgusted. "Seriously? You're thinking about adopting some of Dickson's techniques? Mark my words, he'll be fragged before tomorrow morning. Just you wait and see."

"You're going to be fragged if you don't shut up and get back there with Leeson and his specialists," Harris barked. He'd finally had enough of Carlos.

"Okay. Okay. Don't go postal on me. Don't shoot the messenger. I was just trying to let you guys know how the rest of the unit is feeling."

When he'd faded away out of earshot, Harris glanced at me. "What the pug said is true."

"What's that?" I asked. I was surprised Harris would ever say Carlos was correct. Even in person.

"Dickson is walking a fine line. Troops can only take so much before they pop off."

Harris should know. I could recall one bad day when a young woman named Sarah had put fifty rounds into the back of his skull. Hell, I'd killed him during an early training during the Steel World campaign. That had been my first murder in a long and illustrious career full of bloodletting.

"Still," Harris continued, "I have to take back what I said about Dickson being the most annoying man in this unit. That prize still belongs to Carlos."

I had to smile because I knew that Harris was right.

-27-

We advanced rapidly. It was a good thing too, because this orbital factory was huge. I didn't have the exact estimate, but at forty thousand kilometers in diameter, it was equivalent to the circumference of the Earth.

Lots of sections were unused, partially built, or relatively unimportant, such as storage facilities that held masses of scrap metal and fuel cells. You could easily climb through ten kilometers of twisted metal pipes, empty fuel tanks and the like before you came to anything interesting.

After about twenty kilometers of slogging through long passages and big chambers, we came to a *very* large chamber. Essentially, instead of having fifty or sixty levels of equipment and machines, we came to a zone where the entire tubular station formed a single hangar. It was just one long hollow zone, like a warehouse in the middle of the factory.

"Sir…? Sir?"

It was Dickson. I answered the call immediately. "Go ahead, Adjunct."

"Sir, we've made contact with something… unbelievable."

I called a halt to the main column. Everybody went down to one knee and pulled out their rifles. They aimed in every random direction that could conceivably lead to a threat. Varus troops were among the most paranoid that had ever left Earth—and for good reason.

"What have you got, Dickson?"

He sent me back some footage. Dickson was using his own forward scouts and a few buzzers Kivi had lent to him. He had one of them transmit directly to me.

The most amazing sight came up on my tapper. The light platoon had come out of a long, tubular corridor that was itself some four meters in width, into a massive chamber. In the middle of this squatted something I could hardly believe.

"Is that a battleship?" I asked Dickson.

"Sir, I don't know what class of ship this is—but it's a monster. I would also say it is definitely a warship."

We looked it over, sending buzzers into the vast chamber. They pinged and probed, and we soon determined that the vessel was indeed armed and armored. There were turrets on the top and bottom of the warship. Most of these turrets had no barrels, so they didn't seem to be operable. There were missile tubes as well, prepared to launch all kinds of hell when this thing was finished.

Dickson's group was hunkered down in front of the great ship.

"Hold your position, Dickson."

"Roger that."

I had Kivi send in a flock of buzzers. They skimmed the hull, moving around to the rear of it. The thing was so big, it seemed to take a long time for the little drones to get to the stern.

"This frigging thing must be a kilometer long," I said.

"Correct," Kivi told me, "I'm measuring at least that much, Centurion."

"Look at the armor, too. Kivi, swing a drone down under the belly. There are open spots down there."

Bays yawned on the sides of the ship—two cargo bays.

"It's not ready for flight yet," Kivi said.

"No, I'm not even seeing engines in back. The big guns are missing too—at least the barrels, anyway. But there do seem to be small turrets on the flanks." I said.

"Uh-oh…" Kivi said. "I think we have a problem."

"What?"

Switching from buzzer to buzzer she switched from one feed to another. Her hands were shaking. She was switching inputs so rapidly, she didn't even have time to explain anything.

Finally, she brought up a view from the starboard flank of the monster ship. I saw one of the smallest turrets—and it was moving. It had to be a point-defense gun. It was tracking her buzzer as it flew by.

"That thing sees us, sir!" she hissed. "It's active!"

Her eyes met mine, and I realized what she was telling me. Maybe someone was manning that ship, or possibly it had automated defense systems that were switched on. Whichever case it was, the warship was imminently dangerous to us humans.

Dickson and his lights had begun to ease forward, infiltrating the hangar at the bottom. They were under the bulk of the warship, walking and investigating like a herd of anxious cats.

"Dickson! That thing is live!" I shouted. "Pull back! Withdraw your troops!"

He relayed the order immediately, but it was already too late. More small turrets, placed at strategic angles all around the large cylindrically shaped ship had spotted Dickson and his men. Maybe they had motion sensors, or maybe they'd waited until they had good targets that were too close to run.

The turrets opened up all at once. They hosed down my light platoon with a liberal dose of particle beams. The recruits had no chance. Six of them were blown to smoking fragments instantly, while the rest scrambled away, bouncing in the low gravity. They leapt and dove for any cover they could find, but they were torn apart as the turrets swiveled and chased each of them down.

Other units were arriving about then. No matter which level you were traveling along, they all came out right here in this big chamber. A dozen more turrets came to life. I could see them spitting fire at the new arrivals as well.

Light troops were running everywhere. Shouting, they jammed the tactical chat with cries of pain and requests for help. Dozens died within the span of a minute.

Fortunately, the timely arrival of fresh game had saved the last few of Dickson's ill-fated 1st Squad. They'd been torn up, but they hadn't been slaughtered down to the last man. Dickson himself managed to slip away into the safety of the entrance tunnels. There, he crouched low with the survivors of his team.

In the hangar, the smoke cleared. There was nothing but bloody remains and the random janky motions of the activated defensive turrets.

"We've got to take those things out, sir," Harris told me. "How about we have Sargon, and his boys aim a few belchers at those turrets? Two beams at once, that ought to do it."

I thought about it, but I shook my head. "They'd probably get one or two, but the others are angled so that several can target any single point. What are the odds that they won't figure out where the fire is coming from? They'll focus fire on whatever tunnel we sneak out of and nail our weaponeers."

"What then?"

"We're going to report in to Primus Collins." I made an attempt to contact my direct superior officer but failed to do so. She was already fielding dozens of similar calls from other centurions who'd had their units torn-up as well.

I waited for my turn, and the primus finally contacted me. "McGill," she said, "did your crew set that thing off?"

"Hell no, sir," I lied with conviction. "That's crazy-talk. How could we have done that? My troops weren't even the first ones into the chamber."

She sighed. "Yeah, yeah, of course not. It was probably Manfred's team. He's a hard-charger. He made a big effort to be first, you know. Rumor has it that he wanted to beat you to the goal line today."

I'd been watching the casualty lists, and I could easily see that Manfred had managed to get himself killed. That made him a soft target for the unfair heaping of blame.

"Well, sir, he certainly managed to achieve some kind of first. I hope he's happy."

"He's dead—and he'll stay that way for a while. We don't have any revival machines aboard this factory yet. They're all still up on *Dominus*."

"Oh yeah... that's right," I said feeling a bit concerned. Without revival machines, deaths were permanent. At least

Manfred would have to remain in purgatory until Collins gave the blessing to revive his sorry ass again.

"So…" I said, "how exactly are we supposed to take this entire orbital factory if we're limited to just a few thousand men?"

"That's not your worry, McGill. Your problem is to get past that warship."

"Have you got any suggestions in that area, Primus?"

"I do," she said. "Knock out the turrets. Either that, or circumvent them. Maybe there's a way to slip under the belly of this beast. Or maybe you can go back out on the surface and walk past it that way. As Manfred's dead right now, I'm giving you tactical command of his unit for this action. Find a way past that warship."

Collins closed the connection, and I grunted unhappily. This wasn't going to be as easy as it sounded. There were a lot of turrets, and as far as I could tell, the drydock facility completely filled the interior of the factory. There was no way I was going to lead my men outside the factory again though. None of us had any stomach for being burned off like insects in a flame.

I squatted and took a moment to think. During that time, my adjuncts bitched, carried on, and made jokes about Manfred. I had Kivi feed me replays of various videos, and I studied the warship's massive hull.

"Okay," I said, getting an idea at last. "This is how we're going to play it."

"Uh-oh," Leeson said, "I got a feeling we're not gonna like this."

"Some of us aren't," I admitted. "As close as I can tell, these point-defense turrets are designed to shoot things that are at least a few meters from the surface of the battleship's hull."

"Yes," Kivi said. "That much seems clear from the videos."

"After watching their movements, I've never seen any of them turn their barrels downward. They never aim with an angle that could hit the hull itself."

"Of course not," Harris said, "that would be crazy design. No one wants a gunner or robot to make a mistake and accidentally blow off a fin or something."

Leeson was listening, but he was also squinting with suspicion. "What are you saying, sir?" he asked. "I gotta tell you, I don't like the sound of it so far."

Adjunct Dickson joined us and squatted in the circle of officers. He looked worried—even more worried than Harris or Leeson. Possibly, this was because he'd already lost a third of this command. He also might have had some inkling as to what I was about to propose.

"Here's the deal," I said. "Primus Collins has given me the ball on this one. We're going to use your troops, Dickson. You're going to send them out as fast as you can from multiple start-points."

Leeson whistled, but I ignored him.

"Your troops are going to rush in. Let's put about six in the lead group. Six more will follow."

"After two more waves," Harris laughed, "that should about run you out of troops."

Dickson didn't even smile in return. "What's our mission, Centurion?" he asked.

"Your mission is to race as close as possible to this massive hull and jump up with your magnetics activated. Latch onto that big bastard. Once your troops are crawling all over that hull, start taking out the turrets any way you can."

"Is that all?" Leeson asked. "Maybe you want him to shine your boots, first."

Dickson studied the deck, but he nodded. "My troops won't disappoint you, Centurion."

"I'm sure they won't." I replied.

Dickson knew this was the sort of thing that light troops were all about. They always took the most dangerous missions with the highest casualty rates. Part of the reason for this was because they were the least experienced and therefore the least valuable troops. They also were equipped with the worst gear, but as a benefit, that allowed them to move more quickly.

"I understand, sir. My troops will do it."

"I bet they will," Harris said, "otherwise they'll find a needle stuck in their ass."

Dickson glanced at him but didn't say anything.

Harris grinned.

"We'll do the best we can to cover you," I told Dickson. "We'll send out buzzers to distract the turrets to start with. Once the initial turrets are engaged, Sargon will destroy them with mini-missiles and belchers."

Dickson nodded. He stood up, clapped his hands together, and saluted. "I'm ready to deploy my men, sir."

"All right. It's a go."

Dickson trotted away. At least he hadn't complained. That was one thing I'd noticed about Victrix people. They were insufferably arrogant, but they knew enough not to make jokes and complain all the time on the field of battle.

Less than ten minutes later, the operation commenced. Dickson had carefully arranged his troops, and Sargon had carefully arranged his weaponeers. They all moved at once, right behind a cloud of buzzers.

At first, the turrets chased the buzzers. They spat out beams of fire trying to blow them down. While they were distracted, Dickson's troops sprinted across the open space to the hull.

They moved in great leaps and bounds. The low gravity and their sheer desperation got them moving at an impressive rate of speed. There was something like a hundred meters between safety and the hull of the hulking battleship, and they crossed this ground in seconds.

Unfortunately, the first wave of troops wasn't quite fast enough. The turrets noticed them and switched targets, forgetting about the drones they'd been chasing. Maybe they were programmed to recognize the greater threat the approaching troops represented.

Whatever the reason, stitching fire swept across the charging light troops. Firing hundreds of blazing plasma bolts in rapid succession, they cut every one of the first six light troopers down. Right behind them were the next six—and then six more after that.

In the end, nine humans survived long enough to launch themselves in a final, desperate leap. They flew through the air, using every thruster and grav-boot they had.

They slammed into the metal hull and clung there to the bottom of it, like fleas hugging to a giant dog for dear life. The turrets swiveled, twisted, contorted and even shook with indecision. It looked like they were desperate to get a bead on the troops, to blow them off the hull.

"Sargon! This is your chance. Make it quick, and make it count."

He obeyed me immediately. A dozen beams and missiles leaped up from our undercover spots. The storm of beams and tiny warheads knocked out two, then three of the quivering defensive turrets.

After that, they began to return fire. Sargon was forced to retreat. We lost one weaponeer in the process, and that left me cursing and muttering under my breath. Each of those men was irreplaceable at this point.

Dickson himself, I noticed, hadn't been lounging. He was crawling across the surface of the warship. I hadn't really expected him to take any further action. His role had been that of a decoy—or the bunny-rabbit, as we tended to refer to men like his—but he was on the move, leading his troops up higher on the flanks of the great hull. I was slightly impressed.

"My men are in position, Centurion. Permission to use our grenades."

"You don't have to ask permission for that, Dickson. Blow those turrets up anyway you can."

He worked slowly and methodically. Over the next several minutes, his surviving lights crawled close to turrets that couldn't target them and set charges. Then they slunk away.

One at a time, they popped the surviving turrets that encrusted the nose of the battleship. All of them were soon destroyed.

-28-

Once we had troops crawling over the hull, our progress became much easier. We were able to get my whole unit onto the nose cone of the giant battleship. We destroyed one defensive turret after another.

The ship hadn't been designed for this kind of attack. It hadn't occurred to the builders that infantry might crawl all over it while it was in drydock.

My entire unit was soon working their way over the ship, seeking an entrance. A few platoons from other units joined us. I led a squad of heavies, and we made plans to sneak into the sockets where the big guns were supposed to be placed. Even as we reached one of the big turrets that were currently gaping holes, something went wrong in a big way.

"Sir? Centurion, sir! The roof… it's opening up!"

I looked up, and it was true. The drydock's big topside doors were slowly rolling away, revealing the darkness of open space.

As the vast chamber had been pressurized, some of my men had foolishly had their faceplates open. I lost troops just from decompression. Others were caught by surprise and sucked away from the hull of the vessel as the air pressure from inside the chamber blasted out into nothingness.

The men who were sent spinning away from the hull roared and struggled, using their grav-boots and any kind of propulsion they could devise. Then the point-defense turrets we hadn't yet destroyed began to spit fire at them. Helpless, the troops that had lost their grip on the battleship were torn to shreds.

For a full minute, utter chaos reigned. The tactical chat lines were jammed as troops attempted to deal with this new unexpected twist. Then, things became a lot worse.

"The ship! Centurion, the ship is moving!"

It was true. Somewhere deep under the belly of this monstrous vessel, thrusters had ignited. Our buzzers had videoed these small engines, designed to steer the battleship rather than power it. The big engines in the rear hadn't yet been installed, but the steering jets were enough to lift her off and send the massive ship up into open space.

We clung to the hull, unable to abandon her. If we tried to jump off and fly back into the relative safety of the drydock, we knew we'd be gunned down by the remaining defensive turrets around the stern.

"Everyone hang on!" I shouted. "Try to get inside, any way you can!"

At this point, I was pretty sure that someone was inside the battleship, trying to defend her. Whoever was driving this big battlewagon had tried to use the defensive armament, but when that hadn't worked, they'd switched to escaping the drydock entirely. They were making a run for it, attempting to take the ship into open space.

Letting them escape would have been fine with me—but it wasn't an option now. My entire unit was clinging to the hull of this behemoth as she emerged from her cocoon.

"Ignore all the small turrets," I ordered. "Forget about them. Find an entrance. Get into the cargo hold or crawl into the empty gun tubes."

We looked like ants swarming over a burning log. We crawled everywhere we thought we might find an escape hatch. I moved with a platoon of heavies led by Harris, and our last platoon of lights led by Dickson followed in the rear.

We went for the big turrets on the roof of the battleship. We crept into the tubes that would someday have barrels for fusion cannons, but the weaponeers couldn't fit. None of them were small enough—their heavy kits were the problem. They had the bulky armor that didn't bend as easily as the rest of our suits.

"Dickson, take your lights in first. We can't afford to get blocked by some fat-boy. Sargon... take your weaponeers somewhere else. You're on your own."

"Thanks a bunch, Centurion." Sargon and his over-armored boys crawled away.

Dickson reached the interior passages first. He glanced over his shoulder and urged the rest of us to move faster. He had his light troops inside the ship. They were running all over in the fire control rooms underneath the turret.

When it came to be my turn, I found out I was just too big as well. My Rigellian armor wasn't as thick as a weaponeer's kit but crawling into the tube was more than a tight squeeze.

Inside the empty socket, there was all kinds of heavy machinery. Just looking at it, you knew you could be killed in a dozen ways. There was equipment built to load fusion warheads, along with giant gears and slides to release gases and eject massive cartridges. If just one of these things moved, I would be crushed, mutilated and killed instantly.

Crawling over a set of massive gears I felt the rasp of sharp metal on my armor. The teeth of the gears were like diamond blades. That's where I stopped. The sharp teeth hooked up on my armor, and I couldn't move.

Harris was personally trying to get me through that tight spot. "Centurion?" he said, "exhale as deeply as you can."

"I am, and it's not doing any good."

"Well then, we're going have to cut off an arm or something."

"I suggest," Dickson said, "that you remove that armor and use the spacer suit underneath."

Harris looked at him like he was insane. "An officer with no armor?"

Dickson shrugged. He was looking up at us from the bottom of the turret mount. "It's better than being left outside. For all we know this ship is about to be attacked by our own vessels. Life expectancy on the exterior hull will be rather short, I think."

Harris looked back to me. "It's your call, sir."

"I know it. My mom always said I was too damned big."

I retreated a ways and pulled off my breastplate. Then I had to pull off more pieces of armor than that to get through. The armor itself was shoved in, then I followed, crawling over all those blade-like gears and threaded pipes.

Behind me, I dragged my rifle and a few bottles of oxygen. I was able to wriggle through the hole. The sharp, heavy gears meant to move the barrels tore their way through my spacer suit. When I got down to the safety of the fire control area, alarmed men came up with patches and slapped them all over my hissing suit.

The freezing cold of space came through in those spots and burned me. It was like being touched by dry ice. Slathering on glue and patches, my suit was declared airtight and given a fresh bottle of oxygen.

While I pulled my armor back on, I ordered the troops to push deeper into the ship.

"All right," I said, "time to stop fussing over me. Harris, I want you to take point. Dickson's squad has lost enough."

Harris's lips parted into a snarl, but he nodded and didn't argue. He headed down a random passageway. The rest of us followed. We left the fire control area behind and began looking for whoever or whatever was flying this frigging ship into space.

In my experience, I'd found that alien ships were just that: alien. Their internal design didn't always follow the logic and rationality of human or imperial design.

Sure, there were certain facts of physics that required adherence to a common logical theme. For example, deflectors meant to stop meteor strikes and missiles were often mounted on the front of the vessel. The rear normally had the heavy thrusters to push the ship in a given direction.

Other than that, there were a dozen variations when it came to where best to put the bridge. Sometimes it was placed at the prow, so the pilots could see where they were going. In other cases, you might find the bridge in the protected center, or even in the rear near the engines.

We had no idea which philosophy had been taken by the bears when they built this monstrosity.

"I sure hope they don't have too many more of these things waiting for us at Rigel," Harris said.

The odd thing about the bears was they tended to build big ships—really big ships—but with small interiors. As they were normally about a meter tall, their passages were about a meter and a half high, at best.

We were forced to move in a crouch, hunched over on our way down the passages. A short man like Leeson could pretty much stand upright, with maybe a slight stoop to the shoulders. But a guy like myself who was two meters in height… well, I was damn near doubled over.

I raced along anyways, trying not to hit my head on various lamps and pipes which hung down from the ceiling.

All of a sudden, a lot of firing broke out. Plasma bolts splattered the walls and blazed away. There was someone shrieking, and I realized I could hear their voice through my helmet and suit. This region must be pressurized again, or I wouldn't have heard it.

"What have you got, Harris?"

"Vulbites, sir! A butt-load of them." As he spoke to me, he fired short bursts as did several of his heavy troopers.

"Are they returning fire?"

"Doesn't look like it."

I frowned. "They're just running away, and you're shooting them in the back."

"More like the tail section, sir."

"Harris, ceasefire."

Grumbling, he came back along the tubes and stared at me. His eyes were big, round and unhappy. "Listen, sir," he said, "we can't tell if the Vulbites are setting up traps or killing the men out on the hull—we don't know their intentions. I think we have to assume the worst."

"Were they armed?"

"No, sir. They did not appear to be."

"Are they wearing armor?"

"No, just spacers' gear. A uniform maybe, and oxygen tanks. That's it."

"And you shot them all down anyway? Killing them on sight? What if they're trying to surrender, Harris?"

He looked exasperated. "Then they were damn well out of luck, sir. If you can tell me what a bug-eyed monster looks like when he's surrendering, then you know aliens better than I do. To me, all I saw were some fangs, some spread pinchers, and then a lot of legs churning as they tried to run away."

I thought it over, and I didn't like it. Killing civilians was wrong, no matter what species they came from.

"What if they come to Earth some day?" I asked him. "What if they walk into a supermarket, and they see some folks pushing carts around, and they just start shooting everybody? Our screams and running away could be sinister. Our children and our women- are they harmless or not?"

Harris shrugged. "Sir, sometimes we've got to just go with our gut instincts. Are we taking this ship or not? Because these Vulbites just activated defensive systems and flew this ship into space with us on its skin!"

Harris was pretty much yelling at me by now, and I was pretty much yelling at him. Dickson looked on as if curious, but he wasn't saying much.

Harris finally stopped and just stared at me angrily. "What are your orders, sir?" he practically spat at me.

"If I send you on point again, and you run into more civilian Vulbites, are you going to shoot them?"

"Absolutely, sir."

"What if I order you to shoot only hostiles that you are certain are a threat to this unit?"

"Then sir," he said loudly, "I will gun them all down and let Hegemony or the bears sort them out later."

I was angry, and so was he. I considered ordering him to stand down and putting someone else in charge. Maybe Moller or even Dickson—but I overcame my flash of rage and gestured for him to move ahead. "Carry on."

He stalked away, stooped over, and continued the operation. He ordered his heavies to press hard. I soon heard more splattering plasma bolts.

Dickson fell back and walked with me. "That was very interesting, Centurion."

"How so?"

"I would have handled it differently. A Victrix officer takes his right to command much more seriously."

"So, what would you have done?"

"I would have executed Harris on the spot, of course. Then I might have taken his advice, as it was wisdom from the beginning."

I laughed at that. "That's an interesting mix."

"Well, he is right. Of course, we should gun down every alien we see. They've already killed half your command, and we're in danger of failing our mission."

"Even if the Vulbites aren't military types?"

"It doesn't matter if they're civilians or not. They're opposing us."

"Huh…" I said, and I thought that over. I had to admit he had a point. "So then, why would you shoot Harris?"

"He argued with your direct orders. That's simply unacceptable, whether he's right or not."

"Ah, so anyone who gives me an argument, right or wrong, needs to be executed?"

"Yes, sir. That's what I just said."

Whipping out my pistol, I placed it against his forehead.

Dickson looked comically surprised. His mouth gaped. "Um… what are you doing, Centurion?"

"I'm taking your excellent advice, Dickson. Didn't you just correct me? Didn't you just tell me I handled a command situation incorrectly?"

"Yes, well…possibly I did. Perhaps I didn't think this through."

"No, you didn't. Let me explain something to you. This is Legion Varus. This isn't Victrix. We play by different rules. We fight a lot harder, a lot dirtier than you guys ever could conceive of. Harris and I—we've killed each other. Several times each. But we've also killed thousands of aliens."

"Your point, sir?"

"After you live together for a half-century—fighting to the death together—that changes your relationship with your subordinates. It's almost like we're a married couple or something."

Dickson seemed to think about that. Finally, he nodded.

Despite this introspection, I couldn't help but notice that he could hardly take his eyes away from the barrel of my pistol, which was still planted against his forehead.

"Is this my final lecture on the topic, sir, before I'm dispatched?"

I made a face, pulling the corners of my mouth down tightly. At last, I moved the pistol away from his forehead and tucked it back into my holster. He looked relieved.

"See now? I'm handling this the Varus way, not the Victrix way. Do you understand the difference?"

"I see things quite clearly at this point, Centurion."

"Good. Don't be thinking I won't shoot you on another day, though. We execute our men in the field just like Victrix does—just possibly for different reasons."

"Good to know."

I directed Dickson ahead after that, and he scooted. He seemed to want to get away from me as quickly as possible. That was fine by me.

We pressed onward and spread throughout the gigantic ship like a cancer. With only about fifty soldiers, we managed to sweep the ship clean and kill every Vulbite we found. Eventually, the battleship was left drifting some distance from the orbital factory, but at least it was no longer a danger to the fleet.

We found communications gear, and I was able to convince *Dominus* and other ships in the region not to destroy us.

"McGill? Seriously?" Winslade said. "I might have known that it was you flying that giant bathtub around. Do you have any idea how close you came to being blown out of the sky?"

"I'm actually kind of surprised that you didn't do it yet, sir."

"Our reluctance wasn't due to any love for the troops scurrying inside that hulk. It was because we simply had hopes of capturing her, and it appears that you've done so. That's good work, McGill—but I rather wish you'd left her in drydock."

"Not our choice, sir."

I quickly reported the action that we'd gone through including our summary execution of every Vulbite we could find aboard the ship.

"You did well," Winslade said. "We could have used a few of them to explain how the controls work, that sort of thing, but you know what? They probably wouldn't have cooperated anyway. When was the last time you saw a centipede cut a deal with an ape?"

"Not too often," I admitted. "However, there was one time down inside one of those mounds down on Dark World when—"

"Shut up, McGill. That was a rhetorical question."

"I see, Tribune. Of course."

Winslade paced on the deck of the *Dominus* bridge. He was thinking hard.

"All right," he said, "we're going to send some teleporters directly to that vessel. They'll be a relief group of technicians. Cooperate with them. Make sure they're secure."

"Uh…" I said. "When we're sure there's no threat, Tribune, sir… will we be allowed to use their teleport harnesses to return to our cohort on the orbital factory?"

Winslade chuckled at my suggestion. It was an evil sound.

"We'll see, McGill. We'll see."

-29-

To my surprise, the teleport team that came out from *Dominus* to the battleship did not include only a group of technicians and Fleet pukes. There was also among them one small, shapely female officer. She seemed to have an absurdly high rank to be part of such a mundane mission.

Galina strutted around the battleship with at least two dozen camera drones following her every move. She first demanded the techs explain to her what various sections of the ship did and what state of repair they were in. She then proceeded to talk to her camera drones, with the techs safely out of view, repeating back the information they'd just given her. She was making it look as if she'd figured out everything by herself.

"She's essentially taking credit for the entire capture," Dickson said. "I have to admit, I'm forced to admire both her form and her behavior patterns."

"She's one smooth customer all right," I said. "That's how she maintains her lofty rank."

Dickson glanced at me. "You have inside information about that, do you?"

Harris stepped up. He'd been listening in, and he wore a crap-eaters grin. "More than that," he said. He released a dirty laugh. "McGill knows just how smooth she really is—he can't keep his big hands off her. He's had countless private meetings with that snake-charming woman over the past twenty years."

I shot Harris an unpleasant look, and he stomped away. I could tell he was still stinging about our argument from earlier.

Dickson was left gaping like a fish once again. "Is that true, sir?"

"Yeah, well... I suppose it is. Turov wasn't always such a high-level officer, see. Back about twenty... no make that thirty or forty years ago, she was just another primus running around Legion Varus. She wasn't much different from the rest of us."

Dickson snorted at that. "I don't know. I've seen a number of the officers in Legion Varus. None of them quite look like that."

I laughed, taking his comment for what it was: a joke. He was right, anyway. Galina had long ago refused to store updated body scans. Somehow, probably because her father was a high government official, she'd gotten away with this.

Every time she died these days, she came back looking like she did the first day she'd signed up at age eighteen. It was weird having a relatively old, wise and downright mean soul planted inside the body of a doll-like young woman.

I decided not to tell Dickson any of this. Perhaps he would learn it on his own. Sometimes the best lessons were delivered without warning.

Hours went by as the ship was repaired. We all leaned tiredly on our rifles or sprawled on the deck. Galina was full of energy, however. She hadn't been fighting for her life, after all.

She pranced around the ship, touring every section and giving the lucky future recipients of her video the nickel tour. Once she was done, she came looking for me.

Fortunately, she was in an excellent mood.

"McGill?" she said. "There you are. I have to say, I'm impressed."

"How's that, Imperator?"

"Isn't it obvious? You actually managed to capture a valuable enemy spaceship without wrecking it entirely. That's got to be something of a first for you."

I wasn't sure, but I thought maybe I'd just been insulted. Still, as there was no advantage to acting butt-hurt about it, I grinned and stuck my thumbs into my loose belt.

"That's right, sir. I delivered it all up to you with a bow on it."

Galina smiled back. I could tell she was warming up to old McGill. A less savvy man might have bitched and moaned about her taking all the credit, but I knew that always ended up a loser.

I decided when she showed up to give her the line about it being a gift with her name on it, and what's more, that I was pleased to give it to her. She was the kind of woman who really liked gifts, and I figured it was a good place to work some of the old McGill magic.

Galina stepped close, and she tapped my chest three or four times with one small finger. "We'll have to talk about this later… but I'm moving on now."

"Huh…" I said, "are you talking about returning to *Dominus*?"

"No. I'm going to the orbital factory. This operation isn't over with yet."

I was surprised, and she caught my expression.

"I know, I know," she said. "Normally, I would sit on *Dominus*, but I'm avoiding that duty now. I'm going to be serving in the headquarters unit on the factory until it has been completely captured."

"Wow."

This wasn't her normal mode of operation. Galina liked to stand well back from the front lines. She preferred to direct battles from inside a comfortable office.

Thinking about it, I felt I knew why she was doing this. She had just sent Merton back to Earth in her place, thereby dodging arrest and abuse. If Drusus or whoever was behind the arrest orders refused to accept Merton as a sacrificial lamb, then they might come looking for her.

They also might send orders for her to come back in from the field. That would be much harder to implement if she was on the front lines, rather than sitting in the lounge on Lavender Deck on a nice safe ship.

"The headquarters unit, huh?" I said. "That has possibilities. They'll probably have a cantina setup by now at the very least."

She smiled instead of snarling at me. Again, that was quite a change. Galina had always been a woman who could blow hot or cold like a summer rainstorm on top of the mountain.

"Maybe I'll take you with me," she said.

I half-expected to be executed and revived on the orbital factory with the rest of my cohort, but it didn't play out that way. Probably because Galina was with us, we were allowed to take the teleport harnesses from the techs who are working feverishly to get the battleship underway.

Recharging the harnesses and redirecting their coordinates for a nearby destination, we pressed the buttons and reappeared on the orbital factory. I had my rifle up and ready, but I didn't need it. I looked around as did the rest of my unit's survivors. We were in the midst of the grand headquarters unit.

"We're going to like this, boys," I said, and we did. We were allowed to lounge in relative comfort. We didn't get bunks or anything crazy like that, but we did get sleeping bags on floaters, clean clothes and fresh water.

For a Legion Varus trooper these things were like gifts from heaven. After I'd gotten cleaned up and overseen the revival status of my unit, which was more than half dead at this point, I went hunting for Galina herself.

I found her in a private bubble-tent near the rear of the encampment. She was busy editing down dozens of video feeds. Every one of them pictured her explaining the brilliance of her conquest of the battleship.

Galina was still smiling at me, even though I was interrupting her editing session. That was a bit of a shocker.

Damn. Was this really the same girl who'd been doing her worst to have me tortured and killed repeatedly just a few short months ago? It felt a little weird, but as a male of questionable character who was permanently dedicated to the female form, I decided to go with the flow.

Accordingly, I didn't interrupt her work by talking or falling asleep and snoring on her cot. No sir. Instead, I stayed out of the way while she worked on her video, I waited patiently, only raiding her drinks and her snacks.

I squatted on the floor of her bubble tent until she gestured for me to get up and sit on her cot. It was a single-wide affair, but I didn't mind. I got up and sat on it, and soon found myself stretching out.

My big shoes hung over the end by ten centimeters or more. Still, Galina made no complaint. She worked on her video until it was finished. Then she deep-linked the whole sales pitch straight to Central.

"Do you think it'll work?" I asked her when she was done.

She glanced at me and frowned. "I hope so—and you should hope so, too."

"How's that?"

"Because I'm going to be in a much worse mood if I'm killed and held prisoner in nonexistence at Central like you were."

I chuckled, and I smiled. My eyes were half-closed, and I was feeling sleepy. It'd been a long day with a lot of hard slogging action. Now, with some whiskey and chips in me, I was feeling mighty good.

"McGill…?" she asked watching me.

"Yes sir?"

"I think we need to reestablish our partnership."

My eyes popped back wide open, and I looked at her. She appeared to be serious.

"Uh…" I said. "How's that?"

"We've always accomplished great things together in the past… but I feel that we've moved apart."

"You don't say… you mean like, that part where you were having a hog chain me to a wall and beat me to death over and over again? Then the part where you left me dead for about a year?"

Galina rolled her eyes. "Yes, yes, she said. Let's not bicker and argue about details. Let's think about the future."

"Hmm," I said, "the future… You mean like, the rest of this operation?"

"Not just that," she said. "I'm talking about for the duration of Vengeful Skies."

"Uh… what?"

"Vengeful Skies is the name of this campaign. Didn't you know that?"

"No, sir. I guess I've been out of the loop what with being dead and then all caught up in the fighting and such.

"Right, right. Well, it's really Drusus' idea originally. Although I might be able to take some of the credit for it."

I knew *steal* would fit better than *take* in that sentence, but I didn't snort. I didn't choke, either. I just listened earnestly like a true believer.

"He believes that our fleets and the orbital platforms protecting our planets are all that matters in this war with Rigel," she explained. "Normally, we fight on a planet—a single planet. The point is to bring your fleet to that planet, to defeat all enemy spaceborne forces, and then invade with troops or bomb their cities or whatever."

I nodded, and I poured myself another drink. I pushed one into her hand, and she took it absently.

"This time, however," she continued, "we're facing a true rival power. Rigel's empire spans over several star systems, just as ours does. Therefore, our fleets are much more important."

"I get that, but it doesn't make me like Fleet pukes anymore, though."

"You don't have to, but I suppose as Earth's list of planetary conquests continues to grow, it's only natural that the fleet gains importance."

"Okay, okay—Vengeful Skies," I said. "So, we all work for the Fleet now?"

"Not exactly," she said. "But on this campaign, we're going to be fighting ship-to-ship and taking critical orbital facilities like this one."

Thinking it over, I could see this new point of view. We were in a bigger war. We weren't going to win this by crushing one army on one planet. There was too much involved. The Big Sky project, the protective dome over Rigel—there were all kinds of targets.

"Troops are still important," Galina continued. "Today, for example, you captured a battleship. That couldn't have been done with just fusion cannons."

We sipped our drinks for a minute or so, and Galina kept giving me funny looks. I waited, knowing I didn't need to ask what was on her mind. She was going to tell me, whether I wanted to hear it or not.

"Enough about Vengeful Skies," she said. "We have something deeper to discuss."

"I'm all ears, sir."

"You have mentioned several times that you still harbor some resentment for my unfair treatment of you a year ago."

"Yeah, well, those whips did sting, sir."

"I'm sure they did. But now the situation has changed. I believe that I'm now also a target in this purge of officers"

"Oh…" suddenly, the light went on inside my dusty fridge. To Galina, the mere possibility she was in trouble was truly frightening. If one lash ever landed on her pretty behind, I'd wager she'd consider that more of a tragedy than any dozen torture-deaths of mine.

"Someone is looking for disloyal characters in the military," she continued. "And they're searching for them in a chain that started with you. I'm in that chain, as was Winslade and Wurtenberger."

"I think you're right about that, sir. Graves, hell, he's *still* dead."

She nodded grimly.

I'd still never told her anything about the bunker, or the fact that I'd found it and lied my ass off about the fact to everyone who asked. I'd also let other pertinent things slip my mind—like the fact that Graves had made certain admissions about having been in the Unification Wars and all.

Galina was paranoid, and I now knew what she was up to. She hadn't brought me into her tent, cozied-up with me and let me drink and snore without a good reason. She was looking for allies. She wanted people who were under the same threat she was under to join forces with her.

"You know what you need, sir?" I asked, as if getting a bright idea for the first time today.

"What's that?"

"A counterpunch. If someone comes after you, they should damn-well expect you to go after them."

Galina got up and began pacing around the bubble tent while I rested on her cot. She had folded up the computer table she'd used to edit her videos and set it to one side. That's what gave her enough room to pace.

I was tired, so I tipped my hat down over my eyes. But I gently nudged up the brim so that one of my eyes was exposed. That way, I could watch her as she moved.

The woman was mesmerizing. She always had been, even years back. When she'd first come back to life young, she'd had a nearly perfect figure. After multiple surgeries and a few updated body scans, she now had a *provably* perfect figure. At least, it was about the best that Earth's modern medical workers could sculpt.

I had to admit, being a man of both low standards and low self-respect, I was beginning to entertain certain thoughts while I watched her strutting around in circles.

She didn't seem to notice as she was thinking hard and worrying even harder.

"McGill," she said at last, "both our asses are on the line. This time it's not just you, and it's not just me. It's both of us. Someone means to take us out. You mentioned me needing a counterpunch and I think you're right. We need to find out who they are and take them out *first*. Are you with me?"

I thought about it seriously for a moment. "If this effort will help save Graves, I'd be more interested."

Galina squinted at me. "Sure. It will save Graves, Wurtenberger, you me—even Winslade. What do you say?"

I sat up on her bunk, then I stood up. I approached her and took her small hand in one of my paws.

"Okay Galina," I said, "but if I do this, if I swear to help you through thick and thin, you've got to do the same for me."

"Done," she said. She tugged at her hand to pull it away from me, but I held on.

"I'm not finished yet. I need more than that, because I'm not really in this anymore. I've already been let off by Drusus the consul of all Earth—you know about that, right?"

Galina looked down, and she frowned. "I know what you're saying. You've been pardoned, but I haven't yet. You're also saying Drusus really hates me."

I shrugged. I hadn't actually said any of that. But I had implied it because it was all true. "So," I said, "you're going to owe me one after this."

She squinted up at me. "Are you talking about sex?"

"No, no," I laughed. "The sex—that's all assumed."

She slapped me then, but I barely felt it. I smiled at her. She pursed her lips and gave me a tiny frown.

"No, I'm talking about something bigger than just that," I continued. "You're going to owe me one."

"Owe you what?"

"I don't know," I lied. "You're going to have to forgive me for something, maybe... or you'll have to help me out when I need it at some point in the future—even when you don't want to."

"A favor. You're asking for a favor."

"That's right. Deal?"

Galina thought hard for a second. Finally, she nodded her head. "You've got your deal, McGill. I owe you one."

"Now what?" I asked.

She smiled, then she got up on her tiptoes, and she kissed me. The night went by very pleasantly after that.

-30-

After capturing the drydock, which contained several large vessels, Legion Varus was feeling proud. Drusus himself came out to join the campaign the very next day. He arrived via gateway posts at our headquarters unit. That was quite surprising, as top-level officials rarely ventured out into space when the legions were fighting and dying.

Drusus began holding meetings with all kinds of people the second he showed up. Neither Galina nor I made the list, which was a sheer relief to me. I went back to my unit, planning to get drunk.

Back at my unit's camp, Kivi was working on mapping our next advancement deeper into enemy territory. Each day had turned into essentially a long jogging session, hopping along in low gravity that was less than that of our Moon.

We were advancing rapidly like rows of ants—soldier ants that hopped like kangaroos. Each day carried us farther and farther into the complex. At times, the enemy Vulbites would put up some resistance. Usually, they were factory workers who had somehow armed themselves. We burned them away without too much trouble. Our progress had taken us about a third of the way around the ring so far, and we were advancing ahead of schedule.

It was on a Saturday evening that I got a visit from Galina. I was all smiles to see her. I dared to hope she was finally wanting to see a little bit more of old McGill.

I nodded to her and began talking even before she did. "Hello there, Imperator," I said. "Are you checking up on your fastest-moving unit?"

"No," she said, "I'm checking up on a fool who has managed to ruin both his future and mine."

"Uh…" I said. "Who are we talking about, exactly…?"

She rolled her eyes at me. "Drusus has noted how fast we're advancing. Hegemony has taken note as well, and they've declared you and I to be noncritical personnel since there's little resistance. They're stepping up their demands for our submission to arrest."

"Oh… that's not good."

"It gets worse. Drusus has asked that we attend one last, special meeting. Let's go—the meeting is now."

Galina was very nervous, but I sighed, anticipating the great boredom that awaited me. She had good reason to worry, of course. She'd been dodging requests from Hegemony to report back to Earth for what was called 'processing'. She'd received a number of stern notes that demanded she make various statements and deliver her testimony before an investigatory body.

Galina was having none of their shit. I recalled that she'd been absent when her father had shown up with his little black box to do a swearing-in loyalty test. I was pretty sure now that her father had told her to steer clear of that fateful meeting, which had resulted in Wurtenberger's execution and indefinite storage.

During operation Vengeful Skies, she'd stayed in the field and close to the front lines. She'd even arranged to die once—which I thought she might have done partly to get herself young again. She'd physically aged to about twenty-five over recent years, and so a solid death and a good revive was exactly what she needed to look her best again.

As the action at Dark World was winding down, she'd gone to extreme measures to generate more excuses to send back to Hegemony. Tonight, with Consul Drusus in physical attendance, there was no more evasion possible. He had summoned us both to a quiet, secure module. The module was located aboard *Dominus*, giving us no excuse to ditch him.

"We could hijack a lifter, maybe," she whispered to me as we walked along the passages to learn our fate. "If we had to, we could even crash it into something."

"That's just crazy talk, girl," I told her. "I'm not doing that. I wouldn't even know how."

She flashed me something she had in her pocket, and I knew it in an instant. It was the Galactic Key, a highly illegal object that could hack just about anything.

"Put that thing away," I hissed at her. "Get ahold of yourself."

"That's easy for you to say. You've already been pardoned by our fresh-faced dictator. I haven't."

We reached the module then, and the guards spotted us. Primus Bob himself was there, ushering us inside. Galina looked like a kid who was about to get her shots for school, but she followed me inside.

Once we were in a quiet conference area, the door clanged shut behind us. It was ominously heavy and made of metal.

"Nice setup you've got here, sir," I said. "Uh…what should I be calling you now? Your lordship or something…?"

"Sir or Consul Drusus is fine, McGill. Have a seat."

I flumped myself down in a chair and smiled at him as if I didn't have a care in the world. Galina on the other hand, walked in the way a cat might enter a laundromat with all the dryers going. She seemed to suspect every item of furniture was a possible danger, or perhaps even an alien device bent on her destruction.

She finally sat down where Drusus suggested she should, and she nodded to him. "So glad we could be of service, Consul."

Drusus made a dramatic gesture. The conference table was smart-furniture, and it caught the feed from his tapper. The table lit up, and we saw Galina walking through the battleship and talking about each of its systems. It was one of the promotional videos that she'd sent back to Earth.

"Again, McGill," Drusus said, turning down the volume and looking to me. "You were leading the group that captured a critical vessel. It's the largest of all those that we found under construction here at Dark World. More importantly, it's the only one that wasn't destroyed when we attempted to capture it."

"That's right, sir." I said proudly. "My unit just happened to be the lucky ones to get on the hull and crawl inside. We made the best of it."

Drusus nodded thoughtfully. He turned toward Galina next. "And you played the part of the Legion's spokesman. You did an excellent job of explaining to Hegemony how important this military conquest really was."

Galina was red-faced over not being given the first and only credit for the capture, but she managed not to complain about it. "Glad to be of service, Consul."

Drusus nodded again. "In my mind, this makes you two critical to the success of Vengeful Skies. Unfortunately, you're both wanted for processing back on Earth."

I pretended to be surprised. I even feigned outrage. "Huh?" I said. "What the hell for? I thought I'd been pardoned over all that nonsense."

"You were pardoned and are considered immune to prosecution for a specific crime, McGill. But a new investigation was launched, with all new charges."

I flumped back into my seat again and crossed my arms. "I'm sorry to say it, sir, but this sounds like bullshit to me. The truth is Legion Varus is the most loyal and successful outfit that Earth has. Everybody back home should know that by now."

Drusus frowned and looked at Galina.

She looked like she was about to wet herself, but she managed to speak. "I believe our success on the battlefield speaks for itself, sir."

Drusus seemed to like both of our answers. "I agree," he said after thinking it over for a moment. "As the consul of Earth, I have delayed this investigation and refused to allow Hegemony officials to interrupt this operation. Leverage is the problem now."

He began working on his table display again. A long list of officer names came up. There were around thirty names on the list. Graves was on there, as well as Wurtenberger. Many of them were in Legion Varus, while there were others I'd never heard of.

"Damnation," I said. "Are all these guys accused of treason?"

"Yes," he said. "More names are added every day."

Galina and I glanced at each other. We were both worrying inside. What could we do against a determined witch-hunt coming out of Hegemony? We were like ants in comparison to some of the names on that list.

I grunted unhappily. "As my father used to say, life always ends up with the little guy getting stepped on."

"While you were fighting here at Dark World," Drusus said, "it was easy to put things off. The problem is this stage of the campaign is wrapping up. We're going beyond Dark World, but Hegemony sees this pause as an opportunity for you two to return to Earth. I need a reason to keep stalling the investigators on your behalf. Have you got any ideas?"

"Why no, Consul, sir," I said. "We're no good at stuff like stalling. All we know how to do is fight and die to expand the glory of Earth."

It was a bullshit answer, and Drusus barely glanced at me when I uttered it. Instead, he turned his eyes toward Galina.

She was looking her best. So cute and super-young. Of course, she was far from innocent, and she was certainly full of an evil energy.

"Tell them we'll turn ourselves in after operation Vengeful Skies is completed," she said.

"Interesting," Drusus said, "you don't think your work is done out here?"

"Not at all, Consul. We won't be ready to return to Earth until Rigel lays at our feet."

"That can work, but the problem we're really having is one of timing. If there's a large delay between the time this system is under control, and the moment we commence our next step of the campaign, Hegemony will want to intervene. They're claiming that if you're found innocent, you'll be back to work the next day."

That made me brighten. "Is there any chance of that? That we'll be found innocent, I mean?"

Galina and Drusus both glanced at me.

"No, James," Galina said gently. "That's never how these things work."

"Oh…"

They began to talk, discussing various options. I soon grew bored, and my mind wandered. After a bit, I got an idea.

"Hey," I said, "I know what we can do."

Galina had been in the middle of a useless speech. She looked at me like she wanted me to shut up, but Drusus appeared interested.

"Let's hear it, McGill."

"How about this?" I said. "How about we end this campaign here at Dark World right now? Just declare it to be over and done with."

Drusus looked interested, but Galina shook her head. "The enemy hasn't surrendered yet. They're bugs. We'll have to root them out from every nook and cranny of this vast station. Declaring victory won't fool anyone."

Drusus lifted a finger. "What if we made a decisive strike? What would bring the Vulbites to the negotiating table?"

Galina smiled. It was an evil smile. "I like it. Instead of slogging a step at a time all the way around this massive orbital factory, we'll show the Vulbites we mean business."

"Uh…" I said, not liking where things were going.

"How exactly will we do that?" Drusus asked.

"We'll use the broadsides."

"Genocide?" Drusus asked. "Are you actually suggesting…?"

"It's going to take many months to conquer the surface of this planet. In fact, just running around this ring shooting these giant insects is going to take several slow months. Do you really want to know how long it would take—how many lives will be lost—to conquer all their underground nests? Rigel might gather a fleet and chase us off before we're halfway done."

Drusus seemed conflicted, but he finally gritted his teeth. "You're right. I wasn't looking forward to the final stages of this campaign… but we can't let it drag on. We'll strike the planet itself. Just once, and hard."

My mouth fell open, and it stayed that way.

"Exactly," Galina said. "We'll take out the smallest of their ant hills down there."

"Millions will die..." Drusus said.

He sounded like he really gave a shit. I was impressed.

Galina shrugged. "How else do you conquer a world full of disgusting hive creatures? They won't surrender until they see there's no hope."

"All right," Drusus said. "We'll contact the Vulbites and demand that they surrender. If they don't comply, blow up the smallest of their hives."

I was sitting there dumbfounded. My jaw was hanging wide open, and I was breathing through my mouth like a fish on the dock. "Whoa, whoa, whoa! We're talking about millions of civilian deaths, here."

"*Now* you object, McGill?" Galina said. "Have you forgotten that you blew up a hive here once before, just to save your own legion?"

"Well... yeah..."

She was right, of course. My cohort had been trapped inside a nest, and with no body-recovery possible, they were all permed. I'd participated in an unscheduled bombardment back then, and it had been pretty messy. It wasn't a good memory. "I guess I'm not one to talk..."

"That's right, you aren't," Galina said, and she turned back to Drusus. "Let's end this thing now and move on. Any other action will risk losing the entire campaign."

Reluctantly, Drusus agreed. I felt kind of wadded-up inside, but after we left, Galina was giddy.

"We did it!" she said. "We got out of a perming!"

"Yeah... but the Vulbites are—"

"Come on, McGill. Are you seriously going to cry yourself to sleep over a million bugs? They're disgusting. Besides, they'll recover. They can breed almost as fast as we can revive our troops."

Glumly, I followed her back to our part of the ship. I wondered if the Vulbites would hate us forever after this, even if they did surrender. Someday, I sincerely hoped their ships wouldn't be crowding in orbit over our cities. If that day ever came, I figured they would wreak their vengeance without hesitation—and Earth would deserve it.

"Wait a second!" I said, coming up with an idea. I did a U-turn and marched back to Drusus' module.

Primus Bob gave me a fight at the door, and Galina herself, suspecting a coming disaster, tried to interpose her tiny body. None of this worked out for either of them.

Drusus poked his head out of the door, frowning. "You people are making so much noise, I can't even hear my conference call."

He was already into another meeting. That, right there, was why I didn't want more rank. I'd rather die a couple of extra times a year than face that.

"Consul, sir, can I have a moment more of your time?"

Drusus eyed me and Galina, who was standing in front of me, teeth bared and breathing hard. Primus Bob looked like he was in her camp.

"All right, come in—just you this time."

He put his conference on hold and frowned at me. "What is it, McGill? Make it quick."

"How about this? How about you send us on toward another target?"

"What are you talking about, McGill?"

"Galina—uh, Imperator Turov and me. You can simply order us to go off to the next target on your list. Don't tell anyone, just do it. After all, things are about wrapped up here on Dark World."

"It's… not a bad idea, but I don't see how it will make much difference. If we force the Vulbites to surrender quickly, then—"

"But sir, that's exactly it. You won't have to blow up their hives at all! You can just get us out of here on a special mission, and—"

Drusus was already shaking his head. "It won't work. There's more here than your investigation to worry about. I'll tell you what, though, I like your idea. It will give Hegemony less time to react. I'll write up orders sending you away, then we'll bring this chapter to a close by bombing the Vulbites.

Two good ideas in one day—excellent work, McGill. Now, get out of here."

He sat down and began scribbling with his finger on his desk. I stood there with my mouth hanging open.

After a few moments, he looked up again and sighed. "What is it now, McGill? I have people waiting."

"I know, sir. I'm truly sorry about that," I lied. "I... I just can't stop thinking about what's going to happen to the Vulbites."

Drusus sighed. "I understand. War isn't pretty. Just be glad that you're not in my shoes, McGill. These decisions weigh on a man's soul."

After that, he threw me out of his office for good.

-31-

Galina was not very happy with me. "Why did you have to go back there and make another suggestion on your own? Why couldn't you just shut up?"

"I don't know. I had to try to stop a couple of million Vulbite deaths. It seemed like a raw deal for the locals just to keep our two butts out of prison."

"We're going to have to do that anyway to conquer this place. We might as well do it now and get it over with. If we strike them really hard, and we let them know who's boss, they will surrender. Otherwise, we'll just end up killing more of them."

I had to wonder if she was right. After all, prolonged wars always ended up killing more people and blowing more stuff up. If one side or the other submitted quickly, it would all be over, and the outcome would not be much changed.

When we returned to headquarters, she was no longer in an amorous mood. My hopes for another night of passion were dashed.

The next morning, she sent my unit back to the front lines. I had to endure countless giggles and smirks from my own troops. They somehow knew that I'd been spending nights with Galina.

"This isn't the first time," Leeson said.

"And it probably won't be the last," Harris finished.

Dickson looked at these two in alarm. He made a throat-cutting gesture behind their backs, suggesting I should execute them for insubordination and for razzing me in front of the troops.

I did nothing of that kind. I walked proudly past them all, ignoring them, and strode over to Kivi. She laid out some plans for the next day's march—but the orders to move out never came. Instead, Galina arrived in a state of near panic.

"You idiot," she whispered to me.

All around us, troops stared. At least they were trying not to look like they were staring—but they were.

"Uh… what'd I do this time?"

"You told Drusus to step things up. To announce his intentions to move on to the next phase of Vengeful Skies."

"Yeah… so what?"

"Hegemony has seized upon this excuse to send out agents to arrest us."

I smiled. "Is that all? I can handle some hogs. Don't worry about it."

She shook her head. "No. They're sending back Captain Merton with new orders and troops to back him up. We're talking MPs and… and… I don't think we'll be able to stop him."

"What about Drusus?"

She slapped my chest. I barely felt it, but there were some twitters of laughter behind me.

"Drusus has stopped answering my calls. He doesn't care. Maybe he's decided to give up on us."

I was beginning to understand her freaked out state of mind. "What are we going to do? I mean, besides get permed?"

She had wild, evil eyes. She was thinking hard. I could always tell when her mind had gone to a dark place and lingered there for too long.

"We're going to do *something*," she said. "We're going to do something drastic and we're going to do it right now."

She set off, marching down the passages. I glanced back at my troops, and I thought about just letting her go, but then I walked in her wake. After all, I did have something to do with this. Maybe I could talk some sense into her.

"Uh… where are we going?"

"To *Dominus*," she said. "We have to get there before Merton does."

When we were far from my unit, all alone in the echoing pipes and chambers of the great factory, Galina stopped. She pulled out a tangle of wires and straps and put it on.

"A teleport harness?" I asked.

"Yes, of course. Do you know a way of getting to *Dominus* faster?"

The transport ship was in orbit over Dark World, just like we were, but it wasn't docked to the factory or anything like that. It was safely moored something like ten thousand kilometers away.

I gave myself a scratch and watched her curiously. "Well, if you're going to teleport out there—how am I supposed to join you?"

She shrugged. "I don't know. The easiest way would be to get yourself killed. Go tease a Vulbite or something. I'll put a revival order in for you aboard the ship."

I didn't much care for her idea. For one thing, I was wearing my Rigellian armor, and I didn't want to lose it. I also suspected that I was going to need it when we got to *Dominus,* anyway.

"How about we teleport together?"

"With one harness?" she asked, frowning.

"Sure, it's a short hop."

"That's going to require very close contact, and it's dangerous." she said.

"Not as dangerous as getting myself killed just to be revived back on *Dominus.*"

We argued back and forth for a minute, but I finally reached out and plucked the teleport harness out of her hands.

She squawked a bit. "What are you doing? That's mine."

"Look," I said, "I have the greater mass. I'll put it on, and I'll get a good tight grab on you. We'll both land on *Dominus'* deck in two shakes of a lamb's tail."

She complained and carried on, but at last she agreed. I wrapped my big arms around her, pulling her body to me while she wriggled in irritation.

Before she could shoot me with her pistol or give me any clear orders that I couldn't easily disobey, I activated the harness. We flashed out of existence.

A few moments later we appeared aboard *Dominus*. We were on Gray Deck, surrounded by surprised techs.

Galina didn't care. She stepped free of my grasping hands and cracked me a good one across the face. The blow really hurt more than it should have—and I realized that she had gotten her pistol out. She'd pistol-whipped me in the jaw.

I rubbed at the spot, which would bruise up nicely by nightfall. "That kind of hurt," I said.

"I should frigging hope so. My hair—just look at my hair!"

When I did, I saw that the outermost layer of Galina's hair had burned spots. Apparently, the jump had maxed out the safe limits of a team-teleport.

When you teleported an oversized payload through space too far, it was unsafe. The extra hitchhiker was often burned to a crisp. Of course, that normally required taking a longer jump, something like a hundred lightyears, not just 100,000 kilometers. Still though, there was always a limit. Galina's hair was sending up blue wisps of smoke, which definitely indicated we'd pushed too far.

"Your cockamamie idea ruined my hair," she complained.

"I'm real sorry about that, sir. Maybe you could wear a wig or something."

She lifted her pistol. I wasn't sure if she meant to shoot me or maybe crack me one in the face again. After making a sound of frustration, she lowered the gun and holstered it.

"I should stuff you into the ship's recyclers, just on principle," she said, "but I'm not going to do it. We don't have time for that, we have a mission to perform."

I wasn't quite sure what mission she was talking about, but I was pretty sure it was going to be extreme in nature.

-32-

An alert came through on Galina's tapper, and she halted to read it. "No… oh no…"

"What's wrong now?"

"Dammit! Captain Merton is back. He's just arrived aboard *Dominus*. We have to make our move immediately."

Galina marched through the ship's passageways, walking faster than you would think a short-legged girl could manage. Even I had to lengthen my stride to keep up with her.

As I followed along like a gorilla in her wake, I asked her several times where we were headed. She gave me no informative responses. Occasionally, she would flip me off, giving me a peek at her middle finger over her shoulder. She didn't even bother to glance back at me.

She was working her tapper furiously, too busy to talk. She had something in mind, of course, some kind of scheme. I dared to hope it wouldn't involve millions of deaths.

We climbed a steep titanium staircase, then another. We were heading upward, and we were avoiding the lifts. Could she be trying to hide our destination from prying eyes? Maybe she thought that new-fangled behavioral warning software might tip off our victims.

Whatever the case, we kept on climbing up and up, and I realized we had to be heading all the way to Gold Deck. That's where *Dominus* kept her all-important Command Center.

I began to worry a bit as we got closer to the top. Would she ask me to assassinate Merton again? She'd done so before, but at that time, I'd refused to comply. This time might be different, and that's what had me worried.

Merton was in the right, of course. Any military officer following orders from Hegemony would agree. He could arrest us, and it would all be legal. But the undeniable fact was he'd started working with the mysterious investigators. The same nameless officials who'd been following me and so many other officers around the galaxy. That definitely painted Merton as a target of suspicion.

Before we got all the way up to Gold Deck, Galina decided to stop off on a storage level. This place wasn't often visited. Walking through the hallways, she used her rank to scare off any of the hog-like Fleet people we ran into.

After a few minutes, I realized where she was headed, and I became even more alarmed. "Whoa, Imperator," I said, "let's not do this."

She finally stopped and looked up at me. "Don't get cold feet now, James. We are already in this—we're in this deep. If you want to die again under whips and probes, you can do it on your own. I'm not going down that way."

"But we've got a whole shitload of Fleet-pukes aboard *Dominus*. We can't just kill them all. We'll have to get them to cooperate if we try to take over the ship."

"Then we'll have to do some convincing."

She turned away and marched off again. I stood there, indecisive for a few seconds. Finally, making unhappy sounds, I followed her.

She glanced back and gave me a thin smile. "Don't worry. This will work," she said. "Fleet people aren't like Varus legionnaires. They can be cowed. Just follow my lead, and back me up."

Sighing, I followed her to the back of the storage area. There, in a hidden compartment, a very special machine was parked. Its kind weren't often used these days, as they'd long ago been deemed too expensive. According to Hegemony's accountants, flesh and blood was always cheaper.

Galina dropped the hidden wall, and a gleaming monstrosity of metal and polymers stared back at us. It was tall, about three meters in height and weighed damn-near a ton.

It was a dragon. A fighting machine that amounted to a walking, death-bringing automaton. When a pilot was inside, it resembled a robot, but it was really an exoskeletal combat suit.

Sometimes, the legions still used dragons as auxiliary pieces of armored cavalry. They'd lead ground troops into battle, taking abuse that would destroy armored men. Unfortunately, they'd been destroyed at too great a rate for the weak stomachs of the budget-men back home.

Most of the dragons had therefore been phased out—but Galina had set one apart long ago. The last time I'd seen this thing move was during the Edge World campaign.

Galina held the Galactic Key to a sensor pad, high up on one of its legs and the hatch popped open. She sniffed experimentally. "Did you ever clean Winslade's guts out of this thing?"

"Uh…" I said, giving my ear a scratch. "I don't remember. It was a long time ago."

She looked disgusted. "Well, we're way past that. There's no time for niceties today. Step aside."

Reluctantly, I did as she commanded, and she climbed in.

The dragon looked like it was in pretty good shape. Examining the knuckles on the right arm actuator, I thought to see a few brown traces of old dried blood. Could that be part of what Winslade had left behind? Maybe it was.

Galina grunted as she squeezed into the back of the thing and wriggled into the cockpit. She was a perfect fit, because it had been built for someone of her small stature.

"Unplug me," she said.

Shaking my head, which was full of regrets and misgivings, I did as she ordered. Once disconnected from its outlet, the dragon automatically tucked its own cord away into the leg structure.

Galina started the thing, which purred rather than roared. She experimentally revved the motor and worked some of the actuators.

"Damn," she said, "it's been a long time since I've walked around in one of these things."

"You want me to do it instead?" I asked.

"Hell no. First of all, you wouldn't fit without an interior rebuild. Secondly, I don't trust you to do what must be done today."

"Look, Galina… I don't know about this."

"Shut up. Do you know what I haven't found yet?"

"Huh?"

Galina had something in her small hand, lifting it up out of the head section, which was still open for her to gain entrance. She held an object that looked like a seashell. I knew it to be the Galactic Key.

"James," she said, "I'm going to trust you with this. Don't piss me off, because if you do, I'll cut your head off." She made a few scissoring motions with the claw-like grippers of the machine for emphasis. Then, she tossed the Galactic Key in my direction.

I caught it, but it bounced a time or two before settling into my palms. I shoved it into a pocket. I was still wearing my black armor. I'd been fighting in it for weeks. Thinking that over, I realized that with a dragon and my Rigellian armor, the two of us were a fairly formidable force.

That was doubly true when dealing with a bunch of weak-willed, poorly-trained Fleet pukes.

"What are we going to do, exactly?" I asked. Part of me dreaded the answer.

"We're going to take over this ship, and we're going to kill anyone who gets in our way."

"That's pretty much what I figured…"

Galina put the dragon into gear then, and she began to walk. She was unsteady at first, but soon she had the hang of it again. Her long metal tail lashed automatically, balancing the machine's weight.

Her two raptor-like legs did a lot of squeaking. They needed some fresh oil in my opinion. The squeal of gears and the whine of electric motors filled the passages. The evil machine was on the move.

I followed her, regretting all my recent choices. Galina and I had shared a bed recently, but this was taking things a bit far for a rebound romance sort of thing. After all, was I really obligated to slaughter Fleet people just because I'd slept with her lately? Sure, I'd done stranger things on my own in the past—but not usually for the purposes of self-preservation.

We finally entered an elevator as the stairs were a tight squeeze for the dragon. The ride up to Gold Deck was a strange one. Galina was dry-firing her guns and check-listing her armament.

"This thing is so much fun," she said. "I'd forgotten the feeling of raw power that it brings."

For my own part, I sealed up my suit, lowering the visor and turning on all the combat systems. My nearly impenetrable suit of armor was ready for battle.

Galina tended to get carried away in that suit. I knew this from sad experience. Consequently, I was already thinking of ways I could get her out of that dragon if I had to. I figured the only way I could do it would be through the use of the Galactic Key. Maybe I could touch it to the back of the dragon, when she was distracted by the fun of running down and murdering crewmen.

After that, if I could just get one hand in there, I could yank her butt out of the cockpit. That might be worth it to stop a murderous rampage, but it might not work.

The problem would be the minute I tried to open up her combat suit, she would know she was in trouble. She'd turn on me when it came down to it. Then it would be one soldier in his star-stuff armor against a dragon.

I kind of figured that I wouldn't win. The dragon was just too strong, too well-armed. She had grenades in there—all sorts of stuff.

We reached Gold Deck, interrupting my thoughts. We widened our stance and raised weapons, just in case. Like every elevator in history, it took a damnably long time to open.

"What's wrong?" Galina asked.

"Give it a second."

"Is it jammed or something?"

We waited twenty long seconds, but the doors still didn't open. They didn't open at all.

"Force it open," Galina said. "I'll cover you."

"Uh… How am I going to do that, sir?"

"Use the key, you idiot."

"Oh yeah, right." I pulled out the Galactic Key. I rubbed it on the elevator panel and it lit up. I pushed a few buttons but there was still no action.

Finally, I ripped open the control panel and touched the key to the actuators. The door responded, opening a crack. The far side seemed dark, except for playing flashlights. Someone was there, waiting for us.

"It's busted, sir."

"Dammit, what is Merton playing at?" Galina's dragon lurched forward, and her big metal claws extended.

I stepped out of the way, and an awful screeching sound began. She rammed her claws into the crack, and she began to force the doors open. The motor inside the battle suit revved, and the doors groaned as they were forced open.

When she had them open far enough for a person's hand to pass through, a blaze of gunfire erupted. Plasma bolts splashed into the elevator car. I stayed clear to the right, but Galina was cursing and taking some hits on her dragon's front armor.

"Those fuckers," she said, "someone tipped them off."

She shoved a tube from her chest area up against the hole that she'd forced open. There were three popping sounds, and I heard canisters bouncing around in the elevator lobby. There were shouts of dismay and alarm. Moments later, explosions rocked the deck.

I shoved the butt of my morph-rifle into the crack and together the two of us forced the doors open. Once we'd pried them back a ways, something broke inside the doors. They slid aside with a clang.

It was the sound of doom for the crewmen in the lobby. Galina strode ahead, and I followed in her wake.

-33-

When we stepped boldly into the elevator lobby, we were immediately hosed down by gunfire. Bolts came at us from two directions. Both sides of the elevator had been staked out by Marines.

They blazed away, and I was hit by so many rounds that I was sent staggering. I almost fell—but they couldn't penetrate my armor. Sure, that gunfire hurt. It was like being beaten by pillows with rocks at the center of them—not comfortable. But the important thing was they couldn't take me down.

I switched my morph-rifle to full-assault mode and turned to my right. I returned fire and three unarmored crewmen were gunned down. The rest ran. Galina did the same, aiming her weapons to the left.

In less than a minute, it was all over. There was nothing but smoke, dead people and holes in the wall as far as the eye could see.

"Holy crap," I said, "we must have killed a dozen of them."

"Sixteen by my count," she said. "If you include those fools on the deck over there. They ate my grenades right at the start."

That had to be most of the Marine compliment that Merton kept on Gold Deck. I hoped he hadn't brought up more from engineering.

Galina started marching her dragon again. She was definitely in a killing mood. Before we left the elevator, she blasted the elevator controls. It wasn't going to be moving again until there had been some serious repairs.

"Reinforcements can still come up the stairs," I told her.

"Let them. We're going to kill them all if they do."

We marched toward the bridge itself. Officers walked out of their offices as we passed by, but these were mostly staffers—the kind of soldiers who rarely fired a gun, and when they did, it was always at the gun range.

For the most part, they looked shocked, and their mouths fell open at the sight of Galina's dragon. Some dropped coffee cups from numb fingers. A few scrambled out a pistol, but none of them dared take a shot as we strode by, ignoring them all. They weren't the kind of men who were going to be a problem.

Reaching the bridge, we found the main doors were closed and securely locked.

"Use the key," Galina said.

Taking a deep breath and bracing myself, I did as she ordered.

The doors had not been jammed or disabled, so they opened easily. Two Marines were posted on either side of the entrance. They shouted and fell back, firing steadily.

Galina marched her machine onto the deck with sparks showering off her armored machine. She killed one Marine, and I killed the other.

That was pretty much it. Captain Merton was sitting calmly in his command chair. The navigational nerds, the operations staff, the sensor boys—they were all ducking behind their consoles.

I noticed not all of them were at their posts. These slow-witted fellows were the dregs, the holdouts who hadn't been smart enough to disappear by this time. They stared at us with eyes that were as big around as saucers. They could tell when they were outgunned, and none of them even bothered to lift a pistol and fire a single shot.

"Captain Merton," Galina boomed. She'd turned up her external speakers to a punishing volume. "I believe you and I are overdue for a high-level meeting."

Captain Merton steepled his fingers. "I'm sorry, Imperator. I don't recognize your authority on this ship."

"On what basis?" she demanded, striding forward. Her tail lashed dangerously, knocking over stacks of computers scrolls, coffee cups and keyboards as she went. "How do you dare question my authority aboard *Dominus*? When we are in the midst of an invasion action, I am in command of this vessel."

Merton lifted a finger. "Normally you would be right." He waggled the finger and pointed it toward the ceiling. "But not today, sir. Today, you are under arrest."

Galina laughed. "You're going to arrest *me*? You and what army?"

"As a representative of Hegemony, I require no army. All that is needed is legitimacy."

Here, he produced a computer scroll. He shook it out and presented it to Galina. She stepped forward warily and tried to take it. She fumbled at it for a moment, as it's difficult to grab onto something that small and delicate with the hands of a killing machine.

I took the initiative and stumped forward myself. Snatching the scroll from Merton's soft hand, I lifted the scrap of plastic and slapped it against the dragon's faceplate.

She read it, and she began to curse. "Seriously?" she said. "My rank is rescinded?"

"If you do not comply with the arrest orders, you are no longer an imperator. You are no longer a member of Earth's military at all. That goes for you as well, McGill."

"Uh…" I said, "that doesn't sound too good."

If Galina was intimidated by Captain Merton, it certainly didn't show. She strode around on the deck in front of everyone. The big claws of her dragon battlesuit tore up gouges in the textured metal.

"So, I'm out of the loop of command. Is that it?" she asked. "I don't think so. Merton, here are my orders—and they trump yours."

She took one arm out of her gripper long enough to work her tapper. She selected a video, and she cast it to the main forward screen. Everyone on the bridge could see it. Drusus was on the holoscreens, talking to me and Galina.

I winced a little. I was pretty sure Drusus was under the impression that this conversation was under the radar, but Galina had apparently been recording the whole thing in secret.

Drusus was explaining what he wanted from us. I noticed that the video had been edited somewhat. Essentially, he just commanded us to go off to another destination early. Watching the video, it seemed that Drusus was giving us a free rein to do things in any way we wished.

"There," Galina said. She pointed a clawed gripper at the screen. "Does everyone here recognize that man?"

A lot of heads nodded.

"That is Drusus. He is Earth's consul. None of you have ever seen a man with such a high rank, because most of us weren't alive when the last one ascended. He is essentially a dictator, a ruler of all Hegemony."

While she talked, she was pacing around between all the Fleet pukes. The dragon rasped, thumped and the motors whined.

"In this kind of crisis, we must listen to the consul. Nothing that some bureaucrat from Earth has sent to you on a slip of plastic means anything."

She pointed at Captain Merton here. For the first time, Merton was looking concerned. Earlier, he'd been willing to brave death because he knew he was in the right. But now, he was doubting his own legitimacy.

Galina was always good at that. She was tricky, and political. Her mind worked through tactics and strategy like a master. She was good at such toxic arts, using psychology and underhanded cloak-and-dagger moves. Too bad she wasn't as good when it came to the battlefield.

"So," Galina said, "let me explain a few things to you, Captain Merton. I am displeased with your performance. Due to your compromised status, I do not believe you are able to execute the consul's orders correctly. Unlike the rest of us here, you think you work for Hegemony, even though that authority has been superseded."

Merton looked impressed. He opened his mouth, closed it again, then opened it one more time. "Imperator," he said, "it's possible that you are correct. I will have to consult with the Ruling Council back on Earth—"

"No!" Galina boomed. One of her titanium fists slammed down on a nearby operator's station, smashing it into sparking crumpled metal.

"Did you hear that?" she demanded. She pointed an accusatory claw in his direction. "All of you witnessed that, didn't you? He's trying to go back to the old way. He's trying to deny that Drusus is our legitimate leader. That is an act of sedition!"

Galina continued to stride around, her big metal tail lashing. I knew she wasn't trying to convince Merton of anything—not any longer—she was addressing the staffers and supporting officers on the bridge. She would need their cooperation to bring her plans to fruition.

"This is what I say, Captain Merton." She rounded on him and pointing that big claw in his face. "You are the problem here. You are the one that needs to be placed under arrest!"

"This is absurd!"

"Because I believe you may attempt to consult with rogue elements of Hegemony to undermine this mission, I declare that you are a traitor to Earth. You are hereby sentenced to nonexistence."

Merton knew he was in bad shape. He attempted to dart out of the place, vaulting up from his command chair and heading for the exit.

Galina ran him down, springing into the air and landing on his back with her titanium claws extended. He fell to the deck, bleeding half-crushed, but still alive.

She reached out a gripper and snipped off his head. She lifted her trophy between two claws, holding it high for everyone on the bridge to see.

"That is what happens to traitors on my ship," she told the naval officers that surrounded us.

Not one of them had reached for a gun. Not one of them made so much as a peep of objection. There were a few gasps, of course—but that was all. They stared, they cringed, and they waited to hear their own fates.

"Now," Galina said, walking back toward the command chair, "who here will obey our consul? Who here is no longer thinking of becoming a traitor like Merton?"

Everyone on the bridge lifted their right hand and held it high. I was among them since Galina had made a pretty compelling case, and I had been there myself when Drusus had given us these orders. I dared to hope this would all somehow work out in the end without either of us being permed.

Once we had command of *Dominus,* we checked and found that Drusus had left the system.

Galina was thinking hard. "We only have so much time left to get this show on the road. We have to leave here before Drusus finds out about the extreme methods we're using."

She and I were in Merton's office, which was directly attached to the bridge.

"We have to act quickly," she continued. "We'll drop down closer to the planet and send our lifters to the orbital factory. We must get everyone from Legion Varus aboard this ship."

"But we haven't even finished this campaign, yet."

"I know that! Don't you think I know that, James?"

"You're the commanding officer in charge. If you leave now—"

"Shut up," she said. "I have a plan…"

I let her stew for a while, as I leaned back in the dead Captain Merton's chair with my boots up on his desk.

Galina finally stopped pacing in her squeaking, buzzing dragon suit. When she stopped in front of the desk, I snorted awake.

"Here's what we're going to do," she said. "We'll force the Vulbites to surrender publicly. We'll declare that victory and move on."

"Yeah, well, that sounds good… I guess."

"Come with me."

I groaned, stretched, and followed her back out onto the bridge. Sure enough, a gaggle of officers had assembled. They were standing around Merton's empty command chair. They scattered like hens at our approach.

So, I thought to myself, they *are* conspiring, but they're doing it in a very cowardly fashion. So far, there hadn't been a single assassination attempt. To the best of my knowledge no one had even dared to use the deep-link. We'd been monitoring that closely.

I watched with interest as Galina commanded the communications team to connect her to Legion Varus headquarters. She told Tribune Winslade he was going to have to get all his men onto the roof of the factory again to be picked up by lifters.

"But sir," he complained. "We'll be under their laser fire again."

"You let me worry about that. Get your men into position."

The next few hours were critical. We established control over *Dominus*, using the command crew on the bridge to order engineering to swing the transport around and head closer to Dark World.

According to our rules of engagement, we were not to come within 500,000 kilometers of the planet itself. There had been some worry that *Dominus* could be struck by defensive armament from the surface of the planet, but such defensive systems hadn't really materialized.

The Vulbites only had a few lasers which they'd used to burn troops on the surface of the orbital factory. Not one of our lifters had been destroyed when we invaded. Of course, there had been six Rigellian cruisers and other warships to deal with upon our arrival, but those were all gone now.

As we drifted closer to the violet planet, only the helmsman dared to complain. He mumbled a bit about being ordered to break protocol.

Galina's dragon marched swiftly to the helmsman's side and leaned close to oversee his work. The mumbled complaints became inaudible, and the big ship lowered itself to near orbit.

"McGill," Galina said. "I need you to go down to the fire control room."

This order surprised me. I'd already found a comfortable chair at the back of the bridge. It was probably the most comfortable chair in the entire place. Normally, it was used by navigators while they huddled over computer tables, working on numbers that were full of squiggly symbols and such-like.

"Huh?" I said. "Fire control? How's that, sir?"

"You heard me. Go down to fire control. Make sure that every officer down there is loyal to Earth and check the readiness of this ship's primary armament."

I squinted, getting the upsetting notion that she was still determined to give the Vulbites down on Dark World a stern punishment.

I shook my head. "I'm not going to do it, sir. Remember, Consul Drusus gave me a little free rein, too."

There was a lot of thumping and scratching on the deck as she approached me. The dragon was domineering, but I knew that even if she started shooting, I might well survive inside my stardust armor.

"You're going to have to get yourself somebody else for this one, Galina," I told her.

"All right, shut up," she said. "I'll do it myself. Watch the bridge and make sure none of these worms do anything."

I touched my cap to her, and she was gone.

-34-

About half an hour later, the big ship bucked under our feet. The crewmen looked around, alarmed. One of them marched up to me, throwing me a salute. He was angry and bewildered.

I was sitting in Merton's command chair at this point, resting on my backside with my morph-rifle across my knees.

"Centurion?" the commander said. "Our ground affects batteries have been fired."

I released an angry grunt and got up. I waved at the main display, suggesting they show us what was happening outside. We watched as thirty-two fusion warheads fell, punching through the atmosphere. They dropped onto the nearest Vulbite hives.

The fusion blasts began to flash in rapid succession. All thirty-two warheads struck home causing ripples in the atmosphere and even the surface of Dark World. Down there, it looked like raindrops were hitting a mud puddle. The ground and the sky and the air pulsed in response.

Millions were dying down there. Perhaps billions. We watched until it was over. Once the horrible deed was done, Dark World was bleeding from dozens of radioactive craters stitched across the body of the planet.

Each of those large, quivering mounds contained literally millions of insects. The queens were down at the bottom. They lived in utter darkness in the underground depths.

Once, a long time ago, I had destroyed one of these mounds myself with a strike from the broadsides of a different ship. I'd done it because Legion Varus had lost my entire cohort inside that mound—including Graves and many others. I'd wanted to make sure that those friends of mine were inarguably dead, so we could get them into the revival queues. Otherwise, all of them would have been permed.

Galina came striding in a few minutes later. She was clearly proud of herself.

"Imperator," the XO said, "did you order the firing of our primary armament?"

"What if I did, Commander?"

"Such an action, taken without express permission from Central constitutes a breach—"

"In that case, I didn't do it," Galina said smoothly. "Are you satisfied?"

The commander sputtered for a moment. Finally, he stood tall. "No. No sir, I'm not—"

Galina didn't wait to hear his entire tirade. She shot him with her chest cannons.

Being no more than a normal human in a cloth uniform, he was splattered all over the far wall. A gaggle of lieutenants and ensigns shrieked and scattered. Some of them dripped gore.

"A pity," Galina said to me. "I'd hoped we were further along than this."

She turned to rest of the staffers. "Anyone else wish to lodge a formal complaint? This is your best opportunity."

No one did more than cough or gag.

"All right, then," she said. "Bring up the Vulbite leadership on this box, right here." A titanium claw thumped on the holotable.

Fleet people scrambled to do her bidding. It took a few minutes, but finally a Vulbite queen appeared on our screens. She was a massive beast—a centipede over a hundred meters long. She was a nightmare out of a child's feverish dream.

I noticed that one of the queen's eyes had been burned away and slagged. "Jumping Jehoshaphat!" I said. "Do you know who that is?"

Galina swung her dragon's head in my direction. "You've got to be kidding me. McGill, do you actually recognize this gigantic female centipede?"

"I sure do. That queen was here on Dark World when my unit came through—back during the Glass World campaign."

"So what?"

"I can tell by that burned-out eye she's got. See there on the right? It's the same queen."

"Again, McGill. So, the hell *what*?"

"Graves did that," I told her. "He shot out her eye. And you know what? After he did it, she started listening to us."

Galina stared at me for a moment, thinking hard.

"Queen," she said, turning to the massive alien that watched us. That single black eye of hers seemed to be full of malevolence, but she might have simply been pissed-off about us nuking one of her hives.

"What is it, scale-mite?" the queen asked.

"An insult? You dare to insult your new masters?"

"You are not our masters. The Vulbite people are free and unfettered. We live—"

"You live under the dirty paws of your masters from Rigel," Galina said. "Now, things have changed. You will serve us, or you will be utterly destroyed!"

"Uh… Imperator?" I said, uncertain as to the nature of the diplomatic path she was on right now.

"Shut up, McGill. Look, queen of the bug-things, you must know that Earth is just as ruthless as Rigel."

"Incorrect. In our estimations, Rigel is worse."

"You are wrong. We are the greater evil. We will destroy more of your hives until you understand us."

The queen's head was swaying from side-to-side. I realized she was tipping her single eye to see various inputs—possibly screens of her own. "You have only one ship in near orbit. You are not the top official of Earth. Our analysis of your social hierarchy indicates—"

"Did your analysis predict the smoking crater that has now replaced one of your hives?"

"No," the queen admitted.

"Did your prognosticators tell you in advance when that eye of yours was burned away by this madman standing right here?"

Galina pointed a silvery gripper at me. I sputtered, but I didn't accuse her of lying openly.

The queen studied me. "You were in my nest some decades ago? When I was young and foolish?"

"Yep. That was probably me."

The eye swung back to Galina. "My xenoanalysts will be consumed. They are useless."

"That's a good idea. Perhaps they were confused by our gentle handling of your orbital factory. We didn't behave in our usual hyper-destructive fashion aboard the factory complex because we wished to capture it and use it for our own purposes. Hives full of insects on Dark World, however… these are useless to us."

"I understand. I have no choice but to obey."

That was it. After some truly hardball negotiations, Galina got the big bug to formally surrender to Earth.

I was feeling a bit low about my part in this mess, but at least I could take solace in the fact that it was all over with now. Maybe the bugs wouldn't have surrendered if we'd done anything less.

"You are cruel masters indeed," the queen said. "Rigel is vicious. They abuse us at the slightest provocation. They snip off a foot or a tail from any Vulbite that slightly displeases them. But never have they struck us from the skies and killed us in our millions. Never have they dared lay bare a queen in her birthing chambers. Never—"

Galina cut in on the speech. "All right, all right," she said. "Here's your first order, conquered alien: You are to shut up. You are now a subject of Earth. Explain your new status to the cameras."

Galina had the fleet staffers record the conversation. The alien remained silent for a few seconds before it finally spoke. "We are subjects of Earth."

"Good. That's good," Galina said. "You no longer owe any loyalty to Rigel. Say it."

"We no longer owe any loyalty to Rigel."

The beaten queen repeated everything that was required of her. It was a humiliating and utter surrender. I almost felt sorry for the big bug.

"Excellent," Galina said, summing up. "I now declare this world conquered by Imperator Galina Turov. Make a note of the date, communications staff. Now, take that file and broadcast it back to Earth with the deep-link."

"Shall we encrypt this—?"

"No. Do not encrypt it, there is no need. This is joyful news that should be shared by everyone on Earth."

The terrorized fleet people hastened to obey her. It occurred to me that if Captain Merton had spent all his time shuffling around the bridge inside of a dragon combat suit, he probably would have gotten a lot less backtalk from his subordinate officers.

"Cut the feed," Galina said. The connection was broken, and the bridge staff looked at her expectantly.

"Now," she said, "connect me to Tribune Winslade."

It took a few minutes to get a hold of him. I wasn't sure if Winslade was avoiding the contact, or if he honestly was engaged in combat on the frontlines. Whichever the case was, he came on a few minutes later. He seemed surprised to see Galina—especially in a dragon suit.

"Ah..." he said, "to what do I owe this honor, Imperator?"

"It is indeed an honor," she told him. "For you, Tribune Winslade, are gazing upon the conqueror of Dark World."

"What?"

"Yes. The Vulbite queen has publicly surrendered."

Winslade pursed his thin lips. "Might this have something to do with that vicious ground-strike we witnessed less than an hour ago?"

"Yes," she said, "of course it does. You have new orders coming as well."

"Of course, sir," he said, and he did a little bow-thing, dipping his head toward her. Winslade always knew what to kiss and when.

"You will bring your entire legion and all your gear back to *Dominus*. You will do this as quickly as possible. I will send lifters, and we'll set up gateway posts. It must happen within the next hour."

"But sir," he sputtered. "That's impossible timing. I have units heavily engaged with Vulbites right now. I'll have them pull them back and—"

"Order them to withdraw. It doesn't matter if some of them die. We'll reprint them later. Withdraw on every front, get to a gateway or a lifter immediately and evacuate the orbital factory. Do you understand your orders, Tribune?"

Winslade hesitated. He looked from me to Galina and back again. "Ah… what, may I ask, has happened to Captain Merton?"

"Merton is… resting, and Drusus has left the system for Earth."

"I see. They've both stepped out of the picture, have they? Did they do this by the same expeditious and unexpected method?"

I knew, of course what he meant. He was asking if we had somehow executed both of them.

"No, you fool," Galina boomed. She'd turned up the external speakers on her dragon again. Her voice was now painfully loud. "I'm following Drusus' orders. If you do not obey me, you will be defying the will of the consul of Earth. There is only one possible fate for such people. Do I need to clarify?"

"No, no, Imperator. Not at all. What you say will be done. Now, if you'll excuse me, I have a legion to evacuate almost instantaneously."

The next hour went by in a frenzy. Galina worked furiously to get Legion Varus stuffed into the hold of *Dominus*. The biggest delay was with the lifters. Sending them out to land on the factory was a smooth operation. Getting them loaded with troops that seemed to dribble out of the vast factory took much longer.

Galina was in a rage as the end of the first hour passed. "I have half a mind to leave them all behind."

"Why the all-fired hurry, sir? You've conquered Dark World. You've established your command of this operation. You can leave a couple of legions to hold Dark World for now. I can't see the problem."

"Are you truly retarded, McGill?" she demanded. "How is it you can't seem to understand the most basic of concepts?"

"Uh…"

"I'm not worried about Vulbites. I'm not worried about Winslade, either. I'm worried about Drusus or some other Earth official who outranks me showing up here with new orders. As soon as someone comes out here who is in greater authority than I am, they can countermand everything I'm doing."

"Huh…" I said, "yeah, I guess that's so."

At last, when the tenth lifter touched down on Red Deck, she ordered the bay doors to be slammed shut behind it.

"Time to fly this whale out of here," Galina ordered the helmsman.

"But sir," the bridge crew objected, "we still have troops on the way in the lifters. They're just starting to disembark. We need at least ten more minutes to—"

"No. They can sit in their jump seats for all I care. Launch this ship and get us into hyperspace *now*."

A Fleet officer dared to step forward. "I don't think you understand, sir," he said. "Those troops are liable to be fried by radiation. There isn't enough shielding in the hold, see—"

"I don't care!" Galina shouted. The sound of her voice was astoundingly loud in the enclosed space.

The poor fellow opened his mouth to object or explain further, but she lost her temper at that point. I could have told him it was coming. I'd seen the signs a mile off.

She fired a single mini-missile at the officer who had dared to argue with her. His chest popped red, and he was blown apart into a disgusting spray of vitals and fluids.

"Who was that cretin?" Galina demanded.

A mouse-like voice answered from somewhere. "That was your XO, sir."

"Oh… so I need a new executive officer? Who's it going to be?"

There were no volunteers, so I stood up and threw my hand high. "I'll do it."

"Forget it, McGill." She wheeled around and marched through the group. She finally picked out the weakest, most simpering female lieutenant she could find among the navigational staff.

"You," she said, "you're my XO now. Congratulations."

"But sir, I don't have the rank, I don't have the experience—"

"I don't care," Galina boomed, "are you refusing to obey me?"

The navigator shook her head. She looked like she was about to soil her uniform. I felt sorry for her, but I didn't want to interfere. When Galina was on one of her tears, you just didn't get between her and her next victim—not unless you wanted to be on the dinner menu yourself.

Finally, the bridge crew obeyed her, and *Dominus* shuddered. A large bubble formed around us and yanked us into hyperspace. We were whisked away from Dark World at an impossibly fast rate.

"Where are we headed now, sir?" I asked.

"That's classified," she said in response. "You'll know it when we get there."

-35-

The trip in hyperspace from Dark World to Sky World was relatively short. I wasn't exactly sure where on the star map this place was, but it had to be in the same area as the Eridani star cluster.

Being Galina Turov's strongman, I was given a live tapper-feed hooked up to Gold Deck. That allowed me to see what was happening on the bridge in real time. I was in my unit's module when we arrived, so I used the feed to check up on things.

We reappeared in normal space. I watched as *Dominus* dumped gravity waves and pulses of harsh radiation.

Soon, reports began coming in from the sensor ops. We'd arrived near a hot, white star. I was a little surprised, because F-class stars like this one usually didn't have planets that were habitable. They tended to emit too much harsh radiation for life to exist nearby.

The ship's navigational crew scanned continuously, and they began mapping the place. Usually, this process would quickly show the location and size of all the local planets, as they were the largest gravitational masses and easy to detect.

The weird thing was… there weren't any planets.

"What is this?" Galina growled at the nervous crew. She was still wearing the battle suit when she went on the command deck, and she wasn't in a good mood. "Are you attempting to bullshit your commanding officer?"

"No, sir! We're just not detecting anything large."

"Well, run the scans again."

She strode around in her dragon on the command deck, threatening the navigators, the sensor operators—everyone. They were quite nervous in her presence, and they had good reason to be. There were already two bodies lying on the deck—fresh ones since the last time I'd checked.

No one had come to collect them, because Galina wouldn't let any Blue Deck bios clean up the mess. Maybe she wanted those bodies lying there to remind the others that they should focus on being obedient to her every whim. As far as I could tell, it was working.

"You rat-bastards," she said, clanking near the sensor-ops. "You're hiding something. Where is the planet we're supposed to hit? Drusus wouldn't have sent us out here to do nothing."

"I'm telling you, sir, on pain of death, there aren't any planets in this star system. There are only asteroids. There's a bunch of ragged material out in the local Oort cloud, but I'm not really seeing anything anybody would call a planet."

Angrily, Galina stepped up to the operators station herself. Her front gripper swept aside a man who got in her way, and the sensor op went sprawling. He had difficulty standing back up again. When you were shouldered aside by a three-meter-tall pile of titanium and steel, that was a common consequence.

Galina studied the operator panels. At length, she straightened. "This is very odd... You seem to be telling the truth. Have you altered these sensors somehow?"

"No, no! No, sir!"

Galina marched around in circles with her mechanical tail lashing to keep the machine's balance. At last, she came to a conclusion.

"All right," she said. "I believe you. You mentioned asteroids. Where are they? Are there any ships near them? Why the hell are we out here?"

The sensor ops crawled back to their stations and continued their scans fearfully. They examined the incoming data. One ensign finally shouted and put his finger in the air. "I've got something, sir. I've got a contact."

Galina charged toward him and stared. "What is it? A mining station?"

"Yes, that's what it is."

"Odd… a solitary mining station. Apparently, that's what we're out here for."

"But… look, Imperator. This mining complex is *huge*."

More data was flooding in. They transferred control to the battle computers. That drew up plans and course options for *Dominus* to proceed to the area. The computers did this automatically without anyone having specifically ordered it to do so.

Galina stared at the new data. "What are they mining?"

"These asteroids have very high metallicity levels. In other words, they're almost pure metal."

"Ah… Do we have any mining ships? Do you see any cargo vessels of any kind?"

Eventually, the sensors brought in more conclusive data. Now that we had a more distinct target to aim every dish and projector at, details came in to fill the void—there were no warships in the system that we could see, but there were a number of mining operations, cargo vessels, that sort of thing.

"All right," Galina said. "Now, we're getting somewhere. No planet means no feisty local natives, at least. Let's proceed directly toward the largest mining installation in the system. We will take it—or we will destroy it. There's nothing else here for us to do."

No one argued. The ship's engines thrummed, and I finally decided to climb out of my bunk in my module yawning and stretching.

Sure, I'd been lounging in my private quarters, idly watching what was happening on Gold Deck. I'd kind of been hoping the trip would last a few more days. I'd been enjoying the vacation.

I'd even considered chasing a few skirts down on Lavender Deck—now that the fleet boys didn't have the authority to throw me out of there. But no, none of that was happening tonight. I was going to have to go back to work today, so I dragged on my black armor, unlimbered my rifle and made my way up to Gold Deck.

The Fleet personnel upstairs gave me looks that were both fearful and filled with disgust. I ignored them all. They could think what they wanted to as long as they kept quiet and didn't try anything. Once I reached the bridge, I attempted to get Galina's attention.

Eventually, she marched her machine over to me. "I'm glad you finally showed up, McGill. I need to charge this thing. Watch these men for a while—if anybody does anything weird, shoot them."

With that statement, she headed toward the office that had once been occupied by Merton. There, I knew she would tap into direct power and recharge her suit. She might even get out of it to have a stretch.

Looking around, I spotted the two Legion Varus veterans who were posted at the entrance as guards. I essentially repeated Galina's orders, but with a little more soft-pedalling. "Keep an eye on them—but don't shoot anybody unless you're attacked."

They nodded, and I left the command center. I followed Galina, pulling out her Galactic key which I still had my possession.

I overrode the captain's lock and stepped inside. Galina squawked and jumped. She fumbled to get a pistol out of her pocket.

"Easy, sir," I said.

She was out of her armor and half-naked. She'd apparently needed a break after having spent long hours terrorizing people inside the hot machine.

In her haste, she dropped her pistol on the deck, and it rattled and clattered. "Oh, it's you, James. You dick—did you walk in here just to startle me?"

"No, sir. I'm no prowler," I said. "I came here with important information."

"What?"

"I've been thinking—"

"I know what you're thinking about. These Fleet weasels… they know I'm just one woman in a battle suit. They might start an uprising at any moment. That's why I'm going to blow up all these mining facilities from orbit. If I deploy the legion, I have to either go down with the troops, or I have to stay aboard *Dominus* without support. Either way—"

"Hold on, hold on. None of them are causing any trouble. I think you've got them completely cowed and bamboozled."

She narrowed her eyes. "Then why are you pestering me? If you're wanting personal favors, you can forget about it. I'm much too busy at the moment."

"No, sir. That's not it, either… although it's a shame to hear you say that."

"What then?"

"Sir," I said, "have you considered the possibility that this mining installation is directly linked to Dark World for a reason?"

She stared at me. "What are you talking about, McGill?"

"Metals, sir. Lots and lots of metal. If you want to build a large number of starships at a giant factory orbiting Dark World, you've got to be getting the raw materials from somewhere, right?"

"Of course, you're stating the obvious, James."

"Okay," I said, "but the thing you might not be considering is just how critical this mining installation might be to Dark World's shipyards. When you build starships, you don't just need metals—you need the right ones. Titanium, plutonium, cadmium and cobalt. Millions of tons of that stuff."

She stared at me, then she stared at the deck for a while. She pointed at me and snapped her fingers a few times. "I think you're onto something, James. Everybody tells me you're as stupid as a Vulbite, but at moments like this, I don't believe them."

"Uh…"

"There *must* be a reason why Drusus sent me out here. A few rocks with a mining installation on them? That's not good enough. But if the metals are pure, and rare, and exactly what they need to build starships—this place could be a gold mine, so to speak."

"That's what I'm saying!"

"Okay, then," she said. "I'm going to have to alter my plans. We're not going to destroy all these mining bases, even though it would be the easiest path to crippling Dark World's output."

"I'm mighty pleased you see the light, sir," I said with a grin.

"Good enough. Go back to your unit. Legion Varus is going to invade this mining complex and capture it at dawn."

My heart sank. I'd kind of figured I'd be invited to spend the night. Instead, I was dismissed without so much as a polite hug. On the way back to the modules, I wondered if I shouldn't have kept my mouth shut and let her blow up every installation in the star system.

-36-

Dominus slid across the Sky World system like a shark stalking a seal. The asteroid we were cruising toward was a beast of a thing. It was as big as a small moon, being about a thousand kilometers across.

As we closed in, we could see the largest mining installation. For a while, it seemed like we hadn't even been detected, but suddenly, a single ship rose up from behind the large asteroid. Alarms went off all over the command deck.

"Where'd that ship come from?" Galina demanded. "Can we destroy it?"

The worried sensor ops worked their instruments. They frantically transmitted the results to the tactical team, who sorted through the data.

I couldn't help but notice that while Galina was in her dragon suit, and I was lounging with my morph-rifle in my hands, these Fleet guys were working with more zeal than usual. Was that due to our presence, or merely because they believed in this mission? I tended to suspect the former.

"It's a transport ship," one of them finally said, straightening up and breathing heavily. He'd been working so furiously he seemed to be out of breath.

"A transport ship?" Galina said. "What the hell is that doing out here? Is it ours or theirs?"

"All we know is it's Galactic in origin. It's Imperial."

Galina strode to the holotable. "Contact that ship immediately. Give me a targeting solution—are they firing anything at us?"

"Only scanning beams, sir."

Communications sent out signals that flashed across space to the other ship. So far, we were still out of range to fire on one another. After a tense minute or so, the big view screen lit up with a three-dimensional image that was familiar to me.

"Hello, unknown vessel," the man said with a distinctly French accent. "You are out of your jurisdiction. You should withdraw while you still can."

The enemy captain was Maurice Armel. He was wearing an unusual uniform. I suspected he'd designed it himself. It looked like something from the medieval period. He had a blue cloak with gold trim, and his moustache seemed larger than before.

Armel narrowed his eyes. He leaned toward the pickup to examine the incoming visual data. "What is inside of that mechanical suit?" he asked. "Could that be the most feminine of mice? Galina Turov?"

"Armel," she said, "if you wish to remain neutral, you must leave the system immediately. This is your only warning."

He laughed. "Alas, Imperator, that I cannot do. I work for Rigel these days."

"So I've heard. Your treachery is legendary."

"Is that so? Oddly, as I travel across the provinces, I rarely hear your name spoken. Unless, of course, it is a tale of woe and incompetence."

Galina's face reddened. I could see it even through her faceplate.

The Fleet guys wanted to laugh, but none of them had the balls to do it. Instead, they glanced at one another and clapped their hands over their mouths. They must have known that any outbursts of amusement would definitely cost them their lives at this point.

"What are you doing out here?" Galina demanded.

"I'm defending Rigellian territory, of course. What are you doing? Aren't you supposed to be off conquering Dark World?"

Galina smiled. "We've already finished that, Armel. Your masters are failures. Every star system they occupy will fall before us like a row of dominoes."

"A colorful analogy, but this star system shall not fall as you describe. Do your worst."

With that, the channel clicked off. Galina looked up as alarms flashed red, and a klaxon began to sound.

"What's this nonsense?" she asked.

"They've fired on us. Shells are incoming."

Galina hissed. "I thought we weren't even within range."

The weapons tech shrugged. "We're out of range for our guns. Maybe not for theirs."

"What about missiles?" she asked.

"They'd take a long time to get there, sir. They'll probably run out of fuel long before they reach the enemy ship."

Galina glared and fumed. I could tell she wanted to brain the weapons tech officer with her metal fist, but she withheld her rage for the moment.

"Fire three missiles," she said. "Full burn."

"Sir," the weapons guy said, "by the time they reach the enemy ship, it probably won't be there. Even if it is, the missiles won't have any fuel left to maneuver. The transport is going to easily dodge anything we send toward them at this distance."

"I don't care. Armel just fired a barrage of shells. Maybe that's a bluff, maybe it's not. Either way, it's time for us to bluff him."

Shrugging, the weapons tech leaned over his computer console and did as she asked. *Dominus* shuddered slightly three times.

"Missiles away, sir," he said.

"Good, now it's time to wait. Are we still on an approach course?"

"Yes. We will be within gun range in about ten minutes."

A slow-motion game of chicken began. The tense minutes dragged by, and I discovered I had an itchy place inside my thick armor. It was in a spot I couldn't reach, too. Damn, that was annoying.

I set my morph-rifle on the deck with the blade-like bayonet sticking up. I rubbed the spot on my right side against it. Naturally, the point of the bayonet couldn't penetrate my armor, but a slight scratching sensation made it through. It was better than nothing.

Galina walked over to me while I was performing this maneuver. She seemed disgusted. "Seriously, McGill? What are you, a warthog or something?"

"Maybe more of an ape?" I suggested.

"No," she said. "An ape has hands. An ape can reach around and scratch its own ass without disarming itself in the process."

I got the message and picked my rifle back up. I cradled the gun in my arms until Galina walked away again. After approximately eleven minutes went by, we were close enough to the enemy transport to fire our own fusion cannons.

"Do it," Galina said. "A full broadside barrage from this ship is terrifying."

Thirty-two cannons roared, and our entire ship shook. Coming back our way were only sixteen canisters of flaming death, but their warheads were no less dangerous than ours. Armel's ship wasn't one of the new, big bastards like *Dominus*. It was only built to carry ten thousand troops, not twenty thousand.

Galina kept boring in closer. She didn't flinch as the enemy warheads drew close.

"Sir?" I asked. "Is this mutually-assured destruction or a game of chicken?"

"Armel is a coward. He will not allow his one and only transport to be destroyed—especially while he is aboard it."

Everyone on the command deck, especially all the Fleet pukes were beginning to get nervous. They put up a big digital timer on all the screens just for emphasis. A set of large red numbers read six minutes. This ticked down to five very quickly.

One of the navigational crew dared to step close to Galina. She was the youngest woman of the bunch, and she had short, tight hair. She held out a computer scroll to Galina, and her hand shook as she did so.

"Imperator?" she said, "the navigational team took it upon ourselves to plan out an escape route."

"Oh," Galina said, "that's so nice."

She took the computer scroll from the navigator, and she crushed it in her claws, tearing the heavy plastic apart. The scroll blanked, having been destroyed.

Galina poked out one of her long, curved claws, separating it from the others. She extended this toward the navigational officer. "Very considerate," she said, "but you really shouldn't have bothered."

Then, she thrust her arm forward suddenly. The claw plunged into the girl's chest, killing her, and she fell back onto the deck, sprawling. Galina turned to face the others with her dragon's claws dripping.

"Does anyone else have any bright ideas?" she asked.

They shook their heads and huddled in terror.

"Aw now, Imperator, sir," I said, walking up and standing over the corpse. "That was just plain mean."

She wheeled on me. "Why? Just because she's an attractive female? Can't you control yourself for one minute, James?"

"It's not that, sir. At this rate, we're going to run out of officers long before we get home."

"Fine," she said, and she turned to the new XO she had appointed. "Have that one revived. Put her back on duty within the hour."

The XO made a note and saluted crisply.

"Now, let's see what Armel does," Galina said.

The countdowns continued for a few minutes longer. The missiles were due to reach Armel's ship first and then the broadsides, but the very moment that the timer dropped down to fifty-nine seconds, the contact that was Armel's ship vanished.

"Ah-ha," Galina crowed in triumph. "Like I said, he's running. He would never have the balls to let our missiles get close to his vessel. They could explode with X-rays. There's lots of ways we could kill him, even at this distance."

The XO cleared her throat. "Sir?"

Galina wheeled.

The XO was trembling. "Sir, the enemy shells are still heading directly for us."

"All right, all right. Jump into warp and jump out again. Give it a second or two. I don't care where we come out."

"But sir, there are safety protocols. The navigators don't have time to—"

"Do it *now!*"

Fingers stabbed emergency buttons, klaxons wailed, and the power dropped all over the ship. The unexpected requirement to generate a field on an emergency basis caused every power system on the ship to flicker, but the good news was we warped and escaped certain destruction.

We slid to one side, and the deck lurched sickeningly under our feet. The warheads Armel had fired at us swerved to follow, but they struck at nothing as we vanished from normal space.

I was mildly impressed by Galina's tactical maneuvering. "How did you know he was going to chicken first?" I asked her.

She shrugged. "I know Armel pretty well after fifty years of having to deal with him. We fired thirty-two shells at his smaller ship. He only fired sixteen back at us. *Dominus* has more armament, more armor, greater range. The odds we could survive the hit were better than his odds. Therefore, there was no way he was going to go toe-to-toe with us."

"I never doubted you," I lied.

We came out of hyperspace farther from the asteroid than we had been when we'd first caught sight of Armel's ship, and the system seemed to be clean now. The data coming back indicated Armel's ship was nowhere to be found. Apparently, unlike *Dominus*, he hadn't just hopped a few thousand kilometers away. He'd gone into warp, and he'd kept going.

"He's probably outside this system and headed back to Rigel by now," Galina said.

"He'll report the fact that we're here," I said. "He'll beg for reinforcements."

"Yes, of course," Galina agreed. "We don't have much time. We must land our troops on this asteroid and capture it. We'll take it in few hours."

"I don't know… it's a pretty big complex."

"More defeatism?" she asked. She activated the ship-wide officer's voice channel. "Tribune Winslade. Scramble your troops. You're landing with lifters in fifteen minutes to capture this mining installation."

I knew it would probably take longer than fifteen minutes just to load the lifters, but I also knew the top commanders frequently made impossible demands to get their troops moving as fast as possible. We were, after all, under something of a time crunch. We didn't know how long reinforcements from Rigel would take to get here—but I was pretty sure they would come sooner rather than later.

-37-

After marching my unit down to Red Deck, we boarded our lifter and strapped in. About ninety seconds later, the lifter fell out of the bottom of *Dominus*. We experienced about six minutes of janky flight, and then came the landing which was fast and hard. At least there wasn't any atmosphere to punch through.

The ramps slammed down, sending up a cloud of dust that didn't settle as quickly as it rose. The surface of the planetoid looked quite a bit like the Moon. It was well-rounded unlike smaller asteroids nearby. Many asteroids had random shapes, but this one was old and big. It had been pelted so many times by its neighbors—over possibly billions of years—the surface was pockmarked with craters. Along the edge of these craters were craggy peaks. The surface itself was a blazing white.

The asteroid faced the local F-class sun, as well as a billion other unobscured stars. They all hung in space above us with nothing to obstruct our vision, other than the floating particles we'd kicked up.

Harris was the first to begin complaining, and that didn't surprise me one bit. "Did we seriously come all this way just to invade a rock? There aren't any damned trees, birds, water—nothing."

"It does have a perfect level of gravity," Leeson said. "The troops are hopping around like rabbits. We should make good time when we race off to get killed somewhere."

This didn't impress Harris, who continued to grumble.

The gravitational pull was significantly less than the Moon, but it was enough to keep us from losing our grip and propelling ourselves into orbit. On the smallest rocks, you had to work constantly to stay attached to the surface. If you kicked up too high and too hard, you would fly into space and lose your grip on the asteroid. Even on this world, there was some level of danger.

"A strong man might be able to kick hard enough to actually send himself into a low orbit—or at least fly so high that crashing down might star your helmet. Don't over-do it," I warned.

We streamed away from the lifter and fanned out across the barren landscape. More lifters landed and thousands of soldiers disembarked

"Turov dumped the whole damned Legion out here," Leeson remarked.

"Yep—she's not playing this time," Harris said.

Once our cohort was fully disembarked, we found ourselves standing around on an open rocky plain. There was no sign of the enemy, so we had a look around.

There wasn't much to see. No atmosphere, just a glaring white sun and endless plains of dust and rocks. There were craters everywhere because there was no water to erode them away, and no wind to fill them with grit. Instead, all we saw were endless vistas of stone and dust—lots of dust.

The shadows were stark black. Almost a perfect black, because the sun was so bright. Overhead, the F-class, was a radiation-blasting monster. A burning white eye in the sky.

Finally, orders came in. We had a new waypoint.

"Come on, come on! Go-go-go!" My veterans shouted encouragement to the troops as they advanced to their designated waypoints.

Our modern battle suits had ghostlike illusionary markings within the helmets that appeared in the landscape ahead of us showing various arrows and lines. They were faint, but colored and very visible on the surface of this rock.

Less than a minute after we'd started moving, the lifters blasted off. They left behind plumes of dust and gas.

"Turn your helmets away from the exhaust," Leeson suggested. "A dust storm like that can scar up your faceplate—and I mean permanently."

We were given directions to climb up out of the big crater we'd all landed in. Forming columns and ragged lines, we advanced by units. Our entire cohort soon was trotting at a ground-eating, bouncing pace.

"Do you think there might be alien troops out here?" Dickson asked me.

"No clue," I said, "there might be Vulbites, or Rigellians—who knows?"

Grimly, we jogged forward. Thousands of troops were on the move, kicking up a shitload of dust. The weird thing about marching hard in vacuum was always the absence of many normal sounds. You could only hear your own breathing, grunting and your pounding heart. The others were nearby, struggling just like you were—but you couldn't hear them at all unless they broadcast something over chat.

We had no idea what we'd be facing, or if we'd ever see our own Earth, Moon or Sun again. Just in case, I ordered my two ghosts to stealth and lead the pack. Della and Cooper were specialists who could stealth and thus made excellent scouts. They jogged ahead of the pack then vanished. For another dozen steps, I could make out the appearance of footprints and puffs of dust—then I lost them.

"I hate these big, airless rocks," Leeson said.

"It's not the rock I hate," Harris said, puffing over his mic. "It's that white star above us. There's just no way this suit is cutting out all the radiation. No way. My balls are going to be shooting blanks before we get back to the lifter."

"If you survive that long," Leeson laughed.

"Shut up and save your breath for jogging," I ordered. "I'm seeing some contacts at extreme range. Dickson, take your lights forward. Stretch them into a line, and take the lead. If you run into anything, start skirmishing."

"I've got it, sir."

Dickson sprang ahead. He urged his lights to spread out, and they did so without a peep of complaint. I had to admit, all his harsh discipline had reaped some rewards.

Next came Harris' heavies, the core of our formation. They were in a broad line, but they marched more closely together than the lights did.

In the rear came the specialists, the weaponeers, the bio people and the techs. I had my tech specialists, Kivi and Natasha, release buzzers.

"The range on these is going to be terrible," Natasha told me. "Their wings can't work, they're on very limited propulsion."

"Fly one at a time," I ordered. "Every ten minutes or so, send up another. I need eyes up high."

They did as I suggested. We marched for a kilometer then three, then about five. At that point we reached the edge of the big crater. Once we passed the rim of the crater, I knew we'd be in open sight of the mining complex.

Other units matched our pace, and more were behind us. When we reached the crater wall, hundreds of light troopers were grunting and climbing in loose, shifting dust. They poked their noses up over the rim and aimed their snap rifles toward the mining complex.

The big installation was impressive. One end was buried in what looked like a ridge of mountains. The other end was curved upward, like a giant hook that aimed up into space.

The way these things worked was quite ingenious. One end dug ore, sucking it into a series of large chambers. Each chamber digested the ore, purifying it and melting it down into a ball. At the far end, a rail-gun setup fired these balls up into space for transport to their final destination. That's what that giant hook-like thing at one end of the contraption was designed to do. It was like a giant cannon that fired metal spheres up into space.

When we first spotted the complex, nothing happened.

"Permission to advance, sir," Dickson called back to me.

"Permission denied. Wait until we're right behind you on the rim of the crater."

My lights waited as more and more units pulled up. Farther away, I could see other cohorts on our flanks. Some of them had come to the rim and crossed it. Once I was sure we weren't the only unit to be exposing themselves, I ordered Dickson to advance into the open. He did so with gusto, leading his lights at a trot.

Harris and his heavies were next up. They reached the rim and paused. I was about to order Harris to stop playing chicken and advance in Dickson's wake when suddenly one of the light trooper's indicators went red.

"I've got one down, Centurion. Not clear how it happened. Might have been a sniper."

"Go to ground."

The lights all threw themselves prone. They began worming their way toward any shallow, low point on the plain. They hid behind rocks and rolled into small craters. They panted and wheezed, straining to see who was firing at them.

Another one of my lights went red, and I began to curse. Dickson also seemed annoyed. He was shouting for his troops to take cover and stop poking their heads up.

"Techs," I said. "Get me some eyes up there. What's shooting at us?"

Moments later, we had some live video feed. It was grainy and full of glaring blacks and whites, but I could see humanoid-looking troops wearing spacesuits.

"There's someone out there," I informed my unit. "At this range, they look like men, more or less."

The enemy had placed themselves carefully. The snipers were peeping out from behind rock formations. They were about two kilometers off—as far as they could be on this small planetoid to get a bead on us. When you fought on small worlds, you had to expect the horizon to be very close.

"I can't get a buzzer all the way to that line," Natasha said.

I ordered the whole unit to pause under cover. "Okay, Dickson, switch out sniper gear and put some holes in our new friends."

About a minute later, the snap rifles began to pop I couldn't see or hear the firing except through tactical radio chat. Thirty-odd rifles flashed and popped pretty much continuously.

It was hard to tell at this range how much effect our fire was having, but after a few minutes of peppering every rock we could see, we sent out a few more buzzers. New video showed the enemy was retreating.

I frowned at the grainy images, which were digitally zoomed but had sketchy results. Crouched beings were running on all fours, it seemed like. "That's strange—definitely not humans. They're something like a human, but they run so low to the ground, almost the way a four-legged animal might."

The snipers withdrew, racing away from us toward the mining complex.

"Permission to pursue!" Dickson shouted.

I hesitated for a moment not sure if this enemy was luring us into an ambush or they were truly running from a superior force. Standing tall on the ridge where I'd taken shelter, I looked at both sides. I saw Legion forces advancing all over the place. It did make sense that the enemy would retreat as we seemed to outnumber them.

"All right," I said, "everybody on your feet. We're going after them."

We raced after the retreating enemy, firing whenever we could. We chased them all the way to the mining complex, at which point they vanished. Moving at a dead run, they dove into the structure and disappeared.

"Dammit," Kivi said, contacting me directly. "The metallic readings here are really intense. There are high magnetic fields all over as well. That's why the dust is so bad. If you look toward the sun, you can see a haze. That's all charged dust particles."

I glanced the way she suggested, but only for a moment. "I don't give a shit about dust, Kivi."

"Well," Natasha said, coming to Kivi's defense, "you should, James. We have the same problem on the moon—lots and lots of dust. It sticks to everything, with an effect like static."

"So what? What's the big deal about dust?"

"On any rock without air, dust is a major problem. All kinds of equipment is damaged by it."

I shrugged. I didn't much care about frigging dust. I didn't much care about our Moon, or this radioactive asteroid, either. What I was worried about was who might be running that mining complex and whether or not they were going to require shooting.

We jogged ahead, making good time for perhaps ten minutes. By that time, we'd reached the base of the mining complex. Since we'd driven off the snipers, we'd taken no incoming fire. There didn't seem to be defensive turrets on the complex, either. I dared to hope. Things were looking pretty easy for old Legion Varus.

"Dickson," I said calling a halt for the rest of the unit. "Send your lights in."

Harris stopped his heavies, placing them near the entrance to the complex. The weaponeers began to setup their heavy guns, while the light troopers sprang forward with nothing but snap-rifles in their hands. They were our hunting hounds. They would flush the enemy out in the open.

A few minutes later, I heard scattered fire. "Dickson, what have you got?"

"Nothing, sir. It's not me."

Looking around. I found that some other units and cohorts were showing up. They were engaged off to the east. Just then more firing broke out. I saw flashes up the ridge line, at yet another entrance. 5th Cohort was taking the high ground, where the complex met up directly with the metal-rich surface of the asteroid.

"We should be shooting at something," Leeson said.

Tribune Winslade's voice then overrode all the others. "We've made contact with an unknown number of large humanoid fighters. So far, we haven't seen many of this enemy, but they're well-armed. Be alert, people, and seek any way you can to get into the complex without damaging it."

Sargon complained. "How are we supposed to blast open the door without damaging it?"

I shrugged. I agreed with Sargon. My approach to these things was to blow doors open or cut holes into walls to get inside the target structure as fast as possible. After we'd cleared out the enemy and captured the prize, it was then up to all the techs and engineers to figure out how to patch the holes we'd created.

"You heard the man," I said. "Dickson, you're hugging on that hull like a piglet to its mama's belly. Haven't you found a way in yet?"

"Negative, sir. This interior structure seems to function like a storage bay. It's sealed up tight. Do I have your permission to blow a hole in one of these walls?"

"Find a door instead. There has to be a door."

A few minutes went by. Off in the distance in either direction we saw a few firefights going on, but nothing came out to fight us man-to-man—not yet.

Finally, Dickson called back. "I found an entrance sir, but it's locked."

"I'll be right there," I said and trotted into the bay. My black armored suit glinted in the bright sunlight.

When I arrived, I saw Dickson gesturing furiously at the door lock. His troops tried to spin a large wheel attached to it, but it wouldn't budge.

I stepped near brushing them all aside. "Let a man with some power give it a try."

Reaching into a pocket, I slipped out the Galactic Key. Galina had complained about my possession of it, but even she had to admit that it was for the best right now. She was trapped inside of a dragon on *Dominus*.

Running the key over the mechanism, I put my hands on the wheel and grunted. It spun easily in my hands. "You see there?" I asked. "Dickson, your men are weaklings. We're going to have some extra PT when we get back home."

"Very good, Centurion."

The big door swung open. Light troops raised their weapons and aimed into the passageway beyond. There were various pieces of scattered gear.

With our rifles held to our shoulders, we moved inside. The passageway did seem to be built for large humanoids. Not for Vulbites, and not for bears. If I had to guess, I would say this enemy was about as big as a human of my outsized dimensions—maybe even bigger.

Dickson's men rushed up a short flight of stairs. The door at the top of the steps flew open—it hadn't been locked like the external one. That was when we finally got our answer as to what we were facing.

At the top the steps, a heavily armed and armored soldier stood tall, and the moment the door opened, he hosed us down with plasma bolts. He showered everyone in the vicinity of the stairway.

Light troopers cried out. They fell back, their snap-rifles, hammering and blazing away. Blue fire blazed from a dozen sources, but this tall, broad-shouldered enemy didn't seem impressed. He just held down the trigger on his heavier rifle, spraying away with multiple splattering bolts of energy being fired out every second.

Dickson's men melted. Dickson himself was alive—I could tell from my HUD. I lifted my morph-rifle high and activated the grenade-launcher. I fired a single canister, which thumped off the chest of the soldier we were fighting. It dropped and clattered down among the crawling, dying light troopers.

A moment later, it went off. The big alien was blown off his feet. I rushed forward, and Harris followed. Heavy troopers and some of Sargon's weaponeers rushed with us. At the top of the steps, I was slipping on bodies and blood. I reached the enemy carcass and examined it.

When I investigated this new enemy, what I saw was both unsurprising and disheartening. The dead soldier that had mauled Dickson's platoon was a Saurian.

That only made sense because Armel commanded a legion of Saurians. Apparently, he'd dropped off a garrison of his best professional soldiers here at the mining complex. It was quite rude for him to bug out on these faithful troops. He'd abandoned them, running off with his transport to escape *Dominus*.

Regardless of his reasons, we were going to have to defeat his troops—and Saurians were tough. Room by room, chamber by chamber, they would fight us all the way across this complex. They wouldn't give up until the last one was kicking feebly in his death throes.

-38-

When I reported back to Galina that the factory complex was full of Saurians, she wasn't impressed.

"So what?" she asked, "of course, Armel left his army behind. He's that kind of a bastard. Kill them all and stop bothering me—unless you find something interesting."

Winslade made his report to her next, and he allowed me to listen in. When she was done chewing on him the way she had with me, he got onto a private chat channel with me.

"Well McGill," Winslade said, "it sounds like you and I have our orders. How many Saurians do you think there are inside this complex?"

"It's a pretty damned big facility. Six kilometers long from end to end. I'd have to guess… he probably left two or three lifters' worth of lizards behind."

"Three thousand Saurian troops inside one factory? That's just wonderful. I'm tempted to blow the whole thing up and have done with it."

"Wouldn't blame you if you did, but… Turov might not be happy."

Winslade was quiet for a moment. I could hear him buzzing in the background, talking to staffers. Was he actually considering some kind of detonation?

Finally, he came back on the line with me. "We're going to try something unconventional, McGill. Keep advancing, and keep your faceplates sealed."

Frowning, I relayed his order. We got moving again, and we found our way past the staircases and passages and moved into a large series of tunnels full of hot pipes. This led to the smelters.

Mining operations on low gravity worlds like this one all seemed similar. The easiest way to do mining was primarily through automation. On a rock with super-rich ore, it was a fairly easy process. All the machines had to do was scrape up a load of raw materials from the surface of the asteroid. Compressed into a ball, each chunk was a mix of silicon, metal and dust.

The mining system then sorted out these chunks, deciding what kind of metal was in the chunk and how rich each vein was before processing it. In the end, it was all melted down, cleaned off, and separated out by various chemical processes and temperature adjustments. Different metals melted at different temperatures, and whatever boiled up to the top was the good stuff.

Once the ore had been purified it was allowed to cool and harden again. The final sphere was shot up out of the asteroids minimal gravitational pull with a contraption that amounted to a big railgun. These balls were then caught in orbit by freighters and transported to their final destination. In this case, that destination was supposed to be Dark World.

Right now, due to our interference, the plant was in shutdown. There were no metal balls flying off into space. The rail gun was jammed up with a molten mess, with humans and Saurians shooting at each other in every chamber.

The battle became a serious slog. Even though we outgunned the enemy, they were on the defensive. They were desperate and determined. Man for man, they were bigger than we were. In close quarters, only a heavy trooper stood a chance against a Saurian warrior when it got down to knives and force-blades.

Most of our light troops were dead within an hour. Half the heavies died in the hour after that. But although the fighting was fierce, and it seemed to grind on and on, something changed as the third hour approached.

"Centurion? Look at the roof, sir!"

I followed Dickson's finger. Somehow, of all his light troops, he and two others had managed to survive. He at least had a breastplate, but I didn't credit that alone for his good luck. He was a skilled survivor—as hard to kill as a barn cat.

Looking up, I immediately saw what he meant. "Close your damn visors!" I shouted.

Some of the troops were gasping. After long hours of fighting, they'd gotten overheated. They'd opened their steamy suits and poured water into their faces. That was all natural enough while fighting in a hot factory environment, but a few of them hadn't bothered to button-up afterwards. Those were the men who were in trouble now.

Instant regret was felt by many as the roof of the complex was suddenly stitched with holes. These holes were being punched through with great rapidity. I knew I had to be witnessing an automated light-caliber gun turret, firing shells into the roof—but that didn't make much sense.

I didn't think Galina would do such a thing from *Dominus*. She wanted this factory to be taken with minimal damage.

I knew the answer to the riddle when I saw a face peep down from above. The holes in the roof hadn't been created by *Dominus*. No. It was a pack of sappers. Techs and other specialists who'd been held back from rushing into the complex, as they were essentially noncombatants.

A sabotage team had been deployed on the roof, laying charges spaced evenly over the top of the complex. Again and again, like hammer blows, these small charges popped and punched through the roof.

I saw circles of bright light shining down into the complex from the F-class star outside. The beams cut through the dust like lasers. Anyone's skin that was touched by one of those beams would blister up immediately.

Much worse than burns from the overly bright sun was the sound of escaping oxygen. My troops struggled with their helmets in a panic. The Saurians, on the other hand, were flat-out screwed. Most weren't wearing helmets at all.

I couldn't blame them for having lost their helmets. After all, it was hotter than Satan's nutsack inside the smelters, and I suspected they'd grown tired of living inside a bubble of their own released gases, anyways. Every spacer is treated to the joys of his own personal funk, and eventually they begin to regret their career choices.

"Attack!" I shouted, seeing the enemy was in disarray. "Charge into them and finish this!"

We rose up from our positions of shelter and fired into the enemy. We slaughtered the half that didn't have helmets. Then we moved into close-quarters.

The fight was brief and vicious. It was a mess, but we soon stood panting over about thirty Saurian corpses.

"Let's move up," I ordered, and we marched ahead.

We ran into more Saurians. Every other one was gasping for breath, and we managed to press the advantage, sweeping several large chambers clear of the enemy.

At last, however, we came to an exit near the intake machines. These were quiet, no longer digging up fresh rock. Off to the east stood a massive reactor. It was the primary power source for the entire complex. Inside this final bastion an unknown number of Saurian troops had holed-up.

Leeson, Harris and I immediately cast our weapons aside. We flung ourselves onto the hot, dusty deck of the half-wrecked mining complex and took a much-needed break.

Dickson wandered up to us. He gazed around in confusion. "Centurion… sir…? Aren't we going to prepare for the final assault?"

"Nope," I said.

Dickson pointed at the large swollen shape of the reactor which looked kind of like a giant teardrop-shaped water tank. The exterior was painted white to repel the radiation of the harsh star, and the undercarriage was supported by vast columns of pure metal.

"I'm sure we could do it," Dickson said. "All we'd have to do is set some charges, the way they did to open up the complex roof—"

I stood up and knocked his arm down. "We're not doing that. If Winslade wants to, he can give the order."

Dickson looked baffled. "But… what are we going to do? Wait for them to starve?"

"Not my problem. That reactor—that's too hard to replace, see. If we damage it, that's on us. If Winslade or Galina does it…" I shrugged.

"It can't be blamed on us?" Dickson finished.

"Don't bet on that," Leeson laughed. "The brass will try to find a way to call us destructive dumb-monkeys, but at least we can make a good case if we stay the fuck away from that building."

All around us, more units were straggling out of the complex and looking around. They looked tired and half-dead. No one came within fifty meters of the gigantic reactor. We encircled it, took cover from the glaring sun, and waited for new orders.

Dickson finally moved to take a seat near me. "You know, sir," he said. "The truth is, I'm not used to this kind of campaign. Usually, Victrix serves on more civilized worlds. Planets with air and inhabitants. There's always a local peasantry, of course, and a smaller group of nobility. We're almost always hired to protect the nobles from their peasants."

"Yeah, sure," I said, "we know all about your cushy bodyguarding assignments. That's not how Legion Varus operates. We usually end up on some shithole like this one."

"Always," Leeson corrected me. "Not usually… *always*."

Dickson nodded slowly, considering our words. He certainly couldn't deny the truth of them.

"All right then," he said. "What do you think Varus is going to do next?"

"We're at something of a standoff. We need that reactor to run this mine—so we can't destroy it. But we can't just let the Saurians sit in there forever, either. They might even blow it up—if they are so inclined."

We drank water and complained, using our tappers to play boring games. Now and then Kivi came in with a report from her buzzers, but it was always the same thing. The legion had mopped up the last of the Saurians outside of the reactor. We'd lost nearly half our number, but they'd lost more.

A lot of our final success had been due to Winslade's tactic of popping the pressure bubbles protecting every segment of the mining complex. I was pretty sure Galina, and probably

Drusus, were going to be mad about that. But again, it wasn't my problem.

Harris stood up about a half hour after the lull in the battle had started. He had a look of suspicion on his face. He sidled close to me. "McGill?" he said. "I've got a little suggestion for you."

"What's that, Harris?"

"Tell Kivi to put a trace on Dickson's tapper."

I stared at him for a moment. "Why the hell would I want to do that? I don't like foot-porn any more than you do."

Harris smiled, but the expression flickered out. "No, sir... I see him do things. That tapper of his... I'm a little suspicious of that boy."

"You're suspicious of everybody, Harris."

Leeson sidled up out of nowhere and interrupted. "In this rare case, I agree with Harris."

I glanced from one of my adjuncts to the other, and I shrugged. I told Kivi what I wanted. Within a few minutes, I was able to watch every finger stroke Dickson made on his arm. Every slip of a nail that Dickson generated was tracked and transmitted from his tapper to mine.

What I saw alarmed me, and I got to my feet in a hurry. I charged off, launching myself over broken pipes, scattered tools and rubble. When I found him, I grabbed Dickson by the shoulder and spun him around to face me. He dropped his tapper arm, but I clamped a big hand on his wrist and levered it up. The screen was blank.

"What you got there, Dickson? I asked.

"A new tapper-game, sir," he said, "I'm sure that you and your men would enjoy it. I thought I'd try it out thoroughly before I purchased the early access version, see—"

I let go of his hand, reached into my pocket, and fished out the Galactic Key. I ran it over his arm.

"Um... what are you doing, Centurion?" he asked curiously.

I levered that arm back up again. He strained to pull away from me, but although he was a strong man, he wasn't powerful enough. I wondered if he was going to pull a pistol or a knife—but he didn't.

"Let's just have a little look-see," I said. Using my offhand, I slid the key back in my pocket. Then I poked a fat finger at his arm.

"Sir, I don't know what you're—hey, maybe you should take a pill or something, Centurion. Did you take a hit in the head?"

His history came up. I was able to immediately revisit the last screens he had accessed. There was a face there. A face I hadn't expected to see again—possibly not in my entire existence. The face was Saurian, but it was different than most of them because it was blue-scaled.

-39-

"I know that cold-blooded reptile," I said, pointing to the scaly face on Dickson's tapper. "He's a mean alien, a spy of low repute. What are you doing with Raash's face on your tapper, Adjunct?"

Dickson sputtered. He was amazed and aghast.

"How did you do that?"

"I'm full of tricks. A good centurion always knows what his officers are up to. Answer the question, Dickson."

"What kind of tech are you using? Something illegal, I bet."

Dickson and I squared-off. I'm not a man with a short fuse, but I was about to put him out of my misery right there on the spot. Instead, I lifted my own tapper and poked at it some more. "You liked that, huh? Let's see how you like this next one."

Now that Dickson's tapper was hacked, I was able to lift Raash's ID from his history and call it myself. Dickson stood around bewildered and alarmed. I didn't care about his state of mind. I wanted to find out where Raash was and why Dickson was talking to him.

Raash answered the call. He looked at me with the same level of shock that I must have had in my face when I looked at him.

"Is this the McGill?" he said.

Glancing at the signal data, I was unsurprised to see the call was a local one. Raash was on this rock with Legion Varus.

"It sure is McGill, your favorite ape-descendant," I told him. "What the hell are you doing out here on this sorry ass star system?"

Raash squinted at me. "Are you mentally deficient? I'm working for Armel again."

"Yeah, I kind of figured that. Did you get fired from your job whelping out near-humans on Earth?"

"That is not a proper description of my recent past. You, as a human—"

I cut him off. "Yeah, yeah," I said, "Listen, I don't care what you did. I want to know where you are on this sunbaked rock, and how you fit into all this."

"I understand now," Raash said. "That officer, the man who said he was Victrix—he was a trickster. He is another ape throwing excrement from a tree—just like all of you. Primates are never to be trusted. It should be an axiom of my people."

"That's right, Rash. It should be. But I still want to know what you're doing here? And where are you exactly?"

"These are foolish questions. Both answers should be obvious, even to a creature of your low intellect. I am within the reactor that stands before you. It is the final Bastion of Armel's legions—our command center."

"Uh…" I said, "and why are you out here in the first place?"

"I am a liaison for Cancri-9," he said.

Cancri-9, better known as Steel World, was where the Saurians came from originally. It was their home world. Earth and Cancri-9 had a fate that was twisted together. Saurians and humans both considered themselves to be subjects of the Empire, but we operated more like disrespectful neutrals than allies. We rubbed shoulders as much as we rubbed elbows.

"I get it," I said, "you're a frigging spy, planted inside Armel's Legion by your government back on Steel World."

"Your random and spurious accusations are both pointless and incorrect," Raash said. He went on like that, denying everything.

I knew he was lying, of course. Raash had always been a Saurian spy, and he'd gotten in my way more than once.

Somehow, he was adept at mysteriously showing up all around the cosmos. In the end, he was always spying.

The last time I'd seen him was on City World. He'd had a miniature deep-link machine then, and he'd been using it to communicate with his home planet.

I turned toward Dickson and looked at him suspiciously.

"How do you fit into all this?" I asked him. "Are you a spy, too? Adjunct Dickson, do you work for Steel World or for Hegemony?"

"I work for Earth," Dickson said. "Isn't that good enough?"

"Yeah…" I said. "It probably is for now."

I turned back to Raash, who was just finishing up another tirade about my ancestry. "Okay, okay. So, you guys are both spooks. Dickson here, he's a plant from Central's Internal Security. Am I right, Dickson?"

Dickson didn't answer me, but he didn't have to. In my mind, a lot of things were knitting together.

He'd joined my Legion in a one-sided officer-trade from Victrix. But maybe he wasn't from Victrix originally. I now suspected he was really a hog, planted amongst real Legionnaires to keep an eye on us. I would have to have a very serious conversation with Dickson later on, but right now I needed to get whatever I could out of Raash.

"Hey, Raash, listen up," I said. "Maybe this chance meeting can benefit both of us."

"I do not see how such a thing is possible, human. Every time we've met, one or both of us die—possibly several times."

I nodded. "That's all true, old friend. But in this case, I think our needs coincide. Whether you're working for Steel World, or Hegemony, or yourself—you need to get your tail out of that reactor before Winslade blows it up."

"Such hypothetical impossibilities are unconvincing," Raash said. "Winslade won't blow anything up. He needs this complex. Earth needs this facility."

"We'd like to have it, that's true. But as you know, this *is* Legion Varus. Sometimes funny things happen, and stuff just blows up. In fact, did you know the last time I was out at Dark World I dropped a whole section of that orbital factory down on the planet? Millions of those poor Vulbites died. The Rigellian bears weren't able to rebuild the thing for years."

Raash narrowed his eyes to slits. He did not look happy. "Your threats could never impress a creature with a tail as long and magnificent as mine."

"I'm not *threatening* anybody, Raash. I'm just stating a fact. You know it's true. When Legion Varus and old James McGill come around, well sir, things just tend to blow up."

Raash digested this for a moment. "I will admit that you have a propensity for destructiveness."

"There you go. Now, we're on the same page. I think both you and Dickson, here, had better come clean and help me make sense of all this—before something really, really bad happens."

Dickson and Raash looked like a couple of kids that had been caught stealing candy.

"McGill," Dickson said, "you're sort of out of your league, here. Raash is known to me, and while I wouldn't call him a friend, I would call him a colleague."

"Now we're getting somewhere!" I said, forcing a smile. "You two are in cahoots, is that it?"

"We're attempting to negotiate the ceasefire you're talking about even now. It's time you got out of the way."

I blinked a few times and nodded. "Okay, well, in that case, what can I do to help? How can we end this peacefully before Winslade gets bored? Or maybe Imperator Turov gets nervous. One or the other of those two is likely to blow this place to Hell."

"Madness," Raash said. "You misunderstand the situation entirely, McGill."

"Uh... how's that, exactly?"

"It is *we* who are threatening to detonate this valuable facility. Dickson is attempting to persuade us not to do so."

My jaw dropped low, and I let out a hoot. "I get it now! You *are* repping Steel World! They want the metals contracts for Dark World, don't they?"

"My people have toiled long and hard for their wealth," Raash said. "We will not be denied a contract that secures our future."

I looked at Dickson. "So, that's why they're holed up in there? That's why they've been fighting so hard and half-wrecking the place? These frigging lizards want a cut of the cash for our starship production, don't they?"

Dickson shrugged. "I told you this was out of your league."

I laughed. "If you only knew how many ornery aliens I've had to cut deals with—well, never mind."

Cancri-9 wasn't called Steel World for nothing. Their primary export was metals—but that was only inside Province 921. Did these lizards really think they could force us to cut a deal with them?

"Let those of us who are not intellectually challenged speak together, McGill," Raash told me.

I decided he was probably right, and I tossed the conversation back to Dickson. However, I maintained my hacked link, so I could watch and listen to what was said.

After several minutes of getting nowhere quite slowly, my tapper buzzed. Another call was coming in. This time, it was a legion-wide announcement from Winslade himself.

"Troops," he said, "we're going to make a final appeal to these foolish lizards occupying our power station. If they do not submit to our will, Imperator Turov has decided we shall destroy the reactor entirely. Earth will just have to build a new one at a later date."

"That's insane!" Dickson said aloud. "McGill, Turov must realize that it will take us six months to a year to get this complex up and running again. That would back up the entire project. There will be a vast supply-chain delay."

Raash was talking again, too. "This statement was delivered with the singular tongue of cruelty that every human possesses in its head," he said. "The superior forked-tongued people of Cancri-9 will not submit to Earth."

"McGill," Dickson said, grabbing onto my shoulder with a thin, strong grip. "You've got to do something. This pack of rubes that you work for is going to fuck up everything!"

I considered his words, and my mind conjured up a half dozen ideas. I rejected them all as either unworkable or of insufficient value to attempt. Then the sky brightened, and I glanced upward.

"Sorry, Adjunct," I said. "Looks to me like it's a done deal."

Directly above us was the predatory hulk of *Dominus*. As there was no atmosphere, there was nothing to stop our eyes from gazing directly across space at the huge transport ship.

More significant than the great ship itself was the array of thirty-two fusion cannons that lined her flank. These had already fired a full barrage of shells. We hadn't heard the launch, but we could see the flashes of the muzzles and the streaks of escaping gases. Arcing trails grew behind each of the warheads as they plunged down toward us.

Dickson shouted, and he ran for cover. There was no point in running around like a headless chicken today. It would be downright embarrassing if any of my troops saw me do it. I stood tall and saluted death.

As the warheads streaked down, they seemed to move faster as they drew near. Near the end, I saw Raash's face in my tapper. His blue scales had split into what I calculated was an evil smile.

Could it be he was happy to die? Maybe he wanted to go out in a blaze of glory with all those Saurians trapped with him. As an agent of Steel World, he knew his planet stood to gain from this wild act of violence and destruction.

"Well played, Raash," I said. "Score one for your team."

Everything went white after that.

-40-

After a hasty revival, I found myself standing in a ragged line of officers on the command deck of *Dominus*. Galina was still in her predatory dragon battlesuit, striding around and threatening everyone with immediate death and dismemberment.

"You've put me in a very bad position," she complained. She kept tearing at the deck with her flashy metal claws as she walked in tight circles around us.

I looked dumb and almost bored. The others seemed to be scared shitless.

She stopped in front of Winslade and pointed one long claw at him. I'd seen her stab that claw into the chest of many victims, murdering them on the spot. "You ordered *Dominus* to fire her broadsides, destroying that complex."

Winslade, to his credit, did not flinch. "Not at all, sir. Merely the reactor was wrecked. The rest of the complex is only lightly damaged."

"What good is a mining complex with no power, you idiot?" she demanded.

He shrugged. "It's a minor inconvenience. Ultimately, Hegemony engineers will rebuild it. The odds are very long when it comes to capturing a complete piece of manufacturing infrastructure without damage, sir. They teach us that in the academy, you know."

"You smug little prick. Don't you give me an academy lecture."

"Your orders were to gain control of the factory by any means necessary. I merely followed your instructions."

"Oh, so that's it," Galina said, that claw was up again and pointing. "You plan to palm this all off on me. Finally, you reveal the true nature of this sabotage. You're not just wrecking critical equipment, no you're sabotaging me specifically."

I dared to clear my throat at this point. I could tell things were moving into the red zone.

Galina waved the rest of the claws dismissively in my direction. "You wait your turn, McGill. I'll get to you next."

Feeling I'd done my good deed for the day—or at least, I'd attempted to—I stood around while she reamed Winslade. It was when I noticed the floating drones behind Galina that I caught on. She was doing this in front of cameras—her cameras.

I knew how that was going to turn out. She'd edit her videos and snippets down to the best moments, then send it back to Central with her after-action report. That would be carefully designed to make everything look like the damage to the mining complex was someone else's fault.

Once I knew that, I was well and truly bored. Galina went on and on. At the end, she executed the trembling Fleet officers who'd dared to listen to Winslade and fire the broadsides.

"There," she said. "That should about do it—except for you, McGill."

As she'd promised, Galina got around to addressing me at last. "I understand, McGill," she said, "that you were involved in direct communications with the Saurians inside that reactor. Is this correct?"

I blinked twice, wondering where she had learned this factoid.

"Uh…" I said. "How did you…?"

"So, it *is* true," she said. "Is it not also true that you knew one of the enemy reptiles? That you were *friends* with this alien monstrosity?"

"Well… sort of. Raash and I do go back a ways, but we're not exactly friends. We tend to kill each other a lot."

"Raash? Is that the one?" She then glanced off to her left.

I followed her eyes and spotted a certain Adjunct Dickson. He had somehow quietly snuck onto the bridge with the rest of us.

"I know Raash," she said. "He's that freak with the unique scales, right? A mutant of some kind?"

"That's right. I caught Dickson over there chatting with him. That's how I got involved in the negotiations." I pointed an accusatory finger at Dickson, who looked like he'd swallowed a bug.

Galina's nasty metal head swung to look at Dickson, then back at me. "I'll sort this out later. You're all dismissed."

Once the deck had cleared some, I thought about asking if she would be needing my services tonight as her evening bodyguard. I'm not good at reading moods, but I could figure this one out all by myself. The answer was: *No.*

She'd wanted a clean victory, something that she could take home to Hegemony to clear her name. She hadn't gotten that—she'd gotten a clusterfuck instead. If there was one thing I knew for certain about every high-level officer, it was that they didn't like to be the one left holding the bag—especially when there was nothing but shit in it.

She put away her drones and ordered everyone to go back to their posts.

Winslade caught my attention after the dressing-down ended, and the group broke up. "Why were you talking to Raash?" he asked. "And what does that weird adjunct of yours have to do with all this?"

"It's an unsolvable mystery to me, sir."

Winslade was becoming suspicious, and I couldn't blame him. "Things have been strange lately," he said. "Starting off with you and Galina performing a mutiny, executing Captain Merton, and running off to capture Sky World on your own. I need answers, McGill. Not stonewalling."

"Excuse me, Mr. Tribune, sir, but I've got to go talk to the Imperator."

Winslade snorted with amusement. "*Talk* to her, hmm? I doubt that conversation will go the way you'd like. I rather think you're going to be out of luck this evening, McGill."

He let me go, and I rushed off after Galina. I caught up with her outside of her apartments. I knew she was probably going to go in there, remove her battle armor, and maybe take a shower or something.

Down on the asteroid, the techs were kicking into high gear. They'd put on their heaviest radiation suits and began to patch up every leak they could. They were even using reflective fabric to seal up some of the holes in the roof. The complex wasn't a total loss, but it was heavily damaged. It was going to take our construction crews a month to fix it—longer for the reactor, of course. It was a total loss.

Galina ignored me and walked her dinosaur-like dragon to her office doors. The doors shunted open and began to close—but I reached out a long arm, snagging the tip of her tail.

That tail was strong, and the servos whined and struggled. They were trying to curl up to avoid the closing doorway, but I prevented them from doing so. The door scissored together from both sides closing on the tail. It might have been my imagination, but that seemed to put a slight kink in it.

Galina finally became aware of what I was doing. She yanked the tail in, and I was left standing in front of the shut doors. I thumped on them a few times, but finally turned away in dejection. I hadn't taken two steps away down the corridor before they flashed open again.

A monstrous head poked out into the passageway again. "Give me one good reason why I don't burn you down right now."

"Because, Imperator," I said, "I have critical information. I know why Hegemony has been trying to arrest you and me both."

That got her attention. She stared for a moment, then quickly waved me inside. I followed her clanking machinery. The door closed, and she began to climb painfully out of the dragon.

"This frigging thing," she said. "It's fun to kill people with it, but if you spend all day inside, you get a backache."

"Don't I know it, sir. I spent months living in one back during the Machine World campaign. Did you know—"

"Shut up. I don't care."

I shut up and waited while she climbed out, stretched and washed her face. She spent several minutes in the bathroom during which I grew bored, so I headed over to her couch and made myself comfortable.

She came out of the bathroom with her hands on her hips. "Don't plan on making yourself at home, McGill."

"I wouldn't dream of it, Imperator. In fact, I should be going right now." I made a show of heading for the exit, but she got in the way. "You were saying something about these arrest warrants. What have you found out?"

I told her then about Dickson and Raash. I made an especially big deal out of the fact Dickson had as much as admitted to me that he was a Hegemony spook from Central.

"A spy…" she said, "of course. Right here in our midst. Right here to watch you, me and Winslade. No wonder he's been trying to charm me. It's diabolical."

"That's right, sir. He's been on our tail since City World."

"That's when all this started… He joined Legion Varus, and all of a sudden people start getting arrested. You were turned in first, then Graves got put into cold storage. Such effective evil. I'm shocked we didn't see it."

She was strutting around showing her fine white teeth in an expression that wasn't quite a smile. "We've got to do something about this, McGill. We've got to send the message back to them."

"Uh…" I said. "How's that, sir?"

"He's in your unit. Get him killed."

I shrugged. "I did that just today."

"Right. But now we know we've got a snake. He needs to die again, then we can delay his revival—or tragically lose his files."

"Oh… yeah, that would do it."

"All right. For now, I want you to get him killed. I'll keep him on ice until we get home."

I thought that over and nodded. "Easy-peasy."

"I'm sure you can't feel good about this," she said. It's painful to know you've been spied on, but it's worse to know you're being spied on, and you don't know who is doing it.

I knew this was my cue to start spinning some bullshit. "Yeah, it makes me feel a little weird inside—kinda violated. So... how about tonight, anyways?" I asked.

"How about tonight, *what?*"

Dammit... I was being way too clumsy even for old McGill. It took me a half-second to come up with an indirect approach. "Um... how about I go down to the modules, and I take care of Dickson, nice and clean-like. Then, I'll come back up here and spend the night on that couch right there."

She looked at the couch, and then she looked back at me doubtfully.

"Come on, now," I said. "You've got to sleep sometime, Imperator. You're looking a little tuckered out, and I'm just the man to keep a careful eye on things while you get some shuteye."

She crossed her arms. "If Dickson is dead, I won't need a bodyguard."

"Hold on, now. We know about Dickson, sure... but there might be others. Hell, this ship is probably *teeming* with spies. Who knows how many there are?"

"What are you talking about?"

"On top of that, there are those Fleet-pukes you keep killing every day. Who cleans this place? Do you have a cabin steward, by any chance?"

Galina's expression changed from suspicious to nervous. She was a paranoid woman—and she had good reason to be. People really did want to do her harm. She watched me as I made a show of looking under her bed.

"We're just talking about you playing watchdog, right?" she asked.

Solemnly, I put my hand over my heart. "I swear it. No funny business, just an all-night vigil."

She chewed her lip for a moment, considering my offer. "All right. Go scrape Dickson off my shoes and come back here. We'll hole-up together."

Smiling, I hopped off the couch and strode to the exit. After I marched outside, I made sure her door was shut behind me and double-locked.

-41-

When I got back to my unit's module, I didn't summon Dickson to speak with me. In fact, I made no effort to talk to him at all. Instead, I talked to Sargon. Taking him aside, I told him what I wanted—and he agreed eagerly.

"To tell you the truth, Centurion," he said, "I'm starting to hate that guy. Just about everybody in the unit hates him. Did you know that?"

"I kind of suspected… thanks for the good turn."

"No problem, sir." Sargon laughed.

After checking my tapper messages, two of which were from Dickson himself, I ignored everything and headed for the showers.

I actually did need a shower. As combat operations might not be over with yet in this star system, I figured that I had to take any opportunity to cleanse myself that came long.

To my surprise, when I was about halfway through lathering-up a presence appeared. I washed the soap out of my eyes and looked around.

There was Dickson. He was standing in the showers with his arms crossed. He was fully dressed, and his face looked kind of sour.

"Centurion?" he said. "Could I have a word, sir?"

"You sure can," I said, and I threw him a bar of soap.

He caught it and looked at it with bewilderment.

"Nobody stands around in the showers to talk to people, Dickson. That's weird. Either lather-up or get out."

He grumbled a bit, but he stepped in and began bathing. "This does actually feel good," he admitted.

"Just make sure it doesn't feel too good, Adjunct."

He laughed. "No, sir. I wanted to thank you Centurion. You've been quite an entertaining commander all these months. I've actually learned quite a bit from you."

"Is that so?"

"Now, I hope you aren't offended by my studies of your unique style of leadership. We've both performed side-missions of our own, right? I know for a fact that you've done things like that—that you've moonlighted for Hegemony."

I glanced at him and thought that over. "That's true," I admitted.

"Good," he said, "as long as we understand one another, perhaps we can kick our relationship in a new direction."

"Whoa!" I said. "This doesn't sound like a conversation I want to have while we're taking a shower together."

Dickson laughed. I shut off my water and toweled off. He was still shampooing his hair and luxuriating in the warm water when I walked out.

In the passageway, I saw Sargon standing with his girlfriend Kivi beside him. I jabbed a thumb over my shoulder. "He's all yours."

Sargon nodded. Kivi looked a little concerned, but she followed him into the showers anyway.

Something like twenty minutes later, there was a knock on my module door. Harris threw it open. "Centurion," he said, "there's been a killing."

I stood up and came around from behind my desk, walking sternly. "Who?"

"Sargon nailed Dickson in plain sight."

"Wow…" I said, pretending to be surprised. "Well… you know, Harris, Dickson is an abrasive man. This is Legion Varus, and sometimes our troops tend to get a little ornery."

Harris shook his head vigorously. He was frowning deeply. "No, sir. That's not going to wash this time. We've got an enlisted man murdering an officer while he was naked."

I walked out into the module's common area, and I saw Sargon standing there. He wasn't exactly looking guilty, but he did seem uncomfortable. I made a show of putting my hands on my hips. "Sargon, what the hell happened?"

Harris jumped in excitedly. "He frigging killed Adjunct Dickson! That's a veteran murdering an officer. It wasn't even in the middle of an exercise or anything, just a straight-out fragging."

"Personal issues?" I asked Sargon.

He nodded and studied the floor. His hair was still wet. "He just kept on hitting up on Kivi, you know," Sargon said, "while we were in the shower. Couldn't keep his eyes off her—or shut his mouth."

"Huh…" I said, "all right. Take him to the brig, Harris. He's under arrest and on report."

Harris marched Sargon away, and Kivi came to talk to me. "You aren't going to let them do anything to him, are you McGill?"

"Not really…"

"I mean," she said nervously, "he did beat Dickson to death in the showers, but—"

I put a big finger to my big lips and shushed her. "Stop worrying about it, Kivi. Go get drunk or something."

She left me dejectedly, and I walked out of the module before Harris could come back. I knew he would be demanding all sorts of inquiries and details, and I didn't want anything to do with any of it.

Instead, I walked up to Galina's headquarters and tapped on the door. After she investigated me thoroughly with her cameras, she let me in.

"Is the matter taken care of?" she asked. She checked her tapper. "Ah yes, I see that it is. There's another very special package in the revival queue. Perhaps I'll just…" She flicked her finger over her tapper. "Oh no, how unfortunate. Dickson's data has been temporarily lost."

"That's a damned shame."

She smiled at me then, and it was a wicked thing to see. To make a long story short, I spent the night in her cabin—but I didn't stay on her couch for long.

* * *

We were jolted awake by loud alarms, flashing lights, sirens—the works. Galina and I tumbled out of bed half-asleep and entirely naked. We rolled onto the deck, one of us on each side of her bed. We began dragging on clothing as fast as we could.

"What the hell's happening?" Galina asked me.

"No clue, sir."

She opened up her tapper and angled her arm up at her face, so that the camera only caught the ceiling of her quarters in the background. She contacted Gold Deck demanding to know what the hell had gone wrong.

The XO stood there shivering like a leaf. "It's something big, sir... I've never seen anything like it."

"What are you blathering about?"

"A ship, sir. It's got us in a gravity-beam."

Galina insisted the XO relay the external video feed to her, and she flicked it onto the wall of her quarters. I was in the midst of dragging on my boots, but when I looked at the wall, I dropped one of them. Galina made a strangled-cat sound. My mouth fell open and stayed that way.

"Holy shit," I said.

"It's a Skay," Galina said. Her voice was tiny and full of fear.

There was no denying the reality of what we were witnessing. A massive sphere had appeared in orbit over Sky World. It was nearly perfect—way too smooth and round to be a natural satellite.

As we watched, it boldly approached the planetoid under us. It was a huge thing, big even for a Skay.

"Look at the gravimetrics," Galina said, pointing to the readouts at the bottom of the display. The readings... it's massive. Much bigger than our Moon."

"Looks like it's the size of Mars," I said. "Maybe even bigger than that. We've never seen one that size. I didn't know they grew them so big out in the Core Worlds."

Galina looked at me. Her eyes were huge and scared. "It's got to be here to destroy us, James. You reported that you spotted one of these things at Rigel. Is this the one you saw?" She aimed a finger at the screen. Her voice was accusing, as if this was somehow all my fault.

I shrugged. "I don't rightly know, sir. I only saw it for a minute out of a window. There wasn't much in the way of nearby objects to provide a size reference. It *could* be the same one—or it could be a different one."

She turned back, staring at the approaching monstrosity. "That's great," she said, "there could be more of them on the prowl. We've got to get out of here."

By this time, we both had our clothes on with smart straps reaching for one another across our backs, cinching up and tightening. She ignored her hair, which fortunately was short enough that when she put a cap on it looked pretty good anyway, and we rushed out the door to the command deck.

Once on the bridge, Galina began to stroll around, giving orders. That was when she and I realized she had forgotten to get into her dragon.

Galina was just one small, unarmed and unarmored woman with an attitude. She was a Hegemony officer who had been intimidating everyone, throwing orders around on Gold Deck on a ship which didn't really belong to her.

She glanced back at me, and I lifted my morph-rifle suggestively. Fortunately, I'd thought to put my armor back on.

Galina looked around at the crew after only a single moment's hesitation. To cover for her mistake, she went into action. She gave orders as if she meant them and had been born to deliver them. Inner confidence and a projection of the aura of command was often better than true legitimacy in emergencies. Even mutinous commanders were unlikely to strike you down lest everyone die in the confusion.

"Break orbit," she ordered. "All engines, ahead full. We're getting the hell out of this system on sublight power. Once we're safely away from the mining complex, go into warp."

"Sir?" the XO said, "sir, we're already doing that."

Galina rounded on her. "Then why the hell aren't we moving?"

"Because of that thing, sir. It has gravity beams. They're too strong—they're worse than anything I've ever dealt with."

Galina looked fearfully at the wall displays. The growing Skay was getting larger as it came closer. So far, it hadn't fired a shot, and neither had we. Right then, she and I both knew what it meant to do.

"It's going to eat us," Galina said.

"That's right," I said. "It's going to open up that big mouth and suck us right inside. Then it will tear this ship apart and have itself a big titanium dinner."

The crew looked bewildered. They hadn't dealt with aliens of this nature before.

"Go into warp, now." Galina ordered.

"But sir, that's highly dangerous, we're too close—" the navigator began.

"Go into fucking warp!" Galina screamed at him, her voice cracking.

The navigator recoiled as if physically struck. He waved to the helmsman who moved to obey the order. *Dominus* groaned and heaved under our feet. The lights flickered. We went into warp, and it felt as if the field touched our skins. We'd all just gotten a dose of radiation.

The ship was unprepared. The crew was unprepared—worst of all, no one had typed a destination into the computers.

"We're away, sir," the XO said in relief, "but I think that monster is following us."

"Of course, it is," Galina said. "Can we steer this ship or are we flying blind?"

"No sir, we can't steer now. Whatever direction we're moving in, that's the way we're headed until we come out of warp."

"Full power to the engines," Galina said. "Give it everything we've got."

We all strapped in and nervously studied our instruments. Power levels were good. There didn't seem to be much damage to the ship—I dared to believe we might escape.

Nothing disastrous happened for the next few minutes, so I moved to Galina's command chair. She was taking deep breaths. Her heart rate and breathing slowed down.

"It can't get us in warp," she said. "Right?"

"I don't think so, sir."

She turned to me. "McGill… what are we going to do now? How do we get away from this thing? It's right on our tail."

"That's right, sir. Once one of these big bastards gets their gravity-hooks into you, it'll never give up. At this point, we can jump, but we can't hide."

Galina's breathing increased again. "All right… we're headed in a random direction. There's about a ninety percent chance that we're headed out of the galaxy—either upward or downward out of the disk."

"You are correct, Imperator," the navigator said.

Galina thought about that, and she nodded. "Yes," she said, "after a hundred lightyears or so. We'll be out beyond all the stars in a random direction."

I walked close to her and lowered my voice. "That's not good, sir."

"No, it's not, McGill. None of these Fleet losers know what to do, either. They all hate me, but they know shit when it comes to escaping a Skay."

"To the best of my knowledge, none of them have ever tried to do it," I said.

"Useless!" Galina shouted at the crewmen. "You're all frigging useless!"

I reached into my helmet and gave my nose a thoughtful scratch. "Maybe… uh…"

"What? What?"

"Well… I dunno."

She made a sound of frustration and began pacing the deck. "We'll be flying off into nothingness within a day or less. That's if the Skay doesn't have some super-tech that will blow us out of hyperspace when it gets bored."

I nodded. "That's a distinct possibility."

"We have to do something. We have to save ourselves—and soon."

Galina paced for a while, then finally came to a decision. It was hard for her. I knew that she liked to bail out of situations like this. She didn't want to be the one making the hard, no-win choices. She did some checking on her tapper, then growled in horrific frustration. A few crewmen scuttled away in fear.

"I don't believe it," she said.

"Huh?"

"The damage crews—they went down there to repair the factory, remember?"

"Yeah."

"Well, they took the gateway posts down with them."

"Oh…" I said, suddenly getting it. Of course, they'd taken the gateway with them. They needed heavy equipment from Earth to repair the mining complex.

The second thing that occurred to me, based on Galina's statement, was that she was considering bailing out on everything. *Dominus*, Legion Varus—everything.

She was talking again, so I tried to listen. "We have to come out of warp briefly. We'll aim our prow in a direction that makes sense, then jump back into hyperspace again."

"That sounds dangerous. It's going to come out right on top of us."

"I know that McGill. Don't you think I know that?"

The XO had the balls to clear her throat about then, gaining her a few unwelcoming eyeballs. "Another emergency warp jump?" she asked. "Two in a row? The whole ship might tear itself apart."

Galina threw up her hands. "Well, it's that or we just let this thing run us down and light us up." Her breathing was ragged again. She didn't like making hard decisions on the fly. Especially when she didn't have any training or background in these matters.

"Maybe… just an idea, now… maybe we should wake up Merton again."

"No. Never. He'll screw me somehow, taking credit if we win and blaming me if we don't." She thought about it some more, then she stared at me. "No…" she said. "I've got a plan. I know what we're going to do. Crew, prepare to drop warp, change course and then re-engage."

"That's crazy, sir," The executive officer told her. It was the most daring thing I'd seen the woman do, and I clapped my hands for her in appreciation.

Galina and the XO faced off.

The XO had been chosen for sheer weakness of mind and spirit. She'd never said squat to Galina before, but possibly that was because she was no longer inside of her dragon suit.

Galina wasn't having any backtalk today. She smoothly drew her pistol, aimed it at the surprised officer, and shot her down.

"Do we have any more smart-alecs aboard?" she asked.

No one said a word.

"All right, prepare to execute my orders—and stop looking at me like that. We'll probably survive. If that Skay catches us, no one will ever know what happened to the ship. There will be perming for the lot of you. There won't be any records, nothing. We'll all just simply vanish in the depths of space. Is that what you all want?"

Terrified, several of them slowly shook their heads.

"All right, then. Follow me. Listen up. Obey my orders as rapidly as you can, and we might yet live to see tomorrow."

The crew got busy, and soon the big moment came. *Dominus* shuddered again, and we came out of warp. We hadn't gone all that far, as it turned out—less than a dozen lightyears.

"Turn the ship for Earth!"

"It'll take a moment, sir," the navigator said, "we're getting our bearings.

Galina gritted her teeth, and she turned to the communications people. "Is that damned thing still out there?" she asked.

The techs pointed at the displays. "There it is. It's just coming out now."

The giant cue ball-shaped monstrosity known as a Skay coalesced into existence behind us. It seemed to have grown even bigger than the last time we saw it. With every passing second, it closed in on our tail.

"Communications!" Galina cried, "connect me to Central! Emergency channel override!"

It took perhaps seven seconds for the connection to go through, but it seemed like a lifetime. I can tell you those were the seven longest seconds of my life. At any moment, I felt like the Skay might get tired of the game and decide to open fire. At this range it could destroy us with one shot.

So far, Galina had not ordered a single salvo to be fired at the monster. We didn't want to piss it off unnecessarily. It seemed bent on closing with us and probably devouring us. Perhaps it meant to dissect and study us. Whatever the case, as long as it wasn't shooting, we'd figured it wouldn't be smart to provoke it.

We all knew there was no weapon aboard *Dominus* that could penetrate that massive hull anyway.

"Central?" Galina asked the moment an admiral appeared on the screen. The man quickly got over his initial shock, and he seemed angry.

"Turov?" he said. "What are you doing sitting in Captain Merton's chair? Do you realize that your arrest was scheduled almost thirty days—?"

"Shut up," Galina told the admiral. "Just listen to me. Consul Drusus has given me special and specific orders. *Dominus* is returning to Earth and we're bringing with us an alien spacecraft which may or may not be hostile."

She then tossed video of the massive Skay that was closing on our tail. Its mouth had stretched open. Every Skay had a huge rectangular door cut into the midpoint, somewhere around where an equator would be on a regular planet. This door could roll open and allow gases out or debris, like a spaceship, in.

"This visiting dignitary," Galina said with a straight face, "has demonstrated unclear intentions. We're going to warp now, and we'll see you in a few weeks."

"Are you mad?" demanded the admiral, boggling at the Skay. "Don't bring that thing to Earth! You don't have authorization to do this, you can't—"

Galina's hands gripped the command chair like claws. She leaned forward snarling at the admiral. "We're coming, Admiral. This is your one and only warning. Goodbye."

She reached for the cut-off button, but the admiral spoke with urgency. "Wait. Don't come to Earth! Take it to Mars instead."

Galina blinked twice. She glanced at navigational techs. "Can you do it?"

"One second, sir… course adjusted. We're good."

"Engage!"

She didn't even bother to cut off the transmission to the deep-link. The screen went black. The ship shuddered. For a few seconds it felt like we'd put our brains inside a microwave—then we were gone. *Dominus* jumped back into warp and disappeared, leaving the Skay to trail after us.

-42-

The flight back to our home solar system was a tense one. The techs and lab monkeys informed us the Skay was still on our tail in hyperspace, still making strange attempts to waylay us.

"How is that even possible?" Galina complained. She was back in her dragon suit and marching over the bridge deck plates. Every time she went by, the Fleet people cast her hateful looks. "Nothing can shoot at you while you are in hyperspace. That's how it's supposed to work!"

None of the Fleet pukes had the balls to say anything back to her. But as I was there, lounging around and playing watch-gorilla, I shrugged and gave it my best guess. "Well, sir," I said, "it's possible—just possible mind you—that the Skay have tech we don't. They've been flying in hyperspace for thousands of years. What if they've developed something so advanced—"

"Shut up, McGill," she said, whipping around so hard that her tail slashed the top of a console. That caused a Fleet monkey to duck as his cap was swept off his head by the tip of it. "I know they have better tech than we do. I just can't believe my frigging luck. Why am I getting chased by a Skay of all creatures?"

"Well, sir," I said, trying to be helpful yet again. "Maybe it's because we attacked Sky World. See, that's part of Rigel's property, and—"

She told me to shut up again, and I finally got the message loud and clear when I found myself staring down the fat barrels of her chest-cannons. She didn't want answers. She wanted to bitch.

That was the way it was on the flight home for about two whole weeks. Galina did allow me to stay with her in her cabin, at least that was a pretty fun time for old McGill. Most nights, she was eager to let off some steam in bed.

Don't think there was anything terribly romantic about it. For her, it was just a way to distract herself from the grim situation she had gotten herself into. She had started off by running from Hegemony's internal security a month or two back. As part of that dodge, she'd tricked Drusus into sending us to go off and investigate Sky World.

Now, the chickens were coming home to roost. We'd ended up losing a lot of equipment, destroying a goodly portion of the mining complex we were attempting to capture and pissing off the biggest Galactic anybody from Earth had ever laid eyes on. Normally, the Skay were about the size of our Moon, something like three to four thousand kilometers in diameter. This monster was way bigger, more on the order of five or six thousand kilometers in diameter.

That may not sound like a big deal, but we're talking about spaceships. When it comes to fighting in space, size really does matter. Bigger is almost always better. A larger ship is capable of generating more power, and the amount of power you generated allowed your ship to fire a beam that was deadly at a greater range.

Since obstacles are rare in space, the ship with the greater range could reach out and strike first. Any opposition would be fried before they shot back.

Now, we had managed to get the biggest single ship in history to chase us across the cosmos with bloodlust in its eye. You could just tell the Skay was pissed. It could have done a whole lot of things other than follow our vessel across the cosmos.

It must know, for instance, that we were headed for Earth. It could have taken an angular shortcut early on after our first jump, or it could have veered off to Dark World to protect the space factory. Another option would have been to simply recapture and defend Sky World—but no, it had done none of these things. Instead, it had followed us doggedly, absolutely determined to destroy *Dominus* and capture the irritating meat-creatures that flew her. It was out to consume us and exact revenge.

The legion held multiple boarding simulations to pass the time, as if alien marines were going to raid our ship in hyperspace. That seemed highly unlikely to me. The most likely scenario would be that the minute we got out of hyperspace, if we were close enough, the Skay was going to burn a hole in our butts. No amount of target practice on the snap-rifle range was going to change our fate. Not this time.

At last, the fateful day came. Galina and the XO huddled-up trying to decide how far from Mars we should be when we emerged from hyperspace.

"All right," the XO said, speaking calmly and quietly. She was our third XO in a week, and she'd learned the dos and don'ts through careful observation. None of the previous XOs had been approved for revival, so it mattered.

Her chosen approach, which I approved of, was calm and deliberate—but not in any way argumentative or insistent. She made her point, she stated it clearly and then Galina did whatever the hell she wanted. Even if her orders were batshit-crazy.

"According to Fleet regulations," the XO said calmly, "in this situation we should emerge at a range of approximately one hundred thousand kilometers outside of Mars' atmosphere. That will be far enough out to prevent any sort of radiation exhaust damaging local traffic or satellites. It also will allow ample time for the defenders of the colony to target our pursuer and analyze their best defensive course of action."

"Yes, yes, yes," Galina said, "I know all about your regulations and other assorted nonsense. I'm not interested. I'm interested in the survival of this vessel. I'm interested in the destruction of the Skay."

The XO nodded politely and made no move to argue. She did, however, repeat her point again. That was a danger signal to me. "I understand, sir," she said. "I'm only attempting to tell you—"

"And I'm attempting to tell you that I'm not interested in following regulations. The Skay has an insane range quotient. I looked at the math. You guys have run all the numbers on your defensive boards over there. It can easily strike Mars from one hundred thousand kilometers out."

"That's probably true," the XO admitted, "but—"

"But nothing! If we deliver this monster on their doorstep at that range, Mars will not be able to strike the Skay with all her guns. I know you have a fortress on Phobos and some surface batteries as well. I want them all to open fire on the Skay immediately."

The XO blinked in alarm. "But sir… even combined, I don't think they can take out a Skay—certainly not one of this size and ferocity."

Galina was showing signs of stress. Her claws were scarring up the deck plates something fierce right now. Fresh, bright metal showed under her claws as they scratched and gashed the deck up with every step.

"Here's what I foresee if I follow your ludicrous advice. We will appear one hundred kilometers out. The Skay will appear behind us. It will unload all of its guns on *us* not on the Mars base. The hog commanders on Mars will be out of range and surprised. I know these people, they're just like you. They will sit and watch."

The XO put up one finger then. This was a daring moment for her. "Mars should be able to use both T-bombs and a full missile barrage. It will take some time for these weapons to reach the enemy vessel."

"We won't have that time!" Galina said. "We'll be nearly ten minutes out. That monster is going to lock on, and it's going to eat us before any distracting attacks land."

They moved to the planning boards, and they wargamed it out. The XO became increasingly alarmed as the plans unfolded. "You're going to drop the Skay right on top of Mars? Almost inside the atmosphere?"

"Not *that* close… but it is an interesting idea. If the Skay were to ram into a planet—but no, that would cause too many civilian deaths."

The XO seemed horrified that Galina would even consider such a thing. I could have told her a few stories that would have made her hair stand on end.

"Here's what we're going to do," Galina continued. "The enemy must be forced to deal with Mars the moment we come out of warp."

The XO looked concerned. "Forced to deal with... as in being forced to defend itself against Mars?"

"Exactly. I want every gun on Mars beaming away in a panic the moment we get there. If that doesn't distract it into not destroying us, nothing will."

The XO chewed at her lower lip. She looked kind of pretty doing that. If circumstances had been different... but no. Galina wasn't in the mood to be cheated on these days.

She gave the crew their fateful orders, they laid in the course, and they fell silent. It only served to set Galina off, though. She'd gotten her way, but it was obvious the deck crew wasn't behind her.

"We are about to come out of hyperspace quite close to Mars," she said. "Illegally close. That will be due to an unavoidable computer error. It was not deliberate—do you all understand?"

The crew studied the deck plates in dejection.

"I will personally destroy anyone's career who says otherwise. Jailtime, permings—there is no punishment too severe."

They were silent, but underneath, I could sense an undercurrent of resistance. Galina could sense it too, so she kept talking.

"No one will care about the facts," she told them. "When this battle is finished, they'll care about the final results and nothing else. If those results go in our favor, then we're all heroes. If the results do *not* go in our favor, then it probably doesn't matter anyway. The Skay might have enough firepower to destroy every human in the Solar System."

"Then why the hell did we lead them here in the first place?" I dared to ask.

She wheeled around, marched over to me and punched a steel fist into my chest. I had stardust armor on and plenty of padding underneath, but I still felt that punch. I staggered back.

"Hey," I said.

"What matters, James," Galina said, "is that we'll all be permed if we can't stop one Skay. We've already lit this fuse. Now it's time to set off the bomb and place it as optimally as we can."

The crew obeyed her out of fear. We all watched the clocks as the minutes ticked down. At last, the moment of truth came, and *Dominus* emerged from warp.

-43-

We appeared less than five thousand kilometers above the atmosphere of Mars. Now, five thousand kilometers is a pretty good distance if you're riding a bike or flying an aircar, but when it comes to space battles, it's essentially point-blank range.

It was like a gunfight where both guys have their pistols pressed against the other man's belly. Neither could miss, and neither could afford to hold back.

It wasn't two seconds after we appeared in our home space that the Skay appeared right behind us. There was only one piece of good news to be had, the Skay's mouth was wide open, leaving it vulnerable to attack.

One of the scanner people threw a priority override video toward the holotable which immediately flared into life. We could see the situation clearly. The Skay was behind us—its big, rectangular mouth was open, and it was firing out invasion ships that were as black as space. The sleek vessels poured out like hornets buzzing out of a nest that's just been run over by a tractor.

Within seconds, a hundred of them had been released. They individually flared bright blue lights, which I knew were their engines lighting up afterburners. They pursued *Dominus*, and more of them kept on coming. The Skay must have been manufacturing extras and waiting for this exact opportunity.

Naturally, our own sublight engines were blasting for all they were worth. We were quickly being overtaken by the swarm, but in less than a minute, Mars got involved.

Normally, a pack of hogs and Fleet chair-force boys could sit and talk for hours before lifting a finger to do battle—but not today. We'd brought this conflict home and dump-squatted the mess right into their faces. The fortresses on Mars and the ships parked in orbit around her got into action right-quick.

They made their calculations and realized that they had to fire at the Skay. It was 'use it or lose it' time. The range was so close and the warning time so short that no one could afford to wait until they'd been hit first before releasing every missile, teleport bomb and beam cannon they had.

At first, dozens, then hundreds, then finally thousands of individual particle cannons spoke. Some fired pulses, other fired single beams like threads that burned a lavender light through the thin air of Mars.

These countless beams reached out and drew raking lines across the surface of the Skay. Some of them fired on the ships that were chasing us as well, and a dozen of the sleek invasion ships were destroyed.

After the beams hit, I saw that a great number of the bombs and missiles gushed upward—and they were wisely aiming for that gaping mouth on the front of the Skay.

Taken somewhat by surprise, the gigantic vessel began rolling the door shut. Like sardines wriggling out of a narrowing pipe, a few hundred more invasion ships escaped. They were sleek arrows of black metal. Those that didn't make it flared into pinpoints of brilliant light.

"The bombs are hitting now!" one of the sensor ops said excitedly. "Look!"

He was right. Counterfire from Mars was starting to land. There were strikes inside that closing mouth. I could see bright spots like lightning going off inside.

"Teleport bombs…" I said, "you think we got any teleport bombs in there?"

"Maybe a few," the tactical officer told me. "I've been watching for that. We're getting in some beam hits, but our teleport bombs… I just don't think the Skay is angled the right way. We can only teleport in a straight line, and the angle on that opening… it's just not there."

"Too damned bad," I lamented. "If we'd tossed *one* right into its mouth and hit the core, we could have knocked it out of the fight in one shot."

"It is what it is. They're doing some damage, and they're making it shut its mouth."

Realizing the Fleet people needed a win, I grinned big. "That's right, I said pumping my fist in the air. "There's nothing a Skay hates more than a swift kick in the jaw."

A ragged cheer went up from the tense bridge crew. I'd been hoping against hope that the Skay wouldn't manage to get his mouth completely closed—that one of our strikes might break its jaw, so to speak and damage those massive hinges and gears that slid that mouth open and shut. But we weren't that lucky.

Although a fair number of strikes popped off in and around the opening, it wasn't enough to kill the Skay or even to stop its relentless pursuit of *Dominus*.

The Skay had rolled its mouth shut about a minute after we'd arrived over Mars. Everything else the fortifications had thrown at the hull seemed to bounce right off.

Oh sure, there were burning scars all over the exterior. Craters, molten spots, black scorch marks and gouges appeared all over the place. The Skay was even sent into a slight spin due to being struck hard over and over again, but by no means was it knocked out.

We sailed by Mars with the Skay and its little invasion ships trailing in our wake. But then, as the Skay kept on getting bombarded and blasted right in the butt by Mars, the behemoth began to perform a slow roll. It wheeled on its harassers, like a great beast that finally stops running and turns on the pack of baying dogs.

"Mars has been jabbing at his hindquarters for too long, I guess," I said, and the others agreed.

Everyone was breathless while there was a pause in the battle. The Skay finally answered the relentless attacks from Mars with a massive beam. It was something bigger, brighter and thicker than I'd ever seen.

This blazing light from the heavens stabbed toward the fortifications on Phobos. The rock was small, as moons go, only about eleven kilometers across.

"Holy shit…" I said, gasping.

The whole of the moon lit up and glowed. It was like it was wrapped in the power of the Skay, like the hand of some elder god had reached out to snuff the missile-firing irritant.

When the great beam died at last, we found to our shock and dismay that the entire thing had disappeared. Phobos was gone.

"Whoa," I said, "that's not good."

There were exclamations of horror from the Fleet pukes all over the command deck. "There were seven thousand crewmen assigned to that station," one of them told me. "They were wiped out by a single punch."

"Yeah," I said. I pointed a long finger at the holoplate. "Don't look now, but that bad ol' boy is rotating again. I think its cannon is going to be focused on a new spot next."

Everyone watched in horror as the main gun of the Skay—something which we couldn't even see a barrel or a projector for—turned and aimed toward the colony. That was a cluster of dome-like structures that contained most of the humans on Mars.

As if they knew their fate in advance, we saw a hundred new red flaring rockets leap up from the immediate vicinity of the domes. They'd launched everything they had.

They were already firing dozens of pulsing beams that turned lavender when they punched through the thin layer of cloud cover. But it seemed to me like their fire was a little bit disorganized. They weren't hitting one singular point hard and long enough to bust through the Skay's dense hull and score a kill.

"Those gunners seem a little bit panicked," I said. "They're not acting with careful coordination."

The Skay's big, bright blue beam lit up once more. It leapt out across space, finding the cluster of domes that marked Mars City—and utterly destroyed her.

"Geez," I said wincing in pain for all those lost souls. "That's some hard luck right there."

The missiles and beams that had been coming from that part of Mars stopped pouring up into space. I turned to Galina, who was watching the battle with just as much fascination and horror as I was.

"Galina?" I said. "We've got to turn *Dominus* around. We've got to fire the broadsides."

"What the hell for, McGill?" she scoffed. "It's already closed that big door. We can't penetrate that hull."

"Nope—but we might be able to distract it."

She eyed me for just a second, and I could tell she was considering the idea even though it wasn't her usual response to a situation like this.

Galina fought battles following the logic and rules of predatory creatures everywhere. If a battle was easy, with good rewards, she would pounce and abuse whatever lesser being had dared to stray across their path. But if something looks dangerous, or if it might permanently injure her, she would dance away, awaiting a better opportunity.

Today, however, she seemed uncertain. "I think I understand your suggestion, McGill," she said. "If we do turn and fight, we can use that to our advantage later."

"Uh…" I said. "What are you talking about? Listen, we've just brought doom home to Mars. We've killed all kinds of—countless even—civilians. There had to be kids under that dome. All kinds of people. A lot of them won't be backed up. Some will be missing years of growth and memories. Others will be permed for sure."

Galina wasn't listening. She was looking at the holotable again. "If we turn and do battle right now," she said. "We might not get court martialed."

"Who cares about that? Fire the cannons, we might help out a little."

Galina winced, she looked upset. "We'll lose so much," she said. "You're going to lose that armor. I'm going to lose the Galactic Key. Even this dragon suit is pretty much gone and irreplaceable. "

I rolled my eyes at her. "Come on, Galina," I said. "We're talking about thousands of dead people, maybe a million—and the end of your career."

She showed me her teeth. I knew it was the part about her career that had struck home.

"All right," she said. "We have to do something. Helm, hard about. Unlimber the broadsides."

I whooped and the ship lurched sideways. Say what you want about Galina's harsh techniques, when she gave an order, people moved their butts.

As soon as we turned halfway around, we fired everything we had at the Skay. The fleet people seemed to have been waiting for that order. They were frightened, sure, but they were also itching to get into the battle. They'd already seen horrific strikes performed by the monstrous Skay.

We felt the deck rock under our feet when the broad sides opened up. They all fired in unison. Thirty-two shells, each with smart-guided fusion warheads at the tip, flew toward the back end of the Skay that had turned away from us to abuse Mars.

"Imperator," the XO dared to speak. She came close to the two of us.

"What is it?"

"Sir... perhaps you've forgotten. Those invasion ships the Skay launched earlier... some have diverted to Mars, but most are still chasing us. They're reaching *Dominus* now."

Galina turned on her. "What?"

"Yes—the first two have already adhered to the outer hull. We have indications of drilling, sir—hot drilling."

"What the fuck?" Galina demanded, her voice cracking high. She whirled around to me and jabbed a bladed finger in my direction. Fortunately, it did not penetrate my armor.

"McGill, get to the outer hull. Find any invaders and destroy them." Then she turned to the XO again. She slashed with that same claw that had failed to penetrate my chest and almost took off the head of the XO, who managed to stagger back half a step.

"*You* get us the hell out of here. I don't care if you go to warp, do some amazing maneuvers, put up our shields—whatever. Get away from these invasion ships *now!*"

The XO gave a series of sharp orders. I didn't even hear them fully. I was already tramping away with growing speed. Each step took me farther than the last.

Soon, I was crashing and thumping past Marines, Fleet lieutenants, and dozens of others. Everyone looked stunned, but I didn't care. I had to find out who or what had invaded *Dominus*—and I had to destroy them all.

-44-

I contacted Primus Collins, and she directed me to gather my unit and deal with an incursion on Deck Three. The decks that were designated with numbers instead of colors were supporting decks that weren't used except for maintenance and storage. Deck Three was relatively close to the top of the stack, where Gold Deck itself was located.

The enemy invasion hadn't yet reached Deck Three, itself but was still contained in the rather roomy void zone between the outer hull and the inner hull. Starships, especially warships, were built to be resilient and damn-near indestructible. They frequently had to endure shocks and kinetic strikes. They couldn't be constructed with a thin sheet of titanium that could be punctured by a bullet. No, a serious warship, a capital ship like *Dominus*, had layered armor plates. The inner and outer hulls were both a meter thick or more.

The exterior of the ship had sophisticated defensive mechanisms in place as well. Layered plates out there were smart. They angled in various directions, depending on the need. Explosive reactive armor was built into the systems as well, designed to reduce the power of any strike by explosively ejecting a projectile and deflecting it out into space again. All this came after the shielding, which was generated as a powerful electromagnetic field that could repel objects all by itself.

Apparently, the shielding had failed us in this instance. How, I wasn't sure. These invasion ships were built by an enemy that had technology superior to ours. The Galactics weren't inventive, especially the Skay, but they were thousands of years ahead of us. They'd seen it all. With their massive head start, they'd evaded all our defenses, reached our hull, and begun to dig inside. Within seconds after having adhered to the outer hull, the invaders began drilling their way through the armor.

Normally, if your goal is simply to destroy a ship like *Dominus*, all these elaborate tactics weren't really necessary. A straightforward antimatter bomb, for instance, could have taken out the ship by now. We would have been crumpled up like a tin can on the bottom of the ocean and utterly destroyed.

The Skay clearly had worse intentions for us than simple destruction. It intended to absorb our biomass and add it to the collection of creatures that inhabited its interior. I had seen these freakish biomechanical monstrosities in person. Every Skay had a large and vibrant ecosystem living inside, made up of creatures of its own design. Whether by accident or purposeful intent, these creatures were always nightmarish and surprisingly effective.

"Harris!" I shouted. "Harris, where are you?"

"Heavies reporting, sir," he responded. "Uh… sir?"

"What is it, Harris?"

"Dickson is back, sir."

I snapped my head around in alarm. Galina had told me she'd put him on ice until we got back to Earth. How had he managed to escape purgatory? I decided on the spot to play it cool, like his presence, welcome or not, wasn't a surprise at all.

"Dickson!" I shouted, as if angry he wasn't in position yet.

"On my way, sir!"

Checking my tactical grid, I saw Dickson's light troopers were already on station. Adjunct Dickson himself was right behind them. He had to be wet behind the ears still, having just gotten printed out on Blue Deck.

Say what you want about the man, he was always punctual. He led his platoon of panting lights on a merry race straight up to meet me at the breach point.

"Dickson," I said, "huddle-up. We're about a hundred meters from the hull penetration point. Get your troops ready."

I turned toward Harris again. He had a strange look on his face, and he tilted his head suggestively in Dickson's direction. Did that mean he knew I'd had Sargon take out Dickson? I hoped not, but he seemed to be offering to repeat the hat-trick.

I shook my head at him and pointed toward a big cargo portal. "You'll group up there. You're going to be my power arm. If the lights can hold the invaders, that's fine. You don't have to do anything. But the second they fail, and something wriggles through, your guys are charging in and putting out the fire."

Harris nodded. He looked disappointed but resigned to his fate. "What about Leeson, sir?"

"He's coming. You know as well as I do that the specialists take a little longer to get to the deployment point."

"More like they're bigger pussies," he muttered to himself and wandered away.

Primus Collins contacted me next, asking me what the hell I was doing. I gave her a rundown, and she confirmed I was doing it right.

"I'll send you two more units—but I want you to get closer to that drill-in point."

"Uh... how close, sir?"

"Like, right under it. Encircle the breach. Collins out."

I grunted unhappily. The orders were clear. When in a combat situation, editing your commander's instructions too much was considered bad form.

"Harris, move up! Form up just behind Dickson's picket-line."

There was a lot of cursing, which I ignored. Leeson finally showed up about then, and he was full of advice.

"The void between the inner and outer hull layers is only lightly pressurized," he told me. "But the region will still turn into a windstorm when opened to outer space."

"I know that, Adjunct. Place your weaponeers near the portal, here."

Leeson frowned and ordered his troops into position—but he wasn't done complaining yet. "The vacuum could lift out unprepared troops, you know."

"I know it. Keep your panties on and get prepared."

Once placed, we watched as more and more hotspots appeared on my HUD. Somehow, a dozen more invasion ships had landed on *Dominus*.

In the middle of our unit, the ceiling began to glow. They were burning through now. It was only a matter of minutes—maybe less. Farther away more hotspots appeared. These were encircled by other first-responder units.

Leeson squawked about this, and Harris was determined to stand and point out every nearby hotspot.

"Keep your eyes focused on this one," I told them. "It's going to open up before those do."

As if the Almighty had heard my words, the ceiling above us began to drip and run like wax. Finally, it burst open entirely.

Molten metal sprayed down. Despite the fact I'd ordered the lights to worm backward, a number of them were struck by glowing orange globules. These burned through their thin spacesuits. Their screams were irritating. I had to squelch Dickson's entire platoon from my tactical chat channel.

A windstorm began, but none of my men were lifted away. The depressurization effect wasn't strong enough for that.

"Steady on," I said, "keep your rifles and your peckers straight. When you see something, hammer it hard. Get some revenge for that buddy who's dead at your feet."

When the hole in the ceiling was a ragged rip some four meters across, creatures began to drop into sight. These monsters were different than those I'd previously encountered. They resembled roaches. They had swiveling heads on segmented bodies.

Numerous legs scurried when they came to the edge of the metal tear in *Dominus*' skin, and they did not hesitate. They didn't seem to feel pain from the heat. They just launched themselves through the burning hole and down into our midst.

Each of these giant roaches was something like the size of a lion—a big lion. They were squat rather than long, and I imagined a saber-toothed cat would have been about the right comparison. Weighing in at around five hundred kilograms, they sprang down into our midst.

We had them encircled, so at first, things did not go well for these metal-plated bugs. Dickson's lights hammered them with point-blank full-auto fire. They had metallic armor like insectile shells, which was not easily penetrated.

It took four or five hundred rounds from a dozen snap-rifles to put one out of commission. When the camera eyes were all popped, and the organic ones slagged into gory horrors, they were blinded, but that wasn't enough. Every flesh-like protuberance had to be shot away, and the metallic shell had to be banged on, dented, and finally cut open by relentless firepower.

Despite our early success in containment, there soon came to be a difficulty. Yes, the light troops were putting down a roach at a rate of perhaps one every five seconds. But the enemy roaches were jumping down into our midst at a rate that resembled more like one per second. As a result, despite the growing mass of thrashing, scrabbling, squirming, alien monstrosities, some managed to get close enough to spring into the air and launch themselves on top of my screeching light troopers.

That was when I sent in Harris and his heavies. They used morph-rifles and force-blades to quickly finish the interlopers. Moments later, another one—or perhaps two or three of them—would spring and land amongst the troops again.

"They just keep coming, sir!" Harris told me. "We're killing them. We're killing hundreds, but we're losing men, too. Eventually we're going run out of troops."

"Only if they don't run out of beetles first," I said, "but I'll put in a call for backup."

Primus Collins assured me more troops were on the way, but I hadn't seen any of them yet.

"Leeson!" I shouted. "Get something bigger lined up. We've already suffered about ten percent losses, here."

"Yes, sir. Just hold them for another minute or so, and we'll put the fear of God into these devils."

Dickson's light troops, which had suffered most of the casualties so far, were looking panicky. "Dickson, let your men throw grenades into the central mass of the enemy. One grenade at a time—you call out the trooper who is given the green light."

Grenades began to fly. This achieved a satisfying victory when a full squadron of enemy roaches that had been planning on doing a mass jump all died at once. But still, more and more of them kept falling out of that damned hole in the ceiling. At this point, there were so many heaped-up bodies that fresh roaches had something to hide behind when they first dropped into the kill-zone.

How many could there be? Was there more than one invasion ship attached out there now? That was a horrific thought. I realized I had seen hundreds of sleek ships leaving the mouth of the massive Skay.

More holes were beginning to open-up all over the ship. Like molten pustules, they penetrated the outer hull, allowing hordes of these little demons to enter *Dominus*.

It all depended on what it looked like out there, on the external armor. Maybe there were so many they were lining up out there. I doubted they were waiting their turns calmly, they were probably crawling over one another like a buzzing hive of insects. They seemed to be eager or even desperate to get past one another for their chance to tear apart even a single human. It was a chilling thought, and I couldn't get it out of my head.

Dominus shuddered then, and she shifted from one form of existence to another. It was that point at which I realized that we must have come back out of warp. Either Galina had gone fully crazy at last, or something had changed on the battlefield. I didn't know which it was, but I knew we hadn't spent much time in warp, and we hadn't gone all that far. There hadn't even been enough time to get ourselves out of the Solar System.

Despite the chaos of battle, I tried to do a little math in my dim-bulb of a brain. The Alcubierre effect started off just above the speed of light and slowly accelerated. We'd been in hyperspace for something like twenty minutes… Twenty minutes at light speed…? That wasn't even long enough to get from Mars to Earth. No, we were definitely still inside the Solar System.

There wasn't time to worry about all that now. The enemy was upon us, and if we didn't defeat them, we were all going to be dead anyway.

-45-

"I'm ready, sir. Permission to fire?" Leeson shouted in my headset.

"Permission granted already. Do your worst!"

Leeson opened up then, and I was immediately impressed. In the short number of minutes since we'd been summoned to this inhospitable spot to defend *Dominus*, he had managed to get one of our light artillery pieces set up and operational.

He'd wisely put Sargon himself on the 88. Using his masterful techniques, he cut a swath across the opening where the bugs were still dropping into the ship. He scorched a few Skay minions that way, to be sure. But that wasn't the sheer genius of it.

By aiming upward, he was able to reach up inside the guts of the enemy invasion ship. He didn't just destroy the roaches that were cluster-humping the spot up there, he also managed to damage the invasion ship itself.

We could see secondary explosions after six-seconds of a sickly green beam was applied. He just aimed at the hole in the ceiling and let it sizzle there for a while. Normally, an 88 was used by sweeping lines across a mass enemy formation. This always proved devastating to lightly armed troops.

Instead, Sargon was using the 88 like a fire hose. He cooked one singular point allowing it to burn there for an unusual length of time. Nothing in that path could withstand the beams horrific energy.

It lit up the interior of the hull itself, causing the blackened metal that had cooled to become orange-hot again. Molten and dripping, it set the roaches that dared jump down into the beam to explode into flame. The nightmarish creatures boiled inside their shells, like flash-fried crabs. Dozens of the enemy were slain, and untold damage was done to the ship up above.

"Nice work, McGill," Centurion Manfred said. He was leading one of the other units that had finally joined us as reinforcements. "I like your idea. Let me get my men in on it."

Soon, a dozen other beams leaped up, coming from different angles. These weren't 88s, of course, but old-fashioned belcher cannons. When Sargon's beam sputtered out and his 88 had to be put into cooldown mode for at least 30 seconds, we still had continuous fire from multiple angles to keep the bugs hopping.

My weaponeers joined Manfred's, and we had mini-missiles in the act now, too. The roaches weren't having a good day. Whenever one dared poke a nose or an eyeball or even a feeler into range, our weapons immediately burned the exposed bit away. We sent them scuttling and hissing.

"Heavies," I said. "Harris? Where are you?"

"Yessir?" he said, reporting in.

"You see that pile of dead roaches in front of you? Climb over it and destroy the ones hiding down underneath."

Harris didn't like his new orders much. In fact, he looked a bit shocked, but he also looked resigned. "Just when I think Hell can't get any hotter, sir, you come along and make my day."

"That's my job, Adjunct. Get moving."

Muttering foul words about my family members, he hustled his heavies together and began to climb over the steaming bodies of metal-shelled roaches.

Manfred threw in his heavy platoon to support mine. Soon, sixty troops in armor were rushing to the mound of dead creatures. They scrambled to the top, but when they reached the shifting peak, they encountered resistance.

This indicated that my thinking was correct. The enemy roaches that had survived were hunkering down and waiting for more of their comrades to gather before launching a new offensive.

A vicious fight erupted in the center, directly under the molten hole in the ceiling. Hidden roaches slithered up between the curled-leg corpses of their brethren. Sometimes, they managed to grab onto a human appendage and drag one of our heavies down underneath the pile to be eviscerated. These struggles often ended with the flash of a grenade or the unholy screams of the dying. After about three minutes, it was all over with.

"I think we've got this contained," Leeson said. "All we have to do is stay here and beam that hole when a nose pokes out."

"Roger that," I said, and I contacted Manfred.

"What is it McGill?"

"Let's finish this. Let's send all our heavies up into that hole. Yours, mine and the fresh troops from Centurion Mills."

Jenny Mills spoke up then. Her group had finally shown up and was trotting to fill a gap in our encirclement. "Nice of you to think of me, McGill," she said.

"Let's send all of our heavies into the middle of that stack of bodies. We have to pop up outside the hull. We'll go into their invasion ship and finish them off."

"There's a lot of radiation up there, McGill," Jenny said. "We're still in warp."

"No, we're not. Take a look at your tapper."

She did so, and she made sounds of amazement. "We're not all that far from Mars. What the hell is Turov thinking?"

"I have no idea," I said, "but I do know that if we can seal this breach and get rid of that invasion ship, we can call this exercise a victory."

The three unit commanders agreed, and even Primus Collins gave us her approval after she got wind of our plan. We proceeded, and I went with Harris.

All three of the centurions met in the middle with their adjuncts and their heavy platoons. Together, we had approximately a hundred troops. Using the light ship's gravity and our exoskeletal leg-power, we all sprang upward. Boot-thrusters, anti-gravity repellers…we turned on the works and flew up into that smoking hole.

Once I came out onto the outer hull of *Dominus*, I saw an amazing sight. The invasion ship was a wreck. Sargon's 88 had torn the sleek vessel apart. Apparently, they weren't armored, but just thin metal meant to move nimbly through space, rather than being built to take a punch from light artillery.

We were in the middle of the ship, which was no longer complete. It was torn apart and shredded. Segments had fallen away, revealing the strange guts of the machine and the open outer skin of *Dominus* around us.

After exterminating the few remaining roaches that had any fight left in them, we peeped out of the gaping holes in the invasion ship. We could see other hotspots on *Dominus'* outer hull. In several directions, we spotted nearby scrambling hordes of alien marauders. They were all trying to get into similar breaches they had burned through the ship's armor.

"Hot damn," I said. "It looks like we've gotten behind them."

"We're flanking them, McGill," Manfred said. "This wreck is hiding us, and they don't even know we're here yet."

"Here's what I think we should do. Let's get all three of our units up here onto the outer hull and sweep the whole ship clear."

"That's got to be the most shit-off crazy thing I'd ever heard, Centurion," Harris had the balls to say.

Manfred was standing near him, and he reached out with a massive boot. He kicked him one in the rump. Harris grunted, but he shut up.

"You've got to stop your dog from barking so much, McGill," Manfred told me.

"I know it. I know it. Here, let me relay this situation to Primus Collins."

I contacted Collins, and she was impressed to learn that we were on the outside of the vessel. I suggested to her that we should press our advantage and sweep the hull clean. She immediately put me into contact with Tribune Winslade, who showed me his sharp teeth and even sharper eyes.

"I see you've managed to get outside *Dominus*, McGill," he said. "Is this some kind of ill-conceived escape attempt?"

"No, sir," I said. I explained the situation to him, and he was intrigued.

"I like it," he said, pointing a skinny finger at me. "I'm going to back you up. I'm sending five hundred fresh troops to your location."

True to his word, troops began to boil up behind us minutes later. By that time, we'd brought up our lights and some of our toughest weaponeers with belchers on their shoulders. Soon, there were too many of us to be contained inside of the shambles of the assault craft.

At some point, the enemy roaches spotted us and recognized the threat that we represented. They stopped trying to ram their way down those tiny entrance holes and turned to advance upon us from a dozen directions at once. A massive firefight began.

It was a strange experience. When you have a firefight in pure vacuum, you're not able to hear your own rifle. You can feel the recoil, and you can hear popping sounds transmitted in through your gloves and your shoulder, but the sound is different, and the feel is different.

In no time, we saw men bouncing and half-floating away from the fight. When inexperienced troops fired too hard and too fast, they sometimes broke loose from their magnetic boots and were sent skittering and tumbling away, spiraling out into space.

Fortunately, my heavy platoon was made up of experienced veterans. We had trained and drilled on vacuum-based combat and some of us excelled at it.

Although we blew most of them away at range, some of the roaches reached us. They tore apart one, two, sometimes three men before they were taken down, but the majority were stopped at range by a withering hail of firepower.

Recognizing the threat we represented, it seemed like all of the invaders had stopped trying to penetrate *Dominus*. They turned and charged us instead. We fought for perhaps fifteen minutes straight. In some cases, men ran out of ammo, and were down to force-blades and even combat knives.

Every grenade we had was tossed at the roaches. Every mini- missile was launched. Even our stock of buzzers ran out. Kivi and Natasha used them as explosive drones, finding and killing alien creatures after landing on their backs.

Half an hour after we'd started to push back, it was about over. Every roach that had dared to infest *Dominus* was dead or floating in space above us.

That's when Winslade himself showed up. He appeared on our tappers, of course, rather than in person. He clapped his bony hands together, telling us how proud he was of our skills and how excited he was to be commanding such fine troops. It was a good gesture, and the troops liked it for the most part.

About a minute and a half into his victory speech, however, Galina overrode his transmission. She delivered some unwelcome news.

"Troops," she said, "*Dominus* might soon be engaged in space combat. I want every able-bodied soldier to get back into the ship. Drag as much equipment as you can back inside the hull—but don't take more than three minutes. Even if those enemy roaches are still crawling around out there, withdraw immediately."

She disappeared from our arms, and I began screaming at my troops to obey. We grabbed every scrap of gear we could, oftentimes hauling dead soldiers because their suits and guns weren't too badly mauled. We pulled it all back down into *Dominus* and moved away from the breach point, bumping and thumping as we went.

Leeson had Sargon rapidly dismantle his 88 while the others shouldered belchers. Everyone was in a rush to return to the safety of *Dominus*' inner decks.

"I don't like the sound of this," Harris said. "What the hell's going on, McGill?"

"I don't know, and I don't like it either," I admitted.

The moment I was certain that the survivors of 3rd Unit had withdrawn to relative safety. I used my tapper to contact Galina. As I still was her trusted bodyguard and near-professional night masseur, she answered the call.

"What the hell is going on, Imperator?" I asked.

"The Skay is finished with Mars," she said. "It's looking in our direction again. It's now flying after us in normal space."

"Huh… that's not good."

"I don't think we can outrun this thing, James. If we jump into hyperspace again, it's going to jump with us. If we try to fight it, we'll be destroyed. I don't know what to do."

I could see by her freaked-out face she was telling the truth. She'd hoped that Mars would distract the monster and get it off our tail—but then we'd shot it in the ass and run away. Apparently, the Skay hadn't forgotten about that. It still wanted to eat us—perhaps more now than ever. Galina turned away to chew on her crewmen, who weren't getting the ship underway fast enough for her liking. The connection went dead.

I thought about the situation for several intense moments. All told, something like ninety invasion ships had managed to reach our hull, and they had done us grievous harm. If we hadn't had an entire legion of Earth's finest soldiers aboard, we couldn't have repelled the first assault of the roaches.

It would be worse if we were swallowed by the Skay, or if we were jumped by another hundred invasion ships. Every trick and countermeasure had failed to stop the alien so far. Frankly, I didn't see how we were going to survive.

-46-

In the command center on Gold Deck, things weren't calm at all. The Skay was on track, and it was gaining on us. Even flying at sublight speeds, we couldn't outrun the monster.

"James," Galina called to tell me, "I'm going to jump again. It's all I can do."

"Uh…" I said. "Okay."

I spread the word, alerting my unit and a few others. The ship's official announcement came through the PA system a minute later, and everyone aboard began scrambling.

I reached out to Galina again. Sometimes, she did things in a panic, and she needed a steady hand. "Uh… Imperator?" I said.

"What is it, James? I'm busy fighting a desperate battle, here."

"I know, I know… but… where are we going to go? It's only going to follow us."

She had a haunted look in her eyes. "Yes, it will…" she said, "I'm… I'm taking it to Earth this time. I should never have listened to those fools at Central and brought it to Mars. They had three small bases, but nothing big enough to stop this thing. The full fleet might do it."

"Uh…" I interrupted. "Are you sure that's a good idea, Imperator?"

The screen went blank. She hadn't answered me, and before I could send a text, the ship's deck lurched under my feet. Radiation poured into the hull through every hole the invaders had burrowed. Our spacesuits stopped most of it, but not all. I felt a bit burned and stunned by the gush of hard gamma rays. There was a metallic taste in my mouth. We'd gotten a dose, that was for sure.

"The radiation spiked up to nine hundred rads, sir," Harris told me. "We've got to get out of here."

For once I listened to Harris. Running away as best I could on my numbed legs, I led my troops toward the hatchway that led into the interior of *Dominus*. We piled through and slammed the hatch behind us. I spun the wheel and let the automatic re-pressurization process begin.

Panting, coughing and leaning against walls, men vomited and tried to breathe. We'd left stragglers behind, of course. Anybody who'd died fighting the roaches or who just looked too burned, too injured, or too slow-moving. Well, if we lasted another day or two, they'd live again.

When the air was breathable, we flipped open our faceplates and poured water onto skin that was already beginning to look like it had suffered a sunburn. Troops patched holes in their suits and groaned.

I checked my dosimeter and saw I'd gotten a fairly serious dose. It wasn't necessarily lethal, but it was probably good enough to earn me a recycle if any bio-specialist read the numbers.

We'd stopped the roaches, but this struggle was far from over, and less than half my troops had survived. At least the passages inside *Dominus* felt safe.

The survivors of 3rd Unit crept back to our module and threw themselves down on the bunks. We took showers and ate anti-radiation tablets. We did everything we could, but death stalked us nonetheless.

It took about ten minutes for *Dominus* to jump from the orbital region of Mars to the vicinity of Earth. I was still trying to wash off any particles of radioactive dust that might have gotten into the tears in my suit when we popped out of warp again.

I raced through the ship heading for Gold Deck. My mission was clear in my mind. I had to get Galina to see reason, to realize that she had failed, and *Dominus* was going to have to be destroyed by the Skay.

Then and only then might the super-alien menace stop. Running around the Solar System wrecking everything that we earthmen had spent so long building was crazy, and even I knew it. Sometimes, it was time to take your hit for the good of the team.

It wasn't my rank that allowed me onto Gold Deck, it was the fearful glances I got from the crewmen. Normally, they would have thrown me out.

I played the part of Galina's bodyguard to the hilt. Fully armed and armored, I looked like I was ready to kill anyone who got in between my bloodshot staring eyes and my goal.

"Galina," I said when I finally got within earshot, "let's just stop all this."

She turned to me, and she fixed me with a strange stare. Her eyes were as haunted as mine. She stared at me for perhaps a full second, and I thought perhaps she was seeing the bright light of reason.

But then she shook her head. "No," she said, "we're flying straight for Earth. That thing is on our tail, and our fleet is coming out to meet both of us. After that—this won't be my problem any longer."

I gritted my teeth, turned around and marched off Gold Deck. She wasn't going to listen to me, I could tell—but I was never a man who gave up on things easily. I raced for Gray Deck next.

Outside the ship's battered hull, there were explosions. Reports came in of damaged decks, of strikes and near-strikes. *Dominus* swung side to side, she was surprisingly nimble for a transport of her tonnage.

The Skay was shooting at us. That much was clear—and we were firing back. The broadsides spoke at least four times before I managed to reach Gray Deck, which had been abandoned by the majority of the techs. They'd all been summoned to perform damage-control duties.

I used the Galactic Key which I still kept in the pockets of my armor. Galina had been using her battle suit for so long, she knew she couldn't operate the Galactic Key anyways.

Running over to a locker, I popped the door open. I removed a charged teleport harness, pulled it on and tapped in the presets for Central.

When I teleported to the big building down on Earth, I wasn't greeted with the respectful fanfare that I'd hoped for. Instead, a pair of hogs tried to arrest me.

I had no time for nonsense. I murdered both of them and left them where they lay. Marching out of the Gray Deck equivalent, I found my way to an elevator, overrode all the security protocols with the key, and drove the lift up to the top of the building.

During this long ride upward, a message came through on my tapper. Raising my arm, I was surprised it wasn't Galina—it was Consul Drusus instead.

"What are you doing on Earth, McGill?"

"Oh, nothing much, sir," I said, "I always like to go out for an evening stroll."

He looked down for a moment, no doubt checking my location and direction. "I'm not even going to ask," he said, "how you got here or how you managed to murder two guards already—or even how you took control of an elevator in the most secure building on Earth in the middle of a lockdown."

"That would be for the best, honestly, sir."

"But I will tell you, in case you're looking for me, that I'm not in my office. I'm down below in the control rooms in the depths of Central. If assassination is your goal, you'll never reach me."

"Assassination?" I laughed, but one side of my mouth wasn't working quite right, so it came out a little funny. It was probably the radiation, or maybe a shot to the jaw I'd taken since arriving. One of the hogs had gotten in a few licks. "I'm not here to kill anyone, sir. I'm here to save the Earth."

Drusus blinked once, then twice. He sighed. "All right," he said, "I lied. I am up in my office. Keep coming up."

I'd been about to stop the elevator and reverse course, so I grinned. Old Drusus had gotten cagey with the years. He knew that sometimes I could pull a technological trick that might surprise even an old master like him.

"Clever, sir," I said. "Very clever. I'll be there in a minute."

That minute passed and thirty seconds more before I was clumping down the hallway to his office. I ignored Primus Bob, who waved his fingers at me.

When I reached the big guy's door, I waved the Galactic Key over it. The thing popped open. I hadn't even bothered to knock. I stepped inside and saw a grim-looking group of high-level officers. They were surveying the scene outside.

"Consul Drusus," an admiral said. I didn't know him, but he had an Indian accent and an unsympathetic stare. "We should go down into the depths. To the bunkers."

Drusus shook his head. "By the time we got ourselves down there and set up with all the feeds transferred, this whole thing might be over with. No, we're going to man our stations right here."

I realized then that the leadership of Earth had been utterly surprised by the arrival of the Skay. The battle had been ongoing out at Mars—but now, without warning, it had jumped across the Solar System within a span of minutes. The whole shitbag was about to pop open in the skies over Earth. Galina had truly brought terror to our home world once again.

"Is our fleet in position?" Drusus asked.

"Every ship we've got is up there, sir—everything that could reach us in time."

Drusus nodded. "Give me a roster, Admiral Singh."

"We've got fifty-five capital ships, sixteen battleships and thirty-nine heavy cruisers. Screening them, we've got seventy light cruisers and one hundred and—"

Drusus waved for him to stop. "The smaller ships don't matter," he said. "Only those equipped with heavy guns and armor-piercing rounds will have the firepower to be noticed."

Finally, Drusus raised his eyes to meet mine. I stood there near the door, fidgeting with my beret.

"McGill," he said, "you've got about ninety seconds before our fleet comes into direct conflict with the Skay. If you're going to tell me anything useful, this is your chance."

"It's about *Dominus*, sir," I told him. The Skay wants to destroy *Dominus*. It's… ah… seriously pissed off at that ship."

Drusus narrowed his eyes. "What could you have done that was so upsetting to that monstrous alien ship out there, McGill?"

I shrugged. "That's all a matter of opinion, sir. But it does seem that the Skay has taken offense. It wants *Dominus* dead. It's my belief it won't stop running around tearing a blue streak through our home system until it catches my legions' transport and destroys her."

Drusus thought that over for a couple of seconds. He looked at the displays. "What's Captain Merton doing anyway? He's flying straight toward Earth."

"Uh…" I said. "It's not Captain Merton who's in command, sir. It's Imperator Turov."

Again, Drusus met my eyes. His jaw dropped a little. All of a sudden, I think he understood.

"All right. New orders, everyone. Admiral Singh," he said turning to the Indian-looking fellow. "Change targets. I want all your battleships to use their longest ranged weapons teleport-bombs, everything. Destroy *Dominus*. Blow her out of the sky. I don't want two atoms to adhere together in the form of a single molecule. Do you understand me?"

Admiral Singh began to open his mouth to object, but Drusus drew himself up. He stood tall. "I'm the consul of Earth," he said. "Anyone who disobeys me at this moment of peril for all humanity will be executed and permed. Now, I repeat Admiral, do you understand me?"

Admiral Singh nodded.

"Then carry out my orders."

The Fleet puke turned stiffly and talked to some less important Fleet pukes. They moved slowly but deliberately to follow through with Drusus' fatal command. I could tell that none of them wanted to do it. That the idea of destroying even a single Earthship seemed insane to them. But they did it. In the end, *Dominus* was hit with T-bombs launched by the battleships. Each of them held a few in reserve.

Dominus was still on the run, desperately hurtling away from the pursuing Skay. She was caught by a half dozen gigaton blasts. There was nothing left but a shower of vapor, sparks, swirls of glowing plasma and then an expanding field of light and dust. Even that stuff only lasted for seconds. The Skay plunged into that mess and through it.

"The primary target is still incoming, sir. We're in range now to hit the Skay."

"Hold your fire," Drusus ordered.

"But sir... the longer we wait, the closer that thing gets to our fleet."

"You have your orders, Admiral."

Singh clamped his mouth shut, and his jaw muscles bulged. He was doing everything but biting his own tongue. I was sure that was the only way he could keep it from spitting curses.

Twenty long seconds passed, then thirty. During this tense time, we all just watched on the tactical tables. There were voices, but they were all radio voices, people calling for help. People making reports, that sort of thing.

"I want no one to fire first on our side," Drusus said. "You are free to return fire, but we're not going to start this thing."

This gave the admirals new hope. They lit up and relayed this order, which they liked much better than the previous one, to their captains. Another twenty seconds passed, then thirty.

Admiral Singh frowned at the display. "It's the Skay, sir... it seems to be slowing down."

Drusus lit up. "Give me confirmation. I want confirmation."

"It's confirmed, sir. The Skay has reduced speed."

Drusus thought about that for a few seconds, and he nodded his head. "Withdraw your ships. Turn the fleet around and head back, closer to Earth. Give that thing some breathing room."

"But, sir," Admiral Singh began, "this ship has torn its way through the—"

Drusus drew his sidearm and fired point-blank at the admiral. The shot was a good one. It caught Singh right between the eyes. A neat hole was burned there, and he flopped to the deck, stone dead."

"Good shot, sir," I said.

"Shut up, McGill." Drusus turned to the comms operator, who was looking alarmed all over again. "Broadcast to that Skay. Let me talk to it."

I winced a bit, as Drusus wasn't known for successfully dealing with aliens. He just didn't have a good feel for it.

Channels were opened, and Drusus began his pitch. "Greetings from Earth," he said in a calm voice. "We are the local enforcers of the Mogwa in Province 921. You, our Skay visitor from the Core Worlds, are in forbidden territory. We must ask that you reverse course and return to space owned by the Skay rather than the Mogwa."

There was a period of silence. Drusus was just about to draw in a deep breath to speak again, perhaps to repeat his message, when the Skay finally spoke to us.

"Insects," it said, "by what incredible measure of insolence do you dare to address me?"

"We mean no disrespect Galactic lord among lords," Drusus said, laying it on thick. "We simply mean to alert you to the fact that you are not in a province owned by your people. Province 921 is ruled by the Mogwa."

"Nonsense. In time, all provinces will come to be possessed by the Skay. This is an inevitable reality. It's merely a matter of the passage of time."

"You are of course, correct," Drusus said.

Now, he was impressing me. He was going the right direction without me having to tell him anything.

"But right now," he continued, "in this slice of time, this moment, and this reality, you are engaged in illegal activity. We are the willing subjects of the Empire, and we do not wish to be forced to take action against you."

"Threats?" the Skay rumbled. "The insects dare to threaten the boulder in the midst of their delicate hive? This makes your impudence rise to a new level. You are now ludicrous as well as insolent."

"We apologize, great Skay," Drusus said. "We mean no harm or insult, but we have been conditioned by our Mogwa masters to defend this province against all who enter here."

"Conditioned...?" the Skay said. "Finally, I understand your suicidal nature. The Mogwa would gladly doom your species for their slightest convenience. They are a weak, organic race of outdated design. No doubt they have trained you to compete for the opportunity to lick their filthy appendages."

"That's right," Drusus said. "We are conditioned to behave in such a way that—"

"Your premise is still false, however," the Skay continued, talking over him. "I have every right to be here. I followed a ship that offended my own enforcers. It was causing great destruction in a neighboring province, one which we lay claim to."

Drusus looked around his group of officers for support, but they were mute and worse than useless. At last, he glanced toward me. I put my hands up and gave him an exaggerated shrug. I didn't know what was going on in the Core Worlds. Not this time. For all I knew the Skay had publicly claimed this province. Maybe that's why they've been hanging around Rigel and acting all hoity-toity.

"To the best of our knowledge," Drusus said carefully, "the frontier province between Earth and Rigel is unowned at this time."

"You have now been informed otherwise."

Drusus took in another deep breath and spoke again. "We are capable of injuring you," he told the Skay. "Examine our satellite, we have done battle with your kind in the past and defeated them."

"But the ship I pursued offended me," the Skay said.

"Yes, Overlord," Drusus said. "You're right. We destroyed that ship for having offended you. We hope this will be enough for you to allow us to continue to maintain peace with your kind."

The Skay was quiet for a while.

"It's scanning us, sir. It's running beams all over our ships. Now, it's scanning the Moon, the Earth, and that haze of dust that used to be *Dominus*."

"Good. Let him do it. No jamming, no complaining."

After another tense minute or two the Skay spoke again. "The ship I came to pursue has been destroyed. Let that be a warning to any upstart species out here on the rim of the galaxy. You may not attack a friend of the Skay with impunity.

There will be severe repercussions if this criminal act is repeated."

Drusus heaved a sigh of relief and began to promise profusely that we would never do anything like that again. The Skay never answered any of his platitudes. Instead, it simply turned around and aimed itself toward the rim of the galaxy. Then it flashed away into hyperspace.

"Can we track that thing?" Drusus asked.

"I'm not sure, sir," a sensor op said, "but I think it's heading back toward Rigel. I think its scan revealed that we might be able to harm it."

"He chickened!" I said loudly. "He turned tail and ran off!"

"Yes…" Drusus said, "but that alien is still a threat parked right here in our neighborhood. Apparently, it's been stationed at Rigel like a bulldog guarding its master's house."

I stepped forward, grinning hugely. I began to slap my big paws together. I gave Drusus a hearty round of applause. No one else joined in, but I didn't care. "That was amazing, sir. I honestly didn't think you had it in you."

"What…?"

"You *lied!* You made up pretty-sounding bullshit on the spot. What's even better, you managed to grovel like nobody's business. That Skay had to feel honored just to listen to all that bootlicking."

Drusus didn't know whether to be amused or insulted by my little speech. I think he was so relieved by the final results, he didn't much care what I said.

"Report down to Blue Deck, McGill. You're obviously half-dead on your feet."

"Uh… do I have to, sir?"

"Yes, that's an order."

"Oh well…" I said. "Can I leave some of my stuff, here? Because you know, these bio people—they're outright thieves sometimes."

Drusus smiled. "All right. You can take off that armor of yours. Leave it on the couch over there. I'll have it fumigated, deloused and neutralized for radioactive particles. Just head for Blue Deck."

I started walking, but I turned back. "Oh, uh… can I use the VIP revival center sir?"

"Yes, yes, fine. Just this one time."

Smiling big, I stripped down to my skivvies and left my big black suit on Drusus' fine couch. Then I marched out past Primus Bob. All his sycophantic little buddies complained and pinched their noses, talking about the stink in the place, but I ignored it all.

I rode the elevator down to the nearest VIP revival room. There, I chatted-up a pair of bio-girls until one of them injected me with something cold and deadly. After that, I knew no more.

-47-

When I was revived, I kind of felt that I deserved a vacation. After all, in my own mind at least, I was a hero. Unfortunately, certain malcontent hog-types felt differently about old James McGill and his contribution to Earth's defense.

My tapper spoke to me while my eyes were still bleary, and my uniform was at half-mast. "Welcome to a fine day of victory. You are hereby summoned by Public Servant Alexander Turov. You are ordered to report to the detention level immediately."

I didn't like the sound of that. I'd been arrested in countless ways, but being ordered to show up at the prison door? Well, sir, that was a new one.

Heading for the elevators straight out of the VIP revival, I saw a hog team hustling toward the Blue Deck doors in the opposite direction. Either they didn't know what I looked like, or they were going for someone else.

I wasn't sure which it was, and I didn't hang around to find out. Once they rounded a corner, I broke into a trot. I was still stumbling and dripping from my recent revival. I reached the elevators just as the doors were closing. I shoved my big hand into the crack, and it bounced open again.

To my surprise, my fingers suffered a sharp sensation. I yelled, but I didn't let go of that door. Someone was rattling the buttons in there, trying to get the doors to close. And yes, I was pretty certain they were biting on my fingers.

Being a man who is not easily deterred by physical altercations, I wedged the fingers of my second hand into that crack. Then I forced the doors open a fraction. Inside, I spotted a panicked Winslade. He had a needler in his hand, and he aimed it at my intruding eyeball—but he didn't fire.

"Oh, it's you," he said in a mixture of disgust and relief. "But wait, have you come to arrest me? Hmm? Well, have you?"

"Uh... I don't think so," I said. "There were a couple of hogs just behind me in the hall, though."

"Then get in this elevator or let the doors close, you idiot. Stop impeding me!"

I edged inside and pushed the buttons. The doors swept closed, and as they did so, I saw that same pair of hogs rushing toward us. I gave them a little wave as the elevator whisked us away.

"Fortunately," Winslade said, "they haven't yet revoked my clearances. I've been evading those two for nearly ten minutes now."

"That's a sheer relief, sir. At least they're not after me."

Winslade laughed. It was a nasty laugh. "Oh, they'll get around to you as well. Do you really think that Merton and Dickson and whoever else has made an industry of arresting Legion Varus people has forgotten about you? You are, arguably, the most infamous of us all."

Frowning, I had to admit to myself that Winslade had a solid point. If they were arresting him again, it was only a matter of time until they got around to me. This would be the perfect moment. We were back from our journey abroad, our mission was finished. The Skay had been chased off. Why not finish the witch-hunt they'd started before we even left?

"Do you know what the hell's going on, Tribune?" I asked.

"No, I don't. I'm going up to the consul's office, and I'm going to make my pitch for executive mercy. If you want to come with me, try to be helpful instead of deleterious, please."

"Uh... okay. Whatever that is, I'll try not to do it."

We rode the elevator together up to the top of Central. All the while my tapper made frequent beeps. These were reminder notifications about my previous orders from the Public Servant.

At least he wasn't calling me directly. That would have been hard to dodge.

Winslade noticed my tapper's behavior, and he gave me a nasty chuckle. "So, they really are after you as well. At least there's some level of justice left in this universe. I've done nothing—nothing but serve my world to the best of my abilities."

"Same here—this is bullshit."

"You and me are the victims here, McGill. You fought well on *Dominus*, you saved the ship until Hegemony decided to blow her up. We're the last ones who should be purged."

"It's not just us," I told him. "Imperator Turov is on their short list as well."

Winslade frowned. "That is odd and concerning. Normally, she's immune to any political dirty dealings due to her family connections. If they are going after the Servant's daughter… where will it all end?"

"I wouldn't fret too much. We've got Drusus on our side. He's the consul, and that trumps all these friggers."

"Are you sure about that?" Winslade asked.

"I certainly am!"

He shrugged. "I just hope you're right."

We got off at the top floor, marched past the staffers, and I thumped on Drusus' door. A few seconds later, the doors were flung wide. What we saw inside made both Winslade and I wince in disappointment.

Instead of Drusus and possibly a few of his more attractive staffers, we saw Public Servant Alexander Turov standing in front of us. He was all fresh-looking in his new young body. Behind him were no less than six heavily armed and armored hogs.

I didn't have a combat knife on me, and I was wearing the papery jumpsuit they'd given me after the revival. Winslade was in the same state of unreadiness.

Alexander gave us a predatory grin. He waved for us to enter. "Gentlemen," he said, "you're just in time."

Drusus was in the background, deep inside his gigantic office. He was moving around back there like a ghost in the woods.

"Hi, Consul," I shouted, waving to him.

He might have lifted a few fingers in my direction, but it was hard to tell. He certainly didn't shout out a greeting.

"Come right this way, McGill," Alexander said, "it's fitting that you should witness these next few moments."

Stepping forward, I saluted the burly, unsmiling hogs. They just stared, so I marched between them without a care.

Winslade followed in my wake, glancing this way and that as if he was going to discover some magical way to escape the room. I could have told him there wasn't going to be any escaping today. The door shut behind us with the sound of finality.

We stepped up to the meeting table. To my surprise, new additions to the audience made an appearance. Not one, not two, but eight wavering figures materialized in a circle around that huge conference table. When they were all in place, Alexander moved to stand in the open position at the head of the table.

They were holograms. Each of them wore identical black robes. Even Alexander was wearing his formals. The ghostly apparitions were old, stuffy-looking people. There were five women and three men. Every one of them came from a different location around the globe.

"So… this is the Ruling Council?" I blurted out. "Is that who you guys are? That's cool."

They glanced at me but said nothing and looked back to Alexander. Then Drusus took his spot at the opposite end of that big, big table. Winslade and I were off to one side. We were mere witnesses.

"It has come to our attention," Alexander said, "that an ancient and worrisome treachery from the past has again lifted its ugly head into view. We had thought that this evil from our youth was stamped out long ago. But alas, it is not so."

The ghosts glanced around again. They seemed concerned, but they still didn't speak.

"We nine," Alexander went on, "we all stood in battle for the Unification of Earth. To this day, we are vigilant against those who would oppose us. We have selected a list of individuals, and they stand accused. Two of them are right here. Several others are known to you, Drusus. Under different circumstances, we might have suspected that you were their leader. Fortunately, this has proven not to be the case."

Drusus had been listening this entire time, but now he finally spoke up. When he spoke, the others listened since he was technically higher in rank and prestige than any of them.

"I'm consul of all Earth," he said. "I'm not a traitor, and I know nothing incriminating about these others you've listed as traitors."

"Be that as it may," Alexander said, "you can rest assured that there *are* traitors here."

"What evidence is there? What crimes have been committed?"

Alexander pointed a finger toward the sky. "Have you forgotten about the utter destruction of our four defensive stations? Or the fact millions of citizens died when the stations fell?"

"No, of course not, but—"

"That is our evidence. We *must* have traitors among us. To think otherwise is to play the fool. A great crime has been committed. We, the Servants of Hegemony, are informing you as to whom those miscreants are."

Drusus nodded. It was hard to argue that someone on Earth had played a part in the disaster that had plunged us into an interstellar war.

"There are those among us still," Alexander continued, "who would speak out against the Ultimate Unification. We have never found the leader of that rebel movement, and we believed him dead until recently."

Drusus looked troubled. "You said something about there being a leader, someone that you determined was not me. Who is this leader?"

"Why Praetor Wurtenberger, of course."

To everyone's shock, Drusus snorted with amusement. This caused the councilmembers to murmur with disapproval. I got the feeling the Ruling Council wasn't used to being laughed at.

"Praetor Wurtenberger?" Drusus asked. "Are you serious? I've never known a man who follows the rules more tightly.

Who here has less imagination than Wurtenberger? I'm sorry, but I can't believe this accusation."

"Consul Drusus," Alexander said in a severe tone. "The Council has brought you here for reasons other than witnessing the arrest and expungement of these terrorist individuals. We, the Ruling Nine, decided to recreate the office of consul. We resurrected it from the ancient past because the threat to Earth was so great."

"And I thank you for that honor, but—"

Alexander lifted a hand. "Please, hear me out. When the Big Sky project was destroyed, we needed the power of your office. To prove our wisdom, look at all you have done. You should be proud of your accomplishments. You have captured Dark World and Sky World. You've gained several advantages over Rigel, our greatest rival at the moment."

"That's all true, but—"

"But nothing Drusus, don't be embarrassed by the praise we all wish to heap upon you. The Vulbites of Dark World will soon be churning out superior armor for our troops. The orbital factory will build us fresh ships, fueled by the mining complex on Sky World. We will soon gather a force that will be unstoppable, and Rigel will be placed under siege."

"Um… there is the matter of that gigantic Skay…" Drusus began.

Alexander made a dismissive gesture. "The Skay is yet another impotent and cowardly alien. You ran it off with words alone."

Drusus frowned. "What's the point to all this praise, Servant? Where are you going with all this?"

Alexander attempted to smile. It didn't really work, but he tried. He spread his hands wide. "You've done it all. You've succeeded beyond our wildest hopes. Therefore, your rank and station are no longer needed."

Drusus' jaw loosened, and his mouth fell open. I didn't like the look, and I wondered if I looked that shell-shocked and stupid when this sort of thing happened to me. I suspected that I did.

"We declared you Earth's Consul, and now, by the same power invested in us, we are declaring the emergency to be at its end. We're removing your rank from you. You will, of course, return to your previous role and your previous rank as a praetor and the chief coordinator of Earth defenses."

Drusus began to protest, but Turov lifted his hand again to stop him. "Please, do not take this as an insult. It is instead the highest of compliments. You have succeeded where others would have surely failed. Remember, the rank of consul is always temporary, and we now believe that the time of necessity has passed."

-48-

"We," Alexander said, "the Ruling Council of Hegemony, are all assembled here to formally ask you to step aside and put down the trappings of your high office."

"You're asking me?" Drusus said. "Why don't you command me to step down?"

Alexander met his stare. Now it was my mouth that was hanging open. I looked back and forth between the two men like a golden retriever at a tennis match.

"We're asking you to step down out of politeness and decorum for your high office," Alexander explained.

"No," Drusus said. "That's not why you're asking me. You're asking me to abdicate my position because you cannot order me to do so. I've spent some time, you have to understand, researching the bylaws and the historical precedents. No consul has ever been directed to leave office. Every consul in history ended his reign when his mission was finished—and he was the authority who deemed it finished."

"Praetor Drusus," Alexander said, "let's not make this an unpleasant scenario. If you would simply—"

"No," Drusus said firmly. It was his turn to lift a hand and point a finger into Alexander's face. "I will not step aside—not yet—because as the consul of Earth, I will be the one to declare when our state of emergency has ended. Until that time, you will continue to address me as 'Consul', not 'Praetor'."

Old Alexander blinked a couple of times. I could tell he was honestly surprised. Perhaps he had chosen Drusus precisely because he was the kind of man who was a do-gooder. A boy scout. A guy who always did the right thing, no matter what.

But Drusus had changed over the years. I could have told Alexander that. He wasn't quite as straightforward as he used to be.

"This is most irregular," Alexander said, "perhaps I should put it to a formal vote. Members of the Ruling Council, raise your hand if you agree that it is time for Drusus to step down."

All of them raised their right hands as if swearing a solemn oath. They all looked to Drusus questioningly.

He shook his head. "I'm sorry, esteemed counselors. Although you are all public servants, and I am merely the highest military officer on the planet, you have given me sweeping powers. These will be relinquished—but only when the job is done."

Alexander's jaw seemed to jut out farther than before. "You refuse to step down?"

"Yes, I have said as much."

Alexander turned, slanting his head toward the six hogs and their heavy armor. I now realized why they were wearing combat gear and standing around inside Drusus' office. Right now, that fact seemed downright sinister.

"Look out, sir!" I called, pointing at the hogs.

They were stepping around on his six, but Drusus seemed unconcerned. He turned to face the squad leader of the six hogs.

"Adjunct," he said. "Who am I?"

The lead hog blinked a couple of times. He didn't look like the brightest specimen, even for a member of his benighted kind.

"You're... um... Consul Drusus."

Drusus nodded. "Exactly. Is there anyone in the military hierarchy or the civilian hierarchy who holds higher office than the consul of Earth?"

This appeared to be a real head-scratcher for the hog, but he managed to answer after a few moments.

"No, sir," he said, shaking his head. "That's not the how they taught me in school."

"Right. I'm hereby ordering you to stand down. Move your squad to the entrance. If anyone else tries to enter, stop them."

The hogs stepped around, side-to-side, like cattle who didn't know which way to bolt. But finally, at a signal from the leader, the group followed him to the doorway and set up camp there. They all aimed their weapons at the door and stared at it.

My head whirled back to Alexander. At this point, his teeth were clenched, and you could see them between his thin lips. "This is unnecessary and counterproductive," he said.

"On the contrary. I, as your consul, have determined that this action was necessary. I apologize for any inconvenience or misunderstandings. Servant Turov, please return to your quarters or to your ship up on the roof. Go wherever you like in fact—I've got a war to run. Rigel has not yet been defeated. We just had a Skay nearly destroy our Solar System. The idea that this crisis has passed is ludicrous. If anything, it has intensified."

Alexander, knowing his trump card had been played but failed to strike home, straightened up stiffly. He nodded to his colleagues, and they winked out one by one. None of them spoke to Drusus. None of them even looked at him.

Finally, when Alexander himself marched out of the room, I breathed a big sigh of relief and clapped my hands together.

"That was frigging awesome, sir," I said. "Never have I seen a pack of polecats get face-downed in such a fashion."

"Yes," Winslade dared to say, speaking up for the first time. He'd been pretty much pissing himself while the power-struggle had been in full swing. I guess he wasn't used to cheesing off the Ruling Council of Earth any day of the week. "Very impressive, Consul. I'm glad you kept your position."

"I'm glad you two enjoyed the show. Normally, such debacles happen behind closed doors without witnesses. Now, if you're quite finished, please leave because I have a lot of work to do."

"Oh, yeah… right, sir… but there's just one more thing, see…"

"What's that, McGill?"

"Uh… it's about all these fine, upstanding officers who've been arrested and sentenced to nonexistence. Could you possibly put in a good word for some of us?" I pointed at Winslade, who dared to give a tiny nod.

"Who exactly, is on this list, McGill?"

"You don't know?" I lifted a big hand and began to tick off my fingers. "Right at the top is Wurtenberger. Then there's Imperator Turov, Tribune Winslade here, Primus Graves and little old me, Centurion McGill. There might be others, but I don't know who they are."

Drusus worked his computer. He had permissions that God himself envied. Soon, he was frowning. "That whole list, top to bottom, has been accused of treason and ordered executed within days. Indefinite sentences to follow…"

Drusus looked up at us. "I pardoned you, McGill, didn't I?"

"Yessir, but a spook by the name of Adjunct Dickson informed me that there was a whole new investigation opened up with new charges. Therefore, your pardon didn't apply."

The frown on his face deepened. "Who ordered this? There's no one listed here as the prosecutor. I didn't think you could even create a criminal record with that field left blank."

"Well… I thought maybe *you* did, sir."

"No, it wasn't me. Who else might have done it?"

I thought about that. "Well sir, two culprits come to mind. Servant Alexander Turov himself—or maybe Adjunct Dickson."

"You mentioned that name before. Who is he?"

"A real prick of a man. He was transferred into my unit from Victrix."

Drusus did some more pecking. At last, he looked up at me. "There's no record of an Adjunct Dickson from Victrix. There is one in your legion, but there is no connected service record."

"That's mighty strange."

"It's illegal—or more nonsense from Central."

I nodded. "He does seem like a spook. I traded away a good officer for him, and I've never been sorrier. He can fight see, but he's a hog plant right in the middle of Legion Varus."

"That does make a sort of sense. Someone has to be embedded in the Legion in order to ferret out those they consider disloyal. There must be a very powerful figure at the high end of this group, giving the orders for the removal of such officers."

"Yes, sir."

Drusus nodded to me. "What do you want me to do about it?"

"Well, sir, for one thing—maybe you could, like, cancel the arrest orders?"

"No," Drusus said thoughtfully, "that won't be good enough. If I simply cancel your arrest orders, they'll reinstate them later on, perhaps after I've left office."

He began working his tapper and swirling fingers around on the battle computer. "I think I know what I'm going to do," he said. "I'm going to pardon all of you for the crime of treason against the state. That will mean essentially that the crime you committed has been erased, as if you had never done it. This will not absolve you of future crimes, mind you. But you will not serve any further time in nonexistence for this particular offense."

"You do know that we didn't really do anything, right?"

Drusus shrugged. "That doesn't matter. Technicalities are technicalities."

"You've got the right of that, sir. So… can we go?"

"Yes. It's done."

"That's great, sir. Thanks! But… could you please do one more thing?"

Drusus rolled his eyes. "Really, McGill? What would that thing be?"

"Can I be the one to go down to tell Imperator Turov about her good fortune? I'd like to spring her out of jail personally, sir."

Winslade and Drusus both smiled. They almost laughed. "Sure, you can, McGill. Now, get out of my office."

I turned around, grabbed up my big black armored suit and slung it over my shoulder. I checked the pockets to make sure that the Galactic Key was still there. Fortunately, it was. Then I marched toward the exit.

Just as Winslade and I were about to hit the doors and get out of there, they popped open in front of us. A figure entered. He was holding something about waist high.

The hogs who had been posted there with orders from the Consul were still aiming their weapons at that door. They took their orders seriously, I had to give them that. Old Drusus had told them not to allow anyone to enter, and that was still the single thought caroming around in their empty hog-brains. They opened fire without so much as a question posed or a challenge issued to the intruder.

Primus Bob, walking in with a smug smile and a tray full of steaming coffee mugs, was shot with about a thousand plasma bolts. His body did a little jig, and it flew back out into the office where the other staffers squealed and wrung their hands in horror. Coffee and hot burning blood gushed onto the carpet in a wild, steamy mess.

Winslade and I hopped over Bob and continued on our way. Once we made it to the elevators, Winslade seemed surprised when he saw me punch in a request to be taken down to the prison levels.

"Are you really going down there, McGill? You're mad."

"Uh…" I said. "I was thinking about it…"

"What if someone changes his mind and decides to arrest you anyway?"

I shrugged. "Well then, I think I better put my armor on first."

On the long way down, Winslade fretted with his tapper, and I put on my black armor. It was annoying to find that it hadn't been properly cleaned and cared for as Drusus had promised. They'd probably just left it lying there on the couch the entire time I'd been dead.

Oh, well. As my momma always said, you can't have everything.

-49-

After talking to about twenty stuffy hogs in a row, I finally got an authorization for Galina to be revived again. Unfortunately, there were two round-gut Hegemony boys manning the revival station who didn't like the look of my official orders from Drusus. Like all hogs throughout time, they decided to stand on technicalities to block me.

"This document changes the imperator's status from prisoner to released," a hog officer told me in a prissy tone, "but it's quite another matter to allow a revive."

"What? You're saying she's free to go, but she's still dead?"

"Yes, exactly."

"That makes no sense at all. I'll tell you what, I'll just go up to Legion Varus headquarters and get Tribune Winslade or somebody to sign her revival order."

The hog smiled. Apparently, like any snake hiding in the tall grass, he'd been waiting for this one. "Have a care, Centurion. The imperator is not a member of Legion Varus. Now that your legion is demobilized, Hegemony is responsible for her life/death status."

I don't mind telling you, I was getting a little steamed up by this time. Lots of violent thoughts were coursing through my brain. When I got control of them, I came up with an angle.

"No problem at all," I said. "Consul Drusus is a lenient man. When I meet with him tomorrow, I'll tell him you had no choice in the matter. You were simply forced by careful observation of regulations to ignore and dismiss his orders entirely."

The man blinked his piggy eyes. "You're a centurion," he said.

"There's nothing wrong with your eyeballs, hog," I assured him.

His jaw muscles flexed a little, but he let my insult slide. "No centurion is going to be meeting with the consul of Earth on any kind of regular basis."

It was my turn to smile. I opened up my library of videos, and I played a few of me in Drusus' office. Sure, most of them were old shots before he became consul, but the hog got the point.

He worked on his tapper and shooed me away. "She'll be coming out on Blue Deck."

"The VIP one?"

He snorted and ignored me until I left.

At the bottom floor Blue Deck, various other hogs, bio people and assorted bureaucrats gave me sour glances. I didn't care—they could piss on my shoes as long as they revived Galina. After the deed was done, they threw of us both out the door.

"This is bullshit," Galina muttered.

I was holding her left half up. Her right side was sagging. She was part naked still and drippy. Her hair was a sticky mess.

"Help me get my clothes, you idiot."

I helped her, and she slapped my hands away now and then. I held her up because she would have fallen down without my aid. Once she had some smart cloth on her, and she was able to stagger independently, I led her down the passages as fast as possible.

She finally stopped and eyed me with suspicion. "You're wearing your armor," she said.

"That's right. Your eyes are working real good already."

"Did you just kill someone to bring me back to life? Again? That's not going to help me, McGill. They'll just execute me all over again."

"No, no, no, it's much better than that," I said. "You want the good news first? Or the bad news?"

She swayed and thought about that for several long seconds. With each passing moment, her brain was knitting together, and her coordination was improving.

"Tell me the good news first," she said, "I really could use some good news right now."

"Okay. You have been officially pardoned by Consul Drusus himself."

"Pardoned? Pardoned for what?"

"For treason, of course," I said, and I clapped a big hand on her little shoulder. "Isn't that great? That's way better than just being released. A pardon means that you never did the crime, and you can't be prosecuted for it again."

"But… I didn't do anything in the first place."

I laughed. "That doesn't mean a damned thing to a hog. You're guilty until you're proven innocent and then after that, you're pretty much still guilty anyways. Once you're accused, that stain never goes away. Well, by damn, I made one go away for you today."

She looked up at me for the first time. "*You* made it go away?"

"That's right," I said, "I met with the Consul myself, see, and talked him into it. He pardoned all of us. Everybody in the whole Varus lineup had been accused of improper dealings all the way from me to Praetor Wurtenberger himself. It was quite a bit of diplomacy, I have to say, but—"

Right then, I stopped talking because Galina had come up to me, reached up her small hands to grab my cheeks and pulled me down to kiss her. That was a nice thing, even though she was a little bit sticky and nasty to kiss on, so I went with it.

Grinning, I eased her back down to the floor. We smiled at each other for several long seconds.

"Now," she said. "I want you to tell me that bad news."

"Oh… oh yeah, that part. Well, see… *Dominus* was destroyed."

"Yes, yes. I figured that much out."

"Yeah, that means your dragon suit is gone."

"Oh… of course. It was destroyed with the ship, wasn't it?"

I nodded. She seemed to be taking the news rather well.

"Wait," she said, grabbing me by the cheeks and trying to pull me down to her level. "What about my key? What about the Galactic Key?"

"Oh, that's okay. I managed to get off the ship with my armor and the key. It's in my pocket right now."

Galina heaved a sigh of relief. "So, that's it? Your bad news is we got killed, and my ship blew up. That's nothing. I owe you big-time, James."

"Well, yeah, about that. There is one other thing…" I reached a big fat finger up and into my collar. I tugged there, as I was a bit nervous about telling her this next part.

She stared at me, waiting patiently.

"Uh… a long time ago… I sort of had some very brief, personal contact with your sister." I forced a laugh. "It was almost like we shook hands, really. Nothing to get worked up about."

Galina stood there, stunned. She blinked at me several times. It was like her mind was resetting.

Suddenly, lightning quick, her knee came up and slammed into my family jewels.

I was wearing my armor, but unfortunately, I hadn't had time to put any kind of special padding underneath. I felt that knee, and it left me huffing.

I leaned forward, covering my privates in case she went in for seconds.

"That's for being a horndog," she said, "and you're also an idiot. You can't trust my sister, McGill. She seems sweet and honest, but she is neither. She works for my father, just like we all do. She might even be the one who put the two of us in purgatory."

"Really?"

"You're a total idiot, James." She turned and marched away.

After considering my options, I followed at a safe distance. "Uh… say, Imperator. There is still one more thing."

She stopped. "I can't believe you're even trying this now, James."

"Huh? Oh… no, sir. Not that!"

"What, then?"

"I was kind of wondering if you knew something about these underground bunkers I've been hearing about. Whatever they are, they got us into all kinds of trouble."

"What do you know about rebel bunkers?"

"Nothing. I'm pretty clueless. What could be inside such a place that might get everyone in Hegemony to have their panties in a bunch? They've been trying to perm the lot of us over it."

She came close again, and my hands drifted toward my jewels, just in case. "*Nothing* is down there, McGill. There are no bunkers. There's *nothing*—and don't ever talk about it again. Oh, and give me back my frigging key."

She held her hand out to me, flexing her fingers and making grabbing motions that were positively greedy.

I fished the key out of my pocket and put it in her palm. She felt the weight of it, as if she didn't trust that it was the real thing. After a moment or two she heaved a deep breath.

"All right," she said. "I told you I owed you one, but that is gone now. I forgive you."

She was looking down, and I was looking confused.

"Uh… you forgive me for what again, exactly?"

"For my sister, you idiot!"

"Oh, yeah! Right, right, right..."

She marched down the passage, and we parted ways.

I watched her walk away, and I thought to myself that breaking the bad news to her about Sophia had gone better than expected. All in all, I felt better about it. There was a weight removed and a new feeling of relief in my chest.

I'd been wondering how I was going to go about breaking the details to Galina, and I was glad that I'd finally done it. What's more, I'd done it in-person and clean-like. With any luck, she might even stop hating me in another year or two. Shrugging, I turned around and headed back to Blue Deck. I had more work to do with those hoity-toity ghouls.

The Blue Deck people were nowhere near as happy to see me as I was to see them. I hummed a tune and drummed my fingers on their door till they finally opened it. They stared up at me like a pack of skittery cats.

"What do you want here, Centurion?" asked a bio-officer. She was a primus, and the deck's commander. Her name was Primus Biles, and she was short—but she wasn't sweet. Everything was short about her in fact, the hair, the arms, the stubby legs. Even her squinty eyes seemed smaller than normal.

"I have a little unfinished business here, I'm afraid," I told her.

"I thought we told you to stay the hell away from our facilities."

My temper flared, but I held it in check and forced a smile. "I surely would like to do that, Primus Biles. But you see here, I've got orders from the consul himself. There are other names on this list, not just Imperator Turov. I've got a few more people that need to be revived."

There was a lot of grumbling and venomous looks from Biles, but eventually I got the lot of them out of purgatory. After I'd sprung both Graves and Wurtenberger, you'd have thought I'd get a hug or something—but you'd have thought wrong.

At least Wurtenberger seemed to grasp the situation. "It's upsetting," he said, "but it would seem that I find myself in your debt, McGill. How did this unlikely circumstance arise?"

"Uh…" I said, puzzling out his odd euro-way of talking. "Well sir, it's hard to explain, but a surprising number of individuals have discovered just such a thing in the past."

"Yes, yes, I do believe that's true. What a strange set of circumstances… So, Drusus became consul? I have to admit, I'm a bit jealous about that."

"You thought they'd give you the nod, did you?"

"Well, I am his senior. Did you know that? Was it even mentioned?"

Naturally, I knew nothing about who was senior to whom, and I cared even less. But as it was clearly something Wurtenberger cared about, I lit up with a grin.

"Yes, sir. That was a big topic of debate. You graduated waaay before him. The whole thing was clearly unfair."

Wurtenberger frowned. "Not way before him. I'm only two years older."

"Oh… but hey, you've got to be happy about one thing." I poked a finger at his belly, but I didn't quite jab him in the gut. "You're looking mighty fit."

"Yes. My youth, strength and fitness has returned. I suppose that is one benefit of an illegitimate death."

"That's the damned truth. I practically rely on such events to keep my body in shape."

Wurtenberger wasn't looking great, mind you, but he wasn't a tubby middle-ager anymore. He was more like a lumpy-looking thirty. An improvement, but I didn't think he could keep up with my unit if we took him for a quick jog around the base of Central.

He studied the deck for a moment. I almost yawned, I was getting bored and expecting to be dismissed—but he was still thinking.

It occurred to me that he probably hadn't died for many years. When you got out of the habit, death tended to kink up an inexperienced man's mind when it came on him sudden-like.

"The fact that he pardoned me…" he said at last. "That's somewhat amazing."

"He really is a straight-laced fellow. The only man I know who keeps a bigger stick up his butt is Primus Graves, here."

Graves had kept quiet this whole time, but now he shot me an unpleasant glance. There was no love lost in it.

That's just great, I thought to myself. Another ingrate.

Wurtenberger nodded at last. "Very well. I accept this revival as justice done. I won't forget this, McGill."

The two of them turned toward the elevators. I almost sighed in relief. I thought maybe they'd want me to attend some kind of debriefing, or secret conspirators' huddle, or something. It looked like I was going to be let off easy.

I took the liberty of clapping a big hand on both their backs in congratulations. Graves shook me off, but Praetor Wurtenberger did not.

"Hey," I said, "how about the three of us go out and celebrate?"

"That's a fine idea," Wurtenberger said. "I've spent months laying about dead. It's time to live a little."

"Are you coming, Primus Graves?" I asked our silent partner. "Or is it just the two of us?"

Graves stood stiff and stern for a moment, but then he finally sighed and nodded. "I might as well."

The three of us went out on the town. As luck would have it, we ended up at Unification Square. We sat down at their finest bar and Praetor Wurtenberger bought several rounds of drinks.

In addition to the booze, three triple-burgers, two platters of cheese-fries and a slew of those stuffed potato skins I liked so much was all delivered to our table and consumed. I ate the majority of this food, but old Wurtenberger was in the game with me. He'd lost almost all of his paunch in his most recent death. The bio people had edited it out, I suspected, but it looked to me like he was dead-set on putting it all back on again as fast as possible.

Eventually, Wurtenberger took his leave, and I was left chewing on scraps and chugging the last few beers.

Graves eyed me coldly while I gorged myself on free grub.

"I thought he'd never leave," Graves said.

"Uh... You wanted him to go?"

"Of course. How could I possibly talk to you with him standing around?"

"But I thought he was another one of you traitor-types. One of you guys who know all about the bunk—"

Graves punched me one in the arm. There were a lot of knuckles in that punch. It didn't hurt all that much, but it did shut me up right-quick.

I rubbed at the sore spot and looked confused. "Uh... what was that for, sir?"

"Come on," he said, "let's get out of here and go for a walk."

We left the place and marched across the dark square. There were streetlights still flashing in the distance, but the sounds were all muted here as it was deep into the night by now.

"What do you want to tell me, Primus?" I asked.

"McGill," he said, "have you ever been down in the vaults underneath Central?"

"Well, sure. Many times, actually."

"Right... Have you ever seen the chambers down below level five hundred?"

I looked at him and blinked a couple times. "Oh... you mean those weird rooms full of glass jars and blue lights? You mean the vault of memories? Isn't that what they call it?"

"I can hardly believe it..." he said, shaking his head, "but... of course you've been down there. Why not? You've been to the Core Worlds after all..."

"James McGill can be found in the most surprising places," I admitted.

"Those vaults are their secret of secrets. The inner sanctum of all hidden sanctums—and you know about it." Graves shook his head. "Central prides itself on security, but the place is like a sieve."

I was pretty sure I'd been insulted, but I didn't much care. My gut was feeling good and full. I lifted my head high and belched so hard that it left a little foggy report in the cool autumn air.

"Say, Primus Graves," I said. "What the hell is in the bunker behind the door?"

He glanced at me. "Haven't you learned anything after all these investigations and executions?"

"Nope, I guess not. I'm still curious."

"There's nothing down there, McGill," he told me. "Nothing at all. Forget about it. Never mention it again."

"But we can talk about it now, sir. We've been pardoned by Drusus. A pardon given by a consul can only be undone by another consul. I looked it up."

"You looked it up, huh? Like, on the grid?"

"Yeah..."

Graves rolled his eyes. "It didn't occur to you that that was how you got yourself permed in the first place?"

"Yeah... but I'm in the pardon-zone now."

"Listen, McGill," he said. "The crimes you're coming close to will *never* be pardoned. If they can't get you officially, they'll get you unofficially. Remember that—and keep away from me until our legion is mustered out again."

He turned suddenly and walked away into the night. He left me with my mouth hanging open and an empty feeling in my swollen gut.

"Hey, uh… goodbye to you too, sir. Have a good night."

Graves didn't even throw a hand up over his shoulder in return. Shrugging, I left Unification Square and headed for the sky trains. There was a red eye all-nighter that would take me down to Georgia—but I wasn't ready for that quite yet.

Instead, I brought up my tapper and began searching for names. After a while, I found two of my unit members who had been revived since the disaster on *Dominus*: Sargon and Carlos. I contacted them both and did a little arm-twisting. I offered up some beers and credits. Pretty soon, long before dawn broke over Central City, I was riding home to Georgia in style.

-50-

"No one is as shit-off crazy as you, McGill," Carlos told me.

"That's right," I said. "Just keep flying."

It was about four in the morning, and we were soaring south in his aircar. Georgia was on the horizon, and I was glad to see her hazy skies and forested mountains again.

Somehow, even after he had been accused and convicted of stealing illegal Imperial coins, Carlos had managed to keep his aircar. Maybe it was a form of punishment for him. He was making payments all by himself now, and I knew they were nearly breaking him. To my way of thinking, I wasn't sure if that was a win for Carlos or a win for the bank.

"So... you just want me to drop you off?" he asked.

"Yes, that's right. Just drop me off and disappear."

"You're not going to take me into your shack and give me a beer, or a back rub, or anything?"

"Nope, not today."

Carlos was irritated because he couldn't figure out why I'd twisted his arm so hard to get him to fly me and a few large, strange-looking packages down to Georgia. I'd fed him a line of bullshit, of course, about how the things I was transporting wouldn't fit in the overhead bin on the sky-train.

But he knew that was horse-hockey. If you had too much luggage, you could simply check it, or even ship it. It wasn't that big of a deal. The things I was bringing along, however, weren't checkable or shippable. They weren't even legal.

All the way down to Georgia, Carlos kept giving me sidelong glances and asking me pointed questions. He was pestering the hell out of me. I tried to ignore him and did my best to fall asleep in the passenger seat. I was trying to get a little shuteye before I arrived at home, where I knew I'd be hassled by my parents over my surprise return from the stars.

Eventually, we landed out behind the tool shed, and I startled awake when the skids touched down. Looking around, I realized Carlos was already out the door. The driver's side door was hanging open, and he was rummaging in the trunk.

"Dammit..." I said, grunting as I climbed out and moved around to the trunk. I slapped his hands away from my hastily wrapped-up items.

"That's a tube," he said. "A big, long, hard metal tube."

Carlos had been feeling-up one of the bags, the one that was the more strangely shaped of the two. He stared at me while I grunted and pulled these items out of his trunk. I dropped them in the grass and turned back to him.

"Now, get out of here. Go on, get!" I told him.

He stared at me for a while longer. He pointed at the tube-shaped object. "That's a frigging belcher, isn't it, McGill?"

"I hate to say think, Carlos," I said, "that I'm going to have to kill you and bury you out in that swamp again. I'm going to feel bad this time."

"Again? Bury me in your swamp... again?"

"That's what I said."

He stared at me, and then he turned to look out to the west. It was true that he'd come out here to visit me a few times. Given our long lives and many revives, we both knew there were some missing chunks in our memories. It was possible that I'd murdered him, and he'd forgotten about that—and he knew it. What's more, he knew I could do something like that without feeling any remorse or even a slight regret.

"All right, all right," he said. "I'm going, but if hogs from Central come down here to ask how you burned down this forest, don't mention my name."

"You've got my word on that," I told him. "Thanks a bunch for the ride."

He jumped into his aircar and lifted off. I was struck by a puff of exhaust, gravel and shredded weeds. I cursed his name, picked up the items I'd transported down from Central, and hustled toward the trees.

I wanted to go back to my shack. I wanted to greet my parents. I wanted to check out my tomcat and flop down on the couch—hell, I wanted to sleep until noon. But I knew I couldn't do any of that stuff. Not today. Today, I had to do something crazy before anyone could stop me.

After quietly gathering a few tools out of the shed, I walked toward the trees, carrying my heavy burdens out into the dark swamp. I didn't use a flashlight, just some night vision goggles. In fact, I used the monocle that Etta and I had found. It was made long before I was born, but it still worked.

Pushing my way through the reeds and the chirping insects, I listened to the wild lands. Now and then, things rustled—maybe a gator or a fox. I didn't know which, and right now I didn't care. As long as I didn't hear any boots crunching on the dirt, I figured I was okay.

I kept walking until I found the spot that Etta had discovered. There, I used a power-shovel to clear off the dirt around the hole.

We had buried the hatch over the bunker to hide the spot, but we hadn't done a very thorough job. Fortunately, nothing looked disturbed. As far as I could tell, no Hegemony cops, hobos, or even Etta herself had been out here since I'd left months ago.

Once the hatch was revealed, I turned the squeaking wheel and levered it open. It took me three trips climbing down into the bunker to get all my gear down there. Once inside, I pulled the hatch shut.

It was kind of spooky down there in the dark, I don't mind telling you. The sounds… everything was echoing and metallic. Somewhere, a single drop of water fell every ten seconds or so, making a ringing splash.

After searching for a while, I found the hidden trapdoor that led down to the lower level. I finally found the ring, pulled it up and went down into the deepest, darkest chamber of all.

Inside, at one end was the door with the locked-out key panel still glowing red. I'd kind of hoped it might have reset by now, or forgotten me, or run out of batteries... but it hadn't.

My flashlight played over both the doors, the one we'd failed with so many times it had locked down, and the other one we hadn't touched. They were at either end of the long, tube-like bunker. I scratched my head and face for a minute or so, thinking hard. I'd worked up a sweat, and that always made me itchy.

Finally, I decided to take on the locked door. After all, we'd already failed to open it. There was no point in screwing up the second one and alerting someone like Graves who knew about these places.

Opening up my packages, I unwrapped Sargon's belcher. I rammed an energy canister into the breach at the end, and it glowed into life.

This was quite a series of violations, of course. First off, Sargon was a weaponeer, and he had been formally issued this alien contraption. But that didn't give him the right to take a powerful weapon out of its secure locker just for funsies. Even worse, he'd given it to someone other than the person who had been issued the weapon in the first place.

On top of that raft of charges, any Nairb worth his salt would point out that I had illegally transported said weapon across sector lines. I'd carried it all the way down to my home in Georgia. Prosecutors would have had a field day with the stack of felonies and whatnot I'd committed, which meant I had to get it back to Central before someone noticed it was missing.

Examining the vault door for a while, I decided to go for the hinges. I lit them up with a one second burst on each one. There was some melting and glowing, burning metal, but the door didn't come down. I had to reapply the heat of the belcher again, and soon the whole bunker filled up with a cloud of vaporized metal. Molten droplets dribbled onto the deck and splattered my boots. The whole thing was a mess.

At last, the heavy door fell open with a resounding clang. I coughed and kicked at it until it was out of the way. Setting aside the belcher, I peered into the dark interior.

It was steamy inside, and there were gurgling sounds in the sudden quiet. The whole place reminded me of a fish tank I'd had when I was young. The smells were organic in nature, almost as if the swamp water itself had seeped in somehow.

My hands groped the dank walls of the bunker seeking a light switch, but I found none. I flipped down the night vision monocle, so I could see again. I peered around in the misty darkness.

To my utter surprise, I heard a voice speak.

"Who dares to disturb my slumber?" It was a strange, watery voice. I immediately suspected it was the voice of the dead.

-51-

The voice kind of freaked me out, so I turned on a lantern that was attached to my suit. The voice stopped uttering coherent words. Instead, she shrieked.

"It burns!" she said. "Why do you seek to blind me? Are you the enemy come at long last?"

I put my fingers over the light so that only threads of it shone through. "No, no, ma'am," I said, "I'm just a farm boy who got curious about this old bunker out in my woods."

"A farm boy?" she asked, "do you take me for a fool? No farm boy possesses a plasma weapon like the one you used to burn your way in here."

"Oh… right," I said. "So, you're a smarty pants ghost."

"I am no ghost. I am physical."

"Uh… okay." I was still searching for the source of the voice. At last, I thought I'd spotted it. There was a speaker low to the deck and off to the left. Above that, I saw a tank that was gurgling in the darkness. When my light hit it, you could see bubbles flowing up in the cloudy water and a shadow floating inside.

Straight away, I knew what I was looking at. I'd seen this sort of thing before. It was a disembodied brain, kept alive through some abomination of science. The thing in the tank was unlike most of them because it had eyes. Organic eyes that drifted in the soup with the brain.

The eyes were on short stalks. They hung limply, aiming downward. I wasn't sure how well they worked, but I could tell the thing in the tank probably had no way to focus them. No way to direct them. There were no muscles for that purpose. There were no muscles at all. Just eyes, optical nerves, and a floating brain.

Looking around and investigating further, I saw the tank was fed with filtered water and nutrients. Near the shelf it sat on were more tanks. Seven more.

I moved the beam of light over each of them. Six of the vessels contained a dead, rotted brain like the first one, but the seventh and final vessel was empty. It lay tilted over on its side.

My mouth hung open and my jaw touched my collar. What in the living hell had I found down here?

The one living brain was still talking all this time. She hadn't stopped since she'd first spoken up, but I'd been too stunned to listen.

"Converse with me, farm-boy," she said. "I've been down here a long, long time. It's been decades since anyone's come to meet with me. My companions have perished. You cannot imagine the boredom."

"Uh... no," I said, "I probably can't. But, you know, I've been sentenced to worse things."

The brain in the jar twitched at this. "Impossible."

"Sadly, ma'am," I said, "there truly are worse fates, believe you me." Poking around I found where the pumps and the nutrient reservoirs were. The electrical power was nuclear, I saw—an atomic battery that might well last another century.

"I've waited decades to speak to another being, and I'm saddled with a cretin? What cruel fate of the gods is this?"

"Uh..."

"Tell me, farm-boy, what fate have you suffered that can begin to compare to my personal hell?"

"Well... nonexistence for starters. I've served prison sentences where I was erased for years."

"What? How is such a thing possible?"

"Times have changed I think, since you were out of this bunker. Science has progressed, and we can revive people now. Bring them back from the dead and print them out. We make new copies of them, essentially. In my case, they've executed me and left me for dead for a long time. It's a very cheap form of prison."

"That's... interesting," the brain said. "Intruder, I am pleased that you've not yet murdered me."

"Oh... well, that's not my intention."

"If you're not an assassin, why are you here? You aren't one of my followers. I know that because you've made no attempt to utter any passwords. You've made no attempt to ingratiate yourself to me."

"Uh... yeah, I guess that's true... I'm not really good at that kind of stuff."

"Are you perhaps then, a simpleton?"

"Some would say that, yes ma'am."

"Fantastic. I've lain here in the dark for decades only to be delivered into the hands of an idiot."

"That is indeed your fate, ma'am," I agreed.

A gush of bubbles went up in the tank. Was she sighing or farting? I wasn't sure. I wasn't even sure how she did it.

"Tell me more of these revival machines," the brain said, "how do they work?"

I went ahead and told her everything I knew. That kept her occupied while I searched around and found the various circuitry, tanks, nutrient paste—all sorts of things that were keeping her alive. It seemed to me that she had almost run out of food, and she wasn't going to make it more than another year or two.

Only the fact that the other brains in the tanks had died had kept her alive so long. She was the last one, using up the supplies meant for eight.

While I talked, I set up objects I brought in a second bag. If anything, private possession of these items was more illegal than the belcher itself. Only through my connections in Central City had I managed to purloin something of such great value.

When I was finished, a set of gateway posts stood before me. I was hurrying, as I knew these babies were tracked more closely than any belcher. When some hog bean-counter at Central found out they were missing, there was bound to be an arrest warrant or worse printed out with the name James McGill at the top.

When I had the posts lined up and powered with the atomic battery, I spoke to the thing in the tank again. "Listen, lady. It's been a fine thing talking to you, but I've got to go."

"Please, no!" she said, "don't leave me! You are clearly an imbecile, but this social interaction has been very stimulating."

I sighed. "Okay, tell me your name."

She hesitated. "I cannot be so easily tricked. I will tell you nothing of my past, nothing that can be used to root out the last of us."

Looking around, it seemed to me that she was in fact the last of her kind, but I shrugged. "Okay, whatever. I'll be back in two shakes of a lamb's tail."

She cried. She implored. She urged me not to go, but I stepped between the posts, and I vanished.

* * *

Oddly enough, Dust World was in the middle of its night cycle just as Earth had been when I'd left. The guards watching over this entry point were still on duty, however.

"Whoa, what the hell?"

I heard a shot, and I turned around nice and slow-like. I found a guard aiming his rifle at me. He called over his shoulder for his buddy to join him. It appeared to me that his buddy had been taking a piss among some of the waxy leaved monstrous plants that encircled the lake in the middle of the valley.

"Sam, get over here, man. We've got something."

I heard jangling. Another man trotted toward us in armor. He was messing with his smart-pants, trying to get them to seal-up again.

"Hold on, boys. Nothing to worry about. Just a legionnaire out for a night's stroll."

"No, you're not," The first hog said. He was approaching with his snap-rifle aimed at my gut. "I don't know who you are, but these gateway posts are shut down at night. There's no way you came here from Central without special orders. There's nothing about you on my tapper."

"Okay now, hold on," I said, ambling toward them calmly. I had my hands out to either side, spread wide. "Just relax, I'll show you right here on my tapper. I've got orders from Consul Drusus himself."

When I got close enough, I drew my combat knife and ran it up under his chin strap. It stabbed deep into his brain. His rifle popped off a few rounds, but they missed. He sat down on the dirt, as dead as a doornail.

The other guy who had been taking a piss arrived on the scene about then. I made a show of trying to help the first dead hog back up onto his feet.

"Look at this, Sam," I said, "your partner here seems to have had a heart attack or something."

"I know you," the second man said. "I've seen you out here before. Drop that man and put your hands up."

I did as he said, but when the dead hog slumped, his pistol was in my hand. I'd taken it from his belt. Old Sam saw this, and there weren't any flies on this boy because he just opened up.

He showered me with snap-rifle rounds, which did hurt a little. That was mostly because I hadn't had time to pack any kind of cushion underneath my armor. But the accelerated rounds didn't penetrate. It was like taking hammer blows through a thick pillow.

Fortunately, he never fired at my head. I didn't have my helmet, because I hadn't expected such a hot greeting.

I carefully aimed the first hog's pistol. It was hard to aim as I was rocking a bit each time I was hit. I fired a single clean shot.

"One-tap!" I said, giving myself a little fist pump and a cheer.

Sam fell down on his face and shivered in the dust. Apparently, he hadn't been wearing his helmet while he was pissing, either.

Whistling an old tune, I walked away from the scene and headed cross-country for the caves. There, I knew the Investigator would be lurking.

I made it halfway to the valley wall before I realized someone was following me. That someone was stealthy, but I detected them anyway. I stopped, and my shadow stopped.

Taking a deep breath, I put my hands up to my mouth. "Etta?" I bellowed into the swamp reeds. "Is that you?"

Dust World was so hot up on the surface, no one could survive for long. They all lived in hidden valleys where bubbling springs created oases in the vast desert that covered this planet. Down here at the bottom of a lightless pit, it was really dark at night.

She appeared. She was a slim, mysterious figure. "Daddy? Is that really you?"

"That's right."

She trotted close, and we embraced. "You smell bad—and there's blood all over you."

"Um… yeah," I said, "but it's not mine."

"What happened?"

"Nothing… I just had a little trouble getting out here to see you."

This was a pack of lies, and she knew it. "Why are you here, Daddy?"

"Well… remember when you called me up and said you wanted me to come out here and talk about the bunker with your grandpa?"

"Yes, but that was months ago."

"Right, right. I know. Time kind of got away from me. I went out to Rigel, see and then Dark World. Then there was this new place. I think we're calling it Sky World now…"

Etta shook her head in disbelief. "All right, Dad, whatever. Let's just go talk to grandpa. You can tell him about it."

She led the way and soon I was met with not just the scary old Investigator but Floramel as well. She was the Investigator's wife, now. After living on Dust World for a few years, she had a sunburnt face and a more rugged look to her.

The Investigator was just as tall and strange as ever. His hair was kind of wispy, flying around in the night breezes.

I smiled, telling jokes. I did a little bit of glad-handing and hugging—but the truth was these people kind of gave me the willies.

Finally, I got around to telling them what I'd found and why I'd come. The Investigator was immediately alert. "You've seen a living brain in a jar?"

"Yeah, pretty much. It's in this liquid see, in a tank full of bubbles and nutrients. It's kind of nasty, to be honest."

"And it speaks?"

"It sure does. Freaky to listen to."

"How many others did you find?"

"Uh… Just the one that's alive. The others are all dead and gone."

The Investigator's eyes were intense. They were pretty much always intense. They didn't blink much, but they were always shiny and wet.

"A pity…" he said. "Still, action must be taken."

He turned away from us and began striding away from his cave and back toward town. Not knowing what else to do, we followed him.

Half an hour later, we reached the gateway posts where I'd arrived. There were new guards there now. They were dragging away the bodies of the last ones when we walked up. They trained their guns on us.

"Hold," the Investigator said. "Do you recognize me?"

"We do, sir," the hogs admitted.

"I am the Investigator," he said. "I am he who rules on this planet."

The hogs frowned at that. "This is an Earth-owned world just like the rest of them."

The Investigator lifted a hand, and he waved it toward the village in the distance. "Tell that to my people. If you dare to interfere with my experiment, you will never know peace at this post."

The hogs shuffled, but they finally lowered their rifles because they knew it was true. Dust World people were all killers, through and through. They were scary folk, half-wild and yet smart. If you asked me, they were a little bit nuts from living on this high radiation world for so long.

After a few more intimidating statements, the Investigator was allowed to approach the gateway posts with Etta and Floramel. "These are my technicians," the Investigator explained. "There's something wrong with the posts, and they must be repaired."

The hogs grumbled, but they let him do as he wished.

"There is something wrong with one of them," they admitted. "We can't get back to Earth. We just get transmission error messages."

"You can't get back right now, and you shouldn't try. They're no longer linked to Central. We will repair the system."

The hogs kept their distance. One of them filmed us with his tapper, but I didn't care.

At last, Floramel stood up and nodded her head. "It should be stable now. We can bring through whatever we want."

Without another word to any of us, the Investigator stepped through the gates. There was that bug zapper noise, and he was gone. Etta winced as she watched him disappear. Next, Floramel followed. That left just Etta and I standing in the desert wind.

"What should we do, Daddy?" she whispered to me. "Do we go through or stand around?"

The hogs were scowling at us. Now that the Investigator was gone, they were feeling ornery, I could tell.

"Let's just stay right here and pretend we're working on the posts."

I knelt and opened and closed the access doors at the bottom of the posts. Etta lifted tools and clicked them against the posts. We made rattling sounds, cursed and generally pretended to be working.

The hogs watched us. They cursed and muttered and paced around like guard dogs who had caught scent of a hobo. I noticed, however, that they kept their distance. They didn't trust us.

After ten long minutes, a figure reappeared. He stepped through the gateway posts and stood tall with his arms wrapped around something. It was the Investigator, and I could hardly believe what I was seeing. His arms are thin but long and powerful. They were all muscle and sinew.

He was carrying a massive vessel of water. It must have weighed fifty kilos or more. He walked with a careful, even stride. A moment later Floramel appeared behind him.

"Hurry," she said, "without power, it can't live for long."

The Investigator marched away from the village. Etta and I watched them hurry off toward his labs in the caves.

The new hogs called after them, demanding an explanation. They got nothing, and they didn't dare to leave their post or shoot down a local official.

"Well," I told Etta, "I think I've done my good deed for the day. I'm going back to Earth before this thing breaks down."

"But, Daddy," she said. "You just got here."

"Yeah, well… come with me if you want to."

Etta chewed on her lower lip. "I think I have to stay. I want to see if I can help Floramel and Grandpa. I'm kind of curious about that thing in the tank."

I shrugged. "Of course, you are. Well, it's all up to you. You're a grown woman now."

I hugged her, turned around, and left the way I'd come.

-52-

It was about ten a.m. when I returned to the family farm. I walked out of the swamp carrying all the burdens I brought with me from Central. I was bone-tired by this time and kind of hungry for breakfast. My dad spotted me first, as I was coming out of his toolshed and walking toward my shack.

I didn't make it more than a dozen steps before he charged up and gave me a big sweeping hug. He fell back almost as quickly, scowling. "Holy bejesus, boy," he said, "you smell like an outhouse. What is all this crap that's crusted up on you? And what is this black suit you're wearing?"

"Nothing," I said. "Just some new armor. You don't happen to have a beer handy, do you Dad?"

"Not for a man who stinks to high-heaven I don't. Come over here, boy." He led me over to where a hose with a spray head was coiled up. He twisted the brass nozzle and began blasting me down. A few minutes later I was dripping wet and cursing. He said I could come into the house now.

I stopped off at my shack first. I shed my armor and left it to dry in the sun on the porch. I took a shower, got on some fresh clothes and then headed for the house.

My mom was super-excited, and she had an early lunch going by this time. We ate, and I told them some random tales. Some were true, some were not. Others were glossed-over or flowered-up as was necessary. They ate it all up with a spoon and didn't seem to mind whether I was lying or not.

"It's just so good to have you back home, boy," my dad said. "We've been getting some strange visitors out here, you know. They've been asking about you, and we haven't had any answers."

I stopped chewing on a piece of bacon and glanced up. I was alert for the first time since I'd gotten home. "Strange visitors? Like who?"

My father shrugged. "Hegemony types... hogs—isn't that what you call them?"

"Yeah..." I said. "What did they want?"

Momma frowned and tugged at her apron. "I think they wanted to talk to you, James."

It was hard not to worry, but I did my best. Maybe, even though I'd been officially pardoned by that demigod of Earth known as Consul Drusus, I wasn't completely out of the woods yet.

"Anybody else?" I asked.

"Yes, well, there is that one young woman," my mom said. "The one who came here for Thanksgiving last year."

"You mean Sophia?"

"Yes. That's the name. She dropped by yesterday. She said you'd be coming home, but I told her we hadn't seen you yet. How did she know you were on your way, James?"

"Huh..." I said, "that is a stone-cold mystery." I went to the refrigerator to grab a beer. After that, I watched a ballgame with my dad in the living room. By the third inning, we were both passed out on one of the two easy chairs that dad kept in front of the big wall-screen.

I hadn't gotten much sleep lately, so I slept until afternoon. Then, I woke up and ate again. After that I finally headed back to my shack, telling my parents I had a few things to attend to.

They finally stopped bugging me and trying to give me a list of chores to do. I told them I would get to all of it in the morning. They didn't believe me, but they let me go anyway.

By nightfall, I was peacefully alone in my own place. I almost fell asleep again, but instead, I used my tapper to quietly alert everyone I'd borrowed illegal gear from that I was ready to return it.

I got a flood of worried texts in response. I assured them with absolute certainty I would return all the items in the morning. This was a flat lie, but it got them off my back. After that, I watched another ballgame. I eventually fell asleep again on my crusty old couch.

Along about midnight, there was a scratching at my door. My natural thought was that it was Etta, but I wasn't sure.

My eyes sprung open. It was dark in my shack as night had fallen. I decided not to turn on any of the interior lights. I regretted not having put on my black armor again. It had saved my life more times than I could count.

Shrugging, I took a pistol from under a couch cushion and answered the door, flinging it wide. To my surprise, instead of hogs waiting to arrest me, or Etta returning home for a visit, a different small figure stood on my doorstep. For just a moment, I thought it was Galina, but then I realized the truth.

"Sophia?"

It was Galina's little sister. "Hi, James."

"Hey there," I said, "what brings you out here on this fine Georgia night, young lady?"

"You know why I'm here," she said.

That got my heart pumping a little, I don't mind telling you. Sophia and I had only been together that one, single time. She hadn't seemed overly interested on other occasions. But now... here she was.

Maybe she was more like her big sister than I knew, blowing hot and cold at random. I wasn't sure how I felt about that. Reluctantly, I reached out and unlatched the screen door.

She slipped inside, and in the darkness, she reached up for me. I grabbed her wrists and held her gently at a distance.

"Hold on, now," I said. "That's all over with."

"Why?" she asked.

"Because your sister knows about it, and you and I never had that much of a thing going in the first place. It was just a chance attraction. Besides... your dad wants to kill me."

"My father wants to kill everyone."

"Don't I know it. Look," I said, "I think it's time for you to just turn around and go on back to wherever you came from. I'm in enough trouble."

"Is that the only reason you want me to go? To avoid trouble?"

"No..." I said, "not just that. I feel kind of bad about cheating on Galina."

"You hadn't been with her for a whole year before we were together. She put you to death. She had you tortured."

"Yeah, yeah, yeah," I said, "no relationship is perfect. Time for you to go."

I turned her around and nudged her out the door. Then I slapped her on the butt and closed the screen door behind her.

She stood on the porch, staring at me like a housecat in the rain.

"What?" I asked.

"Did you know?"

"Uh... know what?"

She reached down to her belt. There was a clicking sound. I saw then that she had her hand on a box. A small box with a switch on it.

"Is that an illusion box?" I asked, and then I knew the truth, because it was no longer Sophia standing on my porch. It was Galina.

She had looked exactly like her sister, and the effect had fooled me completely. The two sisters were about the same physical size and dimensions, anyway. I realized it had been quite easy for Galina to imitate Sophia's voice, even without the illusion box.

"I'll be damned," I said, "I haven't seen one of those things for years."

Galina stared at me through that screen door. Her tail was lashing. I could tell she wanted to yell at me, but she couldn't. After all, I hadn't done a damned thing wrong.

Finally, she chewed her lip for a moment and then looked down at the porch boards, which were lit up by the Moon. One of her feet scratched idly at the other.

"Can I come back in, now?" she asked. "Now that you know who I really am?"

I thought about it. This woman was trouble and then some. All the things she had said as Sophia were true. She *had* gotten me killed. She had gotten me tortured and left me dead for nearly a year.

Now why in the hell, with all that bad blood between us, was I going to allow this wicked girl into my home again?

Galina waited on the porch, not saying a damned thing. She just stood there, looking cute. For once, it was completely up to me.

I released a big sigh, unlatched the screen door, and let her slip by me into my shack.

THE END

Books by B. V. Larson:

UNDYING MERCENARIES
Steel World
Dust World
Tech World
Machine World
Death World
Home World
Rogue World
Blood World
Dark World
Storm World
Armor World
Clone World
Glass World
Edge World
Green World
Ice World
City World
Sky World

REBEL FLEET SERIES
Rebel Fleet
Orion Fleet
Alpha Fleet
Earth Fleet

Visit BVLarson.com for more information.

Printed in Great Britain
by Amazon